XX

vax

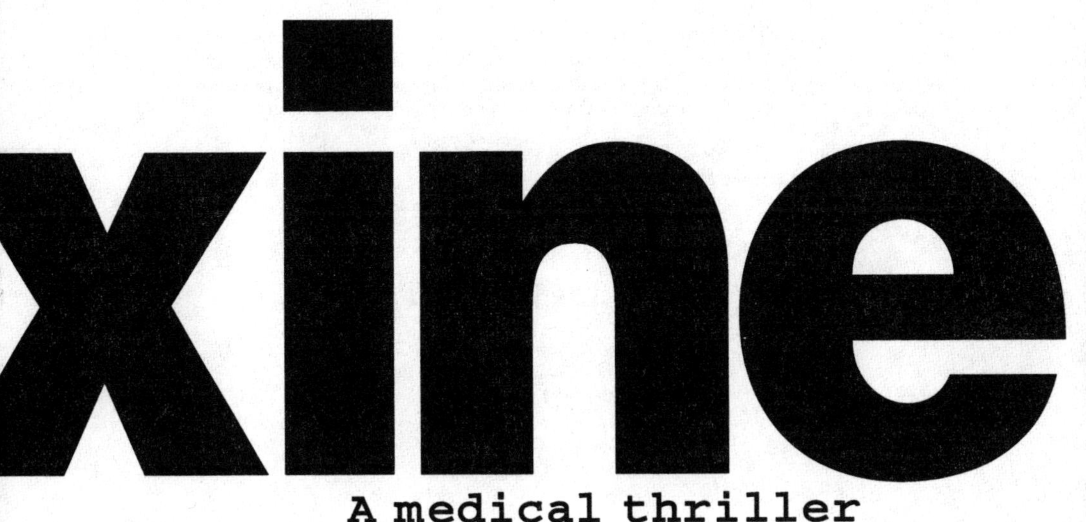

A medical thriller

Andrew Stanway

SMITH GRYPHON
PUBLISHERS

First published in Great Britain in 1996 by
SMITH GRYPHON
Swallow House, 11–21 Northdown Street,
London N1 9BN

A CIP catalogue record for this book is available at the British Library.

ISBN 1 85685 123 0

Typeset by Action Typesetting, Gloucester.
Printed and bound in Great Britain by
Butler & Tanner Ltd, Frome.

To Shirley Russell

ACKNOWLEDGEMENTS

I would like to acknowledge the help of the following who were instrumental in helping me make the transition from thirty years of writing non-fiction to becoming a novelist.

Mary Sandys, my editor; Doreen and Caroline Montgomery, my literary agents; and Professor John Aitken, without whom the technical and medical content of the book would not have been so convincing.

CONTENTS

PART ONE

Washington, DC, 31 March 1998

'*OK, Bart, ten seconds to air!*'

Barton DeWitt, CNN's top industry reporter, tossed back his expensively cut hair and turned to face the waiting Betacam, ready for what he did best.

'*Action!*'

'Following a sensational outburst on last night's *WorldView*, in which Morton Montgomery, CEO of Pharmavax, openly accused the Administration of putting pressure on him to short cut vital testing on Seminon, hundreds of activists are gathering here at the company's headquarters in protest. I have with me Phil Mankovitz of the Seminon Survivors Action Group. Mr Mankovitz, things are starting to look kinda ugly here. Now, some people would say that this sort of demonstration goes way too far –'

'Well, we say it doesn't go far enough!' Mankovitz cut in, his face blazing with anger. 'There's been a cover-up, right? These guys at Pharmavax let their damn vaccine out of the place without it being properly tested. Their security was no damn good. They're gonna have to pay. They encouraged thousands – hell, millions – of people all over the world to put their faith in it, right? And the stuff's *evil* –'

'So, Mr Mankovitz,' DeWitt interrupted blandly, 'what is it you people actually want?'

'We at SSAG are demanding a full congressional inquiry into the whole stinking mess. Pharmavax and the Administration – and that includes the FDA – they're all just as guilty as each other. Hell, they don't care about the way it's ruined people's lives, the way it's wrecked society, just so long as they get rich. We say, these guys are guilty as hell, and they're gonna be made to pay!'

By this time the shouting of the rapidly growing crowd was almost deafening, and Phil Mankovitz's voice was beginning to rasp more and more shrilly in order to be heard. Suddenly, the hostile crowd, which had been systematically heaving at the hastily erected police barriers, broke through and surged furiously across the manicured lawns of the immaculate plaza like a gigantic tidal wave. Dozens of riot-control police managed to hold it at bay a few yards from the front of the Pharmavax building.

The Betacam swung abruptly away from Mankovitz and DeWitt to bring the action live to television viewers across America. As the activists started to throw tear-gas grenades, riot shields went up, and gas visors went down. But within seconds it was plain that, even with their state-of-the-art body armour and sophisticated crowd-control techniques, the police were heavily outnumbered and couldn't hope to hold the mob at bay for long.

Missiles started to fly. A five-pound lump of concrete wrenched from the edge of a raised flower-bed struck the Betacam operator on the head. CNN's live broadcast was blacked out.

• • •

'Christ! Those guys want blood!' Morton Montgomery, Chief Executive Officer of Pharmavax, was watching the surging crowds from the window of the boardroom on the twentieth floor. 'Someone find another news channel! There's as many media people out there as demonstrators – someone else has to be covering it live! C'mon, Jane!'

Mort's secretary calmly surfed through all fifty channels on the six-foot television screen that dominated the far wall of the Pharmavax boardroom. After less than half a minute of zapping through game shows, sitcom re-runs and ranting tele-evangelists, she found another live-news channel.

'... despite the millions of dollars Pharmavax say they put into developing their combined HIV-male contraceptive vaccine, which initially proved effective, the downside is that it is now known to have caused the drastic side-effects that have affected so many people worldwide. Faced with the possibility of huge liability suits, the Administration is insisting Pharmavax pick up the tab. Whether that tab will take the form of direct compensation in settlement of liability claims, or whether Pharmavax will undertake to pour yet more millions into coming up with an effective antidote – well, that's today's hot question!'

• • •

'So how does it feel to be dumped on by the guys on Capitol Hill?' came a dry voice at Mort's shoulder. Colonel Brad Foster, as an adviser to the Pharmavax board, had been involved right from the start; he now joined Mort at the plate-glass window, and both men looked down at the chaos raging below.

Randall Church, Pharmavax's mild-mannered and immaculate CFO, crashed his fist painfully onto the table. 'That lousy, stinking Russian! I knew we never should have trusted him!'

'Damn it, Randy!' Mort lashed out at his old friend. 'I don't pay you half a million bucks a year to give me that I-told-you-so crap! We *did* trust that lousy, stinking Russian. And you remember who was so damn eager we should do that? Those very same guys who are about to dump Christ-knows how many billions of dollars' worth of liability suits on us unless we get our act together and come up with the goods. Sure, it's my fault as well. I should have told them where to get off – stood out for proper testing, is what it comes down to. But I got greedy. Our shareholders got greedy. And the guys on the Hill got the greediest of the –'

'Hey, Mort, this is what they call crying over spilled milk. This company's stock is totally unsaleable, and half the city's staging a riot out there,' Brad observed dispassionately. 'You should be thinking about how to limit the damage *now*.'

He was interrupted by the deafening din of the fire-alarm. Randall Church grabbed the nearest telephone and jabbed the security chief's number.

'Does this mean there's a fire in the building?' he demanded.

'The screen doesn't show a fire anyplace in the building itself, Mr Church, sir,' the security chief's voice came over the telephone broadcast system. 'But the alarm means there's one somewhere inside the perimeter. You want me to go take a look?'

Church raised an eyebrow at Mort, who shook his head. 'No, Fred. Stay inside for now. Anything you find out, you let us know, OK?' No sooner had Church put the telephone down than it rang. He picked it up. 'Yeah? Yeah, he's here.' He handed the telephone to Mort. 'The guys on the Hill,' he said bleakly.

• • •

A few minutes earlier, round the back of the building, a small group of protesters had managed to make their way unseen to a confined area contained and hemmed in by a window-less wall. Working to a carefully rehearsed plan, they raided the transport bay for flammable packaging materials, reduced pallets to firewood and lit a fire under a twenty-foot tank of propane gas.

Then they threw gasoline on the smouldering mass, and ran for their lives.

• • •

'What the fuck do they mean, refute what I said? No way! they can go –'

'Can't you just issue a statement for now, Mort? We can have one ready in a couple of minutes.'

'You heard them, Randy. They want me, live, on the air, now. Or they'll arraign me on every charge you ever heard of!'

Mort's secretary Jane, who had been with Pharmavax all her working life, looked up, fear in her eyes. 'You can't go out there, Mort,' she pleaded. 'It's way too dangerous.'

'At least don't go out there alone,' Brad said. 'I'll come with you.'

'This isn't your baby, Brad,' Mort sighed. 'I may have nothing left to lose, but you're under no obligation to put yourself at risk.'

'*You're* talking to *me* about risk?' Brad joked grimly. 'What do you think got me into this game in the first place? Anyway, I have a personal reason for coming with you. Let's go.'

• • •

As the fire burned more and more fiercely, the liquid propane gas in the tank began to expand. Gradually, the pressure inside the casing increased far beyond anything it had been designed to withstand.

• • •

Mort and Brad made their way through a jam of terrified employees in the marble entrance hall, pausing only for a hurried consultation with a police officer. 'Is it really necessary for you to go out there, sir?' the heavily-armed cop asked. 'See, we'll do our best, but we can't guarantee your safety.'

'We quite understand, officer,' Mort said smoothly. 'We're going out there entirely at our own risk.'

'Right. Well, good luck, sir.'

The automatic glass doors slid open, and Mort and Brad stepped outside. The anger of the crowd hit them like the blast of heat from a furnace. As the door shut behind them, a vast explosion blew out a whole wing of the Pharmavax building. A blinding fireball, belching thick, black oily smoke, rose roaring into the sky.

As though they had been waiting for such a sign, the crowd charged the protective cordon, trampling police, camera crews, crash barriers and everything else that stood in their way. Without a word, Mort and Brad turned and ran for the safety of the building.

PART TWO

Moscow, February 1997

1.

The black, long-wheelbase Mercedes turned off the main highway south of Moscow, and went along a smaller, less frequented road banked by grimy walls of ploughed snow. The birchwoods would remain leafless for at least another two months, but the morning was frosty and clear, and the sky – as so often in Russia – was luminous duck-egg blue. After the car had gone past several private driveways, the passenger leaned forward.

'Next on the right,' he said to the driver. A hundred yards down the bumpy, single-width drive, they passed through a set of heavy wrought-iron gates, which closed automatically behind them with a scarcely audible click as the driver brought the car to a halt in front of the dacha. He got out and opened the door for his passenger, a distinguished middle-aged Russian in a cashmere overcoat and *chapka*, who carried a brief-case.

A younger man, more informally dressed, came out to welcome him. 'Good morning, Viktor,' he called, smiling.

'Morning, Boris,' the elder man replied, looking round at the well-kept grounds of the dacha. Even under the light blanket of snow, the place looked expensively cared-for. In spring and summer, as Viktor knew, it was beautiful; a clearing of neatly edged lawns in a forest of young birch trees. 'The place is looking good, even at this time of year,' he commented.

'I'm lucky to have such a good gardener. Trouble is, he's so good he's started up his own business. Employs ten people now; they look after all the dachas round here. Making good money too. I don't ask how they make a living during the winter!'

'Well, we can't turn the clock back, can we?' Viktor grunted, changing his brief-case to his left hand with a slight grimace of pain.

'Shoulder still bad?'

'Weeks of physiotherapy and massage, and it doesn't seem to get any better.'

'You'll have to give up playing squash.'

'At only fifty-five? I'm not quite ready for that yet.' As if to prove his point, Viktor ran briskly up the stone steps ahead of his younger colleague.

Pausing only for a quick word with his housekeeper, Marfa, Boris helped Viktor off with his coat and laid it on a chair in the hall before showing him through to the large downstairs room where they would talk.

'I see you've been squandering your salary on more antiques,' Viktor observed in a tone of mock disapproval, running his hand over the lyre-shaped back of a fine mahogany chair. 'Biedermeier, am I right?'

'Very nearly,' Boris said, reluctant to show up his superior's ignorance. 'Actually, it's Chippendale.'

'Chipp – what?'

'An English cabinetmaker. I bought it a long time ago in Kalinin, but you may not have seen it. I've moved everything round a bit since you were last here.'

'And how did an English chair come to be in Kalinin?'

'The woman I bought it from told me her great-grandmother was the daughter of a Scottish timber merchant, who married the son of another timber merchant from Kalinin, and brought eight of them with her as part of her dowry. Of course, to buy eight would be – '

'Impossible even for someone paid as much as you are,' his colleague cut in, an indecipherable glint in his eye.

'Impossible, as you say,' Boris agreed, wondering when his colleague would broach the subject he had come to discuss. Viktor Malakhin settled himself into the Chippendale chair, directly opposite Boris, who sat on a battered old chesterfield. His colleagues thought he was crazy not to buy one of the smart new Italian leather sofas that the bigger stores in Moscow were importing. But Boris liked it the way it was, even though the leather was scuffed and cracking, and the springs twanged when anyone sat on it.

His nerves were beginning – not to twang exactly, but to tighten a little. Friends they might be, but the older man was still his boss. And Viktor was clearly taking his time, establishing control of the conversation before it even started.

He gazed round the room at the mixture of old Russian peasant furniture that Boris had rescued and restored over the years, and the rather grander European pieces he had bought on his travels. The morning sun was softened by the dense birch forest crowding the dacha, and the light seemed to burnish the polished woods and enrich the colours of the kelims on the floor.

'Not so very long ago,' Viktor remarked, 'it would have been said that you had acquired a taste for bourgeois luxury during your years in America.'

Boris was spared the necessity of finding an appropriate answer by a soft knock at the door. Marfa, a stout, black-clad babushka from the nearby village, waddled in and plonked a tray down heavily on the only modern thing in the room, a massive glass coffee-table.

'Thank you, Marfa,' Boris said, as she darted a suspicious glance at Viktor who, she was sure, had come to make trouble for her adored Dr Volkov, and waddled out again.

Boris poured black tea into tall glasses and pushed a dish of cherry jam towards Viktor. Instead Viktor took a slice of lemon and leaned back, patting his belly. 'Got to watch this, I'm afraid,' he said.

'At least have one of these,' Boris said, offering a plate of sugary featherlight *hvorost*. 'I told Marfa I was expecting an important guest, and she insisted on making them.' Viktor grinned and helped himself to several.

'She doesn't listen at keyholes, I hope?' he half-joked. 'Now, as we both know, this is far too secret to be discussed in the city – '

• • •

Outside, in the car, the driver pressed a knob on the walnut dashboard. Within seconds an aerial whirred up from the lid of the trunk. As it extended to its full height a small dish sprang out of the top. Turning the knob, the driver altered the direction of the tiny dish so as to pick up the conversation in the room, not thirty feet away. When the signal was at its peak, he pressed the Record key on the in-car stereo system and sat back, a satisfied smile on his face, to read the morning paper.

• • •

' ... and if I were you, I'd start looking for a property in Siberia. Millions of roubles have gone into this, years of expensive research – look, let me spell it out for you for the very last time.

The bosses need hard currency. They have to have an internationally saleable product. And they've been relying on your contraceptive vaccine to solve the country's economic problems. That's why, over the years, you've been given everything you asked for. And now our golden boy says he wants to dump the whole project!'

'But, Viktor, it's dangerous,' he argued. 'I wouldn't abandon it at this stage if it weren't serious. You haven't seen the effect the vaccine has. I have!'

Viktor quickly raised his index finger to his lips and nodded towards the waiting limousine outside on the driveway. Boris quickly picked up the message and cut short the details of what he was about to recount to his boss.

'Ten years as a research scientist have taught me that if things look this bad at this stage, they're unlikely to get better,' Boris went on. 'All I've said is that I want to scrap this whole line of research and start afresh on another approach.'

'They know that; they've seen your report. But there isn't time. They've spent too much on you and your research to let you have however many more years you might need. We need hard currency now. What they want to know is how long it would take you to come up with an antidote to the side-effects.'

'That's easy,' Boris laughed grimly. 'The best antidote would be just to burn the bloody stuff, never use it at all.'

'Boris, old friend, you don't understand, do you? If the bosses can't make money out of your revolutionary contraceptive because it has undesirable side-effects, then they'll make money out of an antidote. Which you are going to develop. Just as soon as you can. Unless you'd rather be investigating the housing market in Siberia.'

'Are you saying that they're crazy enough to try and *market* the stuff at this stage? No one would buy it if they knew what the side-effects were! It hasn't even been tested on humans yet. Anyway, I'd refuse to release my data. I'd rather destroy the whole –'

'Too late, I'm afraid. At this very moment, all your computer files, all your research notes and all your samples are being transported to one of our top-secret research institutes in Novosibirsk. All except the results of the animal testing. Those, scarcely surprisingly, have been destroyed.'

Boris leapt to his feet, knocking the tea-tray to the floor. He was shaking with rage. 'This is appalling. You can't do this. It's criminal – immoral! You, of all people!'

Viktor carefully put his cup and saucer down. 'I know you feel betrayed. To be honest, I don't much like it either. We've been friends for a long time, and I'd rather not have to do this. But the bosses own us both, Boris. And I don't fancy the salt-mines either. So I've been instructed to tell you that that stuff is going to find its way out into the wide world, whether you like it or not. Our plans for it are already far advanced. A few days ago we let it be known that you had reached an interesting stage in your animal testing. And your assistant Chernov – he's one of ours, did you know? – has been told to bait the hook but not deliver the goods. We intend to let our foreign friends come in and help themselves.

'So the best thing you can do – the *only* thing you can do – is to set about developing the antidote. I'm under orders to take you back to Moscow today. Then you're to be sent to Novosibirsk to start work. You can have your old team to work with you. And you'll even be able to travel abroad; in fact, they want you to go to London, to that conference in May, as planned. The only difference is that you're to go as Kandinsky.'

Boris sat slumped, in shock, unable to move or speak. To think that his friendship with Viktor should have come to this! When he was a student, it was the older man who had pulled the strings for him to spend five years doing postgraduate work in immuno-chemistry at MIT, an unheard-of privilege even for KGB operatives in pre-perestroika days. Five years during which he lived under the false identity of Ivan Kandinsky, enjoying to the full everything America had to offer, before returning to Russia to work as a government research scientist under the aegis of the KGB.

It was Viktor who stepped in when Boris went off the rails after his beloved Yelena died of raging septicaemia following a botched abortion. He had been incapable of working properly for months, and if it hadn't been for Viktor, his career would have gone down the drain completely. And it was Viktor who had arranged that Boris should be seconded from the State Industrial Espionage Bureau to head the Russian government's reproductive-biology project in an effort to develop a failsafe male contraceptive vaccine, knowing that after Yelena's death such a project would be close to his heart.

For more than fifteen years, Boris had looked up to Viktor as his mentor and friend. How naive he had been to think that this friendship came without strings attached! There were strings all right, and now Viktor was pulling them!

'I have been asked to do many evil things in my life. But this is the worst. It goes against everything I've ever worked for, as a scientist and as a human being. I really cannot do what you ask. I *will* not do it! I'd rather run any risk – of disgrace, exile, even of being shot –'

'That all sounds very high-minded, Boris,' Viktor observed dispassionately. 'But such dramatic martyrdom is not an option. You'd be no good to us in disgrace, or in exile. And we certainly have no wish to shoot you. We have too much invested in you. But what, I wonder, of your colleagues? Vera Felipova, now. You've worked with her for years –'

'So?'

'She has a little daughter. Remind me of her name.'

'You *know* the child's name, damn you!'

Viktor's smile was bland. 'Of course. Little Lydia. She's nine, I believe. And doing so well at her school. Her *special* school.'

'I cannot believe that even the bosses would sink so low as deliberately to harm a child.'

'Oh, the *child* would come to no real harm. But she only has the excellent education she has by virtue of her mother being such a highly respected member of your team.'

'Are you saying that you would throw Vera Felipova out of her job, just to get at me?'

Viktor shrugged. 'You know yourself how badly we Russians drive, how unreliable our cars can be. And our roads are not at all well maintained, I'm afraid. A dead scientist is, of course, a loss to her profession. But her orphan daughter would no longer be entitled to stay at the special *gymnasium*. And that new lab technician you took on last year – Feliks Vernin, isn't it? A nice-looking young man. He seems to enjoy life, wouldn't you say?'

'You don't need to go on,' Boris muttered, his face thunderous in contrast to Viktor's bland serenity. 'Is there nothing you can do to prevent this – this evil?'

'Absolutely nothing, my friend,' Viktor's steady smile betrayed no emotion whatever. 'Absolutely nothing.'

2.

'Good morning, gentlemen – Veronica. Take your seats, please and we'll get started.'

Brad Foster, colonel commanding A10 Special Ops Task Force, sat down briskly, straightened the papers in front of him and turned round to make a minute adjustment to the overhead projector. He took a sip of mineral water and launched into his well-prepared presentation.

'For the past month, you have all been making detailed preparations for a mission. And I'm confident that you've got everything as near perfect as you can, given that none of you actually knows what the mission is. But I was required to keep you in the dark until today. I now have clearance to tell you that it is codenamed Operation Hot Shot. We should be ready within the week. Indeed, we're under considerable pressure to go at the soonest possible moment.'

'So where're we going, boss?' Major Larry Dougan asked.

'Russia. Novosibirsk, to be exact.'

'Just like in the good old days, huh?'

'Not quite, major,' Brad replied evenly. 'Let me come straight to the point. Our intelligence sources have confirmed that the Russians have come up with a male contraceptive vaccine.'

'Christ!' Dougan exploded incredulously. 'You sure? I mean, come on! Haven't we had people working on that these past ten years? And you're telling me we've been beaten to it by the goddam Russians?'

'That's exactly what I'm telling you, Larry. I was as astonished as you when I heard. But all the indications are that it's true.'

'So where do we come in, sir?' Sam Young, a massive-framed footballer, enquired in his usual blunt fashion. 'If they have it all wrapped up, it doesn't sound like a job for our team.'

'Wrong, sergeant,' Brad replied with a grin. 'Listen up, and it'll come clear. As you all know, since the Wall came down back in 89, the Russians have been in bad financial trouble. Sure, they have massive natural resources, but in all this time they haven't been able to exploit them efficiently. And they've never gotten the hang of playing the international markets. So what do they do? They decide to make use of their other great asset – brainpower. A couple of years ago they redirected all the best people from their germ warfare and space laboratories into the task of finding the perfect contraceptive by the year 2000. And it seems that that's what they've done.'

'Sounds kinda crazy to me,' Larry Dougan interrupted. 'You'd think they'd be more interested in finding ways to feed themselves. The way I read it, they're having a hard time just keeping the lid on the next revolution. Why'd they waste time playing with chemistry sets?'

'Because, Larry,' Brad replied smoothly, 'they reckoned – rightly, I'd say – that if they could find a near perfect contraceptive, there'd be such a massive demand for the stuff worldwide, they'd be able to name any price they pleased. In fact, the guys over at Langley tell me the Russians plan to hold some kind of international auction and let the highest bidder have it.'

'But won't that just mean one multinational bidding against another?' asked Major Veronica Houston, a pretty black woman who only just made the US Armed Forces' minimum-height requirement.

'That's right, major.'

'Well, it's one way for them to sort out their foreign-currency problems,' she observed with a hint of admiration in her voice. 'And any Western governments that wanted to play good guys could help Third World countries, in return for some kind of kickback.'

'Let's hope so. Now, I don't need to tell you that the President has no intention of allowing the United States to be blackmailed on this. Which is where we come in.'

'You mean we're going to go in and actually steal the stuff?' Veronica Houston asked. 'I'd assumed, from our information so far, that this would be just another industrial process job.'

'As far as we're concerned, that's exactly what it is,' Brad replied firmly. 'I want no questions about morality or legality on this one. It's a job just like all the others, and we're under orders. OK, everybody?'

'OK, colonel,' came a chorus of answers.

'The guys at Langley say we can go in whenever we like, so

long as it's soon. I'd like to go this next weekend. Our cover is that we're selling computer components to every industrial outfit in and around Novosibirsk. To make it convincing, we're actually taking a load of computer stuff with us. The gear we really need for our mission will be included in that shipment. The Russians are so desperate for computer parts, they're not likely to give us a hard time. So for the first week Sam will actually be hauling the parts round Novosibirsk and selling the damn things. The manufacturer knows to expect orders as a result.'

Sam Young groaned. 'The things I do for you guys! Do I at least get commission on sales?' he quipped with a smile.

'Only job satisfaction, Sam. Look, this is the best way. You're practically a native Russian speaker, and you know computers like nobody else. You got any better ideas for a cover?'

'No, sir. But I do have some queries. Wouldn't it have been a whole lot easier just to pay some guy on the inside to walk out with the stuff?'

'We thought of that – don't imagine we didn't. You know we only ever set up missions like this if there's no other way. We did have a guy at the research lab, but something spooked him, and the word is that he won't play. Trouble is, all those guys are either KGB, or they're so intimidated they don't dare step out of line. You might think things have changed, but they're not so different from the way they were. No, if we want that data, we're going to have to go in and get it ourselves.'

'One more question, colonel? I assume the information we're going after is stored on datafiles, and you want me and Major Houston to transcribe it from disks. But what if they have a whole roomful of disks? Sure, I know Russian, but I don't know how to tell the difference between stuff we want and stuff we don't. I'm no expert. It could take a helluva long time to transcribe every disk in the place. I don't really go for that.'

'Don't worry,' Brad answered. 'You'll get a damn good briefing before we go. Now, Major Houston will tell us how we get into the joint. Over to you, Veronica.'

Veronica leaned over and pressed a switch on the overhead projector. A satellite reconnaissance shot of a huge scientific complex appeared on the screen. 'It took me a while to guess what this place was, but I reckoned it had to be some sort of government research laboratory, and in Russia – probably Siberia. I kinda narrowed it down to Novosibirsk.'

'You mean the Russians have all their research guys shut up in one place, boss?' Larry Dougan wanted to know.

'Our information indicates that all the scientists involved in this particular project are concentrated there, yes. Go on, please, Veronica.'

As Veronica Houston continued to analyse the satellite pictures of the Siberian research lab, Brad let his mind wander just a little. Damn right Sam was going to need a full briefing as to exactly what information to go for. And he'd given the matter a lot of thought.

'Right, back to you, sir,' Veronica concluded, turning to her superior. 'Who are we going to approach to get the information we need?'

'I've already been looking into possible candidates.' Brad changed the acetate on the overhead projector, to reveal a photograph of a tall, attractive woman in her late thirties, with long auburn hair, smartly dressed and with a decidedly confident air about her.

'Hey, is she gonna come and hold my hand?' Sam quipped.

'This is Dr Jillian Peters. Her boss, Dr Mira Harman, is head of the National Institutes of Health's Human Reproduction Research Lab out at Bethesda. You might think Dr Harman would be the obvious first choice, but my information is that she wouldn't even give us the time of day. This lady, though, is another matter altogether. She's dedicated to discovering a contraceptive vaccine and has been bursting a blood vessel for ten years or more to find one. She's English but resident here since the early 1980s. She was married to another scientist, but her marriage lost out to her job. She's good. *And* she's squeaky clean. So getting security clearance to involve her shouldn't be a problem.'

'Sounds a good idea,' Veronica observed. 'So how are we going to do it?'

'I thought we'd start with you tracking her movements for a few days. It's Monday today – say, Thursday, I'll get alongside her somewhere discreet and put this plan to her. So you have three days to work out the best way for me to get to her, major.'

'With respect, sir,' Sam interjected. 'This all seems kinda late in the day. I thought you said we're going this weekend.'

'We are,' Brad assured him. 'Our guy in Novosibirsk chickened out, but the brass are turning up the heat to go with the original date just the same. I'm under a helluva lot of pressure on this one. Anything goes wrong, the guys on Capitol Hill will think I screwed up, and they're out for my blood if we don't get this thing done – and soon.'

'So let's hope you can talk the lady into cooperating,' Veronica laughed good-naturedly, glancing up at the photo on the screen. 'She looks like she has a mind of her own. It'll take all your charm to get a result.'

'I think you can safely leave that to me, major,' Brad said drily. But, out of sight behind the illuminated projector, he smiled to himself.

3.

For Jill Peters, jogging was about more than just keeping fit. It was her private time, the only moment in the day when she was totally free to think her own thoughts, in the beautiful natural surroundings that reminded her so strongly of her native Hampshire, back in England. Rock Creek Park, north-west of the urban sprawl of Washington, was looking particularly lovely in the early May morning. At seven thirty, the air was still fresh and cool, the sun just catching the creamy blossoms of the dogwood and flowering cherry trees, lighting up the tender yellow-green of the maple leaves and the new shoots of the pignut hickory trees – not that those grew naturally in Hampshire. After several years of early morning runs, Jill knew the park's fifty miles of hiking trails and bridle paths well. This one, her favourite, took her past the Rock Creek Park Horse Center.

'Hi, Karen!' she called. The groom straightened up and waved.

'Hi, Jill. We're seeing you Saturday, right? With Jim? Tell him he can have Jasper.'

Jill pounded rhythmically on through the woodland, bearing south-east towards Rock Creek itself. Come July and August, it would be almost too hot to run by seven thirty, and she would have to get up earlier still. Everyone who could left the city during those suffocatingly humid months, but Jill's work meant she could rarely let up for more than a few days at a time.

Just after turning south along the hornbeam-lined banks of Rock Creek, she became aware of someone running behind her. There were other joggers in the park, many of whom Jill knew by sight. Even though she didn't seriously think the person behind her was in any way a threat, she snatched a quick glance over her shoulder. A man was coming along behind, gradually gaining on her. As he drew level, Jill slowed slightly to let him overtake her, preferring to keep him in front where she could see him.

For a few minutes, he ran in front of her, the gap between them widening. He was a tall, well-built man – in his early forties, Jill judged – and fit enough to be not even breathing heavily. His well-worn sweatpants and running shoes betrayed heavy use. 'Not bad,' Jill grinned to herself, suddenly conscious of her flushed face and sweat-damp hair and wishing she had put on the smart new running pants and matching headband she had bought just the week before. After a few minutes, the man had run ahead, and was out of sight on the winding trail. Jill forgot all about him.

• • •

But around the next bend, he was waiting for her. Jill was used to the conventions of verbal and body-language among joggers, the 'Hi!' that could mean either just 'Hi' or 'Can we talk?', the stance that indicated 'I'm just taking a break, not trying to pick you up.' But this man was standing across the path, arms folded. Waiting for her.

'Damn!' Jill swore silently. 'You ran right into this one, kid!'

She took a deep breath to quiet her suddenly pounding heart and felt for the reassuring cylinder of the rape alarm that lived in the pocket of her sweatpants. Turning back was not an option – she was too far from the place where the Rapids Bridge Trail branched off, and the man stood between her and the Boulder Bridge Trail turn-off. She had to get past him somehow; that was the only way. Her stomach churning with fear, Jill realised that this was not a man who had become fit by reading books about it. As she ran towards him as fast as she could, he called out, 'Dr Peters? I need to talk with you.'

Jill stopped, keeping several yards between them. 'Who are you?' she panted furiously. 'And how do you know who I am?'

'I'm Colonel Brad Foster. Want to see my ID?' He took a small folder from the pocket of his sweatshirt and held it up, open to show his photograph. It was a Pentagon pass.

'No, thank you!' Jill snapped. 'I asked, how do you know who I am?'

'It's my business to know, ma'am,' the colonel replied unperturbed. 'I've been authorised to approach you –'

'By whom?' Jill enquired icily.

'I'm authorised to tell you that, but I need to talk with you first.'

'Look, I don't appreciate this. If you know who I am, you know where I work; you can call me there.' And she tried to push past him. He put out a hand to bar her way, but without touching her.

'There's a seat up ahead. I'd like for us to go there and sit and talk for a while. You'd be free to get up and go at any time.'

'You bet I would! Five minutes. That's all you get!'

'Sure!' The colonel's strong-featured face creased into a disarming grin. 'After all, you have to get home, shower, change and get off to your lab. By the way, you planning to go horseback-riding with Jim this Saturday?' And he turned and loped away from her, towards the bench.

Stunned by his detailed knowledge of her personal life, Jill stayed rooted to the spot. Brad stopped and turned round. 'Look,' he called softly, 'if I'd meant you any harm, I could have gotten to you or your son any time. Relax! Like I said, we just need to talk.'

A few seconds later, they were at the wooden bench. Brad flung himself down, legs outstretched, looking bushed, which Jill knew full well he wasn't. Tense and wary, she sat as far away from him as possible.

'First, I'd like to apologise for scaring you half to death. Sure, I could have called you at the lab. But you would have cut me off. And I'd rather avoid getting snarled up with your boss.'

'Dr Harman?'

'Right. We decided you'd be more sympathetic.'

'Sympathetic to what?' The icy suspicion crept back into Jill's voice.

'Dr Peters, you are a nationally respected scientist, currently working – as you have done for many years – on reproductive biology –'

'The details of my work may be secret, but the fact that I do it isn't. You'll have to do better than that, colonel.'

'What I'm about to tell you is every bit as secret as the work that you do. I have security clearance to tell you this, because we know that your work is also subject to strict security controls. If you don't believe me, you can ring a Pentagon number that I'll give you. Or you can ask anyone you know in the Administration, and they'll refer you to someone at the very highest level who will confirm what I say. I should add that they're not keen to advertise their connection with this project. However, I can assure you I do have sufficient authority to talk to you.'

'OK. So?'

'So I'm involved in a top-secret operation to obtain a male contraceptive vaccine – and one that, by all accounts, has other substantial advantages too.'

Jill leapt to her feet. 'Are you kidding? What are you, some kind of head case? My lab has been working on that for years, spending more millions than I care to think about, and we're still years off coming up with one. When do you think I was born, colonel?'

'Look, I'm not underrating your dedication. I know your marriage even broke up because of it –'

'Damn you! Is there anything you don't know about me?'

'Plenty,' the colonel grinned again, grey eyes crinkling and with a teasing note in his voice. 'But maybe we should talk about that some other time.'

'We'll do nothing of the kind!' Despite herself, Jill had to admit that Brad Foster, with his wiry dark hair greying just the way she liked it, to say nothing of his sheer physicality, was the most attractive man she'd met in ages. Stop it, Jill! she scolded herself.

'If there's anything you need to know about the work I do, you should ask Mira Harman.'

'Yeah, but my dad always said to go for the good-looking ones!'

'Get back to the point, colonel. Your time's running out.' Jill was damned if she was going to be won over by his outrageous charm.

'OK, the point is this. The Russians have created this male contraceptive vaccine, and I and my team have been authorised to go into Russia and steal their formulation.'

'Colonel, this is starting to sound like something you've made up.'

'It's true. And I can prove it.'

'Well, if the Russians have cracked it, why do you need me?'

'On my team I have an explosives expert, a logistics officer, a computer man who is also fluent in Russian – everyone I need but a scientist.'

'If you think I'm about to go off on some crazy raid into Russia –'

'Of course we're not asking you to do that, Jill – may I call you Jill? We just need some information, which you can give us.'

'I'd have to clear it with Dr Harman.'

'We'd rather you didn't.'

'What if I simply refuse? The whole thing sounds highly questionable – even illegal –'

'There's more to it. If you're prepared to listen, that is.'

'Go on.'

'You have a fourteen-year-old son –'

'What does all this have to do with him?' Jill flared up defensively.

'The life you lead doesn't place you in a high-risk category. But can you say the same for Jim in a few years' time?'

'High-risk category for what, for God's sake?'

'It won't be long before he's sexually active, if he isn't already. You remember I mentioned that this Russian vaccine has other substantial advantages? Well, one of them is that not only does it provide life-long contraception but it also appears to prevent infection with the HIV virus. I'm sure you know plenty of women who've lost brothers, husbands, friends or sons to AIDS –'

Jill had to admit to herself that Brad Foster had found her weak spot. More than her own work on the contraceptive vaccine, Jill worried about her son's future in an AIDS-blighted world. And on a wider scale, the spread of HIV would soon threaten America's export markets as Third World populations dwindled. So even if Jim lived a healthy life, it was possible he might not have a job when he grew up. Jill had sometimes wondered if she should switch to AIDS research, but her contract with NIH was a good one, so she stayed.

'What else do you know about this Russian vaccine?' Jill asked, fascinated in spite of her misgivings.

'What it appears they've done is to take tetanus toxoid and sort of bolt on something that makes a man permanently sterile without being impotent, plus another chemical that prevents HIV infection. I don't understand it, but I don't have to. You're the scientist, so I assume it makes sense to you.'

'If you're right, colonel, they have some very clever people working on this. It's what we've been trying to achieve for years.'

'So why haven't you? If you've been working on it all this time –'

Jill sighed. 'Time is what it takes. Do you know how long it takes to test even the minutest development? Every single modification to the –'

'OK, OK, I get the message. So what's the big idea behind this vaccine anyway? Are you allowed to tell me that?'

'The big idea behind *our* work, you mean? I have a well-rehearsed spiel, if you want it.'

'Go ahead.'

'Well, under normal circumstances, when a sperm meets an egg in a woman's reproductive system, it recognises that the egg actually *is* an egg. After all, if you think about it, a sperm meets millions of cells in the woman's body on its way to get to an egg. The sixty-four thousand dollar question has always been: why doesn't it try to get into any or all of those other cells?'

'So why doesn't it?'

'Because there's something about the surface of the egg itself that the sperm recognises as unique – its final destination, if you like. It's as if a key were able to recognise the lock it was made to fit. What my team has been looking for all these years is that lock-and-key mechanism.'

'So this lock-and-key thing is the big breakthrough?'

'Sure. Once you can identify the proteins that make the lock or the key, you can create a vaccine against them. So that when a sperm from a vaccinated man comes up against an egg, it doesn't penetrate it like it normally would. In fact, it will have been programmed not to.'

'The Russian vaccine is a lifelong thing. Does yours last for life too? Once the guy is vaccinated, he can't ever have kids again, is that right?'

'Yes. The vaccines we've been developing are really irreversible sterilisation methods,' Jill answered. 'They're permanent. In fact, all the original ideas about this came from studying men who were infertile, sterile for life.'

'So what happens if a guy wants to change his mind?'

'Well, we're working hard at that one. Ideally, men would only use it once they'd completed their families. But there'll always be people who change their minds. So we're looking at several ways of overcoming the effects of the vaccine when a couple want to have a baby.'

'This far I can understand. But what's all the stuff about tetanus toxoid vaccine? I have a shot for that every few years in my job, but I'm damn sure no one ever told me it was a contraceptive.'

'In itself, it isn't. It's just being used as the carrier for the vaccine itself.' Jill grinned. 'I know, it doesn't seem at all logical if you don't know about the workings of the immune system.'

'Just assume I know nothing, doctor, and you won't be far wrong.'

'Well, for some time now we've been using tetanus toxoid in trials, as the carrier for a female contraceptive vaccine. Like I said, in itself tetanus toxoid isn't a contraceptive; it's just used to make the immune system responsive to molecules it would otherwise ignore, by stimulating things we call T cells. But from what you're saying, the Russians have gone a step byond that and added an HIV antigen on to the tetanus toxoid molecule. Which means the person who gets it is not only sterile, but safe from HIV as well.' Jill's mind was racing at the enormity of the whole idea.

'Quite a lot of guys would think they'd been given the front doorkey to heaven,' Brad smiled. The pretty English scientist, even with sweat-damp hair and unmade-up face, was better looking than the groomed woman in the photographs. And with her face and voice alight with enthusiasm, she was one hell of a sexy woman. In fact, Brad thought, this is probably just how she'd look after making love.

'It'll revolutionise the whole business of contraception,' she went on, almost as though she hadn't heard him. 'At last, it won't be only women who have to take the responsibility. OK, men have always used condoms, but many women don't trust them. And there are always vasectomies, but this will be a *real* advance.'

'You seem to get a real buzz out of all this, Jill,' Brad remarked.

'Of course I do,' she replied. Then her voice became wistful. 'I've dedicated the whole of my professional life to this field of research. And now you're telling me all my work's been made redundant. I suppose I should be really down about this – that someone else has gotten there first. But in fact I'm intrigued. I thought there were only three teams in the world working on this. Clearly I was wrong. There was another horse in the race.'

'So you'll help, then?'

Jill came swiftly down to earth and looked at her watch. 'I'm going to have to get moving, colonel. You'd better get on and tell me exactly what it is you want.'

'OK. My team and I are going to bring home the information about this Russian drug on disks transcribed from datafiles stored at their government research facility at Novosibirsk. How precisely we do that needn't concern you. But they could have hundreds, thousands of files. Now, I said I had a Russian-speaking computer expert on my team. But he's no scientist. He'll need to be told exactly which disks to look for, how they might be labelled, so we don't have to spend a week transcribing every file in the place.'

'What you'd need to bring back would be on no more than one disk, maybe two.'

'All the more reason to know what we're after.'

'Won't their security be really tight? I know what it's like at NIH.'

'We can take care of that,' Brad said dismissively. 'I just need to know the sort of information you guys would need if you were going to replicate their research and make trial batches for testing.'

'You guys? You mean – ?'

'Who else?' Brad grinned. 'So, you see, it's in your interest to ensure we come out with the right information.'

For an instant Jill's enthusiasm dimmed and faltered. 'It seems dreadfully unprofessional, to steal another team's work. Dishonest – '

'Don't forget, we're both following orders on this one. If you refuse to help, as you're quite at liberty to do, there are commercial organisations who would kill for the chance to tell us what we need to know, if it meant they got to develop the vaccine. Also, I happen to know you've retained your British citizenship. I could see the guys in suits giving you a hard time about staying in this country –'

'– if I didn't give you the information you need,' Jill snapped, all her euphoria dissipated. She sighed exasperatedly. 'OK, I can tell you what to look for. But it would really help if you could get your hands on the results of the animal testing. I'm certain we could replicate any of the Russians' basic immunology. But with any new compound, the problem is finding out how it acts in living things. We always start off with animals.'

'Our information indicates they've done some work on monkeys.'

Jill glanced at her watch. 'I have to go, colonel, or I'll be late for work.' She got up from the bench, and started to run down the track to the parking area. Brad quickly caught up, until he was loping easily along beside her.

'Expect a call later today from my computer guy. And call me Brad, why don't you? After all, if this thing comes off, we'll be seeing a lot more of each other.' He drew ahead of her, a hand lifted briefly to wave goodbye. Within seconds, he was out of sight.

4.

'Hi, Jill!' Shirlene Peters emerged smiling from the bean rows in her front yard, brushing the dirt from her hands. 'Art's not back yet. He said he'd be here when you came, but you know how he is. C'mon in and have a cup of coffee. I baked some of those pecan cookies you like.'

'Thanks, Shirlene, you know I can't resist them.'

Shirlene opened the door into the cramped hallway of the modest tract home and she and Jill went in. Jill was genuinely fond of her ex-husband's second wife. After the initial pain of the break-up of her own marriage to Art, and the soul-searching and anguish that had gone into the decision to entrust her son to his step-mother, Jill realised that Shirlene was the best thing that could have happened to all three of them. Jill freely acknowledged that she was so involved in her work, and the inhuman hours it demanded, that if she had to bring up her son as well, she would be short-changing him, emotionally and in every other way. Shirlene had a part-time job that left her plenty of time to devote to her home, her husband and Jim.

Although the two women would never have become friends had it not been for Jim – and indeed, Jill admitted, she wouldn't even have stayed friends with Art, or he with her, if it weren't for Jim – they agreed on most things and respected each other. Shirlene stood in awe of Jill's scientific achievements and envied her her long-boned, elegant looks, while Jill admired the energy Shirlene put into stocking the freezer, tending the tiny garden until it produced riots of flowers and gluts of vegetables, embroidering cushion covers and making baby clothes for her friends. Most important, Shirlene wholeheartedly loved Jill's son and was never even slightly possessive of him.

Jill hung her jacket on the fake-wood coat rack in the hallway. 'I hope they're back soon. I've booked a couple of hours' riding for Jim and me.'

'Oh, Jill honey, you know Art's never all that late,' Shirlene said soothingly, setting out a plateful of the cookies she knew Jill liked. 'I'm not saying it's deliberate on his part, or anything like that, but I reckon it's just his way of getting back at you.'

'Even after ten years?' Jill laughed bitterly.

'Well, I've been thinking about the way he acts towards you. You know, it couldn't have been easy for him. A guy wants to be a hot-shot scientist, sees his wife being promoted way ahead of him, over and over – well, you know what Art's pride is like.'

'Tell me about it! Even when we were both at Cambridge, he was always going to be the one who would win the Nobel Prize. He was a good scientist back then. And I went on believing in him for a long time, even after he stopped believing in himself. But, to be honest, he got a raw deal being married to me. I was always working late, and at weekends, even after Jim was born. I just wasn't cut out for marriage and motherhood, I guess. Not like you, huh?'

Shirlene picked up the tray of coffee and cookies and went through to the lounge, a room furnished with simulated leather sofas and kitsch knick-knacks, which had appalled Jill when she first saw it. Now she was used to it and even regarded the place with a certain affection. It was certainly far more homely than Jill's own Nebraska Avenue apartment would ever be.

The two women settled themselves with their coffee, the cookie plate within easy reach. 'Something else I've been thinking about,' Shirlene said. 'You know how I used to be so sad I couldn't have kids, even though I wanted them so bad? Well, I've come to see that it's best the way it is. Between you and me, Jill honey, Art needs a mother more than he needs a wife. I'm always here for him, which is what he wants. And I keep house like his mom used to, which is what he likes too. And it's what I want.'

'You're so much better for him than I ever was. You put up with all the morose, depressive moods – all his tantrums. I never could.'

'Sure, he's not the easiest guy in the world. But I love him for all that. Don't you have a saying in England – "horses for courses"? Well, that's us.'

Jill drank her coffee, reflecting that although compared to her Shirlene was practically uneducated, she seemed to have a PhD in common-sense. Having Shirlene as a friend made her life so much easier, and Jill trusted her absolutely where Jim was concerned. Mother and step-mother both had his interests at heart, and between them they'd ensured he turned out a good kid.

'You know what Jim said the other day? He said, "I'm luckier than the other kids at school – I've got two moms, and they're both great!" Don't you think that's neat?'

'What's he been up to this week?'

'Oh, the usual things. And I have to tell you, I've taken calls from no less than three of the girls in his class, just this week alone. He's turning into an attractive young man. Course, it's a good thing he inherited your looks and not his dad's!'

Jill laughed and asked, 'What about Art? I never dare ask him how his work is going.'

'He's just bored to death at that AIDS lab. He says it's OK, but I reckon if somebody offered him something different he'd leap at the chance, not that it's likely to happen now. And something else. You remember how he never used to stop running off at the mouth about gays spreading AIDS and killing us all? Well, as the years go by, he's getting worse and worse.'

'You're kidding! He couldn't be more bigoted than he was!'

'Seriously, honey. You know the way things are now, specially in Africa and all those poor countries? He's going round telling everybody, "I told you so."'

'But, Shirlene, with his strict Catholic upbringing, sex was a whole guilt trip anyway, a sort of plague in itself. And all those years of therapy didn't seem to help much.'

'Sure didn't. Cost a bomb, though. You know he's been talking about moving right away, to Florida maybe?'

Jill put her coffee-cup down sharply.

'Don't worry, honey. There's no way we're going anywhere yet awhile. We wouldn't take Jim away from you, and anyways my mom and dad need me close by. No, it's just that he wants to get right away from the job, from the lab, from being in your shadow – sorry to say that, Jill, but it's true.'

'But if you moved, how would he earn a living?'

Shirlene sighed. 'That's a problem. At his age, I guess all he could get would be something in a routine lab in a hospital someplace.'

'He'd be worse off than he is now, Shirlene! I know I'd cut my throat in six months if I had to do that!'

'Sure you would. That's just one of the differences between

you guys, I guess. OK, he'd be bored – I agree with you there. But it's just that he has this dream of getting somewhere right away, maybe still doing some kind of medical research, but away from here, so he doesn't have to compare himself with you all the time. Jill, honey, let's face it: beside you, Art is a failure. As a husband to me, and as a dad to Jim, he's a success. But as a scientist, he hasn't made it, and he isn't going to. Trouble is, he knows it, but he won't admit it.'

'But fifteen years ago, when I first met him, he was good. Where did it all go?'

'You know the real reason he wants to amount to something? Even after all this time, he wants respect and approval from you! I don't know beans about what it is he does all day at that lab, but it makes no difference to the way we feel about each other. My guess is: he's still secretly a little bit in love with you!'

'Surely not!'

Shirlene shrugged her plump shoulders good-naturedly. 'I think that's why he acts the way he does sometimes, like a little kid wanting attention from his mom.'

Jill got up and walked over to the window. She was still feeling slightly strung out after her encounter with Brad Foster and his team at their headquarters the day before, and Art bringing Jim home late was something that always annoyed her. 'If Art doesn't turn up soon, we're going to miss our booking,' she fumed.

'He'll be here,' Shirlene said placidly. 'You're always ahead of time, and he knows it really gets to you when he's late. Just on the odd occasion like this, he can be in control of you. That's all.'

Jill laughed. 'That's the trouble with coming from an army family. Army time is always five minutes ahead of time. My father used to get really angry if people were late. I guess I inherited that from him!'

'And he's been sore about the way you went off to that conference after you said you'd do something with Jim last weekend.'

'I know,' Jill replied calmly. 'But I really can't get into justifying every move after all these years. Jim understands, and that's all that matters to me.'

'There they are now,' Shirlene said, changing the subject with relief as Art's car drew up in the street outside. She gathered up the cups and plates and took them through to the kitchen.

'Hi, Mom!' Jim yelled, filling the narrow hallway as he ambled in, sports bag over his shoulder. He and Jill hugged as if it had been two years rather than two weeks since they last saw each other. Although Jill was tall for a woman, Jim was a couple of inches taller still and seemed to shoot up every week. Jill placed a hand flat on top of his head.

'We'll have to tell Shirlene to stop feeding you on her super-strength plant food!'

'It's not my fault I have an undersize dwarf for a mom! Hey, the guys at school saw that piece in the paper about you speaking at that conference next week in London! They thought it was real neat!'

Uneasily aware that this was sensitive ground, Jill hurriedly switched tack. 'Let's talk about it later. Look, we should get moving. Karen said you could have Jasper today, and we don't want to be late.'

'Great! I'll go get my stuff!' And Jim went bounding up the stairs.

'Sorry we're late back,' Art grunted. Jill mentally bit her tongue and resolved not to let him get to her.

'That's OK,' she smiled serenely. But Art wasn't going to let her go without getting his teeth into her.

'So last weekend's meeting was real important, huh? More important than your own kid?'

'Art, honey –' Shirlene pleaded.

'You'd rather go play the big-shot scientist than come and see your own kid, is that it?'

Jill felt the all-too familiar anger blazing up inside her – how could an intelligent man like Art be quite so stupid? But for Jim and Shirlene's sake, she forced it back down. 'No, Art,' she said evenly. 'That's not how it is at all. You know there's nothing I'd rather do than spend time with Jim. But sometimes my job –'

'You and that damn job!' And Art charged into the downstairs den and slammed the door.

'Oh, Jill honey, he doesn't mean the half of what he says,' Shirlene tried to soothe Jill, who was shaking with suppressed anger. It was a long time since Art had flown at her like that. She took a deep breath.

'Shirlene, I don't think all that was just about my missing a weekend with Jim.'

'You're right; it wasn't. But let's not discuss it right now. You'll bring Jim back the usual time Sunday?'

'Of course. Thanks for the coffee and cookies, and the wisdom, Shirlene.'

Jim came crashing down the stairs two at a time. Jill hoped he hadn't heard the altercation in the hallway. 'Bye, Shirlene.' He hugged her goodbye, and followed his mother out to the car.

• • •

For a few minutes mother and son chatted and laughed about nothing in particular. Then they found themselves stuck in a slow-moving line of cars waiting to turn left at an intersection, and the conversation flagged. Suddenly, Jim said, 'Mom, I heard Dad shouting in the hallway –'

'I'm sorry you heard all that,' Jill said, attempting to sound sensible and unflustered.

'Thing is, Mom, I don't think he was mad at you.'

'Well, he was certainly giving a good impression of it. Look, I'm sorry about last weekend. Did it mess up Dad's plans?'

'It didn't mess up anything, mom. It was fine, really. Dad and me, we went to a ball game, and then I slept over at Scott's house, and Dad and Shirlene went bowling. And it was OK. Really,' he said again.

'So why was your father shouting at me, then?' Jill enquired, mentally chastising herself for the turn the conversation was taking. She had always tried hard to be scrupulously fair about Art as far as Jim was concerned.

'I guess he's kinda worried – about Shirlene.'

At that moment, the traffic started to move forward, and Jill devoted her attention to clearing the intersection before the lights changed. Once they were moving again, she asked, 'What about Shirlene?'

'I don't know. I guess she's sick or something. I didn't ask. And I didn't say anything to you, right?'

'Right. Thank you for telling me. I won't say anything until she or Dad mentions it. God, I hope she's OK.'

'Yeah,' said Jim. 'Me too.'

5.

Mort shuddered to a climax, holding Jill close; they moved in harmony, as they had done so many times over the years. Slowly, Jill relaxed, laying her legs flat, keeping Mort inside her as he smothered her with tiny kisses. After a few seconds, he lifted his head, and took her face between his hands. Flushed, sweaty and breathless, he thought, she looked ecstatically beautiful.

'Great, isn't it?' he smiled down at her.

'It should be,' she grinned back. 'After all, how many years have we been practising?'

'A long time.' Mort rolled to one side and lay on his back. 'A long time,' he repeated thoughtfully.

For a few minutes they lay snuggled together, silent but companionable. Then Mort said, 'I'd like it to go on being good for a long while yet.'

Jill lifted herself up on one elbow. 'Why shouldn't it?' she asked.

'No reason at all,' Mort answered. 'But I'd like things to get even better. I'd prefer to have you all to myself. And when I quit Pharmavax a couple of years from now –'

It was Jill's turn to roll over to lie flat on her back. 'Oh, Mort,' she sighed wearily. 'How many times have we had this conversation? Whenever we start this, I tell you I don't want to give up my work. I'm doing well at NIH, and I really want to finish this project.'

'And how many more years is *that* going to take?' Mort half-jeered. 'Do I have to wait around till we're both too old to have any fun, while you futz around with some half-assed attempt to find a contraceptive vaccine –'

'Mort, what are you saying?' Jill demanded furiously. 'I do not "futz around"! I work damned hard, and you know it!'

'Only too well,' Mort said. 'And I've had enough of your damn job! I've had enough of you working late most nights; I've had enough of you being away at conferences. I've had it up to here with only getting the scraps of your life. Look,' he said in a gentler voice, 'I love you, and when I retire I want to be with you. I don't want to spend the rest of my life alone – I want to spend it with you.'

'We can go on as we are, can't we? I realise I put in too much time at the lab, and I could maybe do something about that. I just don't understand what all the fuss is about.'

'The fuss, dear doctor, is about you being married to your job. OK, I work a sixty-hour week, but I get paid a helluva lot of money for it, and I intend to give it all up just as soon as I've netted a really big project for Pharmavax, so I can retire with a healthy bonus. You slave away for a pittance. And you're not going to get anywhere doing that.'

'How can you say that? Unlike you, I'm still only in my thirties, in case you hadn't noticed. I do good work, and I'm proud of what I do. I'm not about to throw it all up and live in some twilight community with you for the rest of my days!' Jill got out of bed, grabbed her robe and stormed off to the kitchen.

'And another thing,' he went on, following her like a dog. 'For ten years, we've had to have secrets from each other. I've never liked that, even though it's the way it has to be, you working in direct competition with Pharmavax. And I like it even less when you half tell me things and won't let me have the whole story.'

Jill filled the kettle, plugged it in and switched it on. Only then did she turn to face Mort, breathing carefully to keep her temper. 'I never should have told you about that. It was unprofessional, and I feel like I've betrayed NIH. And myself, come to that. I suppose I thought that, after all these years, you'd understand that I had to tell someone, and that you'd also realise why I couldn't tell you everything. After all, there are things happening at Pharmavax that you don't tell *me*. Do you think I like that?'

'That's different,' Mort replied dismissively. 'I have shareholders to think of. You work for the government. Which means Pharmavax's taxes pay your salary.'

'Which, since it's such a *pittance*, shouldn't worry you. Look, are you saying that I'm obligated to tell you everything about my work, just because the government funds us out of taxes? Come on, Mort!'

'I guess what I really mean is this,' Mort spoke deliberately. 'For the past twenty years Pharmavax has been working on developing a male contraceptive pill. We've bought some of the best brains in the industry, and we've put millions into it. Then some guy who says he's from the Pentagon just walks up to you in the park with a crazy story about the Russians having gotten there ahead of us, but with a vaccine. Hell, he probably even told you you'd get to develop the stuff in return for helping him. What I'm saying is: if *Pharmavax* had the Russian formula, we could get it on to the market in half the time you'd take –'

'So that's it!' Jill exclaimed. 'That's the big project you want for Pharmavax, the one that's going to let you retire in a blaze of glory, and a whole stack of performance-related bonuses. Well, let me tell you, you're not going to get it from me! You're just out for one thing – that damn company, its profits and its shareholders. Well, you can't steamroller me, Morton Montgomery. I'm not one of your employees, thank God. Even if I weren't bound by my contract, I wouldn't tell you a damn thing!'

'Isn't it a little late to think of that? You've already told me one helluva lot!'

'Damn you, Mort! Damn you to hell! After ten years – *ten years!* – I thought your loyalty to Pharmavax would be balanced by some kind of loyalty to me. I sure made a mistake in thinking I owed any loyalty to you rather than to NIH, who pay my *pittance* of a salary check!'

'Oh, so the good doctor's being all high minded now, is she?' Mort scoffed. 'No wonder your marriage fell apart. I don't know how the poor guy put up with you for as long as he did.'

Jill took a stainless-steel knife from the wooden knife-block and turned to face Mort. 'I know what makes women like Lorena Bobbitt cut men's dicks off,' she said through clenched teeth. 'And if you don't drop the subject right this minute – '

'OK, OK,' Mort said, as if realising he had goaded her too far. He was relieved when she put the knife back into the slanted wood block on the work-top. 'I guess I should apologise. But I get so angry when I think of all that research Pharmavax could be working on. And I wish we could be together more. I do care about you, and I want to spend the rest of my life with you.'

'You're repeating yourself,' came the cold answer.

'What I mean is with you, not with your career. Look, you're off again this weekend for three days to London. We don't even see each other on the weekends any more. I miss you.'

'Washington is full of women who'd jump at the chance,' Jill snorted.

'Sure. But I don't want them – I want you. If you really can't understand that, then I'd just as soon we split up. Then you'd be free to continue your career, and I'd be free to look for someone who wanted to be with me more than she wanted to slave over a damn work-bench.'

Jill poured out two cups of coffee and took one of them back into the bedroom. She placed it on the dressing-table. Mort followed and lay down on the bed, carefully balancing his coffee so as not to spill it. Jill sat on the edge of the bed beside him.

'Look, we shouldn't be fighting. We don't hate each other. OK, things haven't been going too well for us recently, but we don't have to slaughter each other.'

Mort reached over to get rid of his coffee-cup, then turned to Jill. He drew her down to him, his hand reaching under her silk robe to cup her breast.

'I'm sorry about everything I said,' he told her tenderly. 'If I lost you, I'd be more alone than you can imagine. It's true, what they say about being lonely at the top. Everyone else seems to have someone to talk with, friends, family, whatever. I only have you. With everyone else, I have to watch my back; with you, I can be myself.'

Despite herself, Jill was becoming aroused again as Mort worked his magic on her nipple. She often became excited when they fought, as though her stress and sex hormones were somehow linked right into one another. She stretched out on top of him, her breathing heavier. Confidently, she reached down to feel his hardening erection, drawing down the silky hood to reveal the naked head. Slowly and tantalisingly, she slid herself the length of his muscular body, kissing every inch as she went. Mort released her breast and caressed her hair with both hands as she lowered herself to his crotch.

'Mmm, this is nice,' she murmured as she took him between her lips, moving her mouth and tongue around his erect stalk.

'You wouldn't really have cut it off, would you?' he asked,

with a smile in his voice, yet still sounding for all the world like a little boy seeking reassurance from a threatening parent.

Jill waited a moment, a perfectly conscious dramatic pause for maximum effect, then lifted her head.

'I might have,' she grinned mischievously. 'But just think what I'd be missing.'

6.

'Good afternoon, madam,' the hall porter greeted Jill as she stopped at the reception desk on her way across the marbled hall of the Continental Hotel. 'There's a fax for you.' And he reached, almost without looking, to the pigeonhole above Jill's room number.

'Thank you,' she said, taking it from his hand.

'We've prepared everything you asked for in the Trafalgar Suite, doctor. Do let me or the duty manager know if there's anything else we can do to be of help.'

'You've been a real help already,' she smiled. 'I always like coming here for these events.' The hall porter beamed, delighted to be praised by so distinguished a guest. The management had gone all out to court world-class conferences like this one on fertility control, and the Continental rather prided itself on outdoing the other top London hotels in the way that it ran them.

'Has Dr Harman come down yet, do you know?' Jill enquired, tearing open the envelope.

'You can just see her from here, madam. Over there by the piano.'

'Thank you,' and Jill made her way over to the grand piano, where an anxious-looking girl, probably a student from the Royal College of Music, was playing a piece by Satie; and playing it really rather well, Jill thought to herself as she scanned the brief fax.

'Hi, Jill,' Mira called, catching sight of her departmental deputy, who was also her protégée and closest friend. 'I'm just about to order coffee. Want some?'

'Love to. Thanks,' said Jill absent-mindedly, folding the fax back into the envelope.

'Good news?' Mira enquired, blatantly curious.

Jill grinned wrily. 'Sort of, I guess. It's from Mort, wishing me luck and telling me he loves me. We had a row a couple of days ago.'

'The same one you've had before, don't tell me,' Mira scoffed, scanning the crowded room for a waiter. She raised a finger imperiously to beckon the young man over to their table and turned back to Jill. 'He wants you to throw in your job at NIH and take early retirement so you can jet-set round the world, or sit on your butt in the Caribbean. My dear, I've told you before, the man is a control-freak. He may *say* he's proud of you and what you do, but really he wants you to give it all up and play the adoring wife.' Mira was interrupted by the waiter, who looked scarcely old enough to be out of school.

'Can I get you something, madam?'

'Coffee for two, please,' Mira said. 'Of course, if you leave, it'll be a dreadful blow. Just as we're getting involved in the Phase 2 work.'

'Forget it, Mira. I'm not going anywhere. If that means I say goodbye to Mort – well, so be it. Things haven't been going too well recently. And it's not just my work that's the problem –'

'S – e – x, my dear?' Mira enquired with dramatically raised eyebrows. 'Mr Montgomery showing his age, is he?'

Jill giggled. 'Stop it, Mira. Of course he isn't. That's fine. Well, OK, it's getting predictable, rather too safe. But nine years – nearly ten – is a long time.'

'A long time to be wined and dined at Washington's classiest restaurants? Yes, I can see how that would pall. Years of being escorted to every swanky bash in town? I swear, if I see one more shot of you two swanning down a red carpet and smiling for the cameras, I'll use it to line the cat-tray!'

Jill was laughing in spite of herself, and had to force herself to stop long enough to concentrate on pouring out the coffee, which had arrived with exemplary speed. 'Of course I like all that. Who wouldn't? It's just that, for a while now, I've known that you're right. I've had enough of being Mort's trophy woman. Making a joke of being seen together was great to start with – we must be the only long-term couple in the city who've fooled the gossip columns – but the strain is starting to tell.'

Jill handed a cup to Mira, took one for herself, and sat back in the luxurious armchair. 'And there's something else,' she went on. 'Mort is now CEO of a huge multinational. But I liked him better when he was further down the ladder.The bottom line on the balance sheet is all he cares about these days. He seems to have lost sight of what really matters, forgotten why he went into pharmaceuticals in the first place.'

'You're the only one who imagines he ever went into it for the good of humanity,' Mira observed drily. 'Of course he did it to make money!'

Jill sighed. 'I guess I always hoped he went into it for more than that. But if he ever did, he's certainly lost sight of it now. We're both aiming for totally different things. I just haven't wanted to face up to it.'

'So, you've had a long run,' Mira shrugged. 'Maybe it's time for a change.'

Jill looked at her watch. 'Still half an hour to go,' she commented. 'You'd think that after delivering this paper as often as I have, I wouldn't be nervous. But I still hate waiting like this.'

'Just keep telling yourself you're the best,' said Mira briskly. 'Everyone knows it except you. Sure, you've given them your tyrosine substrate paper a few times, but they're still here to hear it all again. Look at them!'

The foyer of the Continental was the size of a small aircraft hangar, and it was bustling with conference delegates, whose conference badges, complete with photos, made them actually look like airport employees. Above their heads, the central atrium soared through a dizzying perspective of thirty storeys to a glass dome. The noise of three hundred people all talking at once was reduced to a subdued hum in the vast space. On all sides, small groups of delegates were engaged in earnest conversation, discussing professional concerns and golf handicaps with equal fervour.

Mentally running through the roll-call of delegates she met at every conference, all gathered in yet another five-star hotel, Jill couldn't help asking herself whether it was all worth it. After all, it was scarcely four weeks since virtually the same group had met in Rio, at a weekend sponsored by a local pharmaceutical company. Jill had always been deeply suspicious of the industry's attempts to court respectability among academic scientists; she knew only too well that a great many trials were tailored to produce the results the marketing men wanted. That was the main reason she'd avoided the industry like the plague and chosen instead to work in a government research lab. At least there she could feel relatively safe from the appalling commercial pressures that dogged so many of her industry colleagues.

Mira, too, had spent all her professional life as a government servant, and she wore her responsibilities very heavily. She had never married. In a sense she was married to her job, a sort of academic nun. Jill had never been aware of any men in Mira's life; in fact, Mira seemed actively to dislike men and tolerated Mort only for Jill's sake. And Mort certainly had no fondness for Mira, knowing that all his suave charm was lost on her. In fact, one of the worst fights he and Jill ever had was when he unthinkingly referred to Mira as 'that dyke'. Because he so clearly regarded being a lesbian as unacceptable, Jill defended Mira against the accusation without even stopping to wonder whether it was true. Later, she realised, there was no evidence of a woman in Mira's life either.

It saddened her that Mira, to whom she owed so much, should lead such a solitary life, though she understood the reasons for it. Mira's only real relationship was with Jill herself; fifteen years earlier, she had taken the insecure, newly married young research assistant under her wing, sensing the loneliness and insecurity under the intellectual brilliance, and knowing even then that Jill's marriage to Art would founder. Ever since, she had been part-mother, part-confessor to Jill, and a deep affection and respect had grown between them.

The two women had few secrets from each other. Jill made a habit of discussing anything that worried her, professionally or personally, with Mira, because she knew she would always be given sage advice. But she hadn't bargained for the fury Mira unleashed on her when she told her that she had agreed to help the government steal the Russian vaccine formula and that her lab was going to work on it. Even here, in London, Mira seemed unable to let the subject lie for the time being; instead she wasted no opportunity to let Jill know how much she disapproved of the whole exercise. She brought it up again while they waited in the hotel foyer.

'It's just that I feel we're being railroaded into a completely crazy scheme. Once you get involved with cloak-and-dagger merchants, you're in serious trouble. They don't think like we do. They have their own rules. You may think we have problems, as scientists, but these guys are on another planet.'

'Hey, Mira, the "cloak-and-dagger merchants", as you call them, are in the Pentagon.'

'Damn right,' Mira said. 'Proves my point. You know I have this friend in the FBI? Well, we go back a long way, and there was a time when we came very close to being more than just good friends. What finally turned me off the whole idea was the way he lived his life – the lies, the deception, the way I never knew where I was with him. He couldn't help it, but I wanted no part of it. He's married now, to a nice woman, and she told me once she has problems with all that as well. But in that world, even the nice guys have their strings pulled by the not-so-nice guys. And *our* strings are being pulled – by the not-so-nice guys, I suspect – and I don't go for it. I don't care to be made part of it, and I don't like you being involved in this way either. You should know better.'

Jill was uncomfortably aware that Mira felt she had been badly let down. She decided to change the subject. 'Do you realise,' she said, sipping her coffee, 'some of these people are probably here to do the groundwork for industrial espionage?'

'Of course,' Mira replied. 'The way it's going, anyone who signs on for a PhD should be vetted by the FBI first. But unless you lock up all your lab technicians and research personnel in a gulag, what are you to do? Have you ever thought what our department's research would be worth on the open market?'

Jill shivered. 'I don't even *want* to think about it.'

'Well, you should. I have, often. And I don't rate our security as anything like tight enough to protect it.'

'Our security is a pain in the rear, Mira. I spend a measurable amount of my life going through security procedures. And I've been in the department longer than anyone except you. Of course, I realise it's all necessary; I just wish I didn't have to do it all the time.'

'Call me neurotic if you like, but I worry about it night and day. Look, any halfway competent hacker could get into our system, for all the money we spent on it. That's why I make back-ups of every damn thing and keep them under lock and key.'

Jill laughed. 'Dear Mira, what makes your back-ups any more secure than the computer system?'

Mira shrugged theatrically. 'Put it down to my peasant ancestry. My family were the sort of people who'd rather keep their money under the mattress than trust it to a bank, where they couldn't see it.

Of course I know how the system works; I insisted on many of the security precautions being programmed in. So I know just how vulnerable it could be. And this new stuff from the Pentagon – the idea of keeping *that* secure, when we get it, is giving me sleepless nights. I really wish we didn't have to have anything to do with it.'

Oh God, Mira was back on *that* subject again! 'You mean you'd really turn down the chance to work on it?' Jill asked.

'Damn right. And so should you have done.'

'Mira, are you annoyed that they went over your head and approached me direct? Or is it because the stuff's Russian?'

'Of course I'm annoyed at being passed over – who wouldn't be? As for it being Russian, I just don't think any good can come of it, no matter where it comes from. And if it fell into the wrong hands – well, my blood runs cold at the thought! In fact, this time I'm not even going to make any back-up disks. There! That's a measure of how I feel!'

• • •

The handsome Russian, with his dark hair, green eyes and Tartar cheekbones, drew plenty of glances from the knots of gossiping delegates as he wove his way through the chairs and tables, towards the two women sitting by the piano. He'd never met Dr Jillian Peters in the flesh, but he immediately recognised her from a teaching video. He'd been struck at the time by how attractive she was, with her English-rose complexion and unusual-coloured hair. In real life, she was even more stunning than he remembered, her Versace suit revealing the elegant figure the white lab coat had concealed. Her jewellery was good and well chosen, and she wore scarcely any make-up. All in all, she was a far cry from the women who surrounded him at the lab every day, with their thickening bodies and amateurishly bleached hair.

The other woman, Dr Harman, was also striking, handsome and impeccably dressed, her slightly gaunt face alive with sardonic humour as she chatted to her friend. There was an air of detached austerity about her; she would see through any effort to charm her with laser-like accuracy.

He was relieved to see that there was a third chair, unoccupied, at their table. 'Ladies,' he said, bowing slightly, 'may I join you for a moment?'

'Certainly,' Jill replied.

'And may I also introduce myself? I'm Ivan Kandinsky. I know you, Dr Harman, from your review article on the evaluation of glycosylated and deglycosylated porcine zona antigens. I hope we'll get a chance to discuss it, later perhaps? And I've read all Dr Peters' work, with much interest. I'm really looking forward to your talk.'

'Have you just come over from the States?' Jill asked. The man's accent sounded American, even though his manner was anything but. The interesting green eyes twinkled slightly as he answered,

'No, from Russia. But I was lucky enough to spend five years at MIT, which is where I picked up an American accent.'

'So this is your first time at one of these gatherings, then?' Jill asked.

'That's right,' the Russian replied. 'I work in St Petersburg, with Professor Stawowy's group – I'm sure you've heard of his work – ' Jill nodded. 'I always wanted to travel, but we didn't have the funds to come to any big international meetings until recently. Just in the last year, some Western pharmaceutical companies have started to finance trips like this for us.'

Both Jill and Mira knew of the Polish-born Professor Stawowy, whose infertility clinic also ran a research centre. In fact, Jill wondered whether the contraceptive vaccine she would soon be working on had been developed as a result of his work. However, she could hardly ask Ivan Kandinsky outright.

'Have you been to Russia?' he asked, turning slightly to include Mira in his question though it was clear he really only wanted an answer from Jill. Mira, withdrawing into herself, sat back in her chair, leaving Jill to carry the conversation.

'No,' she said. 'But I'd love to one day.'

'You should come to St Petersburg. It would be my pleasure to show you around.' He looked at his watch, as a uniformed conference hostess began to shepherd delegates through to the auditorium. 'Will you excuse me, please, Dr Peters, Dr Harman? There's someone I must speak to before your talk starts.'

As the Russian got up, Jill moved her legs to one side to let him past. The tables and chairs were crammed together, so there was little room to manoeuvre. The Russian's leg brushed her thigh and caused her skirt to ride up, exposing her stocking top. Blushing slightly, Jill pulled the hem down quickly.

'Forgive me,' Kandinsky said, smiling but slightly embarrassed. He laid his hand on her shoulder for an instant.

'No problem,' Jill smiled back.

Mira made a small noise of disgust and impatience as the Russian disappeared into the crowd.

'Come on, Mira. It was an accident. And, anyway, I didn't mind that much. After all, our Mr. Kandinsky is a seriously gorgeous man, you must admit.'

'Maybe. But I wouldn't be surprised if he was trying to eavesdrop. He's Russian. And you know how I feel about them.'

Jill did indeed know. Some years earlier, after working late to finish an article for a journal, Mira and Jill had gone out for a drink together. One drink became several, and both started talking about their early lives. Jill told Mira about her childhood as an army daughter, the only child of an authoritarian, repressive father; she wept, remembering her grief at the early death of her mother, and how she had taken refuge in an academic career and an early unsatisfactory marriage.

And Mira told Jill how she too had lost her mother when she was very young, in horrific circumstances. Mira was only five years old when the Russians came to Danzig. Her father just had time to hide the children and himself under a pile of rubble behind the house, but Mira's mother was caught in the street by a group of drunken Russian looters, who raped her mercilessly for hours before leaving her for dead. Even her neighbours, cowering in the ruins of their homes, were too terrified to come out and help her, and she bled to death where she lay.

A few weeks later, Mira's twelve-year-old brother was rounded up and sent off to a forced labour battalion. Before his thirteenth birthday, he was dead. Mira and her father walked westwards for weeks, scrounging scraps and sleeping in the open, through the wreckage of Eastern Europe. Shocked into muteness, Mira never spoke until she and her father arrived in America. There, a new name doled out by an impatient immigration official, and a new language to learn, freed her to speak again.

'But,' she told Jill, 'my father never could be happy again. I had to cook and clean, as though I was my mother. And I had to excel at school, as though I was my brother. The only thing he didn't want of me was to be his daughter.'

After that conversation, Mira never referred to her childhood again, and only her ingrained mistrust of men, and detestation of all things Russian, ever gave any indication of it. Jill leaned forward and laid her hand on Mira's knee. 'I'm sorry,' she said. 'That was thoughtless of me.'

'That's OK,' Mira said. 'Now, I know about Stawowy. But do we know anything about your Mr Kandinsky?'

'I don't recall reading anything of his,' Jill admitted. 'Why? Do you think maybe Kandinsky is not what he says he is?'

'I just have a feeling about him, I don't know why.'

'You could always ask your friend in the FBI to do a bit of digging,' Jill suggested lightheartedly.

She meant it as a joke and was slightly disconcerted when Mira said, quite seriously, 'I guess I could.'

Jill glanced at her watch; the foyer was almost empty except for a bottleneck of delegates at the door leading to the auditorium.

'I should be in there by now. Well, one thing I have to say for Mr Kandinsky; he quite took my mind off my pre-talk nerves!'

7.

'Just undo one more button on my blouse,' Veronica whispered softly as Brad ruffled her hair to make it even more untidy. She was looking really scruffy, her hands covered in grease, her clothes dishevelled. But she still looked gorgeous.

'What on earth would the pc freaks back home have to say about this?' Brad breathed in her ear as he slipped a button loose to reveal her breasts a little more.

'The hell with them!' she whispered. 'I'm out for a result here. The only thing I'm concerned about is whether the Russians'll fall for it.'

'It'll work OK,' he reassured her. 'An attractive black woman isn't likely to be easily ignored around these parts.'

They'd planned right from the start to use Veronica as a decoy so that they could ambush the tanker, but everything depended on the driver being sufficiently convinced that this particular damsel in distress on the Novosibirsk road was worth stopping for. They had taken the distributor cap out of the rental car, so there was no way it would start. Veronica, looking sexy and helpless, would give any passer-by something to look at while Brad and the others got to work.

But Veronica hardly heard his last words as the sound they were all waiting for alerted their senses. In the distance, just out of sight, a labouring diesel engine strained to pull a heavy vehicle up the long slope from the river.

'Good luck,' Brad whispered, smiling warmly at her. 'I'll be right behind you, here in the bushes.'

'No problems. Just get out of sight before they see you.'

Brad took cover in the undergrowth. Within seconds the huge fuel tanker rounded the bend a few hundred yards away. Brad activated his radio so that everything from now on would be heard by his two sergeants. Sam Young and Nelson Moody had been with him for years and were always on his crack assault team when he undertook covert activities. He knew them. He could trust them with his life, and often had.

'You in place, Sam?' he enquired softly.

'Sure, boss.'

'You OK, Nelson?'

'Right on, sir.'

The plan had been well prepared. They'd thought of everything down to the last detail. But, Brad reminded himself, there was always the unforeseen that kept you on your toes. That was what he loved about the job. He knew he was hung up on the adrenaline fixes, the fear and even the constant danger of death. It was a bit like being a compulsive gambler, but playing with your life.

'I can see the guy's lights,' Sam reported from his concealed vantage-point. 'Ten seconds, and he'll be round the bend.'

Slowly, its huge diesel engine groaning, the vast tanker hove into view, a great leviathan, black, unmarked and mysterious in the Russian night. Nelson could see the driver clearly, as the tanker ground past his hiding-place. Thank God, he muttered to himself, as he saw there were only two men in the cab. They had feared there would be more.

Within seconds the driver had caught sight of the young black woman illuminated in the glare of his headlights, head deep under the hood of her car. The position of the vehicle, slightly across the road, made it impossible for the tanker to pass. With a screech of rubber and a hiss of air brakes, the giant shuddered to a halt, its twenty tyres biting into the cold road surface.

Leaning out of his window, the driver called to Veronica to ask if she needed help. She straightened up and smiled dazzlingly. The driver jumped down from the cab. He hadn't taken more than a few strides towards the stricken car when a scarcely audible hiss made him look round. In a split second Nelson had him in a disabling arm lock, then dragged him, like a doll, into the undergrowth. At precisely the same moment, Sam ripped open the passenger door of the cab and dragged the co-driver on to the tarmac. He spoke in Russian to the terrified man, as he held a gun to his head.

'If you want to stay alive, you'll do exactly as I say. Understood?'

'Da, da!' the man blabbered, shaking with terror.

Brad materialised at Nelson's side. Taking a small, self-adhesive patch from the pocket of his fatigues, he applied it to the squirming driver's neck just above his dirty shirt collar. 'Just hold on to him for a while, till it takes effect.'

In half a minute the thallium cyanide in the patch had seeped through the skin and into the bloodstream of the helpless man, and soon he was slumped on the ground, dying. Nelson removed the patch, and carefully put it in his own pocket. Now even if the dead man were found, no one would suspect foul play until Brad and his team were long gone.

Nelson climbed into the cab and slowly edged the vehicle into the position they'd planned. 'You OK, major?' he called out to Veronica as she grabbed her clothes from the car and made off to change into the warmth of her military fatigues.

'Sure. You can open her up now.'

Nelson jumped down from the cab and ran to the giant wheel that opened the valve that let the the fuel out of the front compartment of the tanker. Quickly, he spun it anti-clockwise, sending gasoline flooding all over the road and the car itself. Sam, meanwhile, bundled the speechless co-driver into the cab, pushing him roughly across to the wheel so that he could drive. Sam clambered in after him and, holding a gun to the man's side, snapped, 'Move her off, and park up ahead.'

The Russian, visibly shaking, eased the stick into the first of its twelve gears. The engine roared as he gently nudged the tanker past the gas-soaked car to bring it to a halt a hundred yards further on. Nelson jumped down from the step and shut off the fuel valve. When he was finished, he slammed on the passenger door with his fist, and the truck lumbered on another hundred yards. Veronica ran to the end of the splashed trail of gasoline, and flicked a lighter. Fire whooshed along the road, and a huge explosion lit the night sky as the car ignited, the area round it scorched by the searing flames of two thousand litres of gasoline.

Seconds later Brad, Veronica and Nelson were scaling the vast belly of the tanker, opening the hatch on the top nearest to the cab. Deftly negotiating the steel walkway that ran the length of the vehicle they passed heavy backpacks to one another. 'Christ!' Nelson exclaimed as he eased himself into the tank through the hatchway. 'I hadn't reckoned on these fumes being so strong. I hope we'll survive in here.'

Flashlight in hand, he let himself down into the drained fuel compartment and was soon out of sight.

With the skill of practised professionals used to working as a team, Veronica and Brad silently passed the equipment to Nelson, and Veronica scrambled down. They were ready to go. Three bangs on the roof of the cab was Brad's signal to Sam to start up. As the monster moved off into the night, Brad came down to join his team in the compartment.

'All according to plan so far, sir,' Nelson croaked, choking on the acrid fumes.

'Sure,' Brad replied confidently. 'But we've only just started.'

Veronica began to cough, her eyes running with the stinging fumes, which were affecting her more badly than she'd expected.

'Don't worry,' Brad reassured her. 'As we get going the wind will clear this out with the hatch open. We'll be OK in a few minutes.'

Soon the icy wind of the tundra had scoured out the fumes, and they were able to breathe more easily.

'Let's check our helmets,' Veronica suggested.

'OK,' Brad agreed. They donned their helmets, transforming themselves into spacemen ready for blast-off. Clipping the connectors into the battery packs around their waists activated their radio transmitters. The head-up display on the inside of their visors showed what the miniature TV cameras fitted into their helmets were seeing inside the dark tank.

'Can everybody hear me OK?' Brad asked, looking round. The image intensifier on his camera enabled him to see the others as if it were daylight.

'Sure,' Veronica answered, giving a thumbs-up.

'OK,' said Nelson. 'Shall I check out the other gear, so we won't be caught out if we get there ahead of time?'

'Might as well,' Brad replied. 'We can take these off now and save the batteries.'

With a judder, the tanker started to slow as the driver, under Sam's instructions, applied the powerful air brakes. He brought the vehicle to a halt and switched off its engine.

'OK, sergeant,' Brad turned to Nelson, 'you're off. Be sure to meet us at the river in exactly two hours. We'll keep radio contact down to an absolute minimum. Any problems?'

'No, sir. Just pass me my pack, and I'll be on my way.'

'Good luck, sergeant,' Veronica smiled.

'Thanks, major,' he said, clambering out of the hatchway.

'Right,' Brad said briskly. 'Let's give him a half hour to get his charges laid. Sam'll know when to move off.'

• • •

Time passed quickly as Brad and Veronica ran through the plans one more time. They'd fine-tuned every detail. Satellite reconnaissance had shown them the entire layout of the facility, and they knew exactly what to do. The only unpredictable elements were the guards themselves and how well armed they were. Security at the facility had been stepped up, and Veronica's information indicated that there could be all kinds of devices that they hadn't encountered on other missions inside Russia. Brad knew about the vibration sensors set in the ground that warned of intruders in forbidden areas, and they had learned, too, from intelligence that the guards could even be armed with laser weapons.

It had been impossible to discover exactly what weapons they were equipped with, but the black, opaque visors of their helmets were designed to give complete protection from any laser weapons the Russians might have. The most up-to-date laser devices altered their frequency every few seconds, rendering coloured protective goggles completely useless. The only answer, the technical back-up boys reasoned, was to have a visor that let through no light at all. That meant equipping the team with miniature TV cameras so they could see. Although all laser weapons had been banned in line with the Helsinki Agreement, there were still large numbers in circulation on the black market in almost every country. They were a terrifying weapon, causing permanent blindness in anyone whose eyes were exposed to the destructive beam.

Brad's team had, of course, brought their own laser guns as well as silent air-powered, Italian-made pistols that fired flechettes. These stainless-steel arrows could penetrate even the kevlar body armour he knew the guards would be wearing. Once inside the body they twisted and turned, causing horrific and irreparable damage.

Having run through everything to Brad's satisfaction, Veronica concentrated on her GPS satellite navigator, as she checked their position against the maps in front of her.

• • •

The roar of the tanker's engine leaping into life shattered the silence.

'Great,' Brad breathed with an audible sigh of relief. 'We're ready to go. I'm not much good at waiting.' As the truck lurched out of its hiding-place on the woodland track and took to the surfaced road again their pulses began to speed as they realised that they were now on the final stage of the journey to their target. Veronica closed the hatch and reached for a large plastic-coated sheet. Using cyanoacrylate, she started to fix it neatly around the walls of the tank above their heads.

'Hope we don't have any hold-ups,' Brad observed. 'We don't have too much air in here.'

'I can't say I'm keen on sitting in here being shaken to pieces, air or no air,' Veronica joked, in an effort to reduce the tension they were both feeling. She shifted her bottom in an effort to get comfortable. 'This suspension is hardly GM's best.'

Up in the cab Sam was also starting to feel nervous. No matter how many crazy missions he'd done with the colonel, he still sweated as an operation swung into action. He knew that once things were under way they'd all be too busy to worry about nerves, but right now he'd have given five years' pay to be somewhere else.

'Pull up slowly at the barrier,' he ordered the driver. Sam had learned Russian at his mother's knee and used it as comfortably as he did English. His grandparents had come out of Russia in the twenties and always spoke Russian to him. He never had to think first in English, then translate – he even dreamed in Russian.

The driver brought the tanker to a halt as instructed. Outside, in the harsh glare of the halogen lights, a guard approached the truck.

'Hi, Igor!' he called to the driver, whom he saw every week on his delivery run. 'How's your old lady?'

'She's much better, thanks,' Sam's captive replied quietly, trying to disguise his fear.

The guard turned as if to walk away, but quickly returned to the side of the cab. 'You OK? You're very quiet tonight.'

'We had some trouble on the road,' Sam interjected. 'Some guy's car caught fire, and we were scared we'd go up with it.'

'I wouldn't want your job,' the guard replied with an understanding grin. 'It must be like driving a bloody mobile bomb. I won't keep you long – just have to check the tanks and the paperwork.'

This was the part of the plan that Sam had been fearing most. They knew that the guards never let a tanker through without ensuring that all the compartments were full of fuel. Breathing tensely, he nudged the barrel of his gun into the driver's heavy jacket, just to remind him it was there.

The guard clambered up the access ladder at the far end of the vehicle and expertly walked along the steel decking in the bright light. One by one, he opened the giant hatches to check that there was gasoline in each compartment. Inside their dark, airless coffin Brad and Veronica froze, motionless. Veronica prayed that the surface they'd created would convince the guard that what he was looking at was in fact a fluid shining in the floodlights.

Brad could feel his heart pounding as the guard edged closer to them, one compartment at a time, agonisingly slowly, checking each tank, his steps becoming louder by the second, as he neared their hiding-place. Veronica held her breath as the guard opened the hatch above their heads. Bang on cue, Sam called out something to him about getting on with it, and before they knew it the hatch had clanged back down again.

Brad and Veronica breathed again. One more phase of the operation over! All they needed now was for the guard to wave them through, and they'd be on their way. Veronica was just beginning to relax her hold on her detonator transmitter, when an eerie sound tightened her taut nervous system yet another notch. At the far end of the vehicle, someone was tapping the side of the tanker. They hadn't prepared for this.

'Must be a guard. Once he gets to us, he'll hear the difference in sound,' Brad whispered in the major's ear. 'Use your detonator, if you have to.'

'When we planned for Nelson to lay his ground charges, we

never dreamed we'd be trapped this way, in a steel coffin!' she whispered back.

'Better pray the frequency works from in here, or we're dead meat!'

Slowly, as if he had all the time in the world, like a schoolboy casually tapping water-filled bottles and taking a delight in the different sounds they made, the guard ambled from compartment to compartment, idling away the time while his partner completed the paperwork in their tiny office at the barrier.

Up in the cab, Sam could hardly believe what he was hearing. In his rearview mirror, he could see the guard working his way along the tanker, inch by inch. He dug his gun a little deeper into the driver's ribs.

'Tell the guy in the office to hurry it up!' he ordered. But the guard was in no hurry and took a leisurely swig from a steaming mug as he glanced at the TV security monitors. Then he turned back unhurriedly to complete the official papers.

'Hey, Andrei,' the tapping guard called to him.

'What?' he replied testily, annoyed at being interrupted yet again in a task he was none too pleased to be doing anyway.

'Come and listen to this! This bit sounds different from the rest. What do you think?'

And the guard hit the side of the tank with his rifle butt. Inside, the clang was literally deafening.

'See what you mean,' his partner called 'Let's take another look inside.'

Brad looked across at Veronica and nodded. She pressed the button on her transmitter, and a tremendous explosion shook the tanker.

'That was a mite close for my liking,' she muttered, wiping her sweating brow with the back of her hand.

The guards, taken by surprise by the explosion at the far end of the compound, waved the truck through in an attempt to get it out of the way as quickly as possible.

The tanker accelerated slowly under the raised barrier and into the road system that serviced the secret laboratory compound.

'We're in!' Brad sighed with relief. 'Nelson's little distraction will have put out half their perimeter lighting, if he's blown the right transformer. And it'll have confused the vibration sensors, so we should be able to ignore them from here on in.'

'All I know is, if I don't get out of here pretty soon, I'm going to feel like a microwaved chicken,' Veronica replied as she tried to stretch her legs after what felt like hours cramped up in their fume-filled coffin.

The truck came to a halt. For a couple of minutes, Brad and Veronica waited, listening to the bumps and bangs on the other side of the tank wall. Then Sam was swinging the hatch open, allowing crisp cold air to flood in.

'You guys OK?'

'Sure. Did you see to the driver?'

'He's safe enough. I put him in the sleeper compartment over the cab, with a sedative patch. He won't be going anywhere.' Quietly and efficiently, he pulled all the equipment out of the tank, then helped Brad and Veronica out.

'That sure feels good,' Brad said, taking a lungful of the freezing air, and stretching his limbs like a cat. 'Let's get going.'

The entrance to the basement of the research building was only a short sprint away. Almost everyone around them seemed to be dealing with Nelson's little diversion, leaving the trio to go about their business undisturbed.

'I'll keep watch up here,' said Brad, as Sam emptied his backpack on to the concrete area at the foot of the basement steps and handed Veronica a large battery pack as he had done many times before. Veronica connected up the leads, and turned it full on. Soon Sam was using a thermal lance to cut the heads off the large bolts that held the ventilation duct's security cover in place.

'The metal's so damn cold, it's taking longer than I thought,' he cursed under his breath.

'Stick with it,' Veronica calmed him. 'We have all the time we need.'

'Hand me the wrench.'

Sam brought his considerable muscle power to bear on the first weakened bolt-head, and it sheared off immediately. Two more, and he was done.

'Brad!' Veronica called. 'We're through!'

The colonel leapt down into the pit to join them. 'I'll just collect these, in case anyone comes by,' he said, picking up the scattered steel bolt-heads and putting them in his backpack. 'Where's that instant glue?' he asked Veronica.

She handed him the cyanoacrylate, then followed Sam, who was already scrambling on hands and knees deep inside the ventilation shaft. Brad entered last, taking the cover Sam had removed and fixing it back in place from the inside.

'You go on ahead,' he said. 'This stuff'll take a few seconds to harden.'

The others crawled along the shaft until they came to a louvred aluminium vent. Sam lay on his back, his football player's legs pushing until the frame gave way and clattered noisily into the room below. Brad joined them; they waited in silence to be absolutely certain that no one had heard anything.

'We're all clear,' Veronica whispered.

It didn't take long to reach the third floor. There were no signs of security guards, and they soon found the department they wanted. Sam quickly got to work with his thermal lance to remove the hinges from the safe that held the computer disks, while Veronica busied herself setting up the transcriber.

'Strange, this,' Sam remarked to the others, as he worked away at the heavy metal. 'You'd think they'd have had this alarmed.' With one swift movement, the sergeant removed the door from its cut hinges, and laid it down on the plastic-tiled floor.

'Right. Your gear all ready?' he asked Veronica.

'Sure. I'll just check the levels. Give me a disk.' The equipment sat on the desk, lights blinking, ready for action. Slowly but methodically, Sam sorted through disk after disk, trying to make sense of the codes, then handed one to his superior officer. Veronica grinned, and fed it into the electronic machine which stored the information before spitting the disk out the other end.

They were about halfway through when Brad whistled their call-sign across the dark room.They froze, praying that the low hum of the transcriber was inaudible outside the room. Brad crouched out of sight behind the half-glazed door. A guard made his way slowly along the corridor, looking into each room, checking that every door was locked. Brad stiffened – they hadn't locked the door behind them! He braced himself against it, so that it would feel locked.

He held his breath as the guard stopped, peered in and tried the handle. The timber gave slightly. Brad found himself unable to press sufficiently hard from his awkward position on the floor. The man outside, sensing something was wrong, pushed again, this time a lot harder. Thinking quickly, Brad moved and let the door fly open, throwing the guard off-balance, so that he fell sprawling into the room. In an instant Brad was on him, delivering a swift fatal blow to the back of his neck, snapping it as if the man were a rabbit.

Calmly, Brad looked up and down the corridor, closed the door and signalled to the others that the coast was clear. Sam got straight back to his task of selecting the disks, as Jill had briefed him, while Veronica went on feeding them into the machine to rob them of their treasure. Outside in the grounds, the noise was still at fever pitch, as men rushed from place to place confused by the lack of lighting.

'Another ten minutes, and we'll be all through,' Sam said.

'Good,' Brad replied. 'Then let's try to get into the animal labs if we can. Dr Peters seemed to think that data would be even more useful.'

Suddenly the dead guard's radio burst into life, a torrent of Russian flooding the tense silence.

'Shit!,' Sam muttered. 'They're asking him to check in at his usual time. If he doesn't answer, they'll know something's wrong!'

'Can't you talk to them, for God's sake?' Veronica asked in a panic.

'No. They'll know it's not his voice. I say we finish this lot and get out. They'll know his route, and they'll be along to check any time now.'

Swiftly but efficiently, Sam and Veronica gathered their equipment together. They replaced the safe's door and dragged the dead guard out of sight behind a pile of boxes. Within seconds, it was as if no one had ever been in the room. The three swiftly retraced their steps out into the night and were soon in the relative safety of the tanker's cab.

'Don't bother with him,' Brad said, gesturing to the unconscious driver. 'You drive, Veronica. We'll cover you.'

Sam leapt up into the bunk high up behind the driving seat,

where the drugged driver still slept on. With one swipe of his rifle butt, he cleared the glass from the side window. Veronica started the engine and pulled away from the shadow of the laboratory block into the glare of the halogen lights on the road.

'Take it gently,' Brad urged. He wound his window down to assess what trouble lay ahead.

'Make for the main entrance. They may still not realise that all this has anything to do with us.' Veronica confidently drove the huge vehicle around the corner of the building, and into the main courtyard at the front of the research block.

'Halt!', a harsh Russian voice challenged her, as its owner brought his rifle to bear on the cab. A gentle hiss from Sam's gun signalled the discharge of a deadly flechette. The guard crumpled silently to the ground.

'Stay calm, major,' Brad ordered firmly. 'We can still get out of here in one piece, with any luck.'

'Think our luck's about to run out,' she replied, putting her foot on the gas. As the giant truck surged forward, its twelve-litre diesel engine screeching in far too low a gear, a guard fifty yards ahead of them lifted a rocket launcher to his shoulder. Veronica, catching sight of it just in time, wrenched the wheel to the left, throwing the heavy vehicle into a sharp turn. The rocket flew past, and exploded in the building behind them.

'I think we can assume they found the guard, boss,' Sam shouted. 'It'll be a fight to get out of here now.'

'We won't make the front gate,' yelled Veronica. 'Just look at that APC. I don't fancy taking that head on. I'm going for the wire!'

Changing up into sixth gear, she pushed her foot hard to the floor. 'Hold on, guys! We're going straight through!' By now bullets were ricocheting off the body of the cab as a dozen soldiers fired at the charging vehicle. Veronica wrenched at the wheel, her white knuckles betraying the effort required to steer the monster around obstacles and the lines of fire from armoured positions along the perimeter fence.

'I'll aim for that other substation block,' she cried, heading for a small, low building like the one Nelson had demolished with his explosion earlier.

'Go for it, girl!' Brad encouraged her, firing his laser gun out of the window at every available target.

'Thank God they don't seem to have any of these,' he observed. 'I wouldn't want to be wearing our headsets in all this.'

'Brace yourself, Sam!' Veronica shrieked. The huge tanker tore into the wire fence where it joined the electricity substation, its vast bulk nudging the building over like a kid's plaything and shredding the heavy steel fence. With a lurch, the front wheels dropped into a wide ditch, bringing the beast to a nose-diving halt. Sam flew out of the front window on to the grass below. Brad and Veronica leapt from the cab to his rescue, stumbling through the rough grass in the blackout.

'Let's go!' ordered Brad, hauling Sam to his feet. 'You OK?'

'Sure. Put my shoulder out, that's all. Do it all the time in football.'

'Major, you bring the things from the cab. I'll take the transcriber. Sam, you cover us. We'll head for the river.'

Veronica ran on ahead in the direction of the river. She hadn't gone fifty yards before she was thrown ten feet into the air by an explosion beneath her.

'Christ, the place is mined!' Brad cursed. He raced over to Veronica. Of all the members of his team, she was the one he could least afford to lose! Both her legs were off above the knee, and she was bleeding uncontrollably.

'Give me a patch, Brad,' she begged, holding out a trembling hand. Without a word, he stuck one on her neck, gave her hand a final squeeze, and dived off into the dark. Later, he would think it all through, grieve for a good friend, but there was no time for that now.

'I hope Nelson's at the pierhead,' shouted Sam, running as fast as he could towards the woodland between them and the river.

'He damn well better be! As soon as we're in the wood, I'll go for the boathouse. Cover me for as long as you can.'

Both men scrambled clumsily into the scrubby woodland, grateful for the meagre cover it offered. It was only a hundred yards deep, and through it they could glimpse the river glistening in the thin moonlight. Guards were already taking up their positions at the pierhead to stop the pair getting to the river. Sam threw himself to the ground behind a tree and, using his laser rifle with its night sight, was easily able to pick off almost every soldier who had come after them.

While Sam held back the attackers, Brad took out the two guards at the pierhead and was soon at the water's edge. His pulse was racing. Where the hell was Nelson, he cursed under his breath. Surely he could see they were in serious trouble!

Sam was holding their pursuers off, but it was plain they didn't have much time. Slowly but surely, the soldiers were advancing on him. Suddenly, out of the blackness, silent as a coffin, a high-speed launch appeared, drifting on the current, its engine dead. Nelson was at the helm.

'Give me a heart attack, why don't you?' Brad cried in a stage whisper.

'Didn't want to draw attention to myself, boss. They don't know I'm here. We better get the hell out of here now, though.'

Brad tied the stern of the powerful vessel to the quayside with a loose knot. 'Don't start the engines till I'm back with Sam. Let's keep the bastards guessing as long as we can.'

Brad tucked himself behind the low wooden building along the quayside and reached for his transponder. This activated a vibrator inside Sam's belt. Three buzzes – their usual signal – would tell him to get going. Within seconds Sam had broken cover and was running like a coyote towards the pierhead. Brad covered him with deadly laser shots, while Sam picked his way through the low bushes and scrub and flung himself into the boat.

'The major not coming?' Nelson called to Brad.

'Fraid not. She didn't make it.'

'That's bad,' said Nelson, subdued for once.

The powerful twin outboards burst into life at the touch of a button. Brad released the rope before leaping aboard himself.

'Let's go!' he yelled.

The sergeant didn't need to be told. He thrust the throttle into full ahead and shot the sleek vessel out into the dark currents of the river. The quayside was now swarming with soldiers firing, with little effect, at the fast-disappearing craft. Brad and Sam crouched low, while Nelson caned the huge engines.

'Time to say goodbye?' Nelson asked with a mischievous smile.

'Why not?'

Nelson took a radio-controlled detonator from his chest

pocket, extended the aerial and, looking back towards the chaotic scene behind them, pressed the yellow button. In the distance, the boathouse and pier blew as the charges Nelson had laid earlier did their job. The two men gave one another a thumbs-up and grinned with a mixture of delight and relief.

'Let's hope Larry's at the rendezvous on time, so we'll be back in time for the ball game,' Brad smiled, as they sped into the night.

8.

'I really love this place,' Mort sighed, lying back on the grass, his hands forming a pillow behind his head. 'You're so lucky, being this close.'

'I know,' Jill agreed 'I never know how you can stand living downtown, especially in the summer.'

Rock Creek Park was looking its best this June afternoon. The weekend should have been a great opportunity for Jill to enjoy some time alone with Mort; Jim was off somewhere with a friend from school and, unusually, they had a few daytime hours to themselves. Instead, she had to tell him their relationship was at an end. Ever since the quarrel before she left for London, she had realised she would have to close the book on the last ten years and do it gracefully.

Ridiculously, the tune of Andrew Lloyd-Webber's 'Tell Me On A Sunday' kept running through her head, and she wished it wouldn't. She was edgy, for all sorts of reasons that had nothing to do with Mort. She fiddled incessantly with twigs picked absentmindedly from the undergrowth, and rolled over from front to back time and again in an effort to get comfortable. The trouble was, the way she was feeling, there was no way of getting comfortable.

Ever since the disks had been delivered to her lab, she'd had nothing but trouble with Mira, who viewed the whole project with deep mistrust. And Mira made no secret of the fact that she was deeply displeased about Jill's involvement in the first place. All this bothered her more than she would have believed possible. She couldn't rid herself of the feeling that she had betrayed Mira's own high ideals.

On another level entirely, she was deeply disturbed by Mira's refusal to make back-up copies of the disks. The whole thing was beginning to feel fraught with problems, and they were getting in the way of Jill's meticulous dedication to her work.

A week of virtually-sleepless nights and long tiring days at her computer, combined with Mira's distant, stony-faced coldness towards her and Mort's wounding comments about her professional life, suddenly became too much for her. Tears started to come to her eyes, and she felt a rock-hard lump deep in the centre of her chest as feelings welled up inside her. For a few minutes she almost forget she wasn't alone, and a giveaway tear escaped and rolled down her cheekbone. Mort noticed.

'What's the matter?' he asked, rolling over to face her. 'You're crying. What is it?'

Jill wiped her eyes with the sleeve of her cotton T-shirt, and sat up. 'It's too much for me, all this. I'm starting to hate myself.'

'I know. I've watched you torturing yourself for days now. Can't you just let it go?'

'What do you mean, let it go? How can I? OK, I wish I'd never become involved. But I did, for better or worse. All my instincts tell me that I should tread carefully with this Russian vaccine, but I know I'm going to find myself under huge pressure to make things happen.'

'Look, you're not in charge. Let Mira take the heat. She's the boss. You didn't ask to get involved. Even if you had refused, the Pentagon would have gotten what they wanted one way or another.'

'But I can't just offload it on to Mira. It's not her style either. She's disgusted with me as it is, partly because she feels I went behind her back, and partly because, the way she sees it, I helped to steal another team's work. I wish I'd never met Colonel Foster.'

'You worry about it all too much. You need to toughen up, or you'll go under. You wouldn't last long in industry with all these scruples.'

'Look,' Jill retorted, leaning back on one elbow. 'I'm not you. I went into a government lab rather than a commercial outfit, precisely so as *not* to have to get involved in this sort of situation. I know you'd get a kick out of it, but that's you – not me.'

'Sure, I understand,' Mort replied gently, trying to defuse the situation.

'No, I don't think you do! The President – God, just listen to me! When did I ever used to care what the damn President thought about anything? – the President has made it absolutely clear that we have to get this vaccine perfected ahead of anyone in the world. There's huge political capital to be made out of the world's first really effective contraceptive vaccine. Imagine, the US government being able to claim they saved the Third World from poverty and disease, and all that stuff!'

'Well, if it comes off, it'll be a real advance.'

'Yes, but you know what'll happen. It'll be just like the space race all over again. The politicians only want to do it to prove that America's still the best. Look what happened once they got to the moon. Everything went ominously quiet. Suddenly, manned planetary adventures weren't all that important any more. Just ask yourself, where have we taken giant steps to since then?'

'Well, you can't deny the government needs to do something to raise our self-esteem as a nation. Half our industries are owned by the Japs; almost every Pacific Rim country outclasses us industrially and commercially. Hell, we need to do something to put ourselves back centre stage. I still want to feel proud to be an American. I'm not ready to settle for Third World status just yet.'

'I even handed in my resignation last week,' Jill continued, ignoring Mort's chauvinistic protestations.

'That's kinda dramatic, isn't it?'

'Hardly matters whether it is or not. They wouldn't release me. Gave me some line about being engaged in work of vital national importance. Anyway, what else would I do with myself? They'd probably blackball me, and I'd end up doing routine blood-testing for some godawful little hospital somewhere in the Midwest. You know what a mafia it is. I'm in, and I can't get out.'

Mort was by now starting to lose patience. Angry, he sat up, throwing a large stone on to the pathway in front of them in fury.

'Jill! Will you get your act together, for Christ's sake? I've had enough of all this self-indulgent crap. You've gotten yourself involved in a great big game here – OK, somewhat against your will, but not entirely. You can't fool me; I've known you far too long. There's a part of you that really wanted to say yes to that Pentagon guy, some sort of self-destructive urge that drove you to become involved. In fact, I reckon you actually enjoy the danger. You live a charmed, ivory-tower life, being employed by the government, and you've gotten bored. So this little game has dropped some nice, new excitement, all neatly gift-wrapped, right into your lap.'

'How can you say that? You are absolutely, totally wrong!' Jill protested angrily. She got to her feet.

'Am I?' Mort stood up too. 'I see all this as some sort of rebellion against your mother. OK, it may be unconscious, but it's real, even so.'

'What the – ! OK, what are you talking about?'

'Well, your mom died when you were a kid. And Mira's sort of replaced her in your life. So, you're getting back at your mom for dying, by punishing Mira. But it'll only damage you in the long run. Anything your unconscious drives you to do like this will harm you. All this acting-out – all the self-pity and woe-is-me stuff – that's just a defence against the old pains.'

'You certainly didn't waste a cent of all that money you spent on analysis, did you?'

Jill rounded on Mort furiously. She was blazingly, uncontrollably angry with him. But deep down, he had hit a raw nerve. She would never admit it to him, but being involved in all the secrecy did make her feel special, privileged in a way.

And Mort wasn't a million miles from the truth about Mira, though she wasn't about to admit that either. There was still a stubborn streak of Englishness in her that mistrusted the American tendency to rely on therapy, and she resented being classified in its terms. But what really annoyed her, however right he was, was his smugness, the fact that he always got everything right.

'Look,' she continued, affecting an icy calm she didn't feel, 'it's all very well you analysing me and the whole situation, but I'm up to my neck in it and I can't get out.'

'Sure you can.'

'Oh yes? How?'

'By simply turning the whole thing over to Pharmavax. We could develop this vaccine standing on our heads. We've been using recombinant technology for years, trying to develop a contraceptive pill for men. Thinking in terms of a vaccine isn't that great a change of direction. And we have the money to throw at it. In fact, I already talked with our bankers about how we could raise a rights issue to fund it.'

'You did what?' Jill exploded. 'What makes you think you can just railroad a government department? Or do you imagine I'll just walk out with the datafiles and give them to you? No way! Can you imagine what would happen to a completely untested drug like this once your lot got their filthy hands on it?'

'What do you mean?' Mort blasted back, as angry as she was. 'We'd play it by the book. The FDA are on our backs all the time. I'm not running a hot-dog stand, you know!'

'Methinks the gentleman doth protest too much,' Jill replied sarcastically. 'You know as well as I do that, given enough pressure from your board and from Capitol Hill, you'd roll over and do anything they told you to do. After all, the only thing that matters is the bottom line, isn't it? You'd sell your soul to the highest bidder! You know what you are? A whore!'

Her emotions boiling, Jill stalked off down the grassy knoll and onto the dirt track. She knew the argument with Mort wasn't really about pharmaceutical ethics. Its roots lay far deeper in their relationship. The fight they'd patched up with sex, just before she went to the conference in London, was such a familiar scene she knew she didn't want any more repeats of it. And when Mort got into his know-it-all mood he reminded her terribly of her father. And it had been to escape him that she'd married Art and come to America! Both men shared that same damn certainty; like her father, Mort always had to know best. And it made her feel so helpless, so controlled, as though she were a child again.

Jill ran off down the path, her feet rhythmically pounding the dirt just as if she were on an early-morning run. She could feel the blood racing in her veins, her head pounding. Then, realising she was being slightly ridiculous, she slowed down and stopped. Running away wasn't going to be the answer.

'Jill! Come back, for God's sake! We can talk about this.'

Mort joined her, breathless from the short run to catch her up.

'I'm done with talking,' she replied coldly, forcing the words through clenched teeth, her nails biting in the palms of her hands. 'You'll get this vaccine over my dead body. And I'm sick of you calling all the shots. First, I'm just a small-time academic working on no-hope projects that your precious company wouldn't waste time on. Then, I'm earning a pittance compared with you. And now you're making out that I'm not capable of handling my first really big break. Well, I've had enough of it!'

She turned to face him, her heart pounding deafeningly, her head swimming.

'We're through, Mort,' she said, panting between gasps. 'Whatever you've done for me in the past, I've had enough of it. I'm old enough and wise enough to stand on my own two feet. OK, when we first met, I needed you to be some kind of good Daddy, but I haven't for some time, and I certainly don't now! So you can get away from me!' she yelled. 'Just go to hell!'

Mort wanted, more than anything, to take her in his arms. With leaves in her hair, and her face streaked with tears, she looked like a hurt little child. Every fibre in his body ached to rescue her, to be the loving father she had never had, to console her the way her mother had before she abandoned her by dying. But he couldn't cross the few feet between them; he didn't dare. It would be useless, even counterproductive. This was something he knew he couldn't control. For once in his life Morton Montgomery knew when to back off.

His feet leaden, and his heart heavier, he walked away. He felt his throat tighten, and red-hot tears cascaded unchecked down his cheeks.

Her words had hit home to his very soul. As he trudged wearily back to the car, he knew that a chapter in his life had come to an end.

9.

The garish yellow halogen light that flooded the parking lot at night-time slanted in through the slats of the blind, casting a pattern of diffused light over the deserted office.The hooded intruder deftly disarmed the electronic security device on the heavy metal door and slid silently into the room. Within seconds, he was at the desk-top, running in passwords from an electronic notepad. It only took a minute for the correct one to be identified, and he was into the system.

It was the work of a few seconds to feed in the virus from a disk he had already prepared. His task complete, he rearmed the security system. Then he left as quickly and as silently as he had come.

• • •

Jill was awake when the telephone rang at four in the morning. She still felt emotionally raw after her row with Mort, and not even a quiet evening at home, with the treat of a carefully-prepared favourite meal, had calmed her to the point where she could sleep. Reluctantly, she got out of bed and made her way to the kitchen.

'Dr Peters,' she answered brusquely.

'Hi, doc. This is Leo from the lab. Security.'

'Yes, Leo. What can I do for you?'

'Sorry to trouble you so late, but I've bad news. There's been a break-in on your floor. I called Dr Harman, and she said to call you too. Would you come down, see if there's anything missing?'

'Sure. Did they mess the place up?'

'No. And it doesn't look like they took anything. If it wasn't for a window with a hole cut in it, we'd never have known anyone'd been in there. We picked it up on a routine patrol.'

'How'd they get in?'

'Through a window, it looks like. Guy left a perfect circular hole in the glass. He used a suction cup and a diamond cutter. We found 'em. But what's really weird is that none of our alarms were triggered. I'd say this was a real professional job. I mean, this guy's no schoolkid looking for what he can get.'

'Yet you say he didn't take anything. How odd. OK, Leo, I'll come down right away. Thanks for calling me. Dr Harman coming in?'

'Yeah, she's on her way.'

Jill went back to her room to get dressed, her mind reeling. They hadn't had a break-in for years. Their security, already tight, had been increased only the year before after some animal rights activists had managed to get past the first-level security. Since then everyone had been doubly careful. Then there were three full-time night security men and dozens of closed-circuit cameras. Whoever got past that lot must have been really determined.

She was suddenly hit by a blinding realisation. Like a whirlwind, she crossed to the telephone, and furiously punched out the numbers as though her life depended on it.

'What in hell's name do you think you're up to?' she blazed.

'Who is this?' the voice at the other end asked, obviously baffled by the aggressive onslaught.

'You know damn well who it is! Taken to criminal activity now, have you? You creep!'

'Jill, what in heaven's name is going on? It's the middle of the night!'

'My lab's just been burgled. I suppose you know nothing about it?'

'Of course I don't. What the hell are you suggesting?'

'You haven't been involved directly, of course, you're far too clever for that. But I bet it was someone in your pay. Can't you just accept defeat, for Christ's sake? You're not going to get your hands on that vaccine, and that's all there is to it. If you think you can get it this way –'

'Jill, you're distraught,' Mort interrupted. 'I don't know what you're talking about. I have no idea who broke into your place. I'm sorry it's happened, but it's nothing to do with me or Pharmavax. Look, just because we had a fight –'

'We didn't just "have a fight". We're through!'

'OK. If you say so.'

'I do say so!'

'Right, but if you think I'd stage a break-in just to get back at you, you're crazy. Sure, I want that vaccine, but I wouldn't go about it that way!'

'Wouldn't you? I know you too well, Mort. You can't bear to lose. But I tell you, if there's anything wrong with my vaccine data or materials when I go over it all in the morning, the cops will be over at your place so fast you won't know what's hit you!'

'Jill! For God's sake, calm down! You've gotten obsessed with all this. It's working with that colonel guy, all the cloak-and-dagger stuff. Look, why don't you talk with Mira, see if you can take some time off? Take a vacation. All this strain – it's making you crack.'

'I'll make *you* crack, you bastard! You'll be hearing from our lawyers if there's even a *sniff* of anything that could link Pharmavax with this!'

Jill slammed the telephone down and stormed off to finish getting dressed.

• • •

Jill arrived at the lab later than usual. She knew she was in a filthy mood; the interrupted night, and yet another blazing row with Mort, had done nothing for her already-frayed nerves. She and Mira had agreed – at least they still agreed on something! – that as much as possible of the outstanding routine lab work should be cleared before they devoted time to the Russian data.

She swivelled the vertical blinds in her office to shut out the glaring morning sun, and slumped down in front of her AppleMac. One fairly undemanding job that she could clear while she was in such a foul mood was the final checking of 'Active Immunisation of Cynomolgus Monkeys', a piece she'd written for the *International Journal of Reproductive Biology,* which was due to be e-mailed through by the end of the week to meet their copy date. She brought it up on the screen, and scowled at the lines of script. Her telephone rang.

At the precise same instant one of her junior colleagues stuck his head round her door. 'Hey, Jill; I'm just clearing all those electro –'

'Rosenberg, go ask Verna. They're her baby – babies, whatever. Just don't bug me about it!' She snatched up the phone. 'Dr Peters!,' she barked.

'OK, OK, I'm sorry.' The tousle-haired technician backed out of her office, and shut the door very quietly. Christ, she'd almost *snarled* at him! It wasn't like Jill to get in such a snit, he thought. What in the hell had gotten into her? A few yards down the corridor, he heard her yell, 'Rosenberg! Come back here!'

When he put his head round the door a second time, Jill was more like her usual self.

'Joe, I apologise. I owe you a beer, OK?'

'Sure,' he grinned.

'It's just that I'm rather short of sleep, and the whole of last week was ODTAA.' The department had several pet acronyms; this one meant One Damn Thing After Another.

'So what else is new?' Joe Rosenberg asked, pulling the Marcel Marceau face he had learned to perfect for such occasions. 'Seriously, Jill, is there any way I can help?'

'I appreciate the thought, but I don't think so. In any case, I have a visitor due in a little while. That was what that last call was about.'

'I mean, I could maybe go so far as to stand you the second beer.'

'Just get outta here, Rosenberg!' Jill laughed. 'Go make someone else's life a misery!'

Alone again, she scanned quickly through the journal article. OK, it wasn't the most inspired piece of writing she'd ever produced, but the facts were in the right order, and the stats were all correct. What more did they want? She quickly printed it, put the sheets into an envelope, scrawled 'To Be e-mailed' and the Journal's address, and skimmed it into the Out tray.

She glanced through the slats of the vertical blinds. Her office overlooked the parking lot, and most mornings she would catch sight of the sperm donors coming in to deliver their daily samples on their way to work. They were a varied crowd: black, white, Asian, Oriental, Hispanic, married, single. But she knew nothing about any of them, not even their names. All deliveries were strictly anonymous. She knew them all by sight, and sometimes wondered what sort of lives they led.

The anxious middle-aged man, always in a hurry, who carried a brief-case: did he spend his evenings skulking round the leather bars, or did he go home to a nice wife and several children? The threatening-looking Afro-American with the shaven head and the Walkman: what was he listening to – gangsta rap or gospel? And what about the angel-faced boy in torn jeans? Computer nerd, hash-slinger, male prostitute – how could you tell? They had only one thing in common, these men: most days, every one of them came and deposited bottled semen in a bin.

Jill glanced at the electronic clock on the shelf above her workstation. She just had time, before her visitor was due, to go down and take a quick look at the morning's samples. Although it wasn't officially her responsibility to make sure this part of the lab's work was done properly, she still felt obligated to keep a watchful eye on it. It also gave her an all-too-rare opportunity to talk with her colleagues.

Added to which, no matter how often she used it, she still got a childish kick out of the Hamilton-Thorn image analyser. The anonymous-looking grey box revealed endless wonders, and afforded endless variations on them. By dint of using a whole range of filters and lenses on the attached microscope, the user could achieve a variety of background effects, depending on what was being viewed.

When Jill got there, she found one of the lab technicians gazing fixedly at the computer's monitor. Yoshi Matsudaira was a very bright postgraduate student from Tokyo, whose devotion to Jill was absolute. When he had first arrived, a stiff, proper little creature who actually bowed before he would utter a word, he had caused screaming hilarity in the lab when, after investing in a rather dubious secondhand Opel Kadett, he had complained that he had a bad case of 'lust in his car', and that there was 'something long with his crutch.'

Jill took the mortified young scientist into her office to assure him that there was no immediate need for ritual suicide and that the more such gaffes he made, the happier everybody would be. He was taken out that evening by his colleagues and driven home insensibly drunk, a turn of events he insisted on attributing to Jill, although she assured him it was nothing to do with her. Within a matter of weeks, he had grown quite relaxed about the casual obscenities that flew around the lab during working hours.

He nodded at the enhanced image on the monitor. 'Looks like one of our donors has problems,' he said. His spoken English had improved so much that he had to be either very tired or fairly agitated before it came out as 'plobrems'. He was right: the sperm on the slide were moving sluggishly.

'Let's junk the whole sample, then,' Jill said. 'It looks as if we have more than enough for today's testing.' Racks of slides and glass vials stood on Yoshi's benchtop, every one neatly labelled. 'Is that the last one?'

Yoshi nodded, and Jill carefully picked up a rack of samples to take through to where they would be prepared for polyacrylamide gel electrophoresis. Yoshi followed her, also loaded with samples.

The first stage was to separate the stronger sperm from the weaker ones, by putting them in a centrifuge in two different concentrations of Percoll gel. The poor-quality sperm would end up in the weaker 50 per cent concentration, leaving the high-quality ones in the 100 per cent concentration. The high-quality sperm were then chemically activated.

Normally, this would be achieved by the eggs in the female genital tract, but in the lab it was done artifically using a calcium ionophore called A23187. Only then were the samples ready for SDS electrophoresis, a process that separated out, by their molecular weights, all the various proteins present in the sperm coat. The next stage was to determine whether any of the separated proteins could interact with antisera obtained from infertile male patients, using the Western Blot technique.

Even though she was technically far too senior to be involved in such work, Jill still liked to watch it being done, and felt that it only made sense to be in daily close contact with the technical team.

The other thing she enjoyed was going down every day to the animal house. Like most people Jill was fond of animals and was happy that NIH made every humanly-possible effort to make sure that the little marmosets and macaques were happy and healthy. The marmosets had the same fertility cycle as humans, which made for frustratingly slow, though accurate, testing of potential contraceptive vaccines.

Jill and her colleagues all knew better than to become fond of individual monkeys, or to read human emotions into their actions and reactions. After all, any one of them could be quietly terminated at any moment. Even so, Jill had never been able to watch with equanimity as a monkey was restrained in a frame while a blood sample was taken, the agonised eyes in the woeful little faces seeming to accuse the animal handlers of a dreadful betrayal of trust. She felt worst of all about one of the macaques who actually liked having blood taken and would put her arm through the bars of her cage for it to be done. The thought of this so-humanly helpful gesture in an animal that would soon be sacrificed for the sake of science moved Jill, not for the first time, to question the use of primates in pharmaceutical research.

She had just entered the elevator to go down to the cages, when her cellular phone rang. Keeping her finger on the Open Door button, she answered the call. It was Leo, the security guard down in the entrance hall.

'Hi, doc!' he greeted her cheerfully, although he wasn't supposed to be so informal in front of outsiders. 'Your visitor's here.'

'Colonel Foster? Send him on up, would you? Thanks, Leo.'

She waited as the elevator went down without her. In a minute or two, it was back. The doors slid open, and Brad Foster stepped out. In linen jacket and chinos he looked quite different from the athlete who had waylaid her in the park. She smiled and held out her hand. His grip was warm and firm.

'Good morning, Colonel. I didn't expect to see you again so soon. What can I do for you?'

Brad came straight to the point. 'Have you put all the Russian data into your computer system yet?'

'Sure, it was the first thing we did. It looks really interesting, even if some of it's in Russian. But the mathematical data are the same in any language, and the language of science is Greek-based, as Russian is, so it's not too hard to understand. Obviously we're getting it all translated. It's taking time, of course, and I can hardly wait! We're going to have a really good time with it!' Jill set off along the corridor towards her office, followed by Brad.

'The reason I ask is that the guys who pay my salary forgot to ask me to make duplicates before handing the disks over to you. Can you run me off a full set? I can get proper authorisation if you need it, though a phone call would be quicker.'

'I'll call, get some proper authorisation just to be on the safe side. I'm slightly jumpy at the moment, colonel. Did you hear we had a break-in last night?'

'Is that so? No, I hadn't heard. Lose anything?'

'Apparently not. It was a very professional job. Someone managed to get past all our security precautions, God knows how, and got as far as this floor. But nothing was missing. Whatever they wanted, they didn't get it.'

'Who else knows about this?'

'The cops came. And our security people are involved, of course. And everyone in this department. But really, there's nothing to worry about. Our computer system is totally secure; the passwords get changed every day. The whole thing's state of the art, and as hacker-proof as anything can be these days.'

'I'm relieved to hear it,' Brad said drily. 'So all you have to do is make one call to get authorisation, and let me have my duplicate disks.'

Jill called Mira into her office while she made the necessary call. Mira stood over by the window, her face granite-hard with disapproval of Brad. His very presence in her lab was something of an affront, and her hostility was almost palpable.

'OK,' Jill rang off. 'Well, let's get to it.'

The three of them went along to the secure computer room. Jill tapped her code into the key pad, waited for an electronic voice command, and fed in her smart card. Mira did the same, then Jill tapped in an amended visitor's code and reached for the card Brad had been given downstairs. Eventually, the door clicked open, and they went in. Jill drew up a chair for Brad, and she and Mira sat down at the keyboard.

It took some time to get in to the system. At every stage the computer required additional verification, and asked questions tailored to each user. This month Jill's verification question was her father's forename. She tapped in 'Gerald', and waited.

It was only when the Russian characters and tabulated figures appeared on the screen that she let out the breath she had been holding since she started.

'There. Look at that!' she beamed at Brad. 'That's what you went to Siberia for.'

Brad leaned over, his head close to hers. 'So it looks good to you?' he grinned.

'You bet!' Jill said gleefully.

But the enthusiasm drained from her face and voice as she whispered, 'Christ, what's happening?'

Empty patches were appearing rapidly all over the screen in half-second bursts. Jill jabbed frantically at the keyboard, but the gradual obliteration of the display continued for half a minute more. When it stopped, there was scarcely a tenth of the information left. None of them said anything; they were all too stunned. Mira reached over to scroll through the rest, and the display rolled up the screen looking like moth-eaten lace.

'I don't believe this,' Jill said. 'This can't have happened. It just isn't possible.'

'So nothing got stolen, huh?' Brad said. 'Looks like your thief left you something instead.'

'How?' Mira snapped. 'Tell me that. This system is the best. Our security is the best. There's no way anyone could have dumped a virus on us.'

'There's always a way. Sure, your system's good. But the guy who did this is even better. However tight your security is, someone, somewhere is always going to be able to crack it. You can keep out ninety-nine percent of the trouble-makers, but if – say – a highly-trained industrial espionage operative wanted to get in, he could do it. Some of them can even do it down the phone line.'

'So what do we do now?' Jill asked wearily, still stunned by the destruction they had been helpless to prevent.

'First thing, you isolate this part of *your* system. Then you'll have to get your IT guys to go through the *whole* system to make sure it's clean.'

'What about the vaccine data, I meant.'

'That's the least of your problems. We just run it all off again, on a different system, from your back-up disks.'

'Thank God that's simple, at least,' Jill sighed, getting to her feet. 'Shall we go over to the main block? They're in the fireproof safe there.'

Mira had not moved. 'No, they're not. You won't find anything there,' she said stonily.

'What do you mean?'

'I said, you won't find anything there. There is no back-up. I didn't do it.'

'What? Why the hell not?' Brad demanded, as Jill groaned inwardly. Oh God, Mira had been serious about not making back-ups after all!

'Security in the main block is laughably inadequate compared with ours, and I didn't trust it. It wouldn't have needed a highly-trained industrial espionage agent to get in; anyone who could get into the safe could have done it. I felt this was far too important.'

'Oh, Mira!' For the first time in her life, Jill was at a loss to understand her friend. 'Oh well, I suppose we can still re-transcribe from the disks Colonel Foster brought back.'

'No,' said Mira, very deliberately. 'You can't do that either. I destroyed them. I didn't want them lying around.' And she got up and walked out of the room. A small electronic bleep from the door told them her entrycode had been cancelled.

Jill slumped in front of the keyboard. 'Just don't say anything,' she muttered furiously to Brad. Methodically, she closed down the computer, straightened the chairs, and reversed the security procedure with the door. Back in her own office, she flung the window open; she had always insisted on working in a room with a window she could open, so she could breathe fresh rather than conditioned air. She breathed deeply a few times to clear her head and calm her fury.

'OK,' said Brad. 'I want an explanation.'

'I don't think I can give you one, colonel.'

'Damn it!' Brad shouted. 'You'd better! And it'd better be good! I lost a fine officer on that mission! I put my own life on the line, and the lives of my whole team. And you two crazy dames just go and lose the whole fucking –'

'Don't swear at me, please, colonel,' Jill said, sounding rather more in control than she felt. There was no way she could come up with an acceptable explanation for what Mira had done, or failed to do. She doubted whether Mira herself would be able to explain it adequately before a board of stony-faced interrogators. 'There is an explanation for the way Dr Harman acted, but it's not one I feel at liberty to give you, and in any case I don't think your superiors would appreciate it.'

'That's not good enough, doctor. Look, I didn't screw up here, you did. But as far as my superiors are concerned, it's going to look as if this whole fiasco was my doing. And it's my job that will be on the line.'

'Mine too,' said Jill, turning to look out of the window again. 'Even though none of this has been my fault. Look, I'm sorry about your job. I'm sorry you lost a member of your team. But I've been shouted at quite enough over the past few days, thank you very much, and I don't want to be yelled at by you as well.'

Infuriatingly, she could feel tears coming into her eyes, and she knew her voice was starting to crack. Recent events – the fight with Mort, the disagreement with Mira, and now the break-in – were starting to pile up on her. So it almost threw her off balance when Brad said gently, 'I apologise. It's not you I should be shouting at. I guess this is as much of a blow for you as it is for me.'

Jill stepped away from the window to get a Kleenex from her purse, and found the colonel blocking her way. He reached towards her face, and wiped away a tear caressingly with his thumb. Jill jerked her head back angrily, but Brad's hand stayed cupping her cheek and jaw. Steady grey eyes looked into hers. 'Would you believe when I walked in here I was planning to ask you for a date?' he grinned. 'Why don't I take you out for dinner this evening? I know a place you'd like.'

Jill moved out of his reach, and spent a moment or two fumbling in her purse while she considered. Colonel Foster, while undeniably attractive, was disconcerting. She didn't know what to make of him, couldn't get a 'handle' on him. He certainly wasn't like anyone else she'd ever met, and the sudden switch from gung-ho aggression to seductive charm felt strange, almost slightly threatening. On the other hand, this last week had been one of the worst she could ever remember. The least she deserved was an evening out. So why shouldn't she accept? What harm could it do?

'OK,' she agreed, dispensing with caution. 'Why not? After all, this time next week, neither of us might have a job.'

'I'll come by your place at about eight, OK?'

'I seem to remember you already have the address,' she said pointedly.

'Sure do. See you then.'

• • •

Jill went immediately to Mira's office. She drew up a chair opposite Mira's desk and leaned forward. 'Mira, we have to talk.'

'Of course.'

'Mira, we're in terrible trouble here. Is there anything you can tell me about this virus?'

'That, I swear, I know nothing about. Except that, like the colonel said, whoever did it is the best.'

'But destroying the disks, Mira! Whatever made you do it? Was it because they came from Russia?'

'Look, I just did it. That's all. Right now, I can hardly explain it myself.' Jill could see she wasn't going to get much out of Mira on the subject. So she said, 'Well, we could both be looking for jobs tomorrow.'

'You won't have any problems,' Mira said. 'I'll exonerate you. After all, this was nothing to do with you. Any lab in the country would jump at the chance to employ you. I don't care that much, really. I'm only four years off retirement. Of course, it won't improve my pension entitlement. But then, if they take legal action against me, I shall be nicely provided-for in a women's penitentiary.'

'It won't come to that. We're going to have to submit a report as soon as we can, though, aren't we?'

'I guess so. And we'll have to get the nerds in to sort out that virus.'

'At least one more or less good thing has come out of it,' Jill said, getting up to go. 'I have a date with the handsome colonel.'

Mira straightened up sharply. 'You didn't say you'd go, surely? Jill, what are you thinking of? A man like that?'

'A man like what, for heaven's sake? OK, so he isn't chairman of a multinational. But you know you never approved of me dating Mort - God knows, you said so often enough. Admit it, Brad Foster could scarcely be more different.'

'Are you so sure of that?'

'Mira, what do you mean?'

'Look, the reason I never liked Mort wasn't that he was rich, or in direct competition with you. I always felt he wanted to control you, mould you into what he wanted you to be. OK, I admit you seem to have stood out against it pretty well, but I'm not sorry to see the relationship come to an end. But to go out on a date with another controlling manipulator –'

Jill realised the conversation was rapidly turning into a fight, and a fight right now – and with Mira of all people – was the very last thing she wanted.

'I don't want to argue with you,' she said firmly. 'We're both upset, and quarrelling about who I go out with is pointless. I don't have to see him again. But it might just be fun. The way things have been going recently, I could do with some light relief.'

'Ach, you know best,' Mira said dismissively. 'So enjoy, enjoy! I have problems enough of my own.'

10.

'What time's this Volkov guy due?' Mort asked his secretary, turning from the window towards the boardroom table.

'Anytime now. Shall I ring down for coffee for you all?' she asked, heading for the door.

'Yes, please, Jane.' Mort turned to the only other person in the room. 'Randy, what do we know about him?'

'Well, he looks pretty interesting,' Pharmavax's CFO replied, engaging his meticulous-accountant mode. When Randall Church started to answer in this tone of voice Mort knew, from years of experience, that he was in for a lecture.

'Make it brief, will you, Randy? The guy'll be here any minute.'

'Sure. Well, he's a Russian research scientist, has been for ten years. All that time he's worked for the government, employed on some secret project. But we couldn't find out what, so it must be pretty special.'

'Did your golfing buddy have any idea what it is he wants?'

'Not really. He was only told to contact me on the green, pass on this other guy's message. He's not a spy or anything, at least not as far as I can make out. Seems to be in the Russian cultural attaché's office.'

'How the hell is anyone supposed to know what these people do in their embassies these days, anyway?' Mort snorted, pulling out a chair at the head of the table and sitting down. 'Sure they give 'em fancy-schmancy titles, but they're all dirty tricks guys, same as they always were. They say the KGB is as busy as ever. All they've done is shift their activities a bit. Still, with jerks like Zhirinovsky banging the drum, they could be back in business for real, any time.' Mort scowled, and rearranged the papers in front of him. 'So we reckon this guy's here on government business, is that it? Come to waste our time with some piss-ant co-operative venture that means we put in the money and the expertise, and they put in damn all!'

'If you don't like what the guy has to say, Mort, we give him the bum's rush. Simple.'

Randall Church had seen his CEO in this sort of mood too many times to be worried. 'But my embassy contact says he's one of their top guys, speaks good English. He's no peasant.'

There was a knock at the door. Mort's secretary Jane opened it, and stood back to let their visitor in. Boris Volkov, immaculately dressed in Armani suit, silk tie and handmade shoes, entered with the confident air of a man used to dealing with top people in high places. Mort stood up and extended his hand.

'Good morning, Dr Volkov. I'm Morton Montgomery. And this is Randall Church, my head of finance. Take a seat, please.'

'Thank you.' The Russian sat down. Both Mort and Church noticed that the man was carrying neither folder nor brief-case.

Volkov gazed round admiringly at the sumptuously furnished boardroom, with its enormous English mahogany dining-table and chairs. The wall at the end was dominated by a vast television screen, and plate-glass windows ran the length of the room which, since it was at the top of the building, meant they had a fabulous view over the city. The Russian caressed the polished mahogany surface in front of him almost reverently. 'You collect antiques?' he asked.

'Not really,' Mort answered. 'I just like certain things. Why, do you collect?'

'Yes,' the green eyes lit up. 'I have always travelled because of my work, and been able to pick up some nice European and American pieces. Next to actually living in the West, it's the best I can do.'

'So you'd like to live here?' Randall enquired.

'Yes, eventually.' Volkov took the coffee cup Mort handed to him, and declined the offer of cream and sugar. 'More than anything, in fact. I don't have to tell you, things aren't that good in Russia. The sort of life you take for granted is beyond the dreams of most Russians, even those who have well-paid jobs, as I do.'

'So, Dr Volkov, how can we help you?' Church asked.

'It could be the other way round, gentlemen. In other words, how I might be able to help *you*. That's why I'm here.'

'OK. Fire away,' Mort said tersely.

'Naturally, you'll have done some homework on me.'

'Naturally.'

'So you'll know that for the past ten years I have been

employed as a research scientist by the Russian government.'

'We turned that up, sure,' Church said. 'But we weren't able to find out what you were working on. Your security's good.'

'Thank you,' the Russian smiled. 'I am sure you would say the same for Pharmavax.'

'Goes without saying.'

'Good. Because what I have to say must not go beyond these four walls. You're not recording this conversation, I hope?'

'No way,' Mort retorted. He grinned conspiratorially at Church. 'I wouldn't want a record of half of what gets said in here.' Both men laughed.

The Russian went on, 'I am, of course, familiar with Pharmavax's considerable reputation in the fields of fertility and contraception.'

'It's one of the more interesting areas we're involved in, certainly,' Mort said non-committally.

'I know you have been working on a male contraceptive pill for many years. Of course, you are not alone in that, but I get the impression you are ahead of the rest. Am I right?'

'We think so. We've dedicated all our efforts, all our best people, and a helluva big budget, to staying ahead.'

'But you are not at the finishing-line yet?'

'I don't think we'd want to go into too much detail about the stage our research has reached until we know you a little better, Dr Volkov,' Mort replied smoothly. 'There's plenty of information in our annual report. I expect you've already read that.'

'Of course. However, I have a proposition to put to you, which I think will interest you. During my years at the government research lab, I came by all the data necessary to make a male contraceptive vaccine.'

Mort and Church caught each other's eyes for a split second, but said nothing.

'I expect you are wondering why our government hasn't already exploited this research. Well, the truth is we ran into problems, and we simply didn't have the technical or financial resources to proceed. You see now why I would like to work in the West. You would never allow such a thing to happen. With your superior technology and experience, you could overcome these problems, and succeed where we have failed.'

'So what are you suggesting, exactly?' Church enquired.

'If this research were allowed to lie unused, it would be a criminal waste of resources, and also of a great opportunity. A company like Pharmavax could make a fortune. And benefit the whole world,' Volkov added hastily.

Church leaned forward across the table. 'Let's get this straight. You're not here on any authority from your own government. You're here on your own behalf. You're telling us you'd be prepared to let us have all this information –'

'Not "have", exactly.'

'OK. You're prepared to sell us the results of ten years of Russian government research, is that right?'

'That's right.'

'Why the heck are you doing this? There's a helluva personal risk involved.'

'Like I said, life in Russia is not good. There have been changes, and things are better than they were in some respects. But we are still a long way behind what you take for granted. The potential waste of this research is just one example among many such failures. You might say I am greedy. Yes, I am. I am greedy for academic freedom. And I want to live a good life such as you have here. I am fed up with the petty restrictions and the inefficiency which make life impossible in Russia.'

'You don't look as if you're doing too badly – Armani suit, Cardin tie –'

'If you have money, you can buy these things,' the Russian said dismissively. 'What I cannot buy is freedom from having my life's work wasted.'

'This all sounds very high-minded, Dr Volkov. It would sound even better, though, if you were suggesting giving us the data for the benefit of mankind,' Mort observed.

'As you say, there's a personal risk involved. Why should I not be paid? If you are not interested, there are companies in Europe who would be.'

'Hold on, my friend. We didn't say we weren't interested.'

'Good. Because there is something else you should know. Someone in this country is already very interested. Sufficiently interested to steal that information.'

Mort raised his head, and steepled his fingers, his expression giving away absolutely nothing.

'Go on,' was all he said.

'I heard, only two days ago, that all the data needed to make the vaccine were stolen from a government research facility in Siberia. It is believed that it was stolen to order.'

Mort pushed back his chair, got up and sauntered over to the window. 'So they stole everything?' he temporised.

'Everything except the results of the animal work, which had not yet been stored there,' the Russian answered.

'I guess we could set that up.'

'Simple,' Church shrugged.

'And you guys don't know who stole the data?'

'There were certain indications that the team was highly professional. Some of their technology might only be available to Americans,' Volkov said cautiously. 'My guess is that it was a special operations job.'

'Christ!' Mort said, still gazing out of the window. 'Are you suggesting that our government, the US Government, sent a team to steal Russian government research?'

'I cannot say for sure. But it seems likely.'

'Hell, any government lab would be bound hand and foot by red tape. It would take them years to produce a saleable product. Randy, do you know what this means?'

Church sighed heavily. 'Guess I do. Pharmavax could get there first, is what it comes down to. So how much do you want, Dr Volkov?'

Mort turned and walked briskly back to the table. 'Hold on a moment, Randy. I have to get one or two things straight. Dr Volkov, we'd have to ask you to spend some time with our vaccine-development team. They'd need to be convinced this was worth going for before I move a muscle. And we'd want to know exactly what kind of problems you ran into. Can you give us some idea of what went wrong?'

'The most important thing is that as a contraceptive it works, at least in monkeys. We got the antigen profile just right. But after a few months, Leydig cells hypertrophy.'

'Run that by me again, will you?' Church interjected. 'I've picked up quite a bit of science over the years, but you guys just lost me.'

'What Dr Volkov means,' Mort interrupted to save Volkov having to go into exhaustive detail, 'is that the body's normal response to one system going down is to rev up others to compensate. The Russians altered sperm production with their vaccine, so the Leydig cells – the ones that produce testosterone in the testes – started to work overtime.'

'Look, I'm no scientist. But won't that mean that any guy who takes this stuff will turn into some kind of a stud?'

The Russian smiled. 'We noticed that effect when doing the animal testing, yes.'

Mort said shrewdly, 'There's more to this than a cageful of mice getting horny, though, isn't there? What about more serious side-effects of excess testosterone, like aggression?'

'Frankly, it was a problem. But I feel sure we could have dealt with it eventually. I am certain Pharmavax could overcome it with little difficulty.'

'Sure. No reason to write off the whole thing. Our steroid team is the best.They'll know how to suppress the high testosterone levels. Anything else we should know?'

'One thing,' Volkov said. He had led them carefully, step by step, allowing them to ask all the questions, until only his last trump card remained to be played. 'We have managed to bolt on HIV protection.'

'Good God! Does it work?' Church asked, amazed.

'Yes,' the Russian answered calmly.

'So, Mort, it looks as if we have ourselves a drug that turns men into studs, and lets them play around without worrying about paternity suits or AIDS. Sounds like a licence to print money. All we need to concern ourselves with are the feminists and the moral majority. They won't go for it.'

'Correction, my friend. It's the amoral minority who really run the country. It only needs you to conjure up some nice fat projected sales figures, and they'll be begging us to get it up and running. Look, it's no secret that one of our main areas of interest has always been vaccine development. You know better than anyone how much we've spent on recombinant technology over the years. And we both know the size of the Third World market. The sale of licences to manufacturers there could set us up for life – hell, for ever!'

'What I also know,' Church cut in, seeing an answer to a longstanding battle between them, 'is that one of your worst headaches has been to devise a delivery system for our male pill. We've spent fortunes on that,' he told Volkov, 'and we still haven't come up with anything we could market. I've been telling Mort to drop it for years.'

'For us too, this was a problem. We have tested every substance – some dating back centuries in Asian history. But delivery is always the problem with any male pill. No woman would trust a man to take it every day.'

'We tried implants, of course,' said Mort. 'But they weren't reliable. Too unpredictable. The level of hormones getting into the body kept varying, so the damn things didn't always work too well. And few men would go for routine hormone shots.'

'That's where the vaccine would have such an advantage,' Volkov continued enthusiastically. 'We envisage a single shot, which would last for life.'

Mort whistled. 'Of course, it would!'

Again Randy Church felt obliged to interrupt. 'Mort, the PR and marketing of this thing will be a major nightmare. Imagine it: the feminists screaming that men already have too many hormones and ought to be castrated; the Catholics saying it's evil and damning us all to hell.The Mothers of America will have us staked out in the midday sun for threatening the sanctity of the family. I reckon you should think about it real carefully.'

'C'mon, Randy, there's not a man alive who wouldn't go for this! Wouldn't you like guaranteed safety from AIDS, and freedom to play around when you liked, knowing you'd always be able to get it up?'

The rather prim accountant just smiled sheepishly at Mort's challenge. Mort turned again to the Russian.

'Well, Boris – may I call you Boris?'

'Please do. Mort?' Boris asked, to gain permission.

'How was the animal testing going when work stopped?'

'Pretty well.This thing definitely works, as a contraceptive. And tests proved conclusively that the HIV protection was 100 per cent effective, at least for the time we did the tests. Of course we didn't do any longterm studies, because we called a halt to the whole programme. The only problem, which I am confident you will be able to fix, was the aggression. I must make it clear that we never got as far as clinical trials. The vaccine has never been tested on humans. It is, of course, possible that the aggression will not manifest itself in human beings.'

'All this is going to take huge amounts of cash, Mort.'

'Damn it, Randy, you know we can raise cash for this, if it's as good as Boris says. Anything we spend, we'll make back a thousand times.'

'But before that,' Church interrupted soberly, 'we've a long way to go. Might I suggest we get Boris to sign a confidentiality agreement before he leaves, and that we then set up meetings with the R and D guys, and the basic immunology team, so that they can assess it for themselves?'

'Good idea. I take it the stuff's all on disk, Boris?'

The Russian nodded. 'You can have it at any time. You will, of course, understand if I hold back some of the vital information until we have arranged everything satisfactorily between ourselves?'

'Sure. So, Boris, how would you want to be paid?'

'Well, I haven't made any firm plans to move here yet, so for the time being I would like the money to be paid into a numbered account at a bank in Europe – I will tell you which one, later. Of course, the payment will only be made if your team is happy that there is something there for them to develop.'

'Quite. So what's the timescale?'

'I can get the data to you on disk within twenty four hours. I can meet your people any day this week. I would want payment from you by the following week. Then you will have the final disks; you will have everything.'

'There's only one thing you haven't told us. How much are you asking for?'

'I've done market projections for a period of five years and, assuming you don't get tied down by the FDA for too long, I reckon my share up front is worth twenty million US.'

'Twenty million?' Church repeated mildly. 'That's a great deal of money.'

'But not unreasonable, I think.'

'Sure isn't,' Mort cut in. 'Randy, we can discuss ways of raising the capital later. Boris,' he got to his feet to draw the meeting to a close, 'we have a deal. We'll see you tomorrow then? Here, first thing – that OK? – with the disks. And we'll have an agreement drawn up for signature.'

They shook hands all round.

When the Russian had left the boardroom and the door was closed behind him, Mort exclaimed, 'Christ, Randy! We're about to make a fortune! Twenty million is chickenshit for this kind of a deal! We can launch that share issue we discussed. Or we can take it out of the Swiss company's budget. You know, a sale and leaseback deal on one of their buildings? And when we get to auctioning licences – Christ, man, we'll be rich!'

'I thought it best not to give the impression that we were falling over ourselves to believe him. I leave that kind of thing to you.' He smiled warmly at his friend, pleased that he was about to have the kind of high-profile success he had wanted for so long.

'Look,' Mort said seriously, 'until the 80s, we made our fortunes developing new drugs and selling them – at vast profits, I might add. Times were good. But those days are gone. Gone for ever.'

'Sure, with the President's crackdown on drug costs and the growth of HMOs, we'll never have it like that again.'

'So, where does that leave us?'

'Buying out generic outfits, wholesalers and HMOs, like we're doing already,' Randall replied.

'Right. But this thing could turn the tide for us. We can get out from under the restrictions of domestic and European cost-cutting, and deal directly with Third World countries.'

'Yeah,' Church agreed. 'And if the AIDS-prevention bit works the way Volkov says, we'll be on the side of the angels.'

'Better than that,' Mort's eyes were beginning to gleam at the thought of the possibilities. 'Think of the gay market in this country, the activist lobbies. If they get wind of this, they'll pressure the FDA into granting licences so damn fast – we'd be able to short-cut all the regulations by supplying it on compassionate grounds.'

'You could go for an IND too.'

'Sure we could and provided the clinical trials work out, I'd have no qualms about sub-leasing it on the quiet to some low-profile outfit so they could run with it on their own, just for the HIV market.'

'Let them try it and take all the risks, huh?'

'Right. If need be, we could indemnify them so they'd stand to make good money if they got it right – and so would we – yet we could quietly underwrite any losses on the cheap if they didn't. I know plenty of outfits that wouldn't be able to refuse. And we'd be in the clear and smelling of roses.'

'I guess I'd be happier with that,' Church replied, visibly brightening. 'In fact, you know a couple of Korean companies, don't you, that have offshore facilities? I bet they'd just love to get round their own regulatory people and manufacture this in the Far East.'

'Now you're talking, Randy, my friend,' Mort said, putting an arm round his colleague's shoulder. 'Let's us concentrate on the contraceptive side of things, and let our Korean friends take the risks with the HIV angle.'

'But Pharmavax's vaccine will still be HIV-effective, won't it?'

'Sure. You don't think I'd throw that away, do you? This is going to be the big one, the one I go out on. And I'm going to be that rare thing in our industry, a hero. I've had enough of us being Public Enemy No.1.'

'Yeah, me too. You'd better get Jane to set up a couple of meetings in-house for this afternoon, see if everyone else reckons it's kosher.' Church gathered up his papers, and put them in his brief-case. 'That Volkov is a good-looking guy, wouldn't you say? You don't see eyes that green too often. Say – .' He stopped what he was doing as a thought struck him. 'What if that story about the Russians giving up on the project was all a load of baloney?'

'You mean, what if he's making a fast buck – or twenty million fast bucks to be precise – and the Russians are going to go ahead anyway?'

'Right. If he's selling out his own side, how do we know he's not selling us out at the same time?'

'We don't, I guess,' Mort sighed and scowled, his enthusiasm temporarily snuffed out. 'Sure, we could go down in flames with this, if we put millions into it and the Russians get there ahead of us. I just happen to believe that if we put enough money and enough muscle into it, we'll beat the bastards to it.'

'It's a risk, Mort. Don't forget there's another horse in the race. I'm not sure I could recommend this to the board, the more I come to think about it.'

'Damn it, Randy, don't play the wimp with me! What "other horse", for Christ's sake?'

'That guy said that a professional team, possibly American, had stolen the information. If it was a special ops mission, properly authorised, then the information will go straight to a government lab. Won't it?'

'Like NIH, you mean?'

'Could be.'

For a few moments, Mort stood looking out of the huge plate-glass window. He smiled inwardly to himself and turned to face his colleague.

'Randy, those government labs haven't half the resources we have. They have to do everything by the rules, red tape every inch of the way. It'll take them a lifetime. If we can't get there first, we shouldn't be in this business. I say we pay Volkov his twenty million, and go for it.'

11.

Brad poured the last of the Frascati into Jill's glass and clicked his fingers to summon a waiter.

'No, really. I've had enough,' Jill protested, feeling light-headed and giggly for the first time in ages. She looked around yet again to see if there was anyone she knew. She was glad Brad had chosen somewhere she would never normally go, as she really didn't want to explain just yet about the break-up with Mort. Not that she had any regrets, she reminded herself, but it was a bit too soon for it all to become public knowledge.

'Not the sort of place you'd usually come to, I guess?' Brad remarked.

'No,' she said cheerfully. 'But after everything I've been through these last two weeks, it's like a shot in the arm.'

Antonio's on Penn Avenue was vulgar and deafeningly noisy. Waiters in black polo shirts moved deftly among the flower centre-pieces, and the aqua-and-pink décor was definitely *Miami Vice*. There was a karaoke unit blaring away, and half the clientèle were joining in loudly. Jill dropped the long-handled spoon into the tall glass with a tinkle, and licked her lips. She had just eaten about a million calories for dessert, but the sheer silliness of the huge ice-cream concoction had appealed to her.

The waiter came to their table and Brad ordered another bottle of wine anyway. Somehow Jill found herself drinking another glass. Going out with a man only two years older than herself was so completely different from dating the rather older president of a multinational. Mort would have a fit, she thought, if he could see her now. She realised, for the first time, that although in those ten years with Mort she had been to the most glittering gatherings in Washington, and had become well-known at all the most upmarket and expensive restaurants, none of it had been half so much fun as this.

Brad half-filled her glass again. 'How about going upstairs?' he asked.

Jill giggled, only slightly fazed. 'Upstairs? Whatever do you have in mind, colonel?' she teased.

'Well, let's just say it involves playing with balls – '

Jill laughed just as she was finishing her wine, and had to spend a moment or two mopping herself up with a Kleenex. It was all thoroughly undignified, but she couldn't have cared less.

'You're a disgusting man, Brad Foster!' For a moment, it flashed across her mind that perhaps it wasn't wise to get tipsy – actually, pretty damn near drunk, she amended – with a man she really didn't know at all. Then she thought: what the hell!

'Do with me what you will, colonel,' she said dramatically, getting to her feet and reaching out a hand to Brad across the table. Going upstairs hand in hand felt completely natural. The physical contact seemed to connect with something inside her, until she felt drawn along by his hard, confident physicality. There seemed no reason to resist.

At the top of the stairs Jill heard the clack of balls and cues and caught sight of a room full of pool tables.

'Is this all you meant?' she said with theatrical disappointment. 'You had me quite excited for a moment.'

Jill hadn't played pool since her college days, and was surprised to find that much of it came back to her. She and Brad played frame after frame, sometimes doing outrageous joke shots which couldn't possibly be taken seriously and, just occasionally, playing very well indeed and for real, until Jill found herself faced with a fiendishly tricky shot which could easily lead to total disaster if she got it wrong.

Taking her time, she leaned over the table, knowing perfectly well that her trimly-proportioned rear, in expensively-cut, black silk evening pants, presented a very sexy view indeed. Behind her, she could feel Brad Foster, standing over her, perhaps closer than was strictly socially acceptable. He leaned round her, covering her hands with his to guide the shot, his body pressed firmly up against hers. The ball flew straight as an arrow, missing all the others that littered the table, directly into the far pocket.

'Attagirl!' Brad shouted, and several other players who had stopped to watch, applauded. Excited and glowing with success, Jill turned round, her bottom propped on the edge of the pool table, her feet apart. Deliberately, she drew Brad to her, wound her arms round his neck, and felt his arms go confidently and reassuringly round her. They kissed for what seemed like an eternity, until someone interrupted, 'Hey, you guys, you done with the table?'

The gleam of anticipation in Jill's eyes was matched by the devil-may-care glint in Brad's. 'Sure,' he said, 'we're out of here. Let's go!'

• • •

Practically before Jill's front door was closed behind them, she and Brad were each grappling for possession of the other. The frenzy lasted only a few minutes, until Jill broke loose, panting raggedly, to catch her breath. Brad reached for her breast, his thumb caressing the nipple under the sheer silk, until the sexual tension between them almost reached snapping point. 'If you go on doing that,' Jill whispered, 'I shall explode.'

'No way,' he grinned. 'Not yet. Not till I'm ready to let you.'

Deliberately, agonising slowly, his gaze never leaving hers, he undid the buttons down the front of her DKNY oyster-silk evening blouse, and eased it over her shoulders and down her arms; it fell to the floor with a whisper. Taking his time, he trailed kisses down her neck and breasts, as he unhooked her bra. Jill had never felt so sexually alive before; in all her years with Mort, nothing had aroused her like this. She was dimly aware that Brad seemed to know her body better than she knew it herself, knew how to make her respond by the slightest touch, until she was desperate for release.

'I can't take much more of this,' she moaned, her voice half-crazed.

'Sure, you can. Give me your hands.' Using her bra, he tied her wrists together in front of her.

Normally, the idea of being tied up would have sent Jill into a panic, but the creature she had become was so far from the cool, professional, in-control Dr Jill Peters that she really didn't care. She felt Brad slide the waistband of her silk evening pants down over her hips and thighs to the floor. She stepped out of them, naked now except for black high-heeled sandals. Brad gently guided her backwards, until she felt the edge of the table; he brought her hands forward and up over her head. 'Lie down,' he ordered. Wantonly, she stretched herself diagonally across the mahogany dining-table, shivering as her back touched the cold wood, and also in anticipation of what was to happen next.

Expertly, Brad tied her wrists to the leg of the table, not painfully, but so that there was no possibility of her moving.

'Let your legs fall over the edge,' he ordered, and she did so. The euphoria of being slightly drunk had long since worn off, to be replaced by something much headier. She felt abandoned, drugged with passion and strung out on the edge of danger. 'Now open them as wide as they'll go.'

Suddenly, Jill felt resistant to doing as he ordered. For an instant, Dr Peters asserted herself, and Jill knew with appalling clarity that Brad had reduced her to an abject, begging animal. He stood between her knees, and forced them apart. Jill shivered as cold air hit her opened thighs and parted lips.

Maddeningly, he teased her with kisses and caresses until she was moaning for mercy.

'I can't stand this any more,' she pleaded. 'For God's sake, just let me come. Please.'

'You'll come when I'm ready,' he told her. He inserted two fingers into her, and beckoned and stroked her inner walls until she was writhing and gasping, driven almost to distraction.

At last, with a scream that could have been heard halfway down the street, Jill shuddered to the orgasm of her life, her wrists straining at their bonds. Still Brad would not let her rest. With one hand he stimulated her already-taut nipples, and with the other he drove her to a second shattering climax.

Moaning weakly, she lay back on the table, limp, sweating and utterly spent. Brad untied her wrists, and gently lifted her off the table. He carried her through to the bedroom, drew aside the patchwork quilt and the duvet, and laid her on the cool cotton sheet.

Almost asleep, Jill curled on her side like a little child as he covered her with the bed clothes. She thought she felt a kiss, and vaguely heard him say, 'Call you tomorrow, angel.' She was asleep even before he had closed her bedroom door.

PART THREE

Washington, DC, 14 October 1997

12. mmontg @ lbx pharmavax.dc.usa

HOW YA DOIN'? HAVEN'T SPOKEN IN A LONG TIME, HUH? HEARING GREAT THINGS ABOUT ONE OF YOUR PROJECTS, GUESS YOU KNOW WHICH ONE. THE GUY I WORK FOR IS EAGER TO SEE THIS THING UP AND RUNNING. SAYS HE'D LIKE TO MAKE THINGS EASIER FOR YOU, ALLOCATE FEDERAL FUNDING TO SPEED THINGS UP. HE'LL EVEN SQUARE IT WITH THE WATCHDOGS TO GRANT YOU AN IND LICENSE, SOON AS YOU GIVE THE WORD. THING IS, MORTIE, YOU GOTTA GET IT RIGHT! AND SOON! CAPISCE? BE SEEIN' YA!

'Welcome back, Sandi,' Mort greeted his head of public affairs. 'Good to have you on the team again.'

'It's great to be here, I can tell you,' Sandi Sidell laughed. 'I mean, it's terrific to be a mother and all, but six weeks of diapers and baby poo is enough for anyone. And I was just going crazy, thinking of all the fun you guys were having with this new vaccine while I was stuck in Maternity!'

Sandi had been with Pharmavax for eight years, working her way up from a postgrad position in Public Affairs until last year, when she was promoted to head up the division. From the company's point of view, the timing of her first pregnancy could scarcely have been worse, and Mort had made it clear that he wanted her back in harness as soon as possible. Fortunately, Sandi felt the same way.

Randall Church was equally pleased to see Sandi. He had been worried sick when she left to take maternity leave, as Pharmavax needed her more than ever at that point to handle the media. He was deeply relieved she was back, since he felt, uneasily, that the new vaccine had the potential to go off like a time-bomb, and he had a share price to protect.

'Hi, Sandi,' he smiled. He'd always had a soft spot for her

and was genuinely pleased that she had done so well so early in her career. 'How's little Jenna?'

'Looks just like her dad,' Sandi announced blithely. 'It was a wrench leaving her this morning. I've been here less than half an hour, and I miss her already. Guess I'll get over it.'

'You won't,' Church replied sagely. 'Our two are away at college and Helen and I miss them all the time. It never changes, you know.'

'OK, OK, enough baby talk already,' Phil Zuckerman, Pharmavax's director of regulatory affairs, cut in. 'Just the four of us – that right?'

'Thought we'd keep it tight,' Mort said as he sat down. It was scarcely five minutes since he'd found an unexpected e-mail message on his pc. He knew perfectly well who it was from, and was more than happy that fate seemed to be dealing him the cards he wanted all along.

'Suits me.'

'Now, for Sandi's benefit, I'm going to start at the beginning, and run through a lot of stuff you other guys already know. The first thing you need to know, Sandi, is that we've picked a name for the product. We're calling it Seminon.'

'Good name. Says it all,' Sandi observed.

'We thought so. Now, I'm happy to say it looks as though things are going well for us. The FDA accepted all the Russian test results, the toxicology, teratogenicity –'

'Hang on, Mort,' Sandi interrupted. 'Teratogenicity – that means birth defects, right? But surely the whole point of this stuff is that there aren't going to be any births?'

Mort sighed impatiently. There were times when he wished that his executive team had the same scientific training he had, so he didn't have to explain things to them all the time.

'Everything that gets developed has to have the same safeguards, in case some idiot kid takes it by mistake – it's been known to happen. Or if we find the vaccine's good for some other use, so women and kids could take it. It's a standard requirement.'

Sandi shrugged, and switched on her pocket tape-recorder.

'To continue: the FDA also accepted all the *in vitro* work and the basic immunology stuff, just as though it had all been done in the US.'

'We were lucky there,' Phil Zuckerman said. 'They could have given us a much harder time than they did. It's almost like someone pulled a few strings.'

'More likely it's because they're so underfunded and overworked, they know they either have to go flat out on this, or put up with egg on their faces for years. They can't sit on an advance like this one, and they know it,' Church put in reasonably.

'I thought they'd drafted in a whole lot more people,' Sandy said. 'Surely that would speed things up.'

'Not so's you'd notice,' Zuckerman replied. 'Back in 91, they had eight and a half thousand full-time staff. Now, even their own management estimates that by next year they'll need seventeen thousand, and a budget of two billion bucks, to do their job properly. That's how fast they need to grow.'

'I'm sure it's safe to say they won't get everything they need,' Church said. 'Of course, that might work to our advantage.'

'Damn well should,' Phil snorted. 'The whole set-up is so goddam inefficient, the way it's run. I mean, thirty-two buildings, spread over eleven different sites in the Washington area! Their labs are state-of-the-ark; about as crowded, too. You remember the time that Watkins guy, the admiral who chaired the Presidential Commission on the HIV epidemic, went round the FDA? He said it reminded him of some Third World research institute. OK, so they've improved a lot since then –'

'We can make all that work for us, like Randy says,' Mort brought his colleague up short.

'Hope they cut corners, you mean?' Sandi raised an eyebrow at Mort. 'Not a chance, I'd say. Look at all the battles there have been over the years about drugs that looked like they could cure cancer and AIDS.'

'I wouldn't be so sure,' Zuckerman resumed. 'There seems to be a groundswell of opinion that patients should be free to make their own choices. It's years since that Katzman piece appeared in the *Post*, which said people ought to be allowed to contractually assume the risks of unconventional therapies for themselves, rather than have the State dictate what they could take.'

Church put in quietly, 'I seem to remember there was a report that showed that nearly half of all drugs cleared by the FDA had severe or even lethal side-effects, which hadn't been identified during testing. There's no way we could afford to take the risk of that happening with any Pharmavax product. I'd be very uneasy if either our own testing, or the FDA's, were skimped in any way on this one.'

'Sure, sure,' Mort said, irritated by his colleague's caution. 'But there's still a strong public perception that if the FDA has passed something as safe, it actually *is* safe. But we're getting way off the point here. The thing is that the FDA has not so far objected to the speed with which we're going ahead on Seminon. There's a reason for that; and I'm telling you this in strict confidence. Phil and I met with a couple of congressmen last week, and they understand how important it is that we get Seminon up and running. So I don't foresee any trouble from the Administration.'

'What about the actual vaccine itself, Mort?' Sandi asked. 'Can you give me something I can use?'

'Sure. Seminon is a contraceptive vaccine for men. They have just one shot of it, and they're sterile for life.'

'How's that work?'

'It's a sperm coat antigen. It stops sperms recognising eggs for what they are.'

'So conception doesn't occur?'

'That's right.'

'So, if this shot works for life, it's kind of like an immunological vasectomy.'

'Exactly. The ideal end-user would be a man who's had all the kids he wants. Of course, it's going to appeal to millions of other men as well, particularly in developing countries. By the turn of the century, hundreds of millions of men, worldwide, will have been sterilised. At the present time, they have to have it done surgically. Seminon will offer a less traumatic way, physically, emotionally and culturally, of achieving the same thing. So in terms of government contracts alone, the market is huge.'

'Another good point about it is that it's a lot safer than a surgical vasectomy. I know if I lived in a country with zilch sanitation and bad hygiene, I'd feel a hell of a lot safer just having a single shot rather than risking surgery in some filthy hospital.'

'Good point, Randy. Of course, in the West we don't hear about morbidity figures in those places. They just hush 'em all up.'

'You say this vaccine is effective for life. But there are always going to be people who change their minds, and decide they want kids after all. What about them?'

'We're working on that too, and we've reached the point where it's starting to look good. Remember all that stuff we did some years back with infertile couples, where the man had antibodies to his own sperm?'

'And they had to take steroids to suppress their own immune systems so the sperms could become active again? Sure, I remember.'

'Well, we're working along the same lines. Not that there's anything new about the idea. Did you know that way back in – now get this – 1932, someone took out a patent on a contraceptive vaccine, produced by innoculating women with semen? And did you know that eight out of ten prostitutes have anti-sperm antibodies? We're as certain as we can be that we're about to achieve pretty much the same thing, so it won't be long before we have a short-term reversal agent which will give couples, say, a month-long window of opportunity, during which time the man will briefly become fertile again. After that, the effect of the vaccine resumes.'

'What's to stop a man taking the reversal agent over and over? Or would that mess up his immune system?' Sandi wanted to know.

'We don't know. Which is why I'm not keen to go that exact same route. Instead, we're trying to create an antibody in another animal, in this case monkeys, which will counteract the antibody produced in response to our vaccine.'

'Let me get this absolutely straight,' Sandi insisted. 'The original vaccine is an antigen, which makes the man's body produce antibodies?'

'That's exactly right.'

'And the reversal agent is also an antibody, which temporarily counteracts the first antibody?'

'You got it! Now, we've already started working with the monkeys on this. And we've made use of all Jill Peters' published research work. The guys in the lab are pleased with the way it's going. You can tell the world there'll be good news soon, Sandi.'

'Can I play devil's advocate here for a moment? What if you

don't come up with a reversal agent, for whatever reason? What are the other options for couples to have children?'

'Sandi,' Mort insisted, irritation beginning to surface, 'there is no question of our not coming up with a viable reversal agent. We're just about there.'

Sandi stuck to her guns. 'Look, Mort, just fill me in, OK? If I get asked that question, I don't want to look like some kind of an idiot. What other options are there?'

'They can freeze sperms, eggs or embryos before the man gets vaccinated. That's always been an option. Then there's ICSI.'

'OK, my turn to play village idiot,' Randall Church said mildly. 'Run that by me again, would you, Mort?' Sandi grinned at the CFO gratefully.

'Intra-cytoplasmic sperm injection. It means taking a sperm and literally shooting it into an egg, in the laboratory. The woman then has her fertilised egg implanted in her womb, and it develops normally.'

'Isn't that fabulously expensive?' Sandi asked.

''Fraid so. At the moment, it's a glorified research tool, but huge advances are being made all over. The teams in Brussels and at Cornell have a head start on the rest, but they're already teaching people all over the world. Even at the best centres, it's only about 50 per cent successful, but it's improving all the time.'

'So it's out of the reach of most ordinary couples at the moment?'

'That's right.'

'We might look at marketing a video-counselling package for potential users. And we could think in terms of setting up our own sperm or embryo banks,' Phil Zuckerman chipped in.

'Sure, we could look at all that. The sky's the limit, if we get this thing right. Which we will,' Mort declared.

'The way I see it, the best selling-point, at least for the US market, is that this stuff's reliable,' Sandi said. 'But think of this. Say I'm a woman, who doesn't want to get pregnant, who meets a guy who says, "Honey, don't worry; I got vaccinated". So how do I know he's telling me the truth?'

Mort flashed a self-satisfied grin. 'You'd ask to see his green spot.'

'I'd do what –!'

'We came up with a marker dye that goes green at the injection site; it infuses the skin and subcutaneous tissue there for life. Short of having it surgically removed, the guy's marked. We're testing it on pigs right now.'

'So all a woman has to do is check the guy's got this little green mark, and she knows she's safe,' Sandi said. 'It's neat. I like it.'

Pregnancy had actually taken Sandi by surprise, and she had thought seriously about having it terminated. But her husband was desperate for kids, and once he knew his wife was pregnant, Sandi had had to go through with it. The last six weeks had been a mixed blessing. With an effort she dragged her attention back to the matter in hand.

'The other really important thing is the HIV effect you mentioned that time you rang. I'll need to know about that as well, won't I?' she asked Mort.

'The vaccine itself is in three parts. The spine of the thing, as it were, is ordinary tetanus toxoid. Then we've fixed on a sperm coat antigen at one end of the molecule, and an HIV antigen at the other. So it's actually a triple vaccine. It protects against pregnancy and HIV, and you get tetanus vaccination thrown in.'

'So why aren't we concentrating on marketing this as an AIDS vaccine, then? Isn't that just as important? More important, even?'

'If we could, we would,' Mort said. 'But there's a whole raft of reasons why we can't do that. For a start, it's not an AIDS vaccine as such. Giving tetanus toxoid boosts the whole immune system. So, if you're perfectly healthy, this antigen gives you added protection against HIV. And if you're already HIV positive, it looks, from the animal work, as though the odds are significantly increased against it becoming full-blown AIDS. What this antigen can't do is *cure* AIDS.'

'Now, the particular HIV antigen the Russians came up with only works in conjunction with both tetanus toxoid and the sperm coat antigen. The guys in the lab will explain why. But since it does work, it's possible that women will want to take it too, for the HIV protection. In fact, as it's a vaccine against sperm antigens it should be just as effective in women as in men. I should add that the HIV protection is being kept under wraps at the moment, until we're good and ready to go public. We have to protect our own interests; we don't want anyone pirating the thing as an AIDS cure.'

'I see. So at the moment you see the market as being sexually-active heterosexual men? Isn't that a bit of a political hot potato?'

'Damn it,' Mort snapped. 'It's a start, isn't it?'

'Keep your hair on, Mort. Just stirring things up,' Sandi grinned, unable to resist taking a sly dig at him. 'Now, everyone's going to ask about possible side-effects. So what about them?'

'Well, it appears that one or two of our employees have been taking Seminon clandestinely. Since we haven't gotten as far as properly-controlled human testing yet, it seemed intelligent to ask these guys to report, informally and in confidence, how they got on with it, and what side-effects they noticed. Needless to say, they've been told that if they leak even a suggestion of the HIV angle, they'll be prosecuted from here to next week. So far it appears that the only problem is a slight increase in libido and performance.'

'And this he calls a problem!' Sandi rolled her eyes at the ceiling. 'Sounds more like a selling-point I can use.'

'We'd have to wait till the Phase 1 volunteer studies to be certain, of course.'

'When are they due to start?'

'They're scheduled to start a month from now,' Zuckerman put in.

'So do we have a launch date yet?'

'I'd like to be able to say we have. But if we do everything strictly by the book, we're looking at four years minimum. Of course, if things continue to go well with the HIV protection, we could maybe swing it a lot sooner than that.'

'So you don't really need me to do anything high-profile just yet?'

'You need to keep up to the minute with this whole thing, Sandi. It's moving so fast, anything could blow up at any time. If, God forbid, the public gets wind of the potential HIV protection, the gay pressure groups – ACT UP and those other guys – could do a number on us tomorrow. That's why I wanted you back so soon.'

'It's important we all know how we stand with the FDA as of today. Don't you agree?' Church asked Zuckerman.

'All we need is enough good results, particularly on the HIV thing, and they'll give us the go-ahead right away,' Zuckerman replied confidently. 'Once we get our Treatment IND, we could go for compassionate use at once.'

'We'd better make totally sure no one gets to hear about people using it clandestinely,' Sandi observed anxiously.

'Damn right. Trouble is, we didn't have too much choice. A coupla gays down in R and D started using the trial batches on themselves. The lives those guys lead, I guess they don't have too much to lose.'

'Are you still sure we should be looking at this as a contraceptive rather than as a major breakthrough in the AIDS war?'

'Quite sure,' Mort insisted. 'Look, point number one: the HIV antigen is ineffective on its own. Point number two: AIDS isn't a worry for most heterosexual couples in the West. Contraception is. More middle-class Americans with high per capita income need a reliable contraceptive than need HIV protection. Of course they'll be pleased to have the added protection, just in case, but what they'll really be buying is freedom from worrying about having kids they don't want.'

'I'm still concerned about these gay guys using the stuff clandestinely,' Sandi persisted.

'I wouldn't waste too much time worrying about them,' Zuckerman said drily. 'One guy told me he'd been talking to his congressman about how to proceed in the event that we fired him. I'm not worried about somebody in Congress finding out unofficially that we may have come up with an HIV vaccine. They'll see the political value of keeping quiet about it until it's ready for the market. But add that congressman, and maybe a few others, to the guys Mort already talked with, and several people in Congress already know about Seminon. That can only be good for us. I foresee a time when they'll be pressuring us to make it available as soon as we can – or sooner!'

Not for the first time, Randall Church wondered how wise Mort had been to appoint Zuckerman as his head of regulatory affairs. He seemed an odd choice. Where many people in his position took every opportunity to tell their CEO why something couldn't or shouldn't be done, Zuckerman was basically a can-do man, a risk-taker. That was what Mort had liked about him from the start, and why he had marched all over Randall Church and his softly-voiced caveats. Zuckerman came to Pharmavax from a small generic outfit that had sailed too close to the wind, stretching the rules and making them work in their favour. Some of the other directors had ended up in jail, but Zuckerman had been cleared on all counts. There were many companies that would not have cared to employ someone with such a background, but Mort had leapt at the chance.

Zuckerman was in his element with Seminon; it was just his sort of project. He knew he and Mort could pull a few strings, lubricate a few congressmen and get where they wanted with it. They'd done it on other projects, and they'd do it again.

They'd played the foreign revenue card heavily in meetings with politicians, to say nothing of the economic implications for the Third World. What Mort and Phil wanted was for Pharmavax to be seen to be bowing to outside pressure, so Phil had been minutely careful in what he had actually said, and had allowed the vote-greedy congressmen to infer exactly what he wanted them to. It hadn't taken long to get them to see things his way. In fact, it was almost disappointingly easy. For years, the economists had been uttering dire warnings about world poverty and its negative effect on America's export markets, so even the most cautiously reactionary die-hards had eagerly agreed that the vaccine could revolutionise the world economic order. And the best bit was that the US government would appear in the guise of beneficent world saviours, while cleaning up financially.

But Phil had a more personal reason for wanting to succeed with Seminon. All his professional life the FDA had been a painful thorn in his flesh. And they'd hauled him into court once, which had cost him his job and his marriage. He'd been waiting to get this sort of edge on them – stick them one in the eye – for years. It was such an irresistible prospect that he quelled any misgivings voiced in the boardroom about possible side-effects with unshakable confidence and apparently watertight arguments.

And the great thing was that Mort was happy for him to do so. Phil knew that he and Mort were two of a kind, though Mort's unscrupulousness was of a more rarefied, intellectual kind than his own. Sure, he could sanitise almost any sort of dirty laundry; it was almost like a huge game to him. For all his very real professionalism, Mort could sometimes pull the wool over his own eyes; Phil, however, never lost sight of the issues. Which was what Mort paid him for, handsomely.

The two men grinned at each other across the expanse of the mahogany boardroom table. 'If they put pressure on us,' Mort said, 'we'll just go along with it. If it suits them, it suits us. Right.' He got to his feet. 'I guess that just about winds it up.'

Outside in the corridor, he fell into step beside Phil Zuckerman. 'We need to talk,' he said.

'Didn't we just spend the morning talking already?'

'Phil, you know what I mean. Meet me down on the waterfront in a half hour. Time I stood you lunch.'

'Right!' Phil didn't need to have it made any clearer. Mort wanted to talk where they couldn't possibly be overheard, not even by Randall Church.

• • •

Few people who haven't been to Washington even realise that it has a waterfront. In summer, the place bustles with both tourists and Washingtonians drawn there by the fairs, the private boats and the expensive seafood restaurants. Now, in October, it was seething with a different kind of activity. Despite the unseasonably sunny autumn weather, people were already out shopping for Christmas. But Mort, as he hurried past the jetties to get to the seafood market, had other things on his mind.

Mort often thought that Zuckerman, with his killer instinct and eye for the main chance, should have had Randall Church's job. And that Randy, with his caution and apparently strong moral sense, should have been head of regulatory affairs. But maybe it was best the way it was. No way would Church have let Mort go as far as Phil had. In fact they had taken such chances in recent months that Mort sometimes felt the whole company could turn turtle at any second. But that edge of danger was what he'd always loved about being CEO of Pharmavax. That, and what he liked to think of as well-deserved fringe benefits.

His meeting with Phil needed to take place well away from any possibility of prying eyes and listening ears, either human or electronic. As Church had pointed out earlier, ever since the notorious fraud troubles in 89–90, things had gotten really tight at the FDA. The old days of corrupt officials were gone, and the new breed were purer than driven snow. But Phil Zuckerman, thank God, was used to dealing with the FDA insiders in a way that got things done. Mort had turned many a blind eye to payments from their Austrian bank account into Phil's offshore account in the Cayman Islands. Hell, he earned it! And it was Zuckerman, rather than Randall Church, who had suggested moving their European funds from Switzerland to Austria. The Swiss banks were far too open; these days the Austrians seemed to have cornered that particular market.

Mort sat down on the stone steps to await the arrival of his colleague. He spent a few minutes watching the aproned fish-vendors on their floating platforms moored to the dock. There was a brisk wind coming in off the Potomac, but the sun was still pleasantly warm.

'Hell of a place to park!' Zuckerman grunted, sitting down beside Mort.

'I like this part of town myself,' Mort said, taking a deep breath of the fresh wind. 'Phil, we need to solve a problem or two.'

'We won't solve anything if I die of starvation. Can't we go someplace?'

'Let's walk,' said Mort, getting up and setting off along the waterfront once more. Phil, his inadequate overcoat flapping, hurried to catch up with Mort's athletic stride.

'So what's the big deal?' he demanded, as they wove through the maundering shoppers.

'We have to be sure the Lugano end is tied up real tight,' Mort answered tersely.

'Well, I did like you asked,' Zuckerman told him. 'I told Fischer in purchasing that he had to buy all the research-quality raw materials for the fermentation feedstock from the Italians. I tell you, the guy didn't like it one little bit. Said quality audit were questioning it.'

'So they damn well should. That's what we pay them for.'

'But you don't want them poking their noses in this time, I guess?'

'Let's say I do and I don't. I want them to approve the quality of the stuff the Italians are supplying, and also to swallow the 30 per cent increase in price. So I want you to make it abundantly clear to Fischer that when I visited these guys in Lugano, they showed me round the labs, and demonstrated beyond all doubt that their product is of better quality than the stuff we've been getting from the UK. Got that?'

'But Mort,' Phil puffed, 'those Italian guys don't *have* labs. You said yourself they were just a re-packaging outfit.'

'You know that, and I know that. But Fischer doesn't know it, and neither do those schmucks down in quality audit. And you're going to see it stays that way, Phil.'

'So where are they getting the stuff from? And what makes it so goddam special that we have to pay 30 per cent over the odds for it?'

Mort stopped, his hands deep in his pockets, and turned to his colleague with a pitying smile. 'I guess hunger's starved your brain,' he said smoothly. 'I never thought I'd have to explain this to *you*.'

'Yeah, well, hurry up with the explanations already! My stomach thinks my throat got cut!'

'The Italians,' Mort started to explain, as if to a small child, 'who have, like you said, a packaging operation in Switzerland, are buying the raw materials from our usual UK supplier. We know the stuff's good, so we know it'll test out if our own guys don't take my word for it. Well, the Italians are simply going to repackage it, and sell it on to us. The only difference is that Pharmavax are going to be paying a higher price. Some 30 per cent higher. And of that 30 per cent, my friend, half is staying with the Italians, and half is going in to my own personal deposit account in Vienna. And if you're a good boy and keep schtum, and if you get Fischer to approve the Italians' raw materials, some of it might even find its way from Vienna to a certain account I happen to know about in the Caymans. What do you say?'

'Well, now you spell it out so clearly,' Phil sniffed, 'I guess I say – OK.'

'Good. You just tell Fischer, on my authority, that the stuff'll give us a better brew and increase our vaccine yield. By the time he's in a position to prove otherwise, we'll be well under way with large-scale production, and it'll be too late.'

'Covered all the angles, haven't you?' Phil observed laconically. 'I like it.'

'Don't think you're going to get your cut for nothing, though,' Mort warned him. 'Those guys down in quality audit are like a self-appointed internal police force ever since the FDA went straight. They'll be like a dog with a bone with this thing. I'll be relying on you to see the bone gets buried.'

'Those guys get right up my ass, you know that?' Zuckerman snorted. 'All that "duty of diligence" bullshit! I just wish we could go back to the days when we used to play those FDA morons like fish on a line. We had us some real fun back then.'

'Not any more, Phil. They're using FBI agents to train their staff now. They work on the assumption that everyone in the industry's crooked until proven otherwise. Hell, these days you can't even do lunch without it looking bad! Remember, some years back, they sent that poor FDA bastard to jail for accepting hospitality?'

'That guy who got gangrene and lost his leg? Hell of a piece of luck. They damn near crucified me too, that other time. If it hadn't been for you standing by me the way you did, I'd have gone under.'

'Sure, I remember,' Mort laid a hand on Phil's shoulder. He didn't mention that Phil being the abrasive, volatile, not-entirely-honest fellow he was, his marriage would have come to grief sooner or later in any case. But he remembered thinking it was bad luck that Sharon had walked out and taken the kids just as Phil landed in court. Bitch showed great timing. Which was why Mort was happy for Phil to salt away cash in the Caymans, so Sharon couldn't get her expensively-manicured claws on it.

'But this deal with the Italians – there'll be nothing for the FDA to gripe about, will there?' Phil wanted to be sure.

'I wouldn't go so far as to say Mother Teresa would approve, but technically it's all perfectly legal. After all, I can buy my raw materials where I choose.'

'Sure. Just like you can choose where to manufacture the vaccine,' Phil answered. He had stopped complaining about not getting lunch, and was now striding alongside Mort, his face alight at the prospect of some more-or-less legal skulduggery. 'The Irish deal's all set up as of this morning. Thank God for the US-Irish

Accord. We had to tread carefully, though, when it came to convincing them it was nothing more than a tetanus vaccine.'

'But they swallowed it?'

'Like sharks!' Phil grinned. 'Put it this way: even if they suspected it was a contraceptive vaccine, they didn't want to be told. They want the incentive to create local jobs more than they want a clean conscience at confession.'

'If it leaked out, can you imagine the trouble? All those right-wing Catholics picketing the joint? Christ, they could even destroy the place if tempers got really hot.'

'Small chance,' Phil said confidently. 'The IDA's been told it's just another tetanus vaccine, and they've chosen to believe us. Which is just as well, because the tax breaks are worth bi-i-ig bucks.'

'You're telling me! Just 10 per cent corporation tax, and the rest repatriated tax free! As opposed to 40 per cent in this country! Wheee-hoo!' Mort punched the air with his fist.

Phil grinned at the sight of his normally-urbane CEO behaving like a little kid at a ball game. 'Guess that'll increase the value of your stock option?'

'And yours, buddy boy. I've started talking up the market price already. And every time Sandi gets a piece in the media, your personal stocks and mine grow nice and fat. That girl's worth every cent we pay her.'

'Bless her cute little ass,' Phil grinned.

'So what we do,' Mort went on, 'is when the vaccine is well in production, we step up the PR so the market price goes through the roof. Then we'll force it higher still by means of a few carefully-orchestrated leaks – maybe even go public on the HIV angle – at which point, my friend, we sell.'

'And collect our pickings.'

'And retire rich!'

'Do I get the idea you have some other nice personal deals going down as well?' Phil joked.

'I sure have,' Mort declared. 'Look, the contract for supplying the fermentation gear alone is worth millions. We had teams pitching for it from Germany, here, the UK, all over. Cork Airport never saw so many corporate jets in its whole history!'

'So who'd you choose in the end? Lemme guess; the one who gave you the biggest kickback?'

'Sure. Now, all you have to do, as of today –'

'You son of a gun!'

Mort laughed. He glanced at his watch. 'Hey, it's quarter after one. Let's go eat!'

Phil put his hands in his pockets and hurried after his boss. 'Thought you'd never ask!'

But at that moment, Mort's cellular phone rang. 'Yeah?' he barked, knowing that only Jane ever called him on it. His face darkened as he heard what she had to say. By the time he put the phone away, he was looking thunderous.

'Looks like neither of us is going to get to eat lunch,' he told Phil. 'We have to find a news vendor right away. Some damned rag is running a piece on us.'

Even before Mort had handed over the money for a copy of the *City Paper*, a weekly known for its investigative reporting, Phil could see that the front page screamed 'SEX VACCINE LEAKS OUT!'

He leaned over Mort's shoulder to read. 'So the stuff's outside the building.'

'Those damn faggots down in R and D have been handing out our vaccine to their boyfriends, is what it says here!' Mort exploded. 'Christ! Guys like that need shooting!'

The two men read on in complete silence. After a few seconds, Phil breathed a sigh of relief.

'Odd.'

'What's that?'

'No mention of HIV. It's all about the contraceptive angle.'

'Perhaps they don't know.'

'Fat chance. Half the reporters on this rag are probably gay. No way – there'll be a reason somewhere.'

'But that's what you wanted, wasn't it?'

'I guess so,' Mort answered, deep in thought as he tried to make sense of the bias the report was taking. 'But the whole idea of the stuff getting out of the building – that we need like a hole in the head.' He looked at his watch. 'Sorry about lunch, Phil. But we need to get back right away. We need to think about how to limit the damage on this, preferably before the end of the day. Look, go ahead without me. There's one other call I need to make.'

Even after six months, Jill's number at NIH was still stored in the memory of his phone.

• • •

She was in the middle of a complicated run of collating when he called.

'It's Mort,' he said. 'I need to see you.'

'I don't think so,' she replied coolly, annoyed at being interrupted, especially by Mort.

'I can understand you're not crazy to hear from me after that night.'

'You're right, I'm not,' Jill answered curtly, barely able to disguise her feelings. 'What do you want?'

'You remember I promised I'd let you know if anything came up on the vaccine? Well, it has.'

Jill's attitude changed instantly. 'Well, what is it? Tell me!'

'I'd prefer not to discuss it like this. I really do need to see you. When would be a good time?'

'I can't manage today. But I could make lunch tomorrow, if it's important.'

'It is. I really have to talk with you. I'll get Jane to reserve a table at Andrio's.' And he rang off. His phone rang, in his hand, almost immediately.

13.

'Mort, thank God I've caught up with you! Where are you? ... So if the traffic's not too bad, you should be here in about fifteen minutes? Look, Jack says he needs you in the animal lab right away ... No, he wouldn't say, only that it's real urgent. I'll tell Fred to have someone ready to park your car, so you can go straight there –'

• • •

He caught sight of his own face reflected in the stainless steel panels of the elevator that took him down to the animal house. Christ, he'd aged ten years! When did that happen? It was nothing to do with thinning hair; he'd always been proud of the fact that though his hair was grey, there was at least plenty of it. And he kept in shape, by working out and playing squash. No, that wasn't it. Rather, it was a look, a sort of deadness round the eyes, as though the flesh had dropped slightly on the bones of his skull. Haggard, he thought. Damn it, I'm looking haggard!

The elevator whispered to a halt. Unlike most elevators, its doors didn't open automatically. Mort had always insisted that not even his status as CEO should give him clearance to go beyond the elevator. He pressed the 'call' button, and stood so that the closed-circuit camera could show his face on the screen outside. Jack Rymer, who ran the animal labs, opened the electronic door, his face tight with anxiety.

'OK, Jack, what is it that's so urgent I don't even have time to go to the john?'

'Trouble, Dr Montgomery, sir,' Rymer answered. 'Big trouble, or I'd never have asked Jane to call you like that.'

Jack Rymer was a long-serving member of Pharmavax's staff. He had been employed by them since he left high school thirty years earlier, and under his management the animal lab had grown from a simple collection of rooms in the basement, to the palatial set-up it was today, housing thousands of rats and mice, a colony of four hundred pure-bred crab-eating macaques, and as many marmosets, all kept underground in a vast compound beneath the main car-park. Even so, for all his expertise and seniority, nothing would induce him to call Mort by his first name, although there was scarcely five years between them.

'Did someone get in?' Mort demanded, as they hurried along the corridor.

'No, nothing like that, sir,' Rymer panted, almost running. The corridor appeared to end in a blank wall; in fact it was the bombproof airlock that everyone had to go through to gain access to the animal lab.

'The amount of money we've spent in the past four years, they damn well better not!' Mort grunted. The two men entered the airlock, and speedily fed in their smart cards, whereupon the door opposite slid open. 'So are you about to tell me, or do I have to play guessing games here?'

'Some of the monkeys broke out of their cages –'

'How the hell did that happen?'

'I don't know, sir. No one does, or if they do they're not saying. Look, this happens in every lab once in a while –'

'Not in this one!' Mort growled. 'Damn it, Jack! We have CCTV surveillance cameras and infra-red night-time beams covering every inch of the place, just so this *can't* happen. You know as well as I do that these monkeys are loaded with several strains of HIV –' He stopped as he saw the look on Jack Rymer's face. 'Oh Christ!' he groaned. 'You don't mean –'

Rymer nodded. Quite apart from the potential danger of diseased monkeys running around the building, he was mortified that the security of the animal lab, *his* animal lab, had been breached. 'Yeah,' he sighed heavily. 'Of all the monkeys in this facility, it had to be the ones we're using to test the anti-HIV properties of Seminon. It could have been someone inside the building, I guess. Anyone who could get samples of that vaccine out of this place, could have gotten round the internal security here –'

Mort strode over to the huge plate-glass window that separated the monkey house from Rymer's office. A macaque monkey was bounding around the ceramic-tiled floor, raging and screaming, leaping from floor to wall and back again, flinging itself furiously at the cages, rattling the stout metal mesh as though trying to get at the monkeys inside. The noise, relayed through a sound system to Rymer's office, was deafening. Mort could feel his nerves being shredded.

'Turn that thing off, for Christ's sake!' he snarled. The instant silence was almost tangible. 'So why didn't you send someone in to sort it out, Jack? You have state-of-the-art protective clothing, syringes on poles, stun guns. What more do you want? A platoon of Marines?'

'See that mess over in the corner?' Jack pointed to what looked like a skein of bloodied rags strewn across one side of the room. 'He did that.' Atop the rows of cages, at the far end, a second monkey perched, glaring balefully at the two men. 'He opened three cages. Those two are males. That was a female. Uh, you really don't want to hear about it, Mort!'

'Tell me, Jack.'

Rymer turned away from the plate-glass window, fighting to keep control of himself. 'Well, he – that one up there – got out somehow, we don't know how. And he let out the other one, and they started screaming around, just like they're doing now. Then he let out the little female. She didn't stand a chance. They – well, they raped her, over and over, and then they started fighting over her. And in the end, they just tore her to pieces. That was an hour ago. They only stopped fighting over what was left just before you got here.'

Suddenly the second monkey swung down the rows of cages, and bounded across the floor. He flung himself up against the plate-glass, baring his teeth in an unheard scream. Rymer and Mort both took a step backwards. The monkey wasn't particularly large, not more than fifteen pounds, but it exuded a ferocity that they could feel, even through the soundproof, bulletproof glass.

'Christ, he's fierce!'

'He's intelligent, too. Look, he's going to try again!'

The monkey leapt up off the floor to hang suspended halfway up the bank of cages. Intently, he fiddled with the catch, while the animal inside, and all the others, leapt up and down howling. Mort found it all the more eerie for watching it in complete silence.

'We can't let this go on. Get your people in there, now!'

Reluctantly, Rymer lifted the internal telephone. 'Dr Montgomery says we're to go in,' he said. 'Yeah – yeah – yeah, I know. I'll expect you down here, suited up, in five.'

The cage door swung open, and the captive monkey was dragged out. It clung pathetically to the wire mesh, screeching and yowling, but it was no match for the larger animal. Mort watched, turned to stone, unable to turn away.

'That's another male,' he said over his shoulder to Rymer. 'What's going to happen now?'

Before Mort's horrified gaze the hapless macaque was subjected to the same fate as the little female earlier. Mort had served in the military, and had seen plenty of real and simulated violence on screen in his life. But this was like nothing he could ever have imagined. The two larger monkeys raped the smaller one, and then started to tear it to pieces.

Sickened, Mort tore himself away from the window and strode out of Rymer's office, breathing deeply to quell his rising nausea. Behind him, Jack Rymer sank into the chair behind his desk, his face buried in his hands.

'I never saw anything like that, sir,' he said, almost sobbing. 'Not in thirty years.'

Mort heard the buzzer at the elevator door, and went through the airlock to activate it. Two technicians clumped out in heavy boots and thick Tyvec coveralls. Both wore industrial leather gauntlets that came to the elbow. In Rymer's office, they halted, horrified, when they saw what was going on on the far side of the glass.

'Hell!' one of them swore. 'Look at those guys, willya? No way I'm going in there!'

Rymer looked up tiredly. 'Contractually, Garcia,' he said, 'you're obliged to.'

'Is that so?' said the technician belligerently. 'Well, I guess I just tore up my contract. I don't care if you fire me, there's no way I'm –'

'That's OK,' Rymer sighed, getting to his feet. 'I don't feel right asking you to do it, anyway. Take your suit off, and I'll go. How do you feel about it, Ebrahim?'

The lanky Sudanese grinned uneasily. 'I don't want to go in either,' he said. 'But I don't want to let you go in there alone. So –' he shrugged.

Mort grasped his shoulder. 'Good man, Ebrahim. Don't worry, Garcia, you won't get fired. Just cover Jack and Ebrahim, OK?'

'OK. Thanks, boss.'

Just then the elevator buzzer went yet again. 'I'll get it,' said Mort. He saw Sandi Sidell's anxious face on the screen, and released the door.

'Sandi, you shouldn't be here!' he said. 'You don't want to see what's happening, believe me!'

'Maybe not,' she replied. 'But I thought I'd come down anyway. Nobody upstairs seems to know what's going on.'

'Good,' said Mort grimly. 'Let's see if we can keep it that way. I appreciate you being here, Sandi, but I still don't think it's wise.'

'C'mon, Mort. I'm a big girl. Let me be the judge of that.' And she strode into Rymer's office.

In half a second she whirled round screaming *'Ohmigod!'* as she buried her face in Mort's shoulder. The fourth monkey, long since dead, was the focus of an obscene tug-of-war between the other two. 'Ohmigod, Mort, you were right!' she cried, shaking.

'Go back upstairs, then,' he said gently, putting his arm round her.

'No, I'll be OK,' she said, stepping away from him. She took a grip on herself and reached for the box of mansize tissues Jack Rymer kept on a shelf. 'Just in case I throw up,' she said bleakly, leaning on the end of his desk. 'It's so weird, watching them all jumping up and down like that, and not hearing it. They never behaved like this before, did they?'

'Jack says never. Look, the guys are coming in now.'

Mort moved closer to the window, as Rymer and Ebrahim entered the animal lab through a door at the far end. Both carried spiked poles, and moved warily along the wall opposite the cages, while Garcia hovered uneasily outside the closed door. Both of the monkeys became absolutely frenzied, and the whole bank of cages was shaking as they stamped, pounded and shrieked at the intruders. One of the escaped monkeys flung the pathetic shreds of the dead one aside and leapt shrieking to the top of the cages. The dominant male stood his ground and bounded from side to side flailing at the two technicians with the disjointed corpse, his teeth bared and bloody.

'Mort, don't they have masks, or electric stun-guns?' Sandi whispered.

'We're not dealing with airborne diseases here, so we've never needed masks. The guns are in that case on the wall, down the far end. We've never needed them either. Those cages are absolutely never opened unless the monkey's doped or dead.'

Rymer and Ebrahim stopped a few feet away from the crazed macaque, their spiked poles well out in front of them. Sandi and Mort could see, rather than hear, some sort of brief consultation going on. Rymer stamped his foot a few times to gain and keep the monkey's attention, while Ebrahim edged slowly round to one side. As he came within range of the cages, the other monkey leapt down and landed on his head and shoulders, raking savagely at his face. He staggered and fell to his knees, dropping the spiked pole and struggling awkwardly to tear the monkey loose, while Rymer cautiously transferred his attention away from the dominant male.

As man and monkey rolled back and forth on the floor, Ebrahim's screams drowned out by the demonic screeching of several dozen demented macaques, Rymer paced round them, trying to find an opportunity to stick the needle on the end of the two-metre pole into the monkey and inject the fast-acting sedative into it. It took only a few seconds, but to Mort and Sandi, transfixed with horror on the far side of the window, it seemed a lifetime. At last the monkey's grip weakened and Rymer was able to haul it off and fling it to one side. Ebrahim crawled away on hands and knees, blood streaming from his face, neck and shoulders.

The dominant male, with no warning, leapt straight from where it crouched on the floor and launched itself at Jack Rymer. The impact sent him sprawling flat on his back, and the pole went flying.

'Mort, can't we get someone else to go in?' Sandi begged. 'That other one is looking for trouble.' Mort was standing up against the window, his clenched fist slowly thumping the glass in frustration.

'No,' he said tersely. He punched the switch on the sound-system and the hellish cacophony crashed into the confined space. 'Ebrahim!' he bellowed over the din. 'Get out! Get the hell out!'

Mort turned the sound off and ran out into the corridor. 'You stay there!' he shouted to Sandi, as Ebrahim, with a huge effort, heaved himself to his feet and started to drag himself along the wall towards the door.

Alone in Jack's office, Sandi watched, transfixed, as the door to the monkey house opened again, and Mort let himself in. Apart from a pole, he had no protection at all. He hurried Ebrahim to safety then, stopping only to take off his suit jacket and wrap it round his left arm, he advanced towards Jack Rymer and the monkey. Unlike Ebrahim, Rymer appeared not to be putting up any kind of a fight. Blood was spurting everywhere. It didn't take Mort long to realise why. The macaque's razor-sharp teeth had gone straight for Jack's throat, and had severed his carotid artery. If he wasn't dead, he would be in a matter of seconds.

With a roar of rage, Mort swung the pole at the beast but accidentally struck an overhead light fitting. Shards of glass rained down. He jabbed the anaesthetic needle into the monkey's thigh, expecting the animal to shriek and possibly turn to attack him. Instead, it sat silently among the broken glass, its teeth and claws dripping with Jack Rymer's blood, and fixed Mort with a cold, burning glare. Mort had never, ever, been so terrified in his life. Almost insolently, it glanced down at its thigh where Mort had jabbed it, touched the spot and slowly, almost meditatively, sniffed its fingers. It gazed up at Mort again, in a more terrifyingly human way than any human ever could.

Mort felt his legs about to give way with fear. Why don't you just roll over, you bastard? he thought. Surely the monkey was about to go under; it couldn't be much longer. How long did the damn stuff take to – ?

'Kraaaggh!' With a rending scream, the monkey leapt again, and fastened itself to Mort's chest and shoulders, its claws ripping his shirt and the skin and flesh beneath. He staggered against the wall, dimly aware of Sandi, her face frozen in a silent scream, falling to her knees on the far side of the glass, her fists beating soundlessly.

Mort flung down his useless jacket and, bracing his back against the wall, grasped the monkey by the throat, straining to push it away from him. He could feel its feet clawing at his chest and belly, and his grip tightened. 'Die, damn you!' he cursed between clenched teeth. He would never know whether he actually did strangle it, or whether the drug finally kicked in. But the red glare died in the creature's eyes, and – an eternity later – the last spark flickered out.

• • •

'C'mon, Sandi. You can fall apart later, but right now I need you to function. First, call the paramedics down here. Then go find me a clean shirt in the closet in my office. Then we have to think how to handle this, what we tell the media.'

'Mort, you were so brave. I never saw anything like that, ever,' Sandi gabbled, still in a state of shock. Mort refused to allow her anywhere near him, and was doing his best to swab the worst of the blood from his lacerated chest. 'Don't worry, you may not be HIV positive,' she went on, her voice shaking. 'They can give you all sorts of shots –'

'Shut it for now, Sandi,' Mort said, not unkindly, jerking his head towards Ebrahim, who was slumped in a chair, breathing weakly, eyes closed and his ebony-dark face almost grey, his Tyvec suit soaked with blood. Only Mort, of the people in the room, knew that the dead monkeys had been infected with deadly strains of HIV, specially developed to test Seminon to its limits and – if Seminon didn't work – totally untreatable.

Poor Ebrahim's days were numbered. And – Mort knew with numbing certainty – however long it took, so were his own.

14.

'Mort, you and I have had dealings with each other for many years. I don't have to tell you that we at the FDA are greatly disturbed at being more or less ordered to grant you a Treatment IND at this stage in the development of Seminon. Jumping the gun in this way runs counter to everything this institution has ever stood for. So I need your categorical assurance that every single result of your testing, whether successful or not, will be made available to our close scrutiny. Of course, I realise that we can only act on the information you make available to us. However, having known you for many years, I am certain that if there is one man in this city whose probity and integrity can be relied upon absolutely, that man is Morton Montgomery –'

Occasionally, there were times when Mort could be honest with himself. The journey by cab to Andrio's was one of those times. He had agreed to tell Jill of any major developments with Seminon, but he could simply have told her to go out and buy a copy of the *City Paper*. But over the years he had come to rely on using Jill as a sounding-board – not for professional concerns; the reason their relationship had worked for so long was that they never discussed those – but for other, more everyday problems, to do with his staff, and the organisation of his own life. Whenever the going got tough, Jill had always listened sympathetically and intelligently. He needed her to do that now.

He still hadn't decided whether to trust her with the news about the appalling effect the vaccine appeared to be having on his lab monkeys. He reached a decision in the cab. If he told her, he'd get into a whole discussion about whether or not he was infected with untreatable HIV, and he simply didn't think he could bear to talk about it with anyone at the moment, not even Jill. Also – Christ, he thought, he must be getting more than usually paranoid! – he no longer knew for certain that he could trust her to keep it to herself.

The night before, he had been too jittery to sleep and had resorted to knocking himself out with pills. Under his immaculate grey-and-white striped Gieves and Hawkes shirt, his body was a mass of scratches and lacerations dressed with layers of lint and band-aid. Every movement he made reminded him of his appalling stupidity in going, alone and unprotected, into a roomful of deranged monkeys. If *that* ever leaked out, the least that would happen would be that his health insurance would be terminated. Well, he'd be paying for that little bit of foolhardy bravado for the rest of his life – and who knew how long that was going to be? This was just the sort of impetuous, even arrogant, behaviour that Jill had so often criticised him for. And here he was falling into the same old traps again.

Jill was already at the table when he arrived. Damn it, she looked good! For a moment, Mort felt a jab of resentment that she could look so radiant and alive, only a few months after they'd broken up. He leaned down and kissed her affectionately. Inwardly, he felt a sense of relief. She obviously understood that he was in trouble, and was having to swallow his pride; so she was going to behave well, make it as easy for him as she could.

'I really appreciate you taking the time like this,' he started, realising that he was genuinely pleased to see her.

'It sounded kind of urgent.'

Mort took a minute or two to order a bottle of white wine and some mineral water, and asked, 'Caesar salad to start?', knowing that was what Jill would choose. Once the waiter had gone, he got straight to the point. He spoke very quietly. Even though he had chosen Andrio's because the tables were spaced far apart, you never knew who might be listening.

'This whole vaccine thing's about to blow up in our faces,' he said. 'Yesterday's *City Paper* has it splashed all over the front page.'

'I'll pick up a copy after lunch. How on earth did they get hold of it? I thought all your staff were bound by confidentiality agreements, same as I am.'

'The staff are, sure. But their friends aren't. And a crowd of gays down in R and D have not only been using the trial batches on themselves; they've been taking it out of the building to give to other people. We wouldn't have known a thing about it if some journalist hadn't talked to some of the men who've been taking the stuff. I'm only thankful that by some miracle no one's said anything about the potential HIV protection. We simply aren't ready to go public with that just yet.'

'Wouldn't you find the publicity useful? It's not as though you engineered this on purpose. If you fire the people responsible, and do it publicly –'

'Sure, sure, we'll do all that. No, the whole point is that while I really do want to get this thing up and running and ready to market as soon as possible, I want to do it at our speed, not at a pace dictated by the public. I don't have to tell you that you can't do this sort of thing in a glare of publicity. I don't want the media looking over our shoulders the whole time.' He shifted uneasily in his seat.

For a moment or two Jill said nothing, but thought instead. Finally, she said, 'Morton Montgomery, I know you too well to believe that this is going to prove to be a disaster for you. Now, you say this stuff works? The fact that people have taken it is clinical evidence of a kind, even if it's not viable in the FDA's terms. Of course, you're going to have to do all the Phase 1 testing, all the dose-ranging and healthy volunteer work, to satisfy the regulations. But your employees and their friends have to some extent short-cut all that. It's only a matter of time before the fact that they've taken the vaccine becomes known, and if the medical evidence is out there walking about in the street – well, what I mean is: you can't un-know what's happened. Neither can the FDA. They can huff and puff but they can't blow your house down. However much they insist on clinical trials, everyone will already know the stuff is effective. The Administration is going to come under pressure from all sides to grant you all the licences you want.'

'I never thought I'd hear you talk like this,' Mort's taunt was soft-edged.

'Look, I don't like this situation. If you really want my opinion, I think it's deplorable. And I have to say I'm glad it's happened to Pharmavax and not NIH. I'm simply being realistic about it.'

At that point, the waiter brought the first course. Jill started on a different conversational tack. 'Now the stuff's outside your control, it's not going to take long before someone finds out how to replicate it, is it?'

'I thought of that too.' Mort picked at his food gloomily. 'OK, we're over the first hurdles with the FDA. But as you and I both know, there are outfits all over the world – in China, Latin America, offshore labs in the Pacific Rim – who don't give a damn about the FDA or any other regulatory body. They'd just make the stuff under another name, throw it out on to the market and rake in the bucks.'

'Bucks that ought by rights to be raked in by Pharmavax.'

'Damn right. And it makes me mad to think that some bathtub braumeister could steal all our work, and cash in on it!'

Jill thought it wise not to point out that the work had already been stolen twice even before Mort got his hands on it. So she said, in as soothing and reasonable a voice as she could, 'Mort, that's a worst-case scenario. It might not happen that way at all.'

'If it does, then there's damn all we can do about it. And another thing: Phil and I have dropped the word to a couple of people in Congress. We led them to understand that if they could set up advantageous trade deals in the Third World for us, then we'd let the US health services have the vaccine for a darn sight less than we could screw out of them if we wanted. You could see them adding up the figures in their heads, counting up the votes; I tell you, their mouths were watering! Chances are they've gone to work on it already. They don't like being made fools of, which is what'll happen if this stuff starts being made by any damn crook who can buy the expertise.'

Jill had been observing Mort carefully. He wasn't his usual self. There was more to this than he was telling her, but she couldn't work out what it was likely to be. He was angry and seemed to be on edge, but his anger wasn't fuelling any constructive thought or action, which normally it did. The Mort she had known for so many years had always relished a challenge; in fact, he almost used to welcome the opportunity to pit his wits against adverse circumstances. She tried to turn him back in that direction.

'Come on, Mort. You've always managed to deal with this sort of situation in the past. You used to enjoy it.'

'But this is the big one. I told you how I always wanted to

head up one really world-class project before I left Pharmavax, retire a rich man. Well, Seminon was it. The way things are going, I'll be lucky to be kicked out the back door.' I'll be lucky even to be alive at the end of the day, he thought.

It looked to Jill as though there wasn't much to be done about Mort's defeatist mood for the moment. 'So what else is new?' she asked brightly. 'What else have you been up to? You realise we haven't seen each other at all for months?'

'I thought that was the way you wanted it.'

'It is. But I still want to know how you are, what you're doing.'

'Quite honestly, I've been so tied up with this, I've done practically nothing else.'

'Morton Montgomery! Not practising what you preach? Is this the man who used to give me a hard time about working a fourteen-hour day? I suppose you're going to tell me you've been working weekends as well?'

'Since you ask, yes I have. And not having you to talk to hasn't made it any easier.'

'Mort, there's no way we could have talked about this. For a start, even now I'm still feeling sore about losing the data. I'm still not sure I can even think rationally about what Mira did.'

'Isn't it the damnedest thing? First, the information gets stolen, and given to you, and you lose it. Then it gets stolen again, and given to Pharmavax and now we're losing it.'

'You haven't lost it! It's just that someone else may have it. Or may not. But yes, it is weird. Like I said to Brad when he first came to me, it's like the plot of a bad B-movie.'

'Oh, it's Brad now, is it? You dating the guy, or something?'

Jill made a determined effort to keep both face and voice noncommittal. 'Since you ask – yes: we're seeing each other. But I'd rather not talk about it. And anyway, you and I have more important things to discuss. There's one thing I still don't understand. I've always believed Pharmavax hired someone to plant that virus in our computer system.'

'We didn't. I give you my word. Look, I know we sail fairly close to the wind sometimes, but we wouldn't do that. For a start, it'd be too risky. Your security's the best, and the chances are we'd get caught. Second: if it were known that we, a commercial outfit, stole from the government, we'd be out of business in seconds. And lastly, I simply wouldn't do that to you.'

Jill believed him. 'OK,' she said. 'I accept all that. So how did the formula get into your hands? You owe it to me to let me know. You can rely on me not to say anything.'

'Of course. I've always trusted you, you know that. But if I tell you that a Russian research scientist smuggled it out of Russia and sold it to us, would you believe me?'

'No. But if you say that's what happened, I suppose I have to. This whole situation is full of bizarre things I have trouble believing. Like: the government sends in a dirty-tricks team to steal the information from the Russians, and all the time it's going to be smuggled out anyway. Talk about crossed wires! So where did this scientist come from?'

'He's worked for a Russian government lab for ten years, and got pissed off with life there. He wanted the good life, and a lot of dollars to enjoy it with. And we wanted the formula. So we paid him a lot of dollars. End of story.'

'I wonder whether he ever will enjoy the good life.'

'If he stays out of jail, he should. He's a good-looking guy, young, intelligent; I was impressed with him. And he's not one of those Russians that look like the rear end of a tank; I guess he came from one of their outlying provinces originally, somewhere in what used to be Soviet Central Asia. You know, dark hair, cheekbones like Rudolf Nureyev. And he had these really weird green eyes, like a cat; even Randy noticed them. I tell you, if he lived here, he'd never sleep alone.'

'Sounds like my kinda guy,' Jill joked. But her mind was racing furiously. Dark hair, green eyes – . Her mind flew back to that brief meeting in London with the shy, charming Ivan Kandinsky. Surely he wasn't employed by the government? She remembered that Mira had known all about the research institute where Kandinsky worked; although for the moment Jill couldn't remember the name, she could ask Mira later. And, for Heaven's sake, in a country the size of Russia there had to be more than one scientist with dark hair and green eyes!

'Does he have a name, your scientist? Are you prepared to tell me?'

'Don't see why not. He's called Boris Volkov. And he is who

he says he is; we checked. He's been listed as working at the government research institute in Moscow for the past ten years. The guy's as kosher as he can be without being Jewish.'

Jill felt every nerve relax. So he wasn't Ivan Kandinsky after all! She looked at her watch. 'I can't stay much longer. I'd like to get away from the lab on time tonight. I have to go over and visit Shirlene in the hospital. Then I have to get home because Mira's coming round.'

'She lost her job, didn't she? Are you any nearer finding out what made her act that way?'

'I never asked her about it again. I don't suppose truly she knows herself. She told me once about some things that happened when she was a little child, which is why she hates Russians like poison. It might have been partly that, or she may have just gotten even more neurotic than usual about security. It's always been a big thing with her, as you know.'

'I'm happy they didn't throw you out as well. I know you had nothing to do with losing the information, but mud sticks. My guess is they probably realised they'd be foolish to let you go. After all, you're the best they have.'

Mort was clearly trying to be gracious. Jill smiled at him. 'It's so good to see you again. I'm only sorry you have such problems to handle. I really wish there were something I could do.'

'Just listen, perhaps? I could do with that from time to time.'

'You gotta deal. And I have to run in thirty minutes.'

'I do too. The animal-testing's taking up everyone's time at present, and I like to keep up with it as it develops. So, let's order. Grilled sea-bass?'

Jill nodded, as Mort had known she would.

15.

'– Of course, sir, I understand what you're saying, perfectly. But there's no way that I, as Commissioner, am going to jeopardise the good standing of this institution by granting a Treatment IND to a company, even one as powerful as Pharmavax, unless I am one hundred per cent sure the testing's been properly done. Put it this way, sir: if anything were to go wrong, the FDA would need to be able to produce documentary evidence that all the rules had been complied with – I agree, sir; we want to see this drug perfected and available just as much as you do – Of course we understand that, sir – But, sir, we at the FDA have a duty to the people of America –'

A thunderstorm broke ferociously just as Jill was leaving the lab, and snarled up the traffic throughout the city. The drive from Bethesda to the hospital to see Shirlene took longer than usual. In the event, she didn't stay long. Shirlene was dopey and ill after chemotherapy, and Jill felt she had better leave.

By a miracle she managed to find a just-vacated parking space within a block of her apartment, and ran like a hare through the rain with her jacket held over her head. She just had time to shower and change when the bell rang, and a few moments later Mira arrived at her door, soaked to the skin. Jill fussed over her and took her wet umbrella and raincoat and hung them in the hallway. She put her sodden shoes to dry on newspaper in the kitchen.

'A good stiff Scotch?' she asked.

'What else?' Mira settled heavily on the sofa. Jill thought she looked tired.

'How's the teaching going?'

'OK, I suppose,' Mira said dully. 'But students these days – ach, they don't *think*! They can't! If they don't see something on a computer screen, it doesn't exist. They have no imagination! Thank God I only have to tolerate them three mornings a week!'

'What about your series of pieces for *Nature*?'

'Coming on nicely. I'd like it if I could get a year's contract with them. We'll see.'

'We miss you so much in the lab,' Jill said. 'Everyone sends their best.'

'Sure they do. More likely they'd send me a bullet.' Mira took the generous drink Jill handed her, and downed half of it quickly. 'I still think I did the right thing, you know.'

'What right thing?' For a moment, Jill couldn't think what Mira was talking about. Then she remembered. 'Oh, that. Mira, I've never understood what that was all about. We never did talk about it.'

'There's nothing much to say, is there?' Mira said shortly. 'Crazy old Mira screwed up. That's all there is to it.'

Oh God, Jill thought, I hope the rest of the evening isn't going to be like this. She poured herself some wine, and sat down opposite her former boss. Just as she was casting about desperately for a harmless topic of conversation, Mira lifted her head, and said, 'I turned up something that might interest you. Want to hear it?'

'Course I do,' Jill replied, immediately interested.

'Remember I said I had a friend in the FBI who was going to do a bit of digging for me? And you recall that Mr Kandinsky you were so taken with in London?'

'Sure. What about him?' Jill's heart was starting to go into a slow plummet.

'For a start, his name is no more Kandinsky than yours or mine. There *was* an Ivan Kandinsky at MIT in the early 70s. I've seen a mug-shot of him in the yearbook, and he's our friend.'

'Mira, you just said –'

'Let me finish. The Ivan Kandinsky who was at MIT from 1970 to 1975, is the Ivan Kandinsky we met in London.'

'So? Isn't that what he said?'

'Just listen, will you?'

'Sorry.' Jill tucked her feet up on the chair seat under her and took a sip of wine.

'Let me confuse you a little more. There is also an Ivan Kandinsky listed as working at the Stawowy Research Institute in St Petersburg. But six months ago, the staff list shows no such name. With me so far?'

Jill nodded. Nothing made any sense, but she wasn't going to annoy Mira further by saying so. The leaden weight in her chest still hadn't shifted, and she just wanted Mira to get to the point.

'However, our Mr Kandinsky's pretty face has shown up somewhere else rather interesting. The FBI keeps records of as many Russians who've lived over here, or visited, as they can. And the CIA keeps mug-shots of all known KGB operatives. For the first time, they cross-referenced the non-existent Mr Kandinsky with the CIA's files. My friend had clearance to show me one mug-shot, so I could identify it. Which I did.'

Mira knocked back the rest of her drink, and held out her glass to Jill.

As Jill poured more Scotch, she said, 'I don't think I want to hear what you're going to tell me, Mira.'

'You don't really need me to tell you, do you? Prince Charming is KGB. Ivan Kandinsky is Boris Volkov. And Boris Volkov is one of their top industrial espionage people. You remember Colonel Foster said whoever broke in to the lab was the best? He is the best. Oh, he's a scientist all right. It was the KGB who sent him to MIT, for Christ's sake! They were training him to work for them since he was a schoolkid. OK, he may be a whizz at recombinant technology, but he's also heavily into dirty tricks. Damn it, Jill, there you were fancying the pants off the guy, and it was him that planted the virus!'

'If anybody but you told me this, I wouldn't believe it,' Jill said bleakly, pouring herself another glass of wine.

'I can hardly believe it myself.' Mira's second drink was disappearing almost as rapidly as the first.

'Well, *I* have something to tell *you* that you won't believe either. Can you just stay sober long enough to give me some advice about how to handle this?'

Mira put her glass down on the coffee-table with symbolic firmness. 'Since I got fired, I do seem to have been drinking more than I used to. I ought to cut down. So what is this I'm not going to believe?'

'I had lunch today with Mort.' Mira raised an eyebrow warily at Jill. 'Calm down, we're not getting back together. He has a problem, that I promised I wouldn't talk about. Actually, I think he has problems he didn't even mention, over and above that.

However, he told me something very important. All this time, in spite of everything he said, I really believed he was responsible for seeding the computer virus. The fact that he then mysteriously came into possession of the data only made me believe it all the more. But he swears it was nothing to do with him or Pharmavax. And this time I believe him.'

'So how *did* he come by the information?'

'He bought it, for a lot of money, from a Russian scientist who offered to sell it to him.'

'And this Russian scientist wouldn't happen to be a romantically beautiful young man with interesting green eyes –'

' – called Boris Volkov. Yes, I'm afraid he would.'

'So Mort knows Boris Volkov is a Russian government research scientist. I take it he doesn't know he's also a KGB industrial espionage expert?'

'I'm sure he doesn't. He would have said, I think. Only you and I know. And the FBI.'

'So it's no coincidence that the information was rendered useless to NIH, and then given to Mort. The Russians, in effect, stole it from us –'

'Brad's team stole it from them first, don't forget. On orders from our own government.'

'In which case, having recovered it you'd expect them to take it home again, wouldn't you? Instead, they sell it to Mort. Why?'

Jill was beginning to feel she needed a third glass of wine, but equally that she should try and keep a clear head. The ramifications and implications were opening up faster than she could keep track of them.

'Is it possible that Kandinsky-Volkov is working independently?' she asked.

'You'd like to think the best of him, I guess. But I saw his cv. This guy has been KGB practically since birth. I'm sorry to say I doubt it very, very much indeed.'

'So what do we do, Mira?'

'Stay well out of it, and let events take their course. Right from the start, I never wanted to have anything to do with this –'

' – and events have proved you right.' Mollifying Mira in this way, with a little flattery, would do no harm, Jill decided.

'There was one other interesting thing my friend told me –'

Mira begàn, but at that moment the telephone rang, and Jill got up to answer it. For a few minutes she chatted with Art, and agreed to pick up Jim an hour earlier the following weekend. The routine they had developed over the years had been thrown into disarray by Shirlene's illness; Art was having to do the housekeeping as well as his job, and was finding it hard to fit everything into the time available. When Jill put the telephone down, she found Mira in the kitchen looking for her shoes.

'I really should go,' she said, glancing at her watch. 'Lord, is that the time? I have to get to the mailbox – that article they wanted by tomorrow.'

'Just tell me one thing,' Jill begged. 'Do I tell Mort?'

Mira shrugged. 'Frankly, my dear, I don't give a damn,' she quoted. 'If he goes and buys information from the Russians, let him handle the consequences. Of course, you may feel you owe it to him to tell him. That's up to you.'

Mira retrieved her still-damp coat and umbrella from the hall. 'Can I call you a cab?' Jill asked.

'No, thank you. The rain's stopped, and the walk will be good for me.'

Jill accompanied Mira out to the landing, and called the elevator. 'Keep me posted, won't you?' Mira said.

'Of course. Good night.' The two women kissed each other affectionately, and Mira waved goodbye as the elevator doors closed.

Jill's brain felt as if ants were scurrying all through it. She poured herself a third glass of wine after all, and sat down to think. It took a fourth for her to arrive at one single conclusion. The real mystery was why the Russian government had sold an apparently viable vaccine to an American company. Money couldn't be the answer. So why had they done it? The one idea that kept returning like an angry wasp to a windowpane was that the formula wasn't what it appeared. Could it, in some diabolical way, be booby-trapped? Jill got up to wash the glasses, and decided that before ringing Mort in a panic, she would sleep on the problem.

• • •

At four in the morning, she woke up. Too much white wine had left her feeling dehydrated and gritty-eyed. She got up to get a glass of water. Standing at the kitchen sink she suddenly remembered Mira saying, 'There was one other interesting thing my friend told me –' But then the telephone had rung, and they had never finished the conversation. As she made her way back to bed, she couldn't help wondering what the 'one other interesting thing' had been.

16.

mmontg @ lbx.pharmavax.dc.usa

HOW YA DOIN'? HEAR THE BAD NEWS? GUYS OUT EAST REPLICATED YOUR VACCINE, BIG MAN NOT PLEASED. WANTS TO EXPORT THE STUFF, NOT IMPORT IT, RIGHT? HURRY IT UP SOME, OK? TALKED YESTERDAY WITH STUFFED SHIRT AT FDA, SAYS YOU CAN CUT THE TESTING SHORT, SO LONG'S THEY'RE SATISFIED IT'S ALL HUNKY-DORY. SO SATISFY 'EM, OK? DO WHAT YOU HAVE TO. BUT MAKE IT LOOK GOOD –'

Jill drove to Art and Shirlene's house to collect Jim, in a distinctly bad temper. Just before she left, Mort had called her to say that Pharmavax were going ahead with scaling-up production of the vaccine. Jill had known Mort long enough to realise that such a decision couldn't possibly be his alone. He could be an unprincipled bastard, but he was no fool, and he'd done well for his shareholders during his years at the helm. Clearly, matters were out of his hands. For the first time in his life Mort was having to bow to pressure. Jill felt half-annoyed with him that he didn't just walk away from the problem, wash his hands of it, and leave the government with egg on its face. But her more rational half knew that the bottom line was all that really mattered to Mort.

The afternoon was unseasonably hot for October, and being held up by a bad tail-back did nothing to improve her mood. She pulled sharply into Art and Shirlene's driveway, not bothering to park neatly – after all, she wouldn't be staying long. She left her purse on the seat and the keys in the ignition, and slammed the door. The yard was deserted; there was no sign of Jim's bike. But the front door was wide open, so she went in.

Upstairs, she could hear the whine of an electric drill. When there was a pause, she called up the stairs. Art's voice came down, 'That you, Jill? C'mon up.'

Except for picking up Jim's things from his room a few times, Jill had never been upstairs, and had certainly never seen inside Art and Shirlene's bedroom. She knocked on the open door to get Art's attention.

'C'mon in,' he called. He gestured towards the bed with the drill. 'Sit down till I finish this.' Half of the room was immaculately neat; in common with the rest of the house it was overdone, a riot of pink frills everywhere. Between the two windows stood a tall case of shelves laden with dolls, and the walls were dotted with trite sayings done in needlepoint. One wall was stripped to the plaster, and Art had fixed a timber frame to it. Neatly ranged against the wall were four mirror-glass panels and various other lengths of wood, battens and shelving. Handfuls of screws in graduated sizes had been neatly heaped on Shirlene's glass-topped dressing-table, and two beer cans tethered in an otherwise empty plastic frame stood by the waste-bin.

'So Shirlene's still not home?' Jill asked, slightly uneasy at being in their bedroom when Shirlene wasn't in the house.

'No. They decided to keep her hospitalised for a coupla days longer. She's been having tests and chemotherapy, but there was something else they wanted to take a look at.' Art determinedly poised his drill at the centre of a pencilled X. The deafening whine filled the room; when it was finished, Jill said, 'Oh, Art; I'm so sorry. I hope everything'll come right.' But Art volunteered no more information, just continued with a series of holes. When he had come to the end of the length of timber, he put the drill down and reached for a can of beer.

'All the years we've been married,' he said, ripping off the ringpull and throwing it in the bin, 'Shirlene's never had a walk-in closet. I've been promising her she could have one for so long, I reckoned now'd be a good time to get it done.'

'She'll be so pleased when she comes home,' Jill smiled, thinking: all the years we were married, Art Peters, you'd never have built *me* a walk-in closet. But more than that, she was glad that Art was doing something Shirlene really wanted, even if it had taken her illness to nudge him into doing it. She perched on the edge of the bed. Art took a swig of beer and put the can down on the dressing-table, then picked up the drill once more. 'I told Jim to be back by now,' he said, wiping the sweat from his face and neck. 'He's over at Scott's parents' place, and they have an indoor pool. Next thing I save for'll be a pool, but just a small one, out in the yard, so Jim can have his friends over.' He started on another row of drill-holes, rendering conversation impossible.

Suddenly the drill met an obstruction, and the bit shattered. A piece of metal flew across the room and ricocheted like a bullet off the far wall. Jill heard Art moan, 'Ah, shit!' One hand clutched the other. Blood was dripping out from between his fingers and spattering his jeans. Jill leapt to her feet.

'Into the bathroom, quick!' she ordered. She turned on the cold tap, seized Art's wrist and held his hand under the running water. Art perched on the edge of the bath, grey in the face and shaky, watching with queasy fascination the reddened water swirling round the sink. There was a ragged tear in the fleshy part of his thumb, and blood kept welling up. 'Put your other thumb there,' Jill said, motioning him to press over the wound to stop the bleeding. 'Where does Shirlene keep the first aid stuff?'

Art jerked his head in the direction of the bathroom cabinet. Thank God for Shirlene, Jill thought, viewing the shelves crammed with household medicines for every conceivable eventuality. At one side, there was a white plastic box with a red cross. Inside Jill found, as she knew she would, everything she could possibly need. Art's hand was bleeding less heavily now. She speedily made a pad out of folded lint, and pressed it over the wound before taping it firmly in place. Then she turned the tap off.

'It's only temporary,' she warned. 'You really ought to see a doctor, maybe get it stitched. Want me to drive you?'

Art shook his head. 'I don't feel so good,' he mumbled.

'Would you feel better if you lay down?'

'I guess so.' Pausing only to kick his shoes off, Art lowered himself on to the bed. 'Hand me that can, would you?'

'Is that a good idea?' Distant memories of school first aid classes told Jill that alcohol wasn't the right thing to give someone who'd just been hurt.

She was taken completely by surprise when Art raised himself up on one elbow, and snarled, 'Look, I don't need you to give me a hard time, OK? Just give me the can.'

Reasoning that one can of beer couldn't do him much harm,

Jill went over to get it. She was horrified to see four empties in the waste bin. 'Art, you weren't drunk in charge of an electric drill, were you?' she laughed, trying to make a joke of it.

'No, I was not,' Art replied, an unpleasant edge to his voice 'Like I said, I don't need a hard time from you, OK?'

Jill sat on the end of the bed, fervently wishing Shirlene were there or that Jim would hurry up and come home. The way the conversation was going reminded her all too uncomfortably of the fights they used to get into when they were married. Art's temper would flare up over what seemed like nothing at the time. He would become vicious almost to the point of violence, and then, like a little boy who realises he's gone too far, regress to almost baby-like behaviour. It would be only a matter of time before he started on the self-pity kick. Shirlene, of course, would have handled the whole thing without turning a hair.

Just get out of that pool, Jim, and come on home, Jill thought. On the other hand – no, don't. Stay away. This could get nasty.

She was surprised when Art asked, in a comparatively civil voice, 'So what's with all these stories about that vaccine of yours?'

'It hasn't been my vaccine for a long time now,' she said, wondering how much he knew. 'It never really was.'

'So you haven't turned out to be the Nobel Prize winner you thought you'd be, huh?' Art said, suddenly nasty.

'Art, I never –' Jill started, then stopped, remembering that getting into a fight with Art could only lead to trouble. She took a deep breath, then went on evenly, 'If I ever got the Nobel, it wouldn't have been for a long, long time. We were years away from finding the answer in our own research. And as for the Russian vaccine, I heard later that there were problems with it. With any luck Pharmavax will have the time and the money to sort them out. I really don't know.'

Art shifted slightly on the bed. 'It's just that –'

'Just that what?'

'Uh, nothing.'

'Art! Just that what?'

'Look, I don't want a hard time from you about this, OK?'

'Art, once and for all, I will not give you a hard time. What is it?'

'Well, I've had that stuff.'

'How could you? It's not on the market yet! It won't be for ages.'

'This guy I know works at Pharmavax, and he's been – well, smuggling it out. I got some from him.'

Personal and professional curiosity both got the better of Jill's determination to soft-pedal the conversation. 'What on earth did you want it for?' she almost exploded. 'I thought Shirlene couldn't get pregnant!' A sudden thought struck her. 'Oh, no! You're not playing around are you? If you dare do anything to hurt Shirlene, I'll –'

'Shut it!' Art snarled. 'I am not cheating on my wife, right?'

'So you're not running any risk of getting AIDS,' Jill was almost thinking out loud. Before she could stop herself, she said, 'The only other reason you'd be taking it is if you were –'

'Go on! Say it! Impotent! Can't get it up!' Art shouted. 'You should know, bitch. It was you who castrated me in the first place!'

Jill got up. 'I think I'd better go,' she said as calmly as she could manage.

But Art had other ideas. He swung his legs quickly off the bed, and grabbed her arm with his good hand. He was a strong man and Jill, though fit, was no match for him. 'No!' he shouted, spitting in her face. 'You'll damn well stay! All these years I've wanted to tell you how much damage you did. Well, now you can damn well listen!'

'Art,' Jill pleaded desperately. 'You're talking about things that happened years ago. I never meant to harm you, put you down or anything. We were both young – it was just our personalities; we were so different.'

'Damn right we were. Should have been at it all day and all night. But no! Miss Smartass Scientist, Miss Castrating Bitch, wanted a career more than a husband, didn't she – ?'

'Art, please let me go!'

'No way! After what you did to me, you can damn well hear me out!'

Jill was becoming really frightened. She'd seen Art in a rage many times, but never like this, never so irrational. She wondered for an instant if he was ever like this with Shirlene and, if so, how she coped with it. He was almost screaming now, his face distorted with anger and hatred. 'Well, let me tell you, bitch, it's different now! Now that I've gotten the vaccine, you'll never be able to put me down again!'

'Art, can't we discuss this some other time?' she tried.

'C'mere!' Art dragged her off-balance towards him; she fell half on top of him, and ended up on the floor. Before she could roll out of the way, he was on top of her, bruising and hurting her with hands and teeth. 'Art! *Stop it!*' she shrieked, praying that someone would hear, and not caring if it was Jim or not. Art clamped a hand over her mouth, leaning his full weight on it, until she could feel her lips being cut on her own teeth; with his other hand he ripped her shirt down the front. He was sitting on her thighs, so she couldn't kick. He started tearing at her bra, mauling her breasts painfully, oblivious to her frantic but ineffectual flailing. She grunted and bucked desperately under the crushing weight. When she felt his teeth sink into her flesh, she thought she would vomit or pass out with the pain, while the scream she couldn't utter built up like a howling migraine inside her skull. Some tiny part of her seemed to stand apart from the horror, like a doppelgänger talking her through what she had learned in self-defence classes. When you're fighting for your life, the instructor told them, there won't be a second chance. *So fight!* With all the strength she could put into it, she rammed the heel of her hand into his nose and, as Art threw his head back, she jabbed viciously at his eyesockets with her knuckles.

Years of jogging and working out paid off. Jill pushed herself up and heaved Art to one side, his nose bleeding. Somehow she extricated herself – afterwards, she would never remember exactly how she managed it – and half-crawled as fast as she could towards the door, her breath coming in agonising gasps. She hadn't made six feet across the room before Art threw himself on top of her again. He grabbed her hair and wrenched her head round. 'Bitch! Bitch!' he yelled, and struck her hard on the cheekbone. Terrified that he really meant to kill her, Jill clawed and bit until she could get out from under Art's crushing weight enough to lift her knee sharply into his crotch. He toppled back on to one of the glass mirror-panels propped against the wall. It shattered under his weight. Art lay among the razor-sharp shards, groaning and swearing. Now on her feet, Jill realised she was bleeding too. She pulled a large fragment of glass out of her right arm – it was hard to tell which was her blood and which was Art's – and stumbled down the stairs.

Thank God she had left the car unlocked, and the key in the ignition! She half fell into the driving seat, her hands shaking so much she could hardly start the engine. The tyres screeched on the blacktop as she reversed out into the road without looking, and promptly stalled. She counted to five to stop her teeth chattering, and managed somehow to jerk the gearshift into Drive.

Fifteen minutes later, out on the main highway, heading home on automatic pilot, she was jolted out of her catatonic state by a siren. A traffic patrolman was signalling to her to pull over. She pulled on to the hard shoulder and wound down the window. The boy was so young; he looked scarcely older than Jim.

'Ma'am, were you aware that you were violating the speed limit?' he stammered, shocked at the state Jill was in.

'No,' she replied, surprising herself by how calm she sounded. 'I wasn't. I wasn't aware of anything, actually.'

'Ma'am, you're hurt,' the poor boy was trying hard. 'Do you wish to lodge a complaint, ma'am?'

'No, I don't think so, thank you.' Good God, I sound just like my mother turning away a door-to-door salesman, she thought irrationally.

'Ma'am, I have to ask you – are you in a fit state to drive?'

'I'm not drunk, if that's what you mean.'

'If you wish, ma'am, I can follow you home. I just need to call in for permission.'

'You're very kind. But I'll be all right, really. I promise to be more careful.'

'If you're certain, ma'am – ?'

Once on the road, Jill looked in the mirror. No wonder the rookie patrolman had looked so horrified. Her cheekbone was swollen and already purple, her left eye puffy, and her Ralph Lauren shirt was gaping open to reveal her torn bra soaked in blood. Blood had dripped from her cut lip and was caked and flaking on her neck, while her right hand was still bleeding where she had gashed it on the broken mirror-glass.

A lifetime later, she found herself safely parked near her

apartment block. For a few minutes, she slumped forward on the steering wheel, her eyes closed, waiting for the shivering to stop. Then she raised her head and gazed unseeingly at the entrance to the block. She struggled to remember the name of the friend Jim had gone to see; surely she ought to try and call him, warn him not to go home. But a tidal wave of exhaustion swamped her; even the idea of getting out of the car, locking the doors, walking to the elevator, finding her keys – was all too much effort. And, she thought muzzily, she'd probably bump into the janitor, or the nice but irritatingly nosy woman who lived in the next apartment to hers. Someone else would have to handle this instead. She reached for her car phone, and punched a number from memory.

'Mira? Can I come round –?'

17.

'Mort, I felt it wiser to leave this message at your apartment rather than at Pharmavax. I'm calling because the FDA should, strictly speaking, have received the results of your Phase 1 trials by now. Now, I'm sure there's some perfectly good reason why we haven't had them, but I must impress upon you the necessity of keeping us fully informed, every step of the way –'

'It's women like you,' Mira said severely, 'who make life tough for the rest of us. All you have to do is file a complaint and let the cops handle it.'

Jill sighed wearily. 'Don't go on at me, Mira, please. If I only had myself to think of, I'd probably do it. But there's Jim to consider, and Shirlene. If they ever knew Art had beat up on me like this, it would change everything for them – and for me.'

'So you don't reckon he beats up on Shirlene?'

'I'm sure he never has. For a start, I don't think he'd want to. There's something about me that brings out the worst in him, but Shirlene's only ever brought out the best. Also, if he did I think I'd know.'

'From what I know of Shirlene, she'd come straight to you, with Jim, if there was trouble at home.'

'I'd like to think she thought of me that way.' Jill suddenly started trembling again as Mira drew back the collar of the towelling bathrobe she had lent Jill, and gently dabbed antiseptic on her grazed collarbone.

Mira had reacted in a practical and unemotional way when Jill turned up battered and tearful at her front door, bundling her straight into a hot tub and leaving the questions till afterwards. Half an hour later, with a mug of hot milk and whisky in her hand, and a tranquilliser already doing its work, Jill felt able to talk.

'In all the time we were married, Art was never like this. Sure, he used to fly into rages, get quite vicious at times, but it was all words. He never hit me. But this time, it was like he was crazy or something, like a rabid dog.'

'Or a werewolf, huh?'

'That's not so far from the truth. You must have read Dr Jekyll and Mr Hyde. Well, that's what it was like. It was horrible –' Jill gasped as the cool antiseptic cream hit the abrasion.

'Sorry. Better let me take a look at the rest of you.' And Mira gently eased the bathrobe off Jill's shoulders.

'Shit! The bastard bit you?'

Jill nodded, tears perilously close to the surface. The perfect set of teethmarks on her breast would remind her all too painfully for weeks to come of Art, her former husband, snarling in a rage, beating and biting her like a mad dog.

'What in heaven's name would have made him behave like that?'

'I don't know. Something was wrong. For all his faults, the Art I've known all these years wasn't the man who did this.'

'So what brought it on? If you didn't say anything to annoy him, what started him off? Was he drunk?'

'He'd had a few beers. Not enough to explain the way he acted, though. Four, maybe?'

'Hmm.' Mira sat back on her heels and threw the blood-stained cotton into the trash. 'But something provoked him, right?'

Jill leaned back, her eyes closed. After a few seconds she said dully, 'There's only one thing I can think of. Art has a friend who works at Pharmavax. Some of the lab technicians have been smuggling out the trial samples of Seminon and selling them. He said he'd had a shot.'

Mira got up and poured herself a drink. 'Want some?' Jill shook her head.

'As far as I remember,' Mira said, her scientist's mind homing in on the most important point, 'there was nothing in the Russian data to indicate that they'd progressed as far as animal testing –'

'Not that we had a chance to examine it properly, don't forget.'

' – nor was there any information about human testing. Do you suppose that means that the Russians had done the tests, but

Brad's team didn't get to the results? Or that that they hadn't gotten past the animal-testing stage?'

'That's the stage Pharmavax's reached. They're due to start controlled human testing any day. But of course the stuff's gone outside the building, so it's as though they already have a sort of uncontrolled human experiment under way. Mort says they're asking anyone who's taken the vaccine to report informally on any side-effects. He's promised there'll be no legal action against them.'

'Well, if there's any basis to our suspicions, Pharmavax will uncover it all sooner or later.'

'And, in the meantime, what if someone else gets beaten up – murdered, even? I think I should warn Mort.'

Mira shrugged. 'Up to you. As you know, I want to stay well apart from all this. In fact, I don't feel obligated to have an opinion one way or the other, now I'm not involved any more.'

'I'll give it some thought.' Jill stood up and walked out into the hallway to inspect her face in the mirror. 'Mira, I can't go into the lab tomorrow looking like this!'

'Nobody was suggesting you should. Tomorrow's Friday, so take the day off. You're entitled. Then, come Monday, tell everyone you got mugged but hung on to your purse. Not only will that account for your black eye, it'll save you having to buy a new purse and go into details about getting new keys and credit cards. And you'll be the heroine of the hour.'

'Dear Mira. You're as full of sound advice as ever. Thank you.'

'Don't mention it,' Mira said gruffly. 'You want to stay the night?'

'I'd better get back. Can I borrow a sweater, just to drive home in?' The blood-spattered Ralph Lauren shirt had been consigned to the trash, along with the ripped bra. 'Sure you can. What about the handsome colonel? You going to tell him about this?'

'I'll have to, I guess. Put it this way: he's more likely to see the bite marks than anyone else.'

'Is he now?' Mira raised one eybrow.

'Mira, you're the one who's been telling me I've been wasting the past God knows how many years! And it's been six months since Mort and I broke up.'

'Sure. But I didn't expect you to replace Mort with a man who's a trained killer. Look,' Mira took Jill by the shoulders and turned her to face her, 'you're a big girl, and what you do is up to you. But you're very precious to me. I wouldn't want to see you hurt. Believe me, there are worse things than bites and bruises. Just don't get too involved, is all I ask.'

'Mira, Brad Foster is not going to hurt me!'

'He'd better not.' Mira's gaze was level and grave. 'But people who've been trained the way he's been trained, who knows what goes on inside their heads? I want you to be very, very careful. Just this once, will you take my advice? Or at least bear it in mind?'

'I promise. Is that enough?' Jill leaned over to hug Mira. 'I really am grateful. Not only for tonight, but for so many things.'

Jill shrugged off Mira's bathrobe and put on a lambswool sweater, which, soft as it was, caused her to wince as it touched the sore places.

'Truth is, I don't feel like being touched by anybody for a bit,' she said ruefully. 'Anyway, Brad's away for a few more days. Come to think of it, so's Mort. He had to go to Geneva. I'll call him as soon as he gets back; I've decided.'

'I think you're right,' Mira agreed. 'Do you know, for the first time since I got fired, I'm glad I'm not at NIH any more? I don't envy you the fall-out from this one. It's a miracle it didn't happen before. Now, are you OK to drive home?'

Jill nodded. 'I feel a whole lot better than when I got here.'

'Good. So keep it that way. And remember what I said about Brad Foster. Just take great, great care –'

18.

'Oh hi, Mort! How's Geneva? Some Russian guy just called – not one of the guys you normally deal with. Well, this was what was so odd – he wouldn't say – no, he wouldn't tell me that either. All he said was that he had this interesting deal he wanted to discuss with you. He said he was staying at the Hilton, so if you don't want to see him I can just call him up and cancel, but I made an appointment for first thing Monday. I hope I did the right thing –'

'Having fun?'

'It was a really great idea to come here. I'm so glad you thought of it.' Breathless, Jill clung on to Brad's arm. 'I haven't done this in twenty years.'

Brad put his arm round Jill's waist and swept her off on another circuit of the ice-rink at Pershing Park. 'Hey, watch out, man!' he shouted angrily as a boisterous black youth cannoned into them and nearly knocked Jill off her feet. 'You OK?'

'Fine.'

Brad was an efficient skater rather than a showy one, his finely-tuned body appearing scarcely to shift balance as he wove between the knots of skaters, guiding Jill effortlessly along with him. The apparent stillness was deceptive; Jill realised she was moving far faster on ice than she ever had before, and she found it exciting rather than scary. It was exhilarating, too, to see how many heads turned to watch them. As she caught the admiring glances, she felt every bit as proud of being Brad's partner as she had when Mort escorted her at society functions.

Brad's skill on the ice was, in a way, a physical counterpart to Mort's intellectual abilities.There was the same element of risk-taking, but in Brad's case there was always an edge of excitement and danger, something Jill now realised she was never aware of in Mort's middle-class, middle-aged lifestyle. It was when she was doing something with Brad that Mort would never have dreamed of that Jill realised how stuffy and middle-aged she herself had become during her years with Mort. Now, she felt as if she was on vacation the whole time.

After some initial nervousness, Jill felt all her old confidence flooding back. It was true what they said: ice-skating was like riding a bicycle. Once you knew how to do it, you never forgot. And with Brad to support and guide her, she felt totally safe. As she felt all her old skills returning, she became more adventurous and experimented with more daring turns and manoeuvres. Every so often, Brad would lift her bodily off the ice as if she were a doll, which made her feel small, feminine and deliciously vulnerable.

'I don't want to tire you out first time. Say when you've had enough.'

Jill was beginning to flag. Although she was perfectly fit, skating wasn't the same as jogging or riding; it involved a different level of concentration and very different muscles. Added to which, it was scarcely two weeks since she had been attacked by Art, and she was still feeling stiff and sore, though the bruises on her face had faded enough to be camouflaged with only light make-up. As she smiled up at Brad gratefully, she felt the cut on her lip pull slightly. It was healing, but not quite right yet.

'Actually, I think I have had enough. I don't want to be a party-pooper, but I'll pay for this tomorrow if I don't quit now.'

'We could always share a long, hot soak in the tub – then I could give you a massage,' Brad said softly so no one else could hear.

'Mmm. Can't wait. Let's go now!'

'Sure.' With one hand in the small of her back, Brad guided her through the circulating masses to the edge of the rink near the exit. In a few minutes they had changed, returned their skates, and were outside. Jill had left her car in a lot on the far side of the Mall, so they had to walk some way to get to it. The early November afternoon was crisp and blowy, the invigorating sort of weather Jill loved.

Relaxed and happy, she took Brad's hand and snuggled up against his shoulder playfully as they strolled along. For some months now, things had been going well between them. Brad had a way of encouraging Jill to do all sorts of things she had never done before, and not only in bed. However, it was in bed – or in the tub, on the table, on the floor, or wherever they happened to find themselves making love – that Brad made Jill feel most alive. For the first time in her life, she was really accepting her own sexual nature. Brad's playful sadism, the bondage games that so aroused her, had transformed the grateful pussycat she had been with Mort to a hungry tigress. Nothing in Jill's carefully traditional upbringing, in her limited sexual relationship with Art or in the predictability of Mort's love-making, had prepared her for what Brad had unleashed in her. The buzz he got from danger, risk-taking and survival was beginning to communicate itself to her, until she could hear the faint siren-song of sexual addiction in her blood. The Dr Peters of six months ago would never have contemplated some of the things Jill got up to now. And, best of all, the fact that Brad usually set the scene for their fun and games meant that Jill felt absolved of all responsibility. In any case, she rationalised, they weren't hurting anybody else. And she adored every gloriously depraved minute of it. She giggled at the thought of what they would do when they got home.

'Happy?' Brad asked, putting his arm round her. He hadn't spoken since they left the ice-rink.

'Yes,' she said contentedly. 'But you seem very quiet.'

'There's something I need to tell you. Can we sit down someplace?'

'Sure – there's a bench over there.'

Brad brushed the leaves from the wooden seat, and they sat down, Jill's bright ski parka rustling against his heavy wool coat. He moved uneasily a few inches along the bench, as though to put a symbolic as well as an actual distance between them.

'What is it?' she asked.

Without looking at her, Brad said, 'I have some bad news. I don't know how to tell you.'

In all the time they had been together, Jill had never known Brad ill at ease or at a loss for words.

'Go on,' she said. 'Try me.'

'Well, I had an army medical a few days ago. Just routine, the usual thing.'

'You have them every year. So what's so special about this one?' But she was thinking, Oh God, they've told him he's got incurable cancer; or he flunked it, and he has to leave the army, or –.

'One of my blood tests was abnormal.'

'OK, which one?'

'I tested HIV positive.'

There was nothing Jill could find to say that wouldn't sound trivial or accusatory. It took what seemed like at least a minute before she could ask, 'Are they sure? I mean, how? Did you have a bad transfusion or something?' Brad remained silent.

'Brad, what are you trying to tell me?'

'I didn't want to have to tell you, ever.'

'Tell me what, for Christ's sake? You're not gay, are you?' Even as she said it, she realised how ridiculous it sounded. Brad was the least gay man she'd ever met.

'I had a thing with a man – once.' Jill was stunned into complete silence. 'But it was all over a year ago. I'm out of all that now.'

Jill got up slowly and started to walk away from him. After a few yards, she turned round. Brad was still sitting there, only now he was looking straight at her, as if willing her not to go.

'Look,' he said, 'I know you're upset. Like I said, I didn't want to have to tell you about it. But it's all long gone. Over. That first time, when I met you in the park, I knew you were something special. That hasn't changed. I'll never go back down that other route. I promise.'

'Your promises are all fine and dandy, Brad. But they don't mean a thing. Right now, I don't care what you do. I don't ever want to see you again.'

Aware that there was too much unfinished business between them for this to be the end of it, Jill thrust her hands deep into the pockets of her parka, and walked determinedly back towards the car. Inside, she was a seething cauldron of emotions.

Damn it! How could she have been so wrong about him? Brad, gay? It wasn't possible. Then she thought: he's sick. Maybe he'll die. Just as it was all getting to be so good. And I'll have lost yet another man in my life.

She had reached the car before the final, chilling realisation struck her. Christ, *I* could be HIV positive! *I* might die of AIDS! A tidal wave of angry, helpless tears welled up and broke, as she fumbled in her pocket for the keys. Brad was standing in front of the driver's door, blocking her way. How the hell had he managed to get there ahead of her?

'Go away!' she spat.

'No.'

'Get – out – of – my – way!'

'No. This'll only take a few seconds, but you're going to listen –'

'I don't want to hear it!'

Jill suddenly found herself trapped against the side of the car, her wrists held level with her head, Brad's face a few inches from hers.

'Well, you're going to hear it, OK? I had just one affair with a man –'

'Oh, I'm glad to hear that!' she retorted sarcastically. 'Why the hell did you have to pick up some cheap little –'

'It wasn't like that! If I told you his name, you wouldn't believe me. We were both at vulnerable stages in our careers, and it just happened. Sure, we could have timed it better if we were going to do it, but you can't always plan these things. Any more than I'd planned to meet you –'

'Oh, leave me out of it, please!'

'The thing is, he and I both hold each other's lives in our hands. We could each destroy the other with a word in the right place. Sure, we'd destroy ourselves in the process, but the bottom line is trust. He has more to lose than I have – he has more power, more influence. And he's done this kind of thing before. You've seen press photographs of him, pretty wife, nice kids; he should be the happiest man on God's earth. But he wants all the rest, and he can't help himself. God knows who else he's trusted.'

'Or fucked!'

'Or fucked, as you say. Anyway, that has to be how I came to get infected. There's no other way it could have happened.'

Brad released Jill's wrists, and stepped back a little way. He sighed.

'Now you see why I had to tell you. But just because I tested positive needn't mean you have to. It happens that way a lot of the time. Will you promise me you'll go and get a test?'

'You don't have to tell me, of all people, about the risks and statistics, thank you. Of course I'll go and get tested. And if I'm positive, what then?'

'As far as we're concerned –'

'"We" – as in "you and I" – doesn't seem to have a lot to offer at the moment. I have a son, in case you'd forgotten! He's called Jim; he's fourteen, nearly fifteen. You may have heard me mention him once or twice?'

'Give me a break, Jill. One of the things I've always envied you is that you have a kid. I don't. And I guess I never will. What I have to live with is the knowledge that my – my friend – pulled every string he could lay hands on to get me transferred to a job that carried maximum risk. That way, he reckoned I'd get killed off in the line of duty, and his hands would be clean. That's how he rates me. And how he values what we had. Forgive me if I sound a little cynical; that's because I am. If he only knew, of all the guys he ever screwed I'm the least likely to dump him in it.'

'So who is he?'

'I'm not about to tell you. It's not that I owe him anything. It's just that I have this – you could call it a moral sense, if you like. Or honour. Whatever. I'll never tell you – or anyone.'

'Did you love him?'

'How the hell should I know? How do you know if you love someone? I care about people. The guys on my team; I care about them. I care about you.'

'What about your family? You never talk about them.'

'Gee, thanks. What family? I was brought up in an institution – found on a garbage dump, wrapped in newspaper. They reckoned I was only a day or so old, so the date on the newspaper is my official date of birth. I never did find out who the jerk was who gave me such a goddam silly surname. I guess he thought it was a joke.' Brad laughed bitterly.

'Oh, Brad,' Jill found herself crying all over again. 'Why did you never tell me?'

'It's not the kind of thing you tell everyone.'

'I'm not everyone.'

'No,' he said, opening a pocket pack of Kleenex for her. 'You're not. I never thought you were. I guess the nearest I've ever come to really loving anyone is what we've had these past few months. You're the last person in the world I'd want to infect with HIV.'

'You may not have,' she snuffled through the Kleenex. 'I'll get tested. I won't be able to think straight until I've had one test at least. Then let's see where that takes us.' She unlocked the car. 'Get in – I'll drive.'

Before Jill started the engine, she turned to Brad. 'There's one thing we might try. That damn vaccine –'

'Source of all our troubles.'

'Ain't that the truth? Anyway, Mort told me part of it is an HIV antigen. He says it looks like it prevents HIV developing into full-blown AIDS. I could ask him if he'd let me have some for you. He's always been generous, and he knows I never actually asked him for anything before. Also,' she laughed grimly, 'I may need it for myself.'

Brad took Jill's face in his hands, and kissed her. 'You're a good woman, Jill Peters,' he murmured softly. She started the car, and they swung out of the parking area.

'There's one thing I should tell you,' she said, as they headed back to her apartment. 'Mira and I think Art getting in such a rage and beating up on me the way he did might have been caused by him taking it. I'd have to ask Mort about the results of the human testing, in case there really is a pattern of aggression. So if I do get the vaccine for you, will you keep a really close watch on yourself? Please?'

'Sure. But I don't think it'll be a problem. We're taught to handle all that. In my line of work, you fly off the handle, you're dead. Or the next guy is. The way we're trained, we can even keep heart rate and blood pressure down. Aggression's a tool to be used. Control's the name of the game. I'll be OK.'

'Mort gets back from Switzerland in a couple of days. I have to call him anyway; I'll ask him then.'

'Will you have been tested by then?'

'You bet. But I won't know the results for a while.'

'Do you want to drop me off on that next corner? I can ride the metro from here.'

'No way. Didn't I hear someone mention a long hot bath and a massage?'

'Are you sure?'

'As Jim would say, sure I'm sure!'

19.

'Mort, this is Jill, calling early Sunday morning. I know you're not back yet, but could you call me the moment you get in? I need to ask a favour from you. I'm leaving to go to Mira's round about mid-day –'

Jill settled herself into the small old armchair beside the electric fire, as Mira busied herself fixing Sunday brunch. For so many years, Mira's cramped but homely apartment had been a sort of haven for Jill. She would go there sometimes to talk business; sometimes to ask Mira's advice about other aspects of her life; but more often than not, she would go simply to enjoy Mira's company. Even after all this time, Mira's laconic, salty sense of humour could still surprise Jill, and her view of the world was often astoundingly penetrating.

There was little in Jill's life that she didn't share with her friend, knowing that outside her own home Mira was the soul of discretion, and would never refer to Jill's private life in front of anybody else.

The apartment was slightly tatty, and furnished with good-quality old-fashioned furniture rather than antiques; nothing had been touched for fifteen years. But the whole effect, though dowdy, was welcoming, and Jill always felt comfortable there.

Mira's cat stalked over to sniff Jill's hand, then hopped up cosily into the chair with her. Most of Mira's colleagues assumed it was because the cat was part-Persian, she'd called him Haji. In fact, he was called Hodgie, after Dr Johnson's cat. Mira always swore that her friendship with Jill dated from the day when Jill, on meeting Hodgie for the first time, laughed and quoted Boswell's account of Johnson saying: 'But he is a very fine cat. A very fine cat indeed.' Actually, Jill had little affection for the spoiled, cantankerous animal, but Mira adored him.

'You got sweeteners with you?' Mira called from the kitchen. 'I just ran out.'

'Sure; I have some in my purse,' Jill called back, reaching for a small dispenser. Mira came in carrying a tray with coffee-pot, cups and a dish piled high with scrambled eggs and bacon.

'I made a whole pitcher of Bloody Mary,' Mira said, heading back to the kitchen to fetch a second tray. 'And I found some unbelievable almond croissants. So I don't want to hear one word about calories, OK?'

'OK,' Jill laughed. Then, more seriously, she said, 'I really appreciate you making the time to chat. I'm in such a mess.'

'I'll say,' Mira observed, putting down the Bloody Mary pitcher. 'You break up with Mort after ten years of him controlling your every move. Then your ex-husband takes it into his head to use you as a punch-bag. And now Superman may have infected you with HIV. I must say you're taking it very coolly. I don't think I'd manage to be quite so phlegmatic.'

'Phlegmatic, nothing!' Jill snorted. 'It's just that I don't see any point in panicking.'

'I still think you're being remarkably calm about it.'

'I can't call the clinic till tomorrow. I can't afford to be anything but calm.'

'What worries me the most is that you're going to ask Mort to let Brad have a vaccine shot.'

'I already have asked him. He called me just as I was leaving to come here.'

'Did you tell him about Art attacking you like that?'

'I sort of felt I had to. He was furious. I always know when he's mad because he goes all silent on me. Anyway, if Seminon does cause that sort of aggression, Mort ought to be the first to know.'

'Jill, the stuff has scarcely been tested! And you're all set to let someone you care about have it!'

'I suppose it does seem crazy –'

'Crazy is not the word!'

'– but none of the people who've had the shot so far has progressed from HIV to AIDS. I don't feel I have a choice. Look, even if I test negative, I could easily become positive in a few months' time. I might end up having to have a shot myself.'

'What about the side-effects, the aggression?'

'You mean I might suddenly start beating up on people?'

'No, of course not. What I mean is: what if Brad gets aggressive? If he goes the way Art went you'd stand little chance of surviving. He's a trained killer. I don't want to have to patch you up a second time, assuming there was anything left to patch up. Are you really prepared to take that risk?'

'I guess so.'

The two women fell silent for a minute or two, while Mira poured the coffee, and passed a cup to Jill.

'Actually, I think I'll have a Bloody Mary as well. May I?' Jill indicated the pitcher.

'Go right ahead, help yourself. Now, you say Mort's asked his employees to report, informally and in confidence, on the side-effects of Seminon?'

'That's right. He's even said he won't prosecute them for stealing the vaccine and using it without authorisation. A sort of quid pro quo.'

'Did he say whether any of them reported undue aggression as a side-effect?'

'No, he didn't. But, let's face it, if any of them had attacked someone, they wouldn't just own up to it, would they? Their immunity from prosecution wouldn't stretch that far.'

'So there could be a whole lot of people out there being beaten to a pulp, and we wouldn't know about it.'

'Even so, the way it affected Art seems very strange. I find it hard to believe that Seminon on its own could produce such – such primitive rage. It really felt as if he wanted to rape me and kill me. And not necessarily in that order,' said Jill grimly.

'You really think rape was what he was after?'

'Thinking back on it, he had an enormous erection. I could feel it. I mean, he never had one like that when we were married.'

'Seminon is supposed to improve sexual performance. But where does ordinary, run-of-the-mill male horniness end, and serious aggression begin?'

'God knows. I don't any more,' Jill said wearily, putting her cup back on the tray. 'The whole thing was so irrational anyway. The only thing I can think of was that he had drunk those four cans of beer.'

'That's hardly excessive,' Mira pointed out.

'But it's more than he usually has. It was a hot day, and Shirlene wasn't there, or she'd have stopped him at two. Do you suppose alcohol could increase the aggression in anyone who's had a shot?'

'It might. It can increase aggression anyway, in some men. Maybe it's that group who are at risk. You'd better tell Mort to start plying his monkeys with Scotch, see if they stage a riot. Mira poured two fresh cups of coffee. 'What did Mort say when you told him about Art?'

'Not much. He never does when he's really angry. But he did say he'd come round this evening. I hope he'll bring a Seminon shot for Brad. And he wants to know what my test says.'

'If it hadn't been for his lousy security, you never would have ended up all bitten and bruised. He owes you one, and he knows it. Come to that, if we're right, he's going to owe one to quite a lot of people. My guess is the stuff's going to get banned if things get any worse.'

'I'm not so sure,' said Jill solemnly. 'Mort's under huge pressure from the government to get results. I reckon they'll lean on him to sort out the aggression problem, even if it means coercing the FDA into turning a blind eye to one or two other things.'

'Just the sort of thing the bastards would do,' Mira grunted contemptuously. 'Of course, the other thing to bear in mind is that anyone who gets hold of the vaccine could – given enough time and expertise – work out how to make it for themselves. If one of Mort's unofficial guinea pigs was made an offer he couldn't refuse, God knows whose hands the formula could get into. There are rogue scientists working in back rooms the world over, producing crack cocaine and designer drugs. What's to stop them adding pirated Seminon to their list of wares? The US government can ban the stuff all it likes, but it'll still go round the world on the black market.'

'Even if Pharmavax backed off at this stage, there are any number of wealthy and sophisticated criminals who'd step in. I'm sure that's one of the reasons the Administration's leaning on Mort.'

With a shrill warble, Jill's cellular phone rang from the depths of her purse. She fished it out, and flicked the switch. The conversation was very short.

'I can't stay much longer,' she told Mira, punching the 'End' button. 'That was Mort. He's coming round to my apartment later on.'

Mira sighed resignedly. 'I just hope to God you're doing the right thing,' she said.

'Me too. But there's only one way to find out.'

• • •

Jill got back to Nebraska Avenue only a few minutes before Mort rang the bell. As she pressed the button to unlock the door to the apartment block, she caught sight of her reflection in the hall mirror. It was two weeks since Art had attacked her, and she hadn't seen Mort since. Although the bruising was still slightly visible, her left eye and cheekbone were no longer puffy and sore, and the cut on her lip had scabbed over and was starting to heal. Even so, with no make-up, she looked like what she was, a woman who a couple of weeks earlier had been viciously attacked.

Mort was shocked. 'My God! When you said the bastard attacked you, I thought he maybe took a swing at you. What was he trying to do – pulverise you? Oh darling, I hate to see you looking like this.'

'You should have seen me this time last week,' Jill answered drily. 'I'm telling everybody I got into a fight with a mugger. I'd be grateful if you could go along with that, for my sake.'

'If you want. But I'd like to see the cops throw the book at him!'

'Oh, Mort, don't,' Jill sighed. 'I already had that out with Mira. I don't want to upset Shirlene and Jim. They don't know anything about this, and that's the way I want it to stay.'

'I'm damned if I see why the bastard should get away with it,' Mort fumed, as he strode angrily through to the living room and flung his overcoat on a chair. He was looking tense, and more tired than ever. Jill poured his usual Glenfiddich and handed it to him. 'Damn it, Jill! You may have found things to complain about in the way I treated you, but at least I never beat up on you. And I certainly didn't swing both ways!'

'Don't give me a hard time, Mort. I'm feeling quite battered, as well as looking it, and I'd rather not have to justify anything to anyone at the moment.'

Mort was instantly apologetic. 'I'm sorry. It's just that neither of those guys is worthy of you. Look, I've dated a few women since we broke up, but I haven't met anyone I'd even cross the street for. We were good together, you and I. We could have all that again –'

'No, Mort, we couldn't. I'm sorry. I appreciate you feeling that way, truly, but we can't turn the clock back.'

'So what's with the AC-DC colonel?'

'Don't talk about him like that –'

'I apologise. But if he's infected you, so help me I'll kill him! Are you in love with him?'

Jill sighed. 'I don't know. Let's just say I care about him, OK? And if Seminon can stop him getting sick, I want him to have it. That's all.'

Mort drained his Scotch. 'I could do with another of those,' he said.

Jill took the glass from his hand. 'There's something else I should tell you, an idea Mira and I came up with. Art had been drinking more than usual just before he attacked me. Is there any possibility alcohol could have a potentiating effect on Seminon? Cause undue aggression, I mean?'

For a few moments Mort said nothing. He gazed at the Scotch in his re-filled glass, swirling it round and round, as though considering what to say. Eventually, he looked up and asked, 'How long ago did Art have his shot? And how did he get hold of it?'

'He didn't say when he had it. He just said a friend who worked at Pharmavax got it for him.'

'That would have been about three months ago, the middle of August sometime. There's no way he could have gotten any since then. Damn!'

'What does that mean?' Jill enquired.

'Just that in the last few weeks, we've been hearing rumours that people have been getting into fights, ending up hurt. Nothing anyone is prepared to put hand on heart and swear to, of course, but we've had one of the guys in the lab off sick for a few days, and another mysteriously lost his front teeth. And one of our trainee technicians – pretty girl – swears she fell off a stepladder. They're all connected one way or another with the trial batch that got smuggled out.'

'Were any of these attacks alcohol-related?'

'How the hell should I know? We didn't think to ask.'

'What about the animal testing?'

Mort took a mouthful of Scotch. 'Not good,' he said abruptly. 'Look, something happened in the lab a while back. And before you ask – I'm sorry, I am not even going to tell you about it. But there's no way I'm letting you have a shot for Foster. I can't take the risk.'

'Something's gone badly wrong, hasn't it?'

'It's only a temporary glitch. We can fix it. Hell, we have to fix it if we want to stay in business!'

'Mort, can't you just call a halt to the whole thing?'

'Not a chance. I'm being all but blackmailed by the Administration. If Pharmavax don't crack this thing, and soon, they'll shut us down tomorrow. Our compliance with the law hasn't been one hundred per cent, since we've been cutting corners – corners, I may add, that we've been pressurised to cut. But we can't prove it. So, legally, we're in the wrong. And I have to say, I violated a few security procedures myself, albeit in a good cause. They could use that against us.They just want the problems ironed out, and Seminon on the market, before the competition gets there.'

'By "competition" you mean cowboys operating outside the law?'

'Right. They say a standing prick knows no law. Hell, a limp one doesn't either. And a guy who's HIV positive sure as hell isn't going to bother with the small print!' Mort said with feeling.

He put down his empty glass and got up to go. He took Jill by the shoulders. 'I'm sorry to let you down over the shot for Foster but I'm grateful to you for suggesting the link with alcohol. We'll look into that first thing, I promise. And you'll promise to let me know the result of your test?' Jill nodded.

He leaned forward to kiss her. In doing so, he brushed against her breast. Unlike the bruises on her face, the bite marks were taking a long time to heal. One or two of the puncture wounds had become infected, and the bruising was still intensely sore. Jill gasped with the sudden pain.

Mort frowned. 'What is it?' he asked. 'You hurt someplace I can't see? Let me look.' His fingers went to the buttons of her cashmere cardigan.

'No!' she cried, stepping back, clutching both cardigan and

shirt to her throat. Gently but firmly he drew her hands away, and unbuttoned her clothing a little. His face darkened thunderously when he saw Art's teethmarks, still an angry reddish-purple against the silky, fair skin.

'Damn him to hell!' he swore. Wordlessly he buttoned up Jill's shirt, then the cardigan. Despite his anger, he kissed her gently. As he stepped out of the door to the apartment, he turned to her and said solemnly, 'Nobody – nobody – does that to you, and gets away with it!'

20.

'Brad? It's about eight-thirty on Sunday evening. Mort was round here earlier, and he says he won't let us have a vaccine shot after all. He wouldn't say much, but I think I can guess why. I'm so sorry. We'll talk when I see you –'

'You the guy wanted to buy a shot of that stuff? Well, I got one. Five hundred bucks in fives and tens says it's yours. You know the McDonald's down on Pennsylvania Avenue? Go in, take a seat, and make like you're real interested in this week's comic strips, OK? I'll come by 'bout eleven-thirty. You're not there, some other guy gets it.'

It was rare for Art to work weekends, but he had a batch of assays to get through before his boss presented the results at the monthly inter-departmental meeting the next day. He quite liked the repetitive work the basic science involved, and he took a pride in making sure everything was done right. Early on he'd hoped for greater things from his career, but he had long settled for a quiet life in the academic backwater of the University Hospital. Deep down he knew, better than anyone except Shirlene, that all his blustering claims to thwarted brilliance were no more than hot air, and were only ever voiced when he had a gripe about Jill. For the most part, Art reckoned, the job suited him well enough. OK, sometimes he got bored, but he liked his departmental head, got along with the technicians, and was known to be reliable around the lab.

In fact, the only thing that bugged Art about his work was that all the long hours and the painstaking attention to detail were being devoted to a section of the community he couldn't abide – gays. Jill used to say he was bigoted, which had led to fights, with Art shouting that Jill was a lily-livered liberal, and that gays were unnatural and perverted. Even Shirlene had once ventured to suggest that he was irrational on the subject; the resultant temper tantrum gave the normally unflappable Shirlene a glimpse of what Jill's marriage to Art had been like, and she wisely kept off the subject after that. She realised that sex and religion were a minefield for him. Art had been brought up in a repressive family, plagued with Catholic guilt about sex, so that his divorce from Jill carried all sorts of emotional baggage. His increasing impotence was simply never discussed.

Jill had found it impossible to tolerate Art's views; Shirlene simply let him rant and rave, knowing that his violent threats against gays would never translate themselves into action. She saw only the confused child, in need of routine and constant reassurance, which she gave him in plenty.

His relatively undemanding job offered him the same sort of security. He was good at the routine stuff which some of his colleagues found tedious, and welcomed the no-surprises aspect of it. He was happy to let the departmental heads and medical chiefs worry about the bigger picture, finding enough pleasure and reward in the tiny details of his daily activities. His only real ambition was to stash away enough money to move to Florida, to the sun. He and Shirlene could have a nice waterside home, Jim could go to college, and he could take up deep-sea fishing again. Dream on, he muttered to himself, as he loaded a batch of samples into the electrophoresis bath.

• • •

Mort slammed the car door and stormed into the entrance hall of the laboratory block. The uniformed janitor, alarmed, looked up from his newspaper. He hurried out from behind his desk as Mort strode past and jabbed at the button to call the elevator.

'You can't come in here, sir,' he called. 'Not without you state your business.'

'You didn't see me, OK?' Mort snapped.

'Sir, I can't permit you to go up in the elevator,' the janitor said helplessly, reluctant to antagonise the expensively-dressed and obviously enraged stranger.

'Lay a finger on me, buddy, and I'll screw you for assault!'

'Sir! Sir! At least tell me who you want to see –'

But it was too late. Mort thrust his way into the elevator and the doors closed. The janitor returned to his desk, wondering whom he should alert. He knew several people were working late, even on a Sunday; running a stubby finger down the dog-eared list of telephone extensions, he started to call people, warning of an intruder.

• • •

Art carefully transferred the last tray of reagents to another bath. Quarter of eight. He'd be able to leave soon. Sunday nights Shirlene liked the whole family to sit round the table to eat, and she usually cooked something special, like pot roast. Tonight was her first Sunday home after leaving the hospital, and she'd made him promise he wouldn't be late back.

Suddenly, he was startled by the sound of the lab door opening. 'Mort! What the hell are you doing here? How'd you get in?'

'I walked in, straight past that bozo downstairs.'

'What do you want?'

'I want you dead; that's what I want!'

Art hastily put the bench between them as Mort stormed the length of the lab. He'd met Mort many times over the years, and had always privately written him off as a tight-ass with enough bucks to keep Jill in designer goodies. But now the guy was angry! And he stank of Scotch!

'What the fuck's this all about?' he demanded, trying not to sound as scared as he felt. For all his habitual verbal aggression, Art was not a violent man. He had been taken completely by surprise by his own attack on Jill, and since then had more or less persuaded himself it had never happened. He retreated as Mort came closer, until he found himself wedged up against the window, trapped by the end of the workbench.

'You know damn well what it's about!' Mort snarled. He grabbed Art by the lapels of his white lab coat and thrust his face close.

'How – how did you know I was here?'

'I went to your house, spoke with your wife. I told her it was important we talk. And it is – very!'

'You can't threaten me!' Art blustered, shaking visibly.

'It appears I can! I went to see Jill, just an hour ago. I saw what you did to her –'

With an immense effort, Art broke Mort's grip and twisted away from him.

'Just where do you get off?' he shouted, making for the door. 'What's between me and my ex-wife is no concern of yours!'

'Well, I'm making it my concern!'

Mort caught him, spun him round and slammed him up against the workbench. The jarring shock caused the equipment to rattle, and knocked over a rackful of glass pipettes. Mort drove his fist savagely into Art's soft belly. Art bent over double, all the breath punched out of him. Mort hauled him upright and sent him flying with a slamming cut to the jaw. Art almost bounced off the wall and crashed to the floor, where he lay, curled up and whimpering.

Mort stood over him. 'Now listen here, and listen good,' he snarled. 'You so much as touch Jill ever again, and I will murder you – personally!'

21.

'Mort? This is Karl. Mort, it's bad news, and I'm truly sorry to have to give it to you. Your test has shown positive, and so has your lab technician's. It's that new Thai strain, which means we won't be able to do anything for you. Look, I can refer you to a whole slew of counsellors, if that's what you want. But my guess is you'd rather we went and got ourselves thoroughly soaked for old times' sake. Any time. Call me when you're ready –'

It had taken a long time for Brad to get his converted warehouse loft the way he wanted it, and he still got a buzz out of the way it looked. The wide, stripped-pine floorboards had a warm honey-yellow glow, and the bare brick walls, which could have looked hard and cold, in fact made a perfect background for the spotlit oriental hangings he had picked up in Vietnam. But the best feature, for him, was the high ceilings. Being over six feet tall, he hated low rooms. He'd looked at plenty of elegant apartments with more fashionable addresses before settling for this one, but they'd all made him feel claustrophobic. And that was something he was not prepared to feel, especially at home. The whole idea of being shut in or constricted, whether metaphorically or in reality, was anathema to him.

On bare feet, he padded over to the Scandinavian stove, added a couple of logs through its open doors, then took the dirty dinner plates from the table and carried them through to the kitchen. Jill came out of the bathroom and walked over to put her arms around him from behind.

'That was a wonderful dinner,' she sighed contentedly. 'I don't know what else you got up to in Vietnam, but you certainly learned to cook!'

'Unhand me, woman!' he growled playfully, bending down to open the door to the refrigerator. He took out a bottle of Moët. 'I thought we'd celebrate your HIV test being negative.'

He found a pair of tall glasses, and he and Jill settled cosily in a pile of huge floor pillows covered with antique tribal weavings. They had already made love before dinner, and Jill was feeling radiant. Sipping the delicious chilled champagne and gazing up at the massive rafters in the roof space, she felt herself relaxing for the first time in weeks.

'I wish I could have told you earlier,' she smiled sleepily. 'Two weeks is a hell of a long time to keep news like that to yourself.'

'Yeah,' he agreed. 'But those courses are so goddam secret, there's no way they'd let a call in or out.'

Jill leaned up on one elbow. 'Brad,' she asked, 'what do you actually do at those things?'

'Oh, they teach us to light fires by rubbing sticks together, stuff like that,' he grinned.

Jill dipped her fingers in her champagne and playfully flicked the drops at him. 'Sure!' she laughed.

Brad took a bottle of scented oil from where it was warming by the stove, and started to massage her feet. Before meeting him, Jill would never have believed that such a simple thing could make her feel so orgasmic. But this was just one of the many doors Brad had opened for her, both sensually and sexually, during their time together.

'Why do I get the idea you didn't spend all your time out East learning about food?' she purred.

Brad grinned. 'Those Vietnamese and Thai women have forgotten more about massage than I've ever known.'

'Don't they walk up and down on you?' Jill giggled. 'I can't say I'm crazy about *you* doing it. A hundred-pound Thai masseuse, OK. Two hundred pounds of you, I'm not so sure!'

Brad turned his whole attention to her foot. Jill still found it difficult to understand the paradox that was Brad. On the one hand, he could be exquisitely tender, loving and sensitive; on the other, she reminded herself, he was a man who killed for a living, and who could push her to her limits of sado-masochistic sex. She had never met another man like Brad, and knew she never would. He was like a drug, and, like any addict, she now needed regular fixes.

'We have something else to celebrate too,' he told her, almost offhandedly.

'What's that?' she murmured drowsily.

'What if I said we didn't have to bother with condoms any more? I hate the damn things anyway, those heavy-duty ones in particular.'

Jill sat bolt upright, almost spilling her champagne. 'What do you mean?' she asked, confused. 'Just because I'm in the clear for now doesn't mean we can stop being careful.' Her mind raced to prevent herself saying something tactless about Brad's own HIV status.

'I'm not positive any more.'

'I don't believe it!' Jill was totally incredulous. 'How did you find out?'

'I had the medics who tested me before test me again.'

'I can't imagine they were that eager. How did you swing it?'

'Pulled some strings,' he replied dismissively. 'Damned medics – they're not about to change the course of my life without me putting up a fight. They weren't too pleased about it, but I got the authorisation, so they had to. And I'm clean. You should have seen their faces!'

Jill just sat there, stunned. Finally, she threw her arms round him, and said, 'Brad, that's wonderful! I can't tell you how pleased I am.'

'Me too. Because I was finding it hard to live with the idea that I could have made you sick.'

'All this time I've been feeling rotten about not being able to persuade Mort to let you have a shot, and it wasn't even necessary! But I still don't understand what's happened, exactly.'

'Well, they were so stunned to find I was HIV negative after all that they checked and re-checked all the samples they tested at the same time as me. And what do you know? They'd mixed up my blood sample with some other poor bastard's.'

'So he's got some bad news coming to him. Poor man,' Jill said pensively. For a moment that seemed to stretch for ages they sat silent, the crackling of the logs in the stove the only sound. Neither knew what to say; the silence seemed to say it all. It was Jill who finally broke the spell.

Calmly, but with an undertone of anger and suspicion in her voice, she asked, 'Why didn't you tell me this before?'

'Because,' he answered, 'after all I put you through, I wanted to be absolutely sure. And until they'd tested me again, and the other guy, there was no point in saying anything.'

Jill added mentally: you could have told me that the minute I got here, you creep! But she pushed the useless anger away. Such manipulative games were an inextricable part of Brad, something she would have to learn to handle for herself. It was unreasonable to expect someone who could exercise control to such intoxicating effect when they were having sex, not to use it in his ordinary dealings with people as well. She might not like it, but she would have to learn to live with it, accept that she couldn't have only the intriguing, exciting parts of Brad without the rest.

Deliberately, she put her glass down, and reached for Brad. She held him close without a word. Finally, she lifted her head and gazed into his eyes. 'I think we should drink to the future.'

They clinked glasses. 'To the future!'

'That sounded like you really meant it,' Brad observed.

Jill lay back against the cushions. 'For the last two weeks, I haven't known whether there was going to be a future,' she sighed. 'Now it looks as though there will be. I feel as if a huge weight has been lifted off my whole life.'

'And I feel like a huge weight's been lifted off my dick.'

Jill giggled into her champagne. 'What on earth do you mean?'

'You know I haven't found it that easy to – well, get it up lately?'

'Have you heard me complain?'

'No. But now I'm not worried about getting sick, or about infecting you, things ought to get a whole lot better.' Brad rolled over on top of her, and started kissing her neck. Then he smiled down at her, and said, 'Champagne doesn't improve with keeping. How about we kill the bottle?' He filled both their glasses, though there was still some left. 'Now, let's get down to some serious business.'

Swiftly he undid the buttons down the front of the shirt – one of his – which Jill was wearing. Jill lay back on the pillows and let herself relax into the delicious sensations. The Moët was finally having its effect on her, and she craved the warmth of the fire on her naked skin. Brad knew exactly how to relax and excite her in turn, playing her body like a virtuoso instrumentalist. He dimmed the lights by remote control, and shrugged off his robe, taut muscles gleaming and contoured in the warm glow from the flames.

'How about I give *you* a massage?' Jill suggested.

Within seconds, she had him face down, his massive shoulders glistening under her soothing hands. With slow, deliberate strokes, she caressed his powerful body, then ran her fingertips over his back, like a spider walking tantalisingly over his skin, until he shuddered.

'Feet apart,' she ordered. 'I'm going to do your butt.'

Taking the oil into the plam of one hand, she rubbed both palms together and spread the liquid firmly over the tanned flesh. Gently she worked the oil into his skin until she felt his buttocks relax.

'You ready for this now?' she asked rhetorically, allowing her fingers to slide down his crack, lingering just a second at his favourite place. He said nothing, only moaned with pleasure, arching his back to get the most out of her caresses.

For a full half hour, Jill deftly relaxed and excited his body, the sight of his glistening oiled flesh arousing her every bit as much as her touch did him.

'Your turn now,' he said, as she finished working on his taut belly.

For Jill, the time passed like a dream, as she found herself released into the hypnotic bliss of total bodily delight. She couldn't tell how much time had gone by when she heard Brad whisper into her ear, 'As this is a special night, I have something very special in mind for you.'

'I'm totally in your hands,' she murmured, relaxed almost into sleep.

'I'm just going to get something. Back in a moment.'

As if in a dream, Jill heard Brad go into another room, and return a minute later. He was carrying a small black leather case. She heard him click open the locks and take out several objects, which he arranged along the seat of the sofa.

'Tonight, goddess,' he whispered as he kissed her, 'I'm going to take you to the extremes of your dreams. This'll be an experience you've only ever fantasised about.'

Once, as they were making love, Jill had shared her most daring fantasy with him, something she had never told anyone else.

So she knew he would be familiar with all the details. Her heart raced at the very thought of it. She told herself that she would simply relax into it, let him make it all happen. She trusted him to take her to her very limits, and to bring her safely back. She closed her eyes, and conjured up the fantasy she used so often when arousing herself.

She felt Brad circle her ankles with what felt like soft cuffs, then her wrists. Lastly, he fastened a collar of soft black leather around her slender neck. Jill sensed herself becoming energised by the excitement this aroused in her, excitement beyond anything she'd normally experienced, and all without Brad doing anything directly to arouse her. It was almost arousal by remote control – her own mind was doing it all. It was as if the leather bonds were a magical focus for erotic sensation, familiar through fantasies, even though in real life she had never done this before. She felt powerless to protest, didn't even want to.

'Stand up,' Brad ordered, and helped her to her feet.

Slowly, agonisingly slowly, he started to kiss her, first her mouth, then her neck and shoulders. Visions of their first love-making, that night after the pool hall, came flooding back. Just as he had tortured her so erotically then, now he covered every inch of her with kisses, occasionally nipping the soft skin with his teeth, until she could bear no more.

'Fuck me now,' she begged plaintively.

'All in good time,' he murmured. He reached between her legs – an electric shiver shot up her spine, and she moaned. 'You're hot! I reckon you're about ready.'

He led her towards the huge, uncurtained fifth-floor window. Jill could see across the street into some of the apartments in the building opposite. But before she had time to take this in, Brad had raised her arms and was looping a rope through small rings on the leather cuffs. Above her head, she could see a brass ring screwed to the under-side of a stout oak beam in the spotlit ceiling, the rope running through the ring from her cuffs. Brad was going to make her fantasy come true, in every detail! Her pulse racing, her heart hammering as though it would burst, she gazed out across the street.

'Brad!' she cried, horrified. 'I can see those people! Can they see me?'

He picked up the dimmer switch, and brought the lights full on. 'They can now!'

Standing behind her, he reached round to cup both breasts, nuzzling into her neck, and whispered, 'See, my angel? You're going to have your fantasy played out just the way you want it. And anyone who wants to can watch you enjoying it.'

Jill managed to force herself a little way back to reality. 'But that's not my fantasy!' she protested weakly.

Brand pinched her nipples a little harder. 'I know,' he smiled wickedly. 'But it *is* mine.'

Jill's mind was in a whirl. She was completely under his spell, and so aroused that she would have had sex in the middle of Times Square there and then if he had told her to. There was nothing she could do; she was totally in his power, unable to move. She could only tremble as Brad continued to push her helpless body to its limits, using both pleasure and pain to excite her and calm her down again, until she could hardly distinguish between the two. At last he asked, 'You ready now?'

'You know I am. You sadistic bastard!' she groaned, her voice cracking with the nervous strain of so many near-climaxes. Also, she was beginning to feel alarmed at where this adventure was taking her. Her fantasy had only been about being tied up and having men tease her to distraction. Brad had already added his own personal twist, and she was apprehensive about what he was going to do next.

Desperately she pleaded, 'If you don't get on with it, I'm going to explode.'

'No, you're not' he said, in a hard, authoritarian tone she'd never heard from him before. 'Not until I say you can.' He unlooped the rope from the brass ring, but kept it attached to her wrists. 'Come here,' he ordered, leading her over to a padded-velvet double piano stool. 'Lie down. On your belly.'

Willing to do anything he wanted as long as it would bring her relief, Jill lay down the length of the stool. Swiftly, Brad lashed her wrists to the legs of the stool, then used the rest of the rope to tie her ankles in the same way. Effortlessly, he turned the stool so that Jill's rear was facing towards the uncurtained window, and massaged more oil into her buttocks and down into her crack. He didn't bother to look up to see whether anyone was watching from the apartments opposite; he knew they'd be there. This was humiliation such as Jill had never dreamed of, even in her most depraved fantasies. Only a tiny part of her brain wondered whether she would ever dare show her face in the neighbourhood again. But the sensation of his fingers delving into her most secret places blotted out even that.

'Stop, please,' she entreated.

From somewhere behind her she heard him tease, 'Ready for me now, angel?'

'Yes,' she moaned. 'You know I can't wait another second!'

Slowly and deliberately, Brad started to insert himself into Jill's waiting body. As she realised what he was doing, she screamed in panic, 'No! Not there, please!'

But he was already inside her, grasping her hips firmly and thrusting insistently. Jill caught her breath, panting wildly. She felt sick with the searing pain, yet at the same time she was on the edge of orgasm. Brad felt enormous inside her – surely he was never usually as huge as that? Almost unconscious with agony, Jill felt Brad bury himself deep inside her with his final thrust, and climaxed as she had never done before. It felt as though mind and soul both left her body, leaving her empty, almost dead.

Brad left her, and went over to the fireside. He sat down, and filled his glass with the last of the champagne. With a satisfied smile, he downed the lot in one.

22.

'What do you mean, she found out? How did she find out, for Christ's sake? Look, I don't want you to waste any time here. Do what you have to do. You understand? Just make sure the bitch never gets in the way ever again.'

'Mira? I'm sorry to call you so late, and on a Sunday night too –'

'That's OK. Nothing but re-runs on the tube anyway! Hold on, while I put Joan Rivers out of her misery.' Jill heard Mira fumbling for the remote control; in a few seconds the canned laughter died a sudden death.

'I've decided I have to tell Mort about Boris Volkov and Ivan Kandinsky being the same person. Too many things have happened with the vaccine over the past few weeks. Also, I know Mort so well, I feel there's more to it than he's telling me. I can't go on any longer pretending something isn't seriously wrong.'

'Mort's not stupid, Jill. He can work that out for himself.'

'Maybe. But you know the sort of pressure he's under, from the Administration. I know that if he can turn a blind eye to something he doesn't want to see, he will. But if I tell him, loud and clear, that I think the Russians have sold him a sort of pharmaceutical time-bomb, he'll have to take notice. Won't he?' Jill was almost pleading for Mira to give her permission to tell Mort of her deepest fears.

'You don't sound like your usual self,' Mira observed perspicaciously. 'Everything OK?'

'Absolutely,' Jill said, trying to force a note of confidence into her voice.

But Mira wasn't fooled. 'Hmmm!' she muttered.

'OK, something happened – with Brad. But I really don't want to talk about it.'

'That's all right. But if you ever decide you do want to –'

'Thanks, Mira. I promise if I ever do want to talk, it'll be to you.'

'Just reassure me – he didn't beat you up, did he?'

'No. It wasn't that.'

'Promise?'

'Promise.'

'Remember; you're very precious to me. You're my dearest friend, and the nearest I ever had to a daughter. I've said it before: I don't want to have to gather up the pieces!'

'You won't have to. I will take care. Oh, Mira; I'm so grateful – for everything!'

'Ach, for nothing! Listen: you rang to ask me if you should tell Mort you think Seminon's dangerous. Well, I say you have nothing to lose by telling him. Let him waste Pharmavax's time and money finding out if you're right or not. Then you can sleep easy, knowing you've done the right thing.'

'Thanks, Mira. But I wonder whether any of us'll ever sleep easy again, if I'm right.'

There was a pause for a few seconds. Then Mira said, 'Can you hold on for a moment? I think Hodgie's trying to get in the kitchen window.' She put the telephone down on the table.

Jill held on for a while, listening to Mira making her way to the kitchen at the back of the ground-floor apartment. She heard Mira call 'Hodgie? Hodgie?' There were various clatterings, followed by a distinct thud. Then there was silence for a minute. And another minute. Jill, perplexed, still listened.

'Mira?' she called. 'Mira, are you OK?'

Complete silence. Jill forced herself to hang on for another thirty seconds. She screamed down the telephone, 'Mira!'

Again, nothing but silence. Countless possibilities jostled in her mind. Hodgie was hurt. Mira had had a fall – or a heart attack. Whatever it was, something was clearly very wrong indeed.

Jill reached out to break the connection, and called 911.

• • •

When she got to Mira's apartment block, there were already several patrol cars, blue lights flashing, in the street. Jill double-parked, and rushed up the steps into the vestibule. A cop stopped her at the door to Mira's apartment.

'Sorry, ma'am. You can't go in there.'

'But it was me who called you!' she panted.

'Right. So you'd be able to identify the deceased?'

'The de – ? Oh God! Is she dead?'

'It looks as if Dr Harman is – well, yeah, dead, ma'am,' the cop stammered. 'Could I see some ID, please?' Jill fished frantically in her purse for her NIH security pass, and handed it over.

'Wait here a moment, please, ma'am.'

It felt like hours, but in reality it was scarcely a minute, before the fat, sweating cop returned and gave Jill back her ID. 'Come with me,' he said.

Feeling sick with apprehension, Jill followed him through the hallway, and into the faded but familiar living-room where she had spent so many happy hours talking things over with Mira. The apartment had been her second home, but now it felt foreign, strange, invaded by cops, investigating officers and police photographers. This was a place she had never been to before, somewhere she would never come again.

'What are all these people here for?' she enquired, stupefied. Mechanically, she followed the cop through to the tiny kitchen. 'If Mira had a heart attack –'

'It wasn't a heart attack,' the crime investigation officer said laconically, getting to his feet and ripping off his mask. 'Who are you?'

'Dr Jillian Peters,' Jill responded automatically. 'I called the police. I know – knew – Dr Harman. I was talking with her on the telephone when –'

The officer bent down and unzipped one end of a green body bag.

'This Dr Harman?'

I thought dead people were supposed to look peaceful, Jill thought irrationally. There was nothing peaceful about Mira Harman now. The usually-immaculate iron-grey hair was straggling all over the place, ripped out of the tortoiseshell combs which had always held it so neatly. Her face was a livid purple, and no one had bothered to close the frantically-staring eyes.

Jill collapsed on to the bench of the dinette unit, sobbing.

'For the record, Dr Peters: is this Dr Harman?' came a remorseless voice.

Clutching a mangled Kleenex to her face, Jill nodded. 'You said it wasn't a heart attack,' she managed eventually. 'Can you tell me how – what happened?'

'Strangulation by ligature,' the crime investigation officer said tersely. 'Homicide one, I'd say.' He unzipped the body bag a few inches further to expose Mira's throat. 'Wanna see?' Jill shook her head desperately. Why did I take so long to realise something was wrong, she wondered frantically. I could have saved her – I should have saved her –.

'Whoever it was, they got the cat as well.' The investigating officer jerked his head in the direction of the draining-board. Hodgie lay on a sheet of newspaper, his eyes half-closed, a sliver of pink tongue showing between the little sharp teeth. Jill got up and went over to look at him. She reached out to the soft, streaky grey-black fur, and felt the cat cooling and stiffening even as she stroked him.

'Why'd they have to kill him too?' she wept. 'I'd have looked after him.'

Her Kleenex was a sodden pulp. The kind-faced fat cop reached over to the roll of paper towel on the wall, tore off a couple of squares, and handed them to Jill.

'Thanks,' she sniffed.

He waited until she had blown her nose and mopped her tears. Then he said, 'I'm sorry; Lieutenant Rafferty says we have to ask you to come down to the precinct, and give a statement.'

Jill nodded. 'Of course,' she said wearily. 'The only trouble is, there's nothing I can tell him. If you were to ask me if I knew of anyone who might want to kill Mira, I'd have to say: no-one. No-one at all.'

'Even so, ma'am, we have to take you in.'

'Take me in? You make it sound as though I'm a suspect!'

'Could be that you are, ma'am,' the fat cop said stolidly.

'Now listen!' Jill snapped fiercely, anger getting the better of fatigue and grief. 'You record and log all calls, don't you? You have the technology to identify voices. Your crime-investigation officer can pinpoint the time of Mira's death pretty accurately at this stage. Less than an hour ago, Mira Harman was still alive. I believe that I actually heard her being murdered, not three minutes before I called you, on my own phone, from my own apartment. Your own records will prove that I called. Now, I may be an intelligent woman, officer, but I have yet to perfect the art of being in two places at the same time! Maybe you'd like to point that out to your lieutenant.'

The officer reached for a clipboard and flipped over a computer print-out. 'Something's a bit strange here,' he said, turning the clipboard towards Jill, jabbing at it with a stubby finger. 'We had two calls on this one. Here's yours. But we had this one too, less'n a minute earlier, from a public payphone way over the other side of town. Just said we'd find a dead woman at this address.'

'How do you account for that?'

'Don't know that I can, ma'am.'

'Well, I certainly can't.' Jill leaned back against the wall, her eyes closed. What kind of person would creep into another person's apartment late at night, strangle them and kill their pet cat into the bargain, then call the cops to say they'd done it? Only someone who knew exactly what they were doing! Jill shivered.

23. Mmontg@lbx.pharmavax.dc.usa

'HI, MORT, HOW YA DOIN'? JUST HEARD TODAY FROM THE FDA THAT YOU HAVEN'T FILED THE RESULTS OF YOUR ANIMAL TESTING YET. SO WHEN DO YOU START TESTING THIS STUFF ON PEOPLE, IS WHAT THE BIG MAN WANTS TO KNOW. WE'VE DONE OUR DAMNEDEST FOR YOU RIGHT DOWN THE LINE. NO NEED TO BE SPECIFIC, YOU KNOW WHAT I MEAN. IF THIS DOESN'T WORK OUT, IT'S NOT GOING TO LOOK TOO GOOD ... ESPECIALLY FOR PHARMAVAX. IN THIS GAME, MORTIE, YOU GOTTA SHIT OR GET OFF THE POT –'

All the following day, Jill stayed at home, her telephone disconnected. She had spent much of the night talking with the police, going over and over the events of the evening until the endlessly-patient Lieutenant Rafferty was satisfied. And now she was feeling jaded and nauseous after too many hours under harsh fluorescent lighting in an airless interview room, drinking endless cups of bad coffee, and she felt half-dead with grief. Of all the things that had ever happened to her, Mira's death was the worst. Not even when her mother died could Jill remember feeling as she did now, utterly crushed, abandoned and lost.

Eventually, Jill knew, she would weep all her tears. But she knew, too, that she couldn't begin to handle the horror and violence of Mira's death and her own loss until she knew who'd done it, and the police released the body so she could lay her friend to rest. In the meantime, she would just have to carry on.

That night, she knocked herself out with a couple of sleeping-pills. In the morning, thick-headed and puffy-eyed, she forced herself to get out of bed and reconnect the telephone. The first call she made was to the lab.

'You don't have to come in, Jill,' she was told. 'Take all the time you need.'

'Thanks,' she replied. 'But I want to come in. I need to get back to work.'

Then she called Brad, who had heard about the murder on the news the night before. He was kind, said all the right things, suggested dinner – which she turned down. 'I don't feel like going out for a while,' she explained. She didn't add that since that night at his apartment her feelings about him had been unsettled or she'd have asked him round. But her confusion was going to have to be put to one side for the time being. Mira's murder had pushed everything else to the very margins of her life.

'I understand,' he said. Then, just as she was about to hang up, he added, 'Something you should know. The FDA are going to call Mort in for a formal meeting. I've been told to sit in.'

'But why on earth should you – ?'

'They want me there as some kind of an observer, I guess. They haven't told me too much about it, so there's nothing I can tell you.'

'I need to call Mort,' Jill said, still foggy from the Restoril.

'Sure. Talk to you soon.' Brad rang off.

Jill still had Mort's number programmed in to her phone. His secretary answered.

'Oh, hi, Jill!' she gushed. 'Isn't that terrible, about poor Dr Harman! And you found her! It must have been just awful for you –'

'Thank you, Jane,' Jill cut her off, unable to handle the woman's heavy-handed sympathy, which felt uncomfortably like ghoulish curiosity. 'I'd like to speak with Mort.'

'He's on his other line right now. Can I have him call you back?'

'Yes, would you? I'll be going in to NIH in a little while, but at the moment I'm still at home.' Jill took the phone into the bathroom with her. She was washing her hair when it rang, and she had to ask Mort to wait while she reached blindly for a towel.

'I'm very sorry about Mira,' he said straight away. 'I know how close you both were. Hell of a thing to happen. Have the police come up with anything?'

'Not really,' Jill answered. 'I spent most of the night before last talking with them, going over and over the same things. There was nothing I could tell them.'

'Sounds a bit like the news reports – they just say the same things again and again. I guess there's nothing else they can say. No traces, nothing stolen, no apparent motive. And it wasn't a sex crime.'

Jill felt tears starting to flood her eyes. 'No. And I'm glad it wasn't. Mira couldn't have borne that!' she said vehemently. 'There's one really weird thing: they got this other call just a minute before I rang. That means someone called them practically before she was dead, and from the other side of town. I don't begin to understand it. The cops have the idea that someone broke in specifically to kill her. They said it was "a slick job", whatever that means. I told them it made no sense. I mean, I know you never got on with her, but you can't imagine anyone wanting to kill her, can you?'

'Of course not, though it sounds very much as though that's what happened. And the killer got in through the kitchen window?'

'She had one of those locks where you can leave the window open a little to let in some air; the cat used to go in and out that way. The killer forced it – very professionally, they said. The creepiest thing of all, though, is this other call.'

'I can't make that out, any more than you can. Well, I'm sorry all this has happened. I'd like to suggest dinner sometime, but my life, right now, is more complicated than ever –'

'I know, the FDA meeting.'

'How did you hear about that?'

'Brad just told me. He's been asked to attend, as some sort of observer.'

'The hell he has!' Mort exclaimed. 'Well, I shall be curious to meet him.' Jill's heart sank. A meeting between Mort and Brad was the one thing she had hoped to avoid.

Mort went on, 'In view of what you told me about the side-effect of alcohol on vaccinated men, I'd be glad to have you along. Would you mind if I ask the FDA if you can come too?'

Jill unwound the sodden towel, and started to comb out her damp hair. 'If you like. I seem to be in as deep in all this as if I'd developed the vaccine in the first place. But you may not want me there when you hear what I have to tell you –'

And she proceeded to tell him everything she knew about Boris Volkov.

• • •

Jill arrived at NIH only a little later than usual, to find her colleagues uneasy and subdued, shocked by Mira's murder.There had been several calls for Jill the day before, mostly from the media. One stood out from the rest: call Frank Osborne at the FDA, followed by a direct-line number. Osborne had been FDA Commissioner for the past two years, and with the Administration for thirty years before that. Jill had met him on countless occasions, liked his old-fashioned courtly manner, and knew his reputation for caution and unimpeachable honesty. If anybody did things by the book, he did, a quality which had earned him well-deserved promotion early on in his career, back in the days when discrimination against blacks was more or less accepted. Jill rang him straight away.

'I guess you've already spoken with Morton Montgomery,' she said, the preliminary courtesies out of the way.

'Indeed I have,' the Commissioner answered in deep, reassuringly measured tones. 'He asked if I would mind if you attended the preliminary hearing at the FDA, but I told him I was going to invite you in any case, in your official capacity in the field, to look into the development and manufacture of a Pharmavax product. My own scientific training was many years ago now, and I need a younger and better informed mind such as yours to call on. Of course, if you feel your long friendship with Dr Montgomery precludes any such involvement, I shall quite understand.'

'I'm afraid there's a great deal more to it than that, Commissioner.' For the second time that day, Jill recounted her fears and suspicions about the Russian vaccine, and about how Pharmavax had come by it.

'I see,' Osborne said, in a professionally non-committal voice. 'It sounds like we shall indeed need to have you at the hearing, in the light of all this. I'll want a formal statement from you, if you'd be good enough to prepare one and have it notarised.'

'For what it's worth, Commissioner, there's something else I can tell you. I have personal experience of one of the side-effects caused by Seminon.'

'And what might that be?'

'Uncontrollable and violent aggression. I was attacked, by someone I've known a very long time.'

'I'm sorry to hear that,' Osborne said kindly. 'And this person had taken Seminon?'

'He told me he had, yes.'

'And in all the time you've known him, he has never exhibited any aggressive behaviour?'

'He used to shout and lose his temper. But as far as I know he was never physically violent. And this was more than just hitting. I have the marks to prove it.'

'In that case, we'll need written evidence from your physician. Can you provide that?'

'Yes. But the person who could have given you the best evidence was Dr Harman,' Jill said, suddenly feeling exhausted even though it was scarcely ten o'clock. 'I went straight to her place after – after I got hurt.'

'I understand you and Dr Harman had worked together for many years?'

'That's right. She was very special to me – a good friend.'

'And a good scientist, I've always understood. Of course, having to leave NIH in disgrace must have been a severe blow for her. I suppose the police will investigate any possible link between her death and the destruction of the computer data at your lab?'

'They spent hours going over that. But I don't see how there could possibly be one. Mira did some digging around through an old friend at the FBI, and came up with everything I just told you about Volkov, whom we both met in London as Ivan Kandinsky. I've passed all that on to Morton Montgomery. But there's no way the Russians could have found out that she'd made the connection, and once she'd gone public on the information, there'd be no point in killing her.'

'It would seem logical to assume that, I agree,' said Osborne. 'Even though Dr Harman's death has no bearing whatever on the Pharmavax hearing, it seems more necessary than ever that you be there. Is this coming Friday morning convenient for you?'

Despite the courteous wording, Jill knew that this was an invitation she was in no position to refuse.

• • •

The moment Jill had been dreading had finally arrived. Mort and Brad arrived at the FDA's Headquarters within seconds of each other. Neither waited to be introduced.

'So we meet at last, colonel,' Mort said coolly.

'My pleasure, sir,' Brad answered. The two men formally shook hands.

Jill was finding the whole situation nightmarishly unreal. She had never wanted Mort and Brad to meet and now, of all the men in Washington, they were to be yoked together in an uneasy alliance.

Mort introduced Brad to his colleagues. Jill already knew both of them, and had always got along particularly well with Randall Church, who had taken the trouble to ask his wife, Helen, to invite Jill to dinner at their home on several occasions. Phil Zuckerman she had never liked; she didn't trust him, and always sensed that he wouldn't hesitate to put his own interests ahead of Pharmavax's.

Mort fetched a cup of coffee for Jill. He turned his back on the rest of the gathering, effectively cutting her off from them. She forced herself not to look at Brad, though she was sure he was watching them both like a hawk.

'How've you been?' Mort asked in a low voice.

'A lot better. Thanks for asking.'

'I wish I could say the same. What you told me last Tuesday, about Volkov, has knocked us all sideways. All we can do now is work flat out on some sort of a containment strategy.'

'I told the Commissioner too. It's going to come out anyway.'

Mort scowled for a second. 'I guess you're right,' he said. 'Do you know, the damnedest thing happened that day we spoke; you won't believe it. A crowd of Russians called up, made an appointment, and came to discuss buying our stuff in bulk – some Government contract. They didn't need me for that, but they insisted. Only the CEO would do. It was all perfectly straightforward, so I saw them. Took a half hour, less maybe. Then just as they're about to leave, one of these guys says something like:

"Oh, by the way, Dr Montgomery, we know all about one of our scientists illegally selling state industrial secrets to your company. And we know the formula had certain flaws." And then he has the gall to say, "We very much regret the problems you've been having!" And then these Russians claim – "in strictest secrecy", if you please! – that their government labs have come up with an antidote to the side-effects of the vaccine! If it hadn't been for Phil and Randy, I'd have thrown them out of the building!'

'You're right. I don't believe it,' Jill said. 'But frankly, I don't know what to believe any more. Is it possible that the Russians still haven't realised we know Boris Volkov is KGB?' Even as she spoke she realised, if that were so, then it was probably the Russians who had killed Mira! Suddenly she longed desperately to be a million miles away from the whole mess. 'Have you told the Commissioner about the antidote?' she asked.

Mort nodded. 'Thought I'd better. Like you said, it'll all come out in the end.'

The Commissioner's aide began to take people's coffee cups and range them neatly on a tray. 'Time we made a start, I think,' Osborne said. They took their places at the conference table. Osborne indicated that he wished Jill to sit on his right. Brad and Mort sat as far away from one another as was physically possible.

At the head of the table, the Commissioner arranged a series of folders in front of him. 'Here I have a digest of Pharmavax's lab reports on the official animal testing, and the – uh – unofficial human testing of Seminon. And here,' he laid his hand on a second folder, 'I have Dr Peters's observations on the alleged side-effects of Seminon which, although she has not been officially authorised to make them, have nevertheless been formally submitted. This meeting will, of course, bear in mind Dr Peters's former involvement with the project, and her own professional record, which is not in question at this time.'

No-one uttered a word as photocopies of the relevant documents were distributed round the table.

• • •

The morning dragged on interminably as Frank Osborne questioned everyone minutely. Every hour, they paused while the tape in the recording machine was replaced, and those who wanted to took a comfort break. For minutes at a time, Jill's attention wandered as the FDA Commissioner painstakingly went over things she had already pondered a hundred times. Finally, having already put the very same question to Mort, Osborne asked, 'Dr Peters, in your professional opinion, is it likely that the Russians' claim to have developed an antidote is one we should take seriously?'

'They could have done it,' she replied cautiously. 'But it would be one heck of an achievement if they had.' She was reluctant to say more. Mort's answer had obviously not pleased the Commissioner, and she didn't want to upstage him. She glanced at him quickly. The look on his face said, 'Go on! You tell 'em!'

Gratefully, she went on. 'It would mean completely reformulating the vaccine to keep all the beneficial effects, yet at the same time modifying it so that Leydig cells weren't adversely affected. Perhaps there's some combination of vaccine and hormone stimulation they've come up with. All I know is, we're nowhere near finding any answers ourselves.'

'Which means,' Mort chipped in, 'that if they do have an antidote, they have to be a whole lot smarter than we've ever given them credit for.'

'They came up with the vaccine in the first place,' Jill reminded the meeting. 'And that was way ahead of our own capabilities.'

'Not necessarily,' Randall Church reminded her. 'It looks as if their original research was far from perfect. But we were all fooled; it did look good. And now it's blown up in our faces.'

'I have to say,' Frank Osborne said, 'that this is something that was bound to happen eventually. Up until 1987, we kept things real tight here so that this sort of thing simply would not occur. But once we started the Treatment INDs, it opened the floodgates to precisely this kind of accident.'

'C'mon, Frank,' Mort interrupted. 'Everybody – industry and public alike – welcomed the law being changed to allow people to try imperfectly-tested drugs that might – just might – save their lives. Sure, there was no requirement to prove that a drug which shortcut the system was totally safe before it was given a Treatment IND. In fact, if you remember, the Office of Management and Budget came in for a hell of a lot of flak at the time. People said they were trying to undermine the whole regulatory process. But they felt, as we did, that it was morally reprehensible to deny potentially life-saving drugs to people prepared to assume the personal risk, while you guys made us spend ten years jumping through hoops.'

Osborne responded to Mort's outspoken attack by clearing his throat and observing mildly, 'Of course, it's all too easy to forget experiences such as the Suramin scandal.'

'What was that?' Brad enquired. He hadn't uttered a word all morning, but had listened keenly to everything.

Osborne leaned forward on his elbows. He was a big, impressive-looking man which, combined with his deliberate way of speaking, seemed to lend an additional authority to anything he said.

'It wasn't a happy story, colonel. Suramin was a drug that had been used for treating sleeping sickness in Africa. In the test-tube, it was discovered that it prevented HIV from replicating, rather as AZT – which is also known as zidovudine – does. Both drugs inhibit reverse transcriptase – that's an enzyme,' he added helpfully, by way of explanation. Brad shrugged. 'Well, in Phase 1 trials it all looked worth pursuing, even though some of the men taking it developed fever, and liver and urinary abnormalities. But in Phase 2, when it was tested on forty-one gay men, a lot more trouble started to surface.'

'I remember,' Jill broke in. 'Two of them eventually died. And some of the others developed severe renal and adrenal problems.'

'Exactly,' Osborne confirmed. 'The thing about those trials was that they were a calculated risk. IND, colonel, stands for Investigational New Drug; it's a form of licence granted in certain circumstances to reputable pharmaceutical companies who appear to have a promising new drug. Of course, there are safeguards. But what it means is that drugs which may save lives can be given to people two or three years earlier than would otherwise be the case.

'In fact, until now there has been every reason to expect that such a licence would be granted to Pharmavax to test this new vaccine, particularly since, as I understand it, it appears to protect anyone who takes it against HIV in the first instance, and against HIV developing into AIDS. But as we have seen, for reasons apparently beyond Dr Montgomery's control, the vaccine was being unofficially tested by humans in any case.'

'Frank,' Mort interrupted belligerently, 'All our safeguards were in place, and you know it. All our work so far has shown that Seminon gives protection against HIV, which certainly comes well within the FDA's own "immediately life-threatening" category. Also, it satisfied your condition that there should be no comparable or satisfactory alternative; you only have to compare our results with those of the Concorde Study on AZT. And, lastly, we were engaged on active research on it. It wasn't as if we just put it on the market and walked away. In fact, since the very first signs of trouble, we've increased our R and D commitment way beyond our initial estimates. Randall Church can give you the figures.'

'That sounds a little disingenuous,' Frank Osborne observed mildly, 'since you had everything to gain by so doing.The question to be decided at this meeting is whether or not you showed the due diligence the law requires. At first sight, it appears you did not.'

'To get an answer to that, you'll have to go way over my head,' Mort replied, a hard edge creeping into his voice. Jill could tell that his temper was beginning to fray. 'Right from the start, we've both been over-ruled on this. By the guys on Capitol Hill. Perhaps Colonel Foster could tell us something about that –'

'Mort, it's my duty to caution you to be very careful what you say,' Osborne advised. Brad's face remained completely impassive.

After a few moments, Mort simmered down. He went on, 'I need hardly remind you that the industry has always been very wary of Treatment INDs. In theory, patients who take unproven drugs give informed consent, but we've never been given a say in designing the forms they sign, so we're always wide open to liability suits. If we hadn't been given every incentive to go ahead on this one – OK, Frank, I'm not going to name names – we never would have allocated the budget and the resources to it that we have. If this goes wrong, there's no way even an outfit the size of Pharmavax can underwrite the cost. Our insurers have already washed their hands of anything to do with Seminon.'

Jill looked up, surprised; this was the first she had heard of it.

'So we're going to be looking to the government to bail us out if this really hits the fan.'

'I think that lies outside the competence of this meeting to determine,' Osborne said quietly but in a voice that allowed no argument.

Over the past weeks, as Jill had watched Mort and Pharmavax struggling in a quick-sand of accumulating difficulties, her initial fury at being denied the chance to work on the vaccine had given way to a feeling of relief that the problems weren't hers. It was starting to look like her worst nightmare come true. Used as she was to dotting the Is and crossing the Ts, she had to admit that it could have happened at NIH. And if anyone at her lab had chosen to smuggle the vaccine out and use it clandestinely, there would have been no effective way to stop them either. For one act of greed and irresponsibility, Mort was paying dearly.

Frank Osborne ostentatiously looked at his watch. 'We've been at this for four hours,' he said. 'And I think we've covered all the ground we can at this time. There is a strong likelihood that we shall have to meet again, after the findings of this meeting have been fully discussed by my colleagues. In which case, you will all be notified.' He got heavily to his feet. He was no longer a young man, and he was looking tired. 'Dr Peters, gentlemen; thank you for your time.'

There was a relieved scraping of chairs as everyone stood up. Mort immediately made his way over to Jill and took her arm. 'Can you do lunch?' he asked urgently. 'I need to talk with you right away.'

Aware that Brad had his eye on them, Jill gently disengaged her arm. 'I don't really have time for lunch. I'm sorry. I've lost a whole morning, to say nothing of the time it took to prepare my statement.'

'It's important. Look, I brought the car. Let me drive you. Phil and Randy can get a cab.'

Jill nodded. 'OK. But I'd like to talk with Brad a moment. Be right with you.'

By this time Brad was gazing out of the window, pointedly ignoring everyone else in the room. Jill walked up behind him and stood close to his side. 'Mort says he wants to talk, so he'll drive me,' she said. 'Is your offer of dinner still good?'

'Sure. Tonight?'

Jill nodded. 'Just one thing,' she whispered. 'I really do want to see you, but I don't think I'll stay over. Do you mind?'

A strange look crossed Brad's face for an instant. Dismissively, he said, 'I guess not.'

• • •

Jill waited until Mort had turned on to the Beltway before she reminded him, 'You said you had to talk.'

Mort sighed heavily. 'You don't know the half of it,' he said. 'I'm in a worse mess than those guys know. I'll have to tell them about it eventually, I guess. But, like Frank said, we had enough to keep us going for over four hours in there. And I don't feel ready to go public with all this yet.'

'With all what?' Jill demanded. 'Mort, tell me!'

'OK. Three things. First, and worst, some cowboy outfit somewhere – Southeast Asia, probably – has discovered how to replicate Seminon.'

'Oh, no! How did you find out?'

'Well, you know the quantities we've been working with – tiny pre-production amounts? We've been keeping tabs on all reported cases of people having shots, so we can monitor the side-effects.'

'And?'

'And the number of people we're hearing about is more than could possibly have obtained the vaccine from us. A lot of them aren't choosing to be too specific about how they got the stuff.'

'Any idea who? Or where?'

'None. But we're working on it. Meanwhile, remember all those Pharmavax stocks I gave you? Better sell them while you can. Once this gets out, you won't be able to give them away!'

'Oh, Mort, I'm so sorry. And the second thing?'

'Almost as bad. It's the side-effects. I didn't tell you before, but we had some real bad trouble in the lab. We managed to hush it up, but it's only a matter of time before it gets out. Some of the monkeys went crazy, and – Oh, Christ, this is the worst – they killed someone. Jack Rymer, who managed the animal house for thirty years – they actually killed him. I was there.'

Jill fell silent. The questions jostled in her mind. How had Mort reported Jack's death? Could Pharmavax identify what had caused the monkeys to become homicidal? Was that what had caused Art to become so violent? – but this certainly wasn't the moment to ask any of them.

Mort went on, 'We tried the monkeys on alcohol, and you were right – it made things even worse. And, in addition,' he sighed heavily, 'we've been hearing from some of our unofficial human guinea pigs that they've been having fits of uncontrollable rage, getting involved in all kinds of violent behaviour. I'm afraid it all bears out your theory. And as if that weren't enough, there's another effect, which I guess you won't know about. Most of the men started off real pleased with themselves because Seminon made them into such studs. Unfortunately, after what you might call a honeymoon period, they're all finding they're suffering from a kind of testicular burn-out. Can't get it up, no longer interested, that kind of thing.'

'Are these effects permanent?'

'God knows. Too soon to tell.'

'And what about the violence? Is there any chance the aggression might wear off along with the libido?'

'Again, too soon to tell, as far as the humans are concerned anyway. We didn't leave the monkeys alive long enough to find out. It damn well better had! Can you imagine the lawsuits, if it turns out Pharmavax's made people impotent, and turned them into homicidal maniacs into the bargain?'

Jill shivered. 'There seems to be no end to it,' she whispered. 'It just gets worse and worse.'

'Bet you're glad you never got involved, huh?'

Jill nodded. 'I wish there were some way I could help you,' she said.

'I'd be the first to tell you, if there were. You could have dinner with me from time to time, talk things over. That is, if the colonel's prepared to let you off the leash.'

Jill winced at Mort's unwitting choice of words. She glanced at him briefly, but his face was expressionless, only furrowed with concentration as he wove in and out of the mid-day traffic.

'Of course,' she said, as blandly as she could manage. 'Do I dare ask about the third thing?'

'Oh, that!' Mort laughed bitterly. 'Well, some might see it as a ray of hope on an otherwise dark horizon. I don't happen to be one of them. This Russian antidote we've been talking about all morning – well, those guys who came to see me earlier this week offered to sell it to me! For twenty million bucks! Christ, I'll be lucky to have twenty cents to call my own, this time next week!'

'But shouldn't someone look into it? See whether they really have come up with an answer?'

Mort laughed grimly. 'Well, if anybody does, it sure as hell won't be me! You know what they say: fool me twice – ? The wisest thing I can do right now is put what resources we still have into developing an antidote of our own. Hell, I'm up against a wall here; it's the only thing I *can* do!'

24.

'Those Russians have some goddam nerve, wouldn't you say? Another twenty million bucks for some lousy antidote we don't even know exists? Tell Montgomery there's no way those guys are going to squeeze one more red cent out of this country, period. Did he say if he knew who'd developed it, supposedly? Like, was it the same guy as before? Well, find the fuck out, for Christ's sake, Schwartz!'

Once again, Brad had excelled himself in the kitchen, and Jill decided simply to relax and enjoy the endless tiny courses of delicious Vietnamese food he produced.

'If I tried to do this, it would take me a week,' she smiled, helping herself to more duck in ginger and black-bean sauce. 'To say nothing of another week to do the dishes.'

'It doesn't take too long, once you know how. There must be things you do every day in the lab, which I couldn't do even in a week.'

'Only because you're not a scientist.' She finished the last mouthful of spring roll and leaned forward to ask, 'Speaking of which, it does seem strange that you were asked to be at the FDA this morning. I still don't understand why the Pentagon is taking an interest.'

'They have a good enough reason, but I can't tell you – at least, not right now. To change the subject, I have to confess I didn't entirely understand a lot of what went on this morning. I don't mean the science stuff; I mean the way things work in your industry.'

'What, for instance?'

'I always thought the FDA was a research facility. Have I misunderstood something here?'

'A lot of people assume that. In fact, on most drugs they don't do any original research. They just regulate other people's work.'

'So how do they know who to grant all these licences to?'

'You really want a whole lecture?' Jill asked. Brad nodded. 'Well, back in 88, there was a new regulation, which encouraged industrial companies such as Pharmavax, or academic research departments like NIH, to consult with the FDA at a very early stage in the development of any new drug. Before that, it was possible for a company to spend years putting a new product through its paces, only for the FDA to send them right back to the drawing-board. But by becoming involved earlier, the FDA could help design the trials, and save a lot of time. They even started doing some research of their own to speed up the process.'

'Sounds like they were trying to help.'

'They were. And of course they were hoping to prevent dangerous products coming on to the market. Do you remember the scandal about an IUD called the Dalkon Shield?'

Brad shrugged. 'Not really my field. But go on.'

'Some of the women who used it suffered serious pelvic inflammatory disease. Huge numbers became infertile because of the rampant infection. The lawsuits were horrendous, and the manufacturers went to the grave.'

'Sounds like they deserved to.'

'They didn't set out deliberately to kill anybody. Turned out the design was faulty. The FDA's simply trying to prevent anything like that happening again.'

'Presumably it doesn't look too good if multinationals start to go belly-up?'

'It certainly doesn't. Pharmaceuticals are a huge source of foreign revenue, whether in the form of direct exports or licences to manufacture abroad. And you wouldn't believe the size of the domestic market – the legitimate domestic market.'

'So what's the illegitimate domestic market?'

'Ever heard of buyers' clubs? In practice, there's nothing to stop a special-interest group, such as AIDS victims, or a leukaemia support group, tracking down a drug manufactured abroad, importing it and distributing it to their members. This might be a drug which the FDA would never sanction in a million years, because it was dangerous, or not properly tested. Once a drug is on the market, there's always the possibility that it can be replicated. A lot of poor countries are boosting their foreign income by illicitly manufacturing drugs apparently identical to the branded Western product that companies like Pharmavax have spent millions developing.'

'Only apparently identical?'

'There's no control over where they get their raw materials. No way of verifying their production processes. There are labs all over the Third World, employing non-union labour for a few cents an hour, but you can bet someone at the top is getting very, very rich indeed. Even some of the cocaine barons, who are obscenely rich anyway, are diversifying into pharmaceuticals.'

'So what about Seminon? What if that gets manufactured illicitly and sold on the black market?'

Jill held her glass out to be filled. 'That was one of the many things Mort had to talk about today. He has reason to believe some cowboy outfit has found a way to replicate it.'

Brad seemed less surprised than Jill expected. 'But it took Pharmavax months to come up with anything at all,' he observed. 'And the Russians had already done the research.'

'I know,' Jill sighed. 'But we have no idea when this other lab got hold of the stuff. They could have come by some of the very early trial batches. We just don't know. And he said it's been causing frightful aggression in the monkeys in Pharmavax.'

'So if your theory about alcohol having a bad effect on anyone who takes it is correct –'

'I'm sure it is. When Art attacked me he'd had had four beers. I'm just worried that a lot of other people are going to get badly hurt.' Just in time, she stopped herself telling Brad about the appalling fate of poor Jack Rymer.

'What would you say if I told you I'd had a shot?'

'If you had a – ? Brad, you haven't! Don't tell me you've taken the cowboy stuff!'

'Well, when Mort wouldn't let you have one, I still thought I was HIV positive, so I went out and found one for myself.'

'Oh Brad, how could you be so stupid? God knows where they got their raw materials! Anything could have gone into it!'

'Just don't squawk at me, OK?' Brad said irritably. 'It's too late now. Anyway, I've had so many shots of stuff you wouldn't believe over the years – protection against anthrax, nerve gas, you name it – I doubt it'll make much difference.'

Jill leaned forward on the table, her head in her hands.

'Oh God, I never thought –'

'Never thought what?'

She chose not to meet Brad's steady gaze. The silence lengthened, second by second. Finally, she said, 'What we – you – did the other night –'

'Just plain ol' fun,' he grinned mockingly.

Confused and embarrassed, Jill stammered, 'No, it wasn't. I think it happened because of the Seminon, the same way Art got so violent after he'd had it. Look, that wasn't something I'd ever done before –'

'C'mon, that shy English rose act won't fool anyone! You loved it!'

Jill shrank away from him. He reached across to take her hand. 'I'm sorry,' he apologised. 'Look, if it bothers you, we won't do it again. If I promise there'll be no surprises, will you stay over tonight?'

'Brad, I can't. You've had a shot of Seminon, don't you see? And knowing what I think I now know, I'd rather not stay. It's not that I don't trust you. But I don't want to risk it. I've seen what that stuff can do, twice now. And to be honest, it frightens me.'

'I'd say I'm the one who should be frightened, wouldn't you? What's going to happen next, doctor?'

'Brad, I just don't know. No one does.' Oh yes, they do, she said inwardly. But there was no way she could tell him about what had happened at Pharmavax, that Seminon had made the monkeys murderous. And mad.

25.

'Dr Montgomery? Good morning to you. This is Mick Roche calling from the Irish Development Agency. Is this true, what we hear? That the splendid new factory you have near Carrigaline is really manufacturing a contraceptive vaccine? Because if that's so, Dr Montgomery, you're going to be in bad trouble. We've played fair with you now, given you a good deal, and it seems that you might have been lying to us. Now you know as well as I do that the Irish government, and the Irish people, won't stand for such a diabolical drug as this Seminon seems to be being manufactured here in Ireland. We're sending a man down today from Dublin to fetch samples for testing, and if the rumours are true – well, Dr Montgomery, you're going to have rather a lot of explaining to do!'

Joe Rosenberg struck his forehead in mock frustration.

'I vowed – I swore – I wouldn't forget your birthday this year! And dammit, I did! All the years I've known you, your birthday has always been exactly one week before mine. And if we Pisceans can't hang together –'

'Rosenberg, get up off the floor!' Jill laughed. Her birthday on March first had passed unnoticed by practically everyone. Art and Shirlene – well, Shirlene at any rate – had sent her a beautiful bouquet of flowers, and Jim had made her a huge card showing Father Time with his scythe – just wait till you hit thirty-nine, my boy, she thought – which was propped on the shelf above her workstation.

But Mort had been preoccupied with crisis after crisis at Pharmavax, and Brad had never even asked when her birthday was, nor how old she was, and had certainly never volunteered the same information about himself. The year before, Mira had taken her out for dinner, but this year Jill had simply switched off the television and gone to bed early.

And, at the lab, Joe was the only one who remembered – albeit three days late. Sometimes his clowning got on Jill's nerves, but he had a kind heart for which she could forgive him almost anything. Being twelve years younger than she was, he felt free to flirt theatrically, while at the same time regarding Jill as his very own Dear Abbie. But best of all, from Jill's point of view, was that he was deadly serious about his work – no clowning then!

'If you're free this evening, I could maybe take you out for a strictly kosher burger,' he suggested. 'I mean, I'd really like to.'

'It's sweet of you, Joe,' Jill answered. 'I'd love to do that. And it'll be nice to see Cindy again. I haven't seen her in so long. How is she?'

Cindy was Joe's live-in girlfriend. Jill liked her a lot, and was constantly urging Joe to marry her, but both of them were burdened with what they described as prototype Jewish mothers. Once Cindy had come right out and said to Jill, 'Look, I'm a nice Jewish girl, right? If Joe and I have kids, we'll do everything our mothers want. But as for getting married, with the mikvah and the chupah and me shaving my head and all – forget it!' So for some time Cindy had been waiting to make sure she was well and truly pregnant before going through what Joe called 'the whole Orthodox schmeer.' But three times, she had miscarried. They both wanted kids terribly but knew she couldn't go on losing babies like that without wrecking her health. Now, for the fourth time, Cindy was bravely trying again.

'I don't think she'll be able to come,' Joe said. 'We've got to twelve weeks, and its kinda, like, dicey for a while. She's been told to take things real easy.'

'And she doesn't mind you taking time off for a strictly kosher burger with another woman? Joe, do you realise what a treasure that girl is?'

'Sure I do,' Joe smiled wistfully. 'You keep telling me. Even my mom says she's too good for me. And if a Jewish mom says that – well, believe me, compliments don't come any higher.'

'Maybe we could do the burger at lunchtime. I'm sure Cindy likes to see as much of you as she can in the evenings. Does "taking things easy" mean she's given up her job?'

'Yeah,' Joe sighed. Then he looked Jill straight in the eye. 'Jill, how much longer am *I* going to have a job?'

'Why on earth are you asking?'

'Well, Cindy and me, we watch the news, we read a lot, we see what's going on. With Seminon, I mean.'

'For God's sake, you haven't taken it, have you?'

'No way! Knowing what I know from working in this place, do you think I'd go within a mile of that stuff?'

'So what are you worried about, exactly?'

'Well, I've been thinking a step or two beyond the immediate side-effects. People are getting real angry out there, and it's only a matter of time before NIH bows to pressure and starts cutting back on reproductive biology research. Isn't it?'

Jill had had the same fears herself, and the suggestion had certainly been voiced at a very senior level in the past, though more recently the opposite view had begun to prevail. But there was no point in telling Joe that until something had been definitely decided.The trouble was, events were moving faster than decisions could be taken.

Joe went on, 'You know how much I like it here. I've worked for you ever since I graduated, and I always thought there'd be a real future for me, a career rather than a short-term job. But the way things are going –'

'The way things are going is this,' Jill said firmly. 'We're under enormous political pressure, more than we ever were before the Pharmavax fiasco. It can only be a matter of time before somebody – and why not us? – comes up with a safe version of Seminon. Don't forget, apart from the side-effects, the Russian vaccine does work as a contraceptive. My own belief is that it was the combination of the different antigens that caused the problems. I reckon we should just try to settle for a good contraceptive vaccine, and dump the whole HIV angle.'

'It would certainly simplify the immunology,' Joe agreed. 'You know, it's really weird when you think about it. Here you have Cindy and me, trying to have kids and not being able to, while the vast majority of the population is busting its collective ass not to get pregnant. Then just as Cindy gets pregnant, we hear that millions of guys are not only infertile but can't even do it at all.'

'That's because Pharmavax let it be believed that they were further along with their reversal agent than they really were,' Jill reminded him.

'Further along?' Joe almost shouted. 'Shit – excuse me – it looks like they sold the whole damn world a bill of goods on that one. Though they were mighty careful not to be too precise about how far they'd gotten. Well, I suppose one good thing came out of it – the HIV protection.'

'Rosenberg, Rosenberg, you haven't been keeping up, have you? The HIV effect doesn't look like it lasts, after all.'

'So that's two holes they've gotten into! Well, it ties in with what somebody told me the other day, that they met this guy who's gay, and his partner took a shot for HIV protection, and then started beating up on him – after ten years together! So this guy's taking legal action for assault. But the worst thing is that the other guy's HIV level is back where it was before, plus he can't get it up any more. Sounded like they were both so mad they'd go and put a bomb under Pharmavax one of these fine days.'

'You must have read about all the pressure groups – the Seminon Survivors Action Group and a whole lot of others. They're becoming unbelievably powerful in political terms.' Jill didn't add that they were also becoming frighteningly violent, so much so that Pharmavax had stepped up its security since the trouble started, and Mort drove a different car from the company pool every day so that he could run the gauntlet of protesters and media without being identified and set upon. It was only a matter of time, though, before someone got seriously hurt.

'Look, you can tell Cindy from me that your job here is safe, for the foreseeable future. Like I said, we're under more political pressure than ever, and – strictly in confidence – the bosses are talking about taking on more staff to sort out the contraceptive vaccine once and for all.'

Joe ran his hand through his hair, making it untidier than ever. 'How's that going to help?' he asked exasperatedly. 'We can only go so fast, looking at all the other sperm coat antigens as possible candidates for another vaccine.'

'Of course,' Jill answered evenly. 'But if we had enough money – money we could really throw at it – and enough skilled people, we could probably come up with something in five years rather than ten.'

'Even so, in those five years, how many more people are going to be attacked and hurt, killed maybe? And why should all these men put up with being impotent for however many years, and even then with no guarantees?'

'God knows,' Jill sighed. 'All I know is that this whole business is producing some very rich endocrinologists, who claim they can reverse the impotence with hormones.'

'But they can't, can they? The whole point about hormones is that they're naturally released by the brain at regular intervals throughout the day. Having the whole lot in a single shot, or even as a series of shots, isn't going to work! Someone's going to have to come up with some sort of timed device for releasing hormones into the bloodstream in eight to fourteen pulses every twenty four hours, so as to mimic nature.'

'I can't believe it's beyond the capabilities of our state and commercial labs to come up with the right combination of hormones, and a timed delivery system. Someone'll do it, even if we don't. Roll on the day, whoever gets there first!'

'I don't know why everyone isn't flat out trying to find a reversal agent for the problems we have already,' Joe said. 'Think of it, all those people took the stuff honestly believing they'd be able to take a reversal agent when they wanted.'

'Be fair, Joe,' Jill chided. 'Pharmavax never promised a reversal agent, only said they were working on developing one. And if it hadn't been for their employees smuggling Seminon out of the building, it never would have been let loose in the world until it was ready. You can't blame them for that. If someone's really determined they'll get past the best security system.'

'You can blame them for everything else, though,' Joe said angrily. 'I'd think a whole lot better of them if they came up with a viable reversal agent. Trouble is, it all takes so damn long! I was telling a guy over at the synagogue just this weekend that we've been working on our project for eight years and that it looks like it'll be another nine before we have a usable vaccine, and he was, like, stunned. He seemed to think it could all be done in a matter of weeks.'

'Not this side of the millennium, Joe,' Jill said drily.

'Speaking of which, did you see that piece where the writer talked about how society has always felt a sense of doom and angst at the turn of every century, and now at the end of the twentieth century it's the worst yet. I tell you, it started me thinking.

Like, maybe we're experiencing some sort of worldwide terminal entropy, sexually, morally, economically, you know? I mean, who's to say there'll even be a human race come the end of the twenty-first century?'

There were times when Jill had to remind herself that, for all his ability, Joe Rosenberg was still very young and had a tendency to overdramatise. But at the same time she remembered how idealistic she and her contemporaries had been at the same age, when Russia was The Enemy who wanted to nuke the West, and the prophets of doom were convinced AIDS would kill off most of the world's population within a generation.

'Oh, I expect there'll still be some of us around,' she grinned. 'Joe, sitting around and schmoozing isn't going to get those X-rays done. If we're going to take time off for a burger –'

'OK, OK,' he said, reaching for her empty coffee-mug, as her telephone rang.

'Dr Peters. Oh hi, Fran!' Joe raised the empty mug questioningly, to ask if she wanted another. She shook her head. 'Health Editor of *Cosmo*,' she mouthed.

'That's OK. Sure, I have a minute. Yes, of course ... well, the trouble is it's hard to predict what the side-effects will be, and in what order ... reduced libido, of course ... yes, some loss of body hair eventually, though we haven't done any research to find out whether men are having to shave less often ... no, I think the loss of muscle will probably prove to be a very long-term effect ... yes, but when men take steroids to build up muscle, that's really not the same at all ... breast enlargement in men? Yes, it's a distinct possibility, but I shouldn't make too much of it just yet ... yes, of course, they'll all eventually develop reduced semen volume, and that's bound to make the sensations of ejaculation different, if they can ejaculate, that is ... no, I wouldn't say that; it's just that ... yes, I see what you mean ... yes, he's quite right; some men who've had both testes removed can still get erections ... well, not weird so much as fascinating. That's what I like about human reproductive biology; there's nothing predictable or straightforward about it.

'The main thing is, Fran, it's impossible to predict accurately how any individual is going to react; it's the same with the Pill, or HRT ... no, it's not as simple as that; if it were ... the trouble is getting the testosterone into the body in a way that mimics nature, and taking it orally just isn't good enough ... of course we're working on it, but it's not going to happen overnight. That's OK; it's a pleasure. Just fax me the article before you go to press, if you're going to quote me, would you? Any time, Fran ... yes ... yes, of course ... Fran, I have to go ... 'bye ...'

26.

'So you reckon Foster's a loose cannon, is that right? After all these years! Shit, I really need that, with an election next year! Look, find out all you can, OK? Through the usual channels, I mean. Just make sure no-one knows what you're doing. And whatever you dig up, I want to know about it ... Sure, sure, great idea; send him! If he fulfils his mission and comes back with what we want, great. And if he doesn't, we can send someone else. But either way, it looks like we can't lose. Doesn't it?'

'Remember your friend Volkov-Kandinsky?' Brad asked. 'The guy who got us all – not to say most of the world – into this mess? Well, it seems he's dropped out of sight, totally.'

Jill took a sip of wine. Behind an expression of absorbed interest, her brain was racing. Top KGB operatives don't just disappear, she thought. Not unless something's happened to them. 'Go on,' she said.

'That's it,' Brad answered dismissively, wiping his plate clean with a piece of bread. 'There's nothing more.'

'How did you find out?'

'The Russians asked us straight out if we knew where he was. They really want to catch up with Comrade Volkov. They've invested a hell of a lot in him; turns out he's their top industrial espionage operative. And he can apparently cut it as a scientist as well. Losing him would be like losing a valuable piece of equipment; money down the drain.The difference is that equipment can be replaced. Of course, what they want almost as bad is Pharmavax's twenty million. They feel they have a moral right to it, reckon it belongs to them. They can ill afford to write off that kind of money, and Mort was paying for Russian government research, after all.'

'So they feel they were made to look pretty stupid.'

'Exactly. All in all, I don't give much for the poor bastard's chances when the KGB catches up with him.'

'If he stole the twenty million, he could be anywhere by now.'

'Living a life of luxury?' Brad shrugged. 'It's possible. But I don't think so. The Russians reckon he's still in the country. They know he went back to Russia from here, but they lost track of him after that. And with all the corruption they have over there, there's no way they're ever going to recover the cash.'

Jill sipped her wine thoughtfully. 'I met him only once, for a few minutes, at a conference in London last spring. He didn't strike me as a thief, or a con-artist. I really thought he was what he said he was: a government research scientist, same as me. When Mira discovered he was KGB, I couldn't believe it. I'm not sure I can even now.'

'Sounds like he made quite an impression on you.'

'He did! For one thing, he was drop-dead gorgeous,' she laughed. 'Even Mira – who wasn't that crazy about men in general and Russians in particular – admitted as much. But seriously, I'd never have said he was –' she searched for the right word ' – dishonourable.'

'They train those guys to make you believe anything,' Brad observed cynically.

'Well, if you ever do find out what's become of him, I hope you'll tell me.' Jill looked at her watch. 'I must go. I'm working such long hours right now, I can't manage late nights.'

'I hoped you might stay over.'

Playing for time, Jill unscrewed an earring and dropped it into her purse. She felt racked with indecision.

'Look, I realise sex hasn't been that great lately,' Brad went on. 'Uh, this is kind of embarrassing. When you said you didn't want to stay over, part of me was actually relieved. The thing is, I've always been able to get an erection at will and maintain it for as long as I wanted. Hours if necessary. For some time after my Seminon shot – when was that, last November? – it was even easier. But now, for the first time in my life, I find I can't do that any more.'

'It happens to everyone sooner or later,' Jill said soothingly.

'That, angel, is a load of crap, and you know it. It doesn't happen to me. Now, I want you to level with me: is this a side-effect of Seminon?'

Jill got up and walked over to the window. Eventually she

turned to face him and said, 'Yes, apparently it is. Oh Brad, I'm sorry!'

Brad exploded in rage. 'You're sorry!' he shouted. 'Christ, the medical profession's a mess! First, I'm told I'm HIV positive. So I take a shot of Seminon, which I'm told will protect me. Then it turns out I'm not HIV positive after all. But we're very sorry, colonel, you're going to be impotent instead! Great!'

Jill turned and leaned her aching head against the cool windowpane, her view of the street blurred by tears. 'I wish the government had never sent you to Russia in the first place,' she whispered.

She felt Brad come up behind her, and put his arms around her. 'I shouldn't shout at you,' he said, snuggling into her neck. 'Whoever's to blame for this whole mess, it sure isn't you. And in a way I'm not surprised. I guess I thought maybe it wouldn't affect me the same way it affects everyone else. But I was wrong.'

She turned in his arms, buried her tear-stained face in his chest and held on to him like a drowning woman. Normally, his muscular bulk was reassuring and solid, but now she felt as if even Brad, vulnerable and assailed by doubts, were drifting beyond her grasp. He stroked her hair.

'I love you, you know,' he said suddenly. 'I never thought I'd say that to anyone.' He held her comfortingly for a minute, and went on stroking her hair. Then he said, 'One thing I need to know. This side-effect, is it permanent?'

Jill stepped away from him, and reached for her purse to get a Kleenex. 'No one knows yet,' she sniffed. 'I wish they did. It looks as if it might be.'

'Well, I guess I'll have to wait and see.' Brad emptied the wine bottle into Jill's glass, and handed it to her. 'I have to go away for a while, quite soon. I don't know how long for – it shouldn't be more than a couple of weeks, maybe three. I'll miss you. I'd like to try and change your mind about staying over tonight. Sex as such may be off the menu, but there's still a hell of a lot of things we haven't tried yet.'

Jill drained her glass, put it down, and came over to Brad. She put her arms round him.

'I love you, too' she said, wondering whether the pity she felt for him now could really be called love. Certainly it felt pretty much like it. 'So, yes – I'll stay.'

27.

'Mort, it's Sandi. Look, I have to come and talk to you right away ... I know it's only eight thirty, but I've had three calls already this morning, from the *Washington Post*, and the *New York Times* and a TV news station, all shouting about something going wrong with Seminon – the pirated stuff, not ours, thank God – and I don't know what to say to them. ... Because some computer nerd has been correlating statistics on domestic and public violence for the police, and has come up with some unbelievable figures for perpetrators who've also had Seminon. And of course the little maggot had to go public. ... Mort, does this mean people are starting to act like those crazy monkeys? Oh, shit, I've got more phones than people here! Look, Mort, this can't wait – we need to think of something to tell everyone now!'

The skills Brad needed to identify his target in Vienna were not that different from those he had used in Vietnam and Cambodia. Two weeks of patient, methodical search, involving long hours of waiting, and stretches of 'dead time', were nothing new to him. The difference was that instead of working in impoverished villages full of rooting pigs and mangy dogs, or sleazy downtown bars, he was surrounded by palatial baroque grandeur. And the sleek, richly-fed Austrians thronging the Karntnerstrasse in their loden coats bore no resemblance to the slight-boned, underfed Asians.

Brad didn't work in Europe as a rule, preferring the raw edge of the Far East, where he had carried out several missions to track down US personnel listed MIA but possibly still alive even after twenty years. He also relished the discipline of working on his home turf. He spoke no European languages fluently, though he understood some German. The fabled beauty of Vienna and its wealth of art treasures meant nothing to him; what he did know, though, was that this was a city Jill would love to visit. For a fleeting moment, he wished she were with him. The shops looked stylish and inviting; she'd have the time of her life with her American Express card. Then he shook off the idea; even if they were useful as a cover, an untrained person was about as much help on an operation as a migraine.

There was a complacency, a smugness, about Vienna and the Viennese that slightly displeased Brad. None of the people he saw on the streets would know what it was to live on the edge of things, as he did. Many of the women looked as if the most demanding thing in their lives would be to decide where to buy new designer collars or winter coats for their expensively-groomed boxers or poodles. Brad took a detached pleasure in being able to move among them, in designer cords and heavy winter overcoat, indistinguishable from the mass of other men. His leather brief-case, even though it was larger and heavier than the cases most people carried, lent weight to his assumed identity as a wealthy American about to open a secret bank account.

Switzerland had lost its crown as the confidential banking centre of the world. And in any case, the Pentagon's computer experts had accounted for every deposit of twenty million dollars, in whatever currency, that had been paid into any bank in Switzerland since Boris Volkov dropped out of sight. Several deposits in Viennese banks had looked more promising, and in the past two weeks Brad had eliminated all but one. His route brought him to the heavily-ornate entrance of the last bank on his list. All along, he had had a feeling about this one, and had consciously left it till the end.

'I have an appointment with Herr Schneider.' He gave his most engaging smile to the glacially-beautiful receptionist, and showed her his specially-produced ID.

Efficiently, she called the manager's office, then said in only-slightly accented English, 'Please take the elevator to the sixth floor, sir, and someone will meet you.'

At the sixth floor Brad was escorted along a close-carpeted corridor hung with paintings even he could recognise as eighteenth-century portraits, and shown into a small room high up under the mansard roof of the former palace, with dormer windows which gave a wonderful view of the skyline and treetops of central Vienna.

Herr Schneider had the same slightly sleepy look that Brad had noticed in many Viennese. However, he knew this was deceptive. The Viennese hadn't overtaken the Swiss as confidential bankers to the rest of the world by sitting around eating cream-cakes all day. And they didn't appoint idiots to manage their top banks.

For a minute or so, Brad curbed his impatience while the two men exchanged the usual pleasantries. At last, the bank manager asked, 'And how may I be of service to you?'

Without a word, Brad took an electronic scanner from his brief-case and spent a few seconds checking the room for bugging devices. Herr Schneider went through the motions of affecting to be shocked. 'I assure you such precautions are not necessary,' he insisted.

'I like to be certain,' Brad said imperturbably, and put the equipment away.

The bank manager attempted to steer the conversation. 'I believe you said you wished to open an account with us?'

'That's right,' Brad answered. 'That's what I said. But it's not what I want.'

The bank manager smiled urbanely. 'May I ask what it is that you do want?'

'Information.'

'About some of the services we offer, perhaps?'

'About the services you've offered in the past few months, to one particular customer.'

'Ah,' Schneider shrugged and spread his hands, palms upwards, with a bland smile. 'You understand that confidentiality is at the very heart of what we do here. I could not possibly tell you anything about any of our customers.'

'And if I said I had authority from the Pentagon?'

'You are not in Washington now, Mr Lauterbach. Your authority may empower you to ask me for information; it does not oblige me to give it. There is nothing I can tell you.' Schneider half got up from his chair, as if to show Brad out of his office.

'Sit down,' Brad said quietly. Astonished, the bank manager did so. 'The information I want concerns an account opened since July last, in the amount of twenty million US dollars, or a comparable sum in any other hard currency.'

'Even if I were prepared to discuss this with you, which I repeat I am not, you must of course realise that we have had many deposits of similar amounts.'

'I have an account number, and I know that substantial funds have been drawn out on two occasions, at three-monthly intervals. I'd bet quite a lot of money that another withdrawal is due any day now.'

'That may be so. But, I repeat, I can give you no information about any of our customers. I must ask you to leave.'

Brad leaned back in his chair. 'I've been told to obtain certain information about that account, and about the person who withdraws the money. I'm not about to go home without it.'

'In that case –' Schneider picked up the telephone on his desk. He had already punched out a couple of digits when his studiedly bland expression changed. He looked disbelievingly for a second at the telephone, and darted a frightened glance at Brad. 'What have you done?' he demanded.

Brad grinned. 'Let's say I have trade secrets too, Schneider.' The bank manager, his face sheened with sweat, tried all the telephones on his desk; every one of them was dead. Once again, he made as if to get out from behind his desk.

'Don't even think about it. You wouldn't make it,' Brad said equably. Schneider sat down again. 'Now, let's try to do this the friendly way. You tell me what I want to know, and in return I'll forget that I ever saw details of a certain account that came up on a computer screen not so long ago. Tiny amounts skimmed off over a period of years, nothing anybody would notice, yet eventually Herr Schneider becomes a rich man.'

Schneider didn't bluster or panic. He simply said, 'How do you know about this?'

'Let's just say, we have the technology. Of course, we can do this the unfriendly way if you prefer. Unless you have a superhuman pain threshold, I can get the information out of you in a couple of minutes. The Ice Queen downstairs knows only that at nine twenty-five, a Mr Lauterbach from Milwaukee came up to the sixth floor. I can get out of this building without anybody noticing, and I sure as hell won't do it as Mr Lauterbach. Poor Herr Schneider, on the other hand, will be found dead at his desk

– a heart attack caused by overwork, maybe? This Frau Schneider,' – Brad angled a heavy silver photograph frame towards his victim – 'and all the young Schneiders?'

Schneider looked directly into Brad's eyes, his gaze resigned. 'I do not believe the Pentagon sent you,' he said. 'Even the Americans would not send such a – a bandit!'

'Bandit? I like it,' Brad said pleasantly. 'OK, let's say that the Pentagon don't know how far I'm prepared to go to get the results I want. But I still intend to get them, Schneider.'

'Very well.' The stocky bank manager deliberately put his hands flat on the desk, to signal to Brad that he was getting up, and heaved his body out of the antique chair. 'I will call up the records of the account you want on the computer.'

Brad reeled off the account number from memory. Schneider looked up, shocked at a stranger having such protected information. Brad laughed.

'You don't think your computer security's that great, do you, Schneider? It didn't take our guy too long to crack it.'

Schneider darted a look of murderous rage at Brad, then turned his attention woodenly to the computer. Within seconds figures began scrolling up the screen.

Brad peered over Schneider's shoulder. 'Hey, I was right!' he exclaimed. 'This is the one I want! And, look, half a million bucks paid out in October, and another half million due to be picked up – shit, tomorrow! Hey, Schneider, you just got back the rest of your life as a gift. If you want to keep it that way, you'll tell me how this money gets paid, and who to.'

The bank manager sighed heavily, and punched a few keys. Seconds later, more information appeared. 'As I thought,' he said. 'There are certain accounts where any payment is collected by an agreed courier. This is one of them. In this case, a woman comes here with a bag or a suitcase, and takes the money. As you say, she is due tomorrow.' He closed down the display, and swivelled back to look at Brad.

'I must say to you, I object very strongly to what you are making me do. It is against all my principles.'

'Just like creaming off a few schillings here and there, huh? Don't let it get to you, Schneider: you'll still sleep nights. What time does this woman come?'

'The October payment was collected at mid-day, according to the record.'

'So you have the money, all stacked up nice and ready?'

The bank manager nodded. 'That is correct.'

'I'd be kinda curious to see what half a million dollars looks like. How about you take me on a tour of your vault, let's say as a courtesy to a valued depositor?'

'You are asking a very great deal,' Schneider said through gritted teeth.

'Sure I am,' Brad answered. He picked up the photograph frame. 'Nice-looking woman, Frau Schneider. Bet she'd look even prettier in black, with one of those little lace veil things they wear at funerals.'

• • •

Schneider didn't utter a word as the elevator took him and Brad past the ground floor, down into the old cellars of the palace. Electronically-operated gates had been fixed to the old stone pillars, and piles of bullion, paper currency and deposit boxes were stacked high in racks that in former centuries had been used for storing fine liqueurs and wines. A constant hum indicated that the light level, temperature and humidity were all electronically controlled.

Schneider went through intricate security procedures to open a series of gates. At last he and Brad came to an arched stone alcove at the end of the cellars. Herr Schneider reached out and laid his hand on top of a stack of dollar bills. 'You can verify the account number,' he said. 'I'm sure this is the currency allocated for collection by the courier tomorrow. It is in used notes, of mixed denominations.'

Brad glanced at the computer-printed figures on the papers that wrapped the bundles of currency. He nodded. 'That's it. I'll need to see the identity photograph you hold of the courier,' he said coolly.

'I realise that nothing I say will carry any weight, Mr Lauterbach, but I sincerely hope you do not intend to harm this woman.'

'No way,' Brad shrugged off the suggestion. 'It's not her we're interested in. We don't even want the money. What we're after is the guy who deposited it.'

'There has never been any contact with the depositor,' the

banker said. 'So I have absolutely no idea who that money belongs to.'

• • •

Even though Schneider had said the courier was likely to arrive towards noon, Brad took no chances. Long before the bank opened in the morning, he was stationed on a bench behind a newspaper, keeping an eye on the main entrance. In fact, it was mid-morning when the woman appeared. If the cropped blonde hair and single earring had not served to identify her, the battered leather hold-all would have. She stayed in the bank less than half an hour.

When she came out, Brad had to move fast, or he would have lost her in the crowd. It took no more than a few seconds for the receiver in the pocket of his overcoat to pick up the faint bleep of the minute transmitter he had inserted in a bundle of hundred dollar bills. Herr Schneider had been left in no doubt as to what would befall him if he substituted another stack of currency for the one he had shown Brad, but even so, Brad felt a slight relaxation in the tension he always felt at the beginning of an operation, when the reassuring bleep came through his earpiece. Keeping his gaze fixed on the white-blonde head, shining like a beacon a few yards in front of him, Brad plunged into the crowd.

• • •

Sipping the black tea in its tall glass, Brad gazed out of the window of the train at the never-ending flatness of central Hungary. His location display, disguised as a Sony Watchman, lay on the table in front of him, enabling him to keep track of his quarry without actually having to be in sight of her. The woman was occupying a seat at the far end of the next carriage.

Not knowing where his journey would end, Brad had booked himself through to Moscow. From Vienna to Budapest, the journey was completely uneventful. There was a long wait in Budapest, where Brad and the woman changed trains. As they wound slowly eastwards, the journey looked like being equally tedious. There was one brief moment of alarm, during a prolonged stop in Nyiregyhaza, when the monitor indicated that the distance between transmitter and receiver was now more than a hundred feet.

Although the woman had shown no sign of getting off the train, Brad hurried the length of both carriages, scanning the platform as he went. After a couple of minutes, he saw the boyish figure, dressed in black leather bomber jacket, Doc Martens and jeans, come out of the ladies' restroom; obviously she had decided against using the cramped facilities on board the train, and had taken the bag with her.

For a heart-stopping moment, Brad feared she might already have delivered the contents of the bag, and kicked himself mentally for not having kept an even closer eye on her. But, reassuringly, the tiny green dot appeared at one end of the Watchman's screen, and moved slowly towards the centre.

Except for brief halts at Kisvarda and Zahony, the train would not stop again until they reached the Ukrainian border, so Brad took the opportunity to catnap, his earpiece firmly in place. On the line between sleeping and waking, his mind ranged over the events of the past few weeks. Going into Russia, ostensibly as a tourist, to find Volkov, had been his own idea, and it had taken some time and effort to convince his superiors that it was worth doing. Once persuaded, though, they made it quite clear that if he failed, his neck was on the block. For some time now, Brad knew they'd been eager to get rid of him, that his very existence had become an embarrassment. Bastards probably hoped he'd get shot by some Russian mafioso, so they'd never need to hear of him again. Half-asleep, Brad smiled grimly to himself. They'd even probably managed to kid themselves the Seminon fiasco was all his fault too!

Every few minutes, he would jerk himself awake and glance at the monitor. For an hour, the little green dot stayed where it was. Then, as the train drew nearer to the border, Brad saw it move towards the centre of the screen. The pitch of the electronic tone in his earpiece heightened. His quarry was on the move!

She was in her early twenties, attractive in a waiflike, slightly butch way. Brad had seen plenty of similarly-dressed young women on the streets of European cities during the past two weeks, but this one was prettier than most, delicately-built, and with the face of a street-wise angel. She strode the length of the carriage, and swung past him, almost catching him on the side of the head with the battered leather bag which she carried slung casually from one shoulder.

Brad hunched himself over the map he had bought in Budapest. He was as certain as he could be that even if she had noticed the well-dressed man outside the bank, she wouldn't match him up with the scruffy tourist in parka and backpack that he had become, but he wasn't about to take any chances. The green dot travelled across the screen and stopped; Brad leaned over to see into the next carriage. It was the dining car. Some time later, she retraced her steps.

The train was held up for an hour at the Ukrainian border town of Cop, and everyone's tickets and documents minutely examined by very young, granite-faced guards. Ahead of them, further east, Brad could see the forbidding bulk of the Carpathians, capped with snow. Eventually the train started moving again, winding its way slowly through the mountains towards Lvov. The light was just starting to fade as the train started to slow at the approach to the junction where the line to Minsk branched off to the north. But instead of regaining speed, the train ran slower and slower, its air brakes hissing as it lost speed.

Brad lowered the window and leaned out. The line snaked round in a wide bend, and he could see some way ahead. There was a level crossing a few hundred yards on. A truck was stalled across the line. His pulse suddenly racing, Brad glanced the length of the carriage to check that the woman was still there. She was gone! Just as the train slid finally to a halt, the earpiece started to bleep shrilly.

Brad grabbed the Watchman and his backpack and raced for the door. He wrenched the window down. Way up at the front of the train, he could see a knot of people gathered, gesticulating, between the engine and the truck. Every instinct told him this was no ordinary incident. Swiftly scanning the landscape, he was just in time to catch sight of the crouched figure running for cover in the dense woodland. He reached outside to open the door, flung out his backpack and leapt down on to the gravel.

The air was sharply cold, and Brad was suddenly glad of his parka. He raced for the trees, keeping watch for the shining silver cap of hair, as visible as a rabbit's scut in the rapidly-gathering dusk. Unaware that she was being followed, the woman darted through the forest clearly confident of where she was going. Behind him, Brad heard the train start up and resume its journey towards Kiev.

The forest thinned, and, a few hundred yards ahead, the girl stopped at a narrow country road. After a quick glance in both directions, she crouched down in the undergrowth, invisible to any passer-by. Brad crept with jungle stealth until he was within sixty feet of her, then he too settled down to wait. In a few minutes, the truck that had stopped the train appeared round a bend in the road, a dilapidated farm vehicle, with a high-sided, open back, full of rusting implements and bales of hay. The girl stood up and ran to meet her accomplice.

Brad followed hard on her heels, making the most of the thinning cover, so that the girl had no idea he was following her. The door to the cab of the truck jammed, and she had to put the bag down and heave with both hands to open it. It took Brad scarcely two seconds to vault over the tailgate and flatten himself among the hay bales and harrows. The idling engine spluttered, and the truck set off again.

It was dark by the time they arrived at an isolated scatter of deserted buildings, unlit and uninhabited. The truck turned in through the vast door of an old barn and juddered to a halt. Brad stayed motionless, his flechette pistol in his hand, as the driver opened his door and jumped down. Brad raised his head just enough to see the man, who slammed the door and came round as if to unload something from the back. He never made it. A tiny hiss, and the deadly flechette found its target in his throat. The man fell to the ground, kicking and writhing for a second or two, then silence.

Brad leapt over the side of the truck, and came face to face with the stunned girl. She caught sight of her friend, and just had time to scream, 'Kolya!', when Brad grabbed her by the throat and slammed her up against the side of the truck, the pistol jammed into her belly.

'You speak English?' She nodded. 'Good, because I don't speak German. Where are you taking the money?'

The huge blue eyes gazed steadily into his, and he felt the ridges of her windpipe rise and fall under his hand as she swallowed, before replying, 'I shall not tell you anything.' Her accent was heavily German, the voice curiously rough-edged.

'You want to play tough? OK, we'll play tough.' Still the wide blue gaze never faltered. She was trained, this one, and trained well. It would be a challenge to break her. And Brad enjoyed a challenge.

Still keeping the pistol rammed firmly into her stomach, he released her throat, and took a length of nylon cord from his pocket. 'Hands over your head!' he ordered.

'No!' she spat.

He hit her sharply in the mouth with the barrel of the pistol. Only a muffled yelp escaped her, but she obeyed him and raised her hands. He grabbed both her wrists in one hand and swiftly tied her hands together, securing them to the door handle above her head. Even with blood trickling down her chin, she still glared at him.

'Damn you!' she cursed. 'You can do what you like. But you won't make me talk.'

Brad only chuckled. He turned on the truck's lights, illuminating the squalid, debris-filled barn, and sat down on the floor a few feet in front of the insolently defiant girl.

'I have plenty of time,' he said. 'I can wait.'

Nonchalantly, whistling quietly to himself, he carefully inspected the flechette pistol, then cleaned it, laid out and counted his ammunition. Painstakingly but efficiently he checked and then repacked all his equipment.

'Always a good idea to take care of your things, don't you think?' he remarked conversationally. Still the girl remained silent. 'You don't have a whole lot to lose any more. Your driver friend's dead. I have the money. I have the time. What do you have?'

'Nothing, as you say,' the girl muttered.

'Except the name of the guy you're taking the money to.'

'I don't know any name.'

'Sure you do. C'mon, you can tell me.'

'I said, I don't know any name.'

Brad sighed and got to his feet. 'You want to do this the hard way, huh?' He held his pistol to her head.

'You can shoot me, if you wish. Why don't you do it?' The girl looked levelly at Brad, contempt burning in her eyes like acid. 'I have told you, I do not know any name.'

Whoever had trained this girl had made a good job of it. She had the sort of guts and coolness he looked for in his own team. What a waste of a good operative!

'All you have to do is tell me who you work for.'

There was no answer.

Brad took a length of piano wire from his pack, tied it round the door handle, brought it down to encircle the slender neck and secured the other end with the first.

'You know this trick, I guess? Sure, they'd have taught you. So, you'll know that all I have to do is kick your feet away, and it's goodnight, sweetheart!'

'So do it, damn you!' the girl spat.

'I may. And then again, I may not,' Brad said softly. 'Or we could find some other games to play. Like I said, I have the time.'

He grasped both lengths of piano wire just above the girl's head. There was so little slack that even that slight pressure caused the wire to bite; she gasped and pulled her weight up on her bound wrists, stretching her head back to lessen the pain as blood seeped into the neck of her shirt. After a few seconds, Brad let the wire relax.

'Want me to do that again?'

There is always a moment when a skilled interrogator knows that something has snapped inside his prey. There was no visible change in the young woman, but Brad sensed it, and grinned. 'OK,' he coaxed her. 'How about we start with you? Who are you?'

'Helga Steinberg.'

'So, Helga, how does a nice girl like you come to be mixed up in all this?'

'Schneider – at the bank. My sister is – his girlfriend.'

Brad laughed out loud. 'The guy's even more of a player than I thought! I hope he's been paying you well. How much do you reckon he's making out of this?'

The girl only closed her eyes weakly. If she shook her head, the wire would cut her painfully.

'Doesn't matter. Now, Helga, who gets the half million every three months?'

'My people.'

'You're going to have to do a little better than that. Who are your people?'

The girl was struggling to speak. Brad went on, 'Do you know Boris Volkov?' The nod was almost imperceptible; the girl's teeth were gritted against the pain, and tears were starting to run down her face.

'So it's Volkov who gets the money?'

'Nein,' the girl whispered, losing control of herself and reverting to her native tongue.

Brad thought for a moment. 'So you know Volkov. But Volkov doesn't get the money. Is he one of your people?'

'He – works –' she winced, struggling to speak through her agony.

'He works for your people? So all you have to do is tell me where to find them, and you can be out of all this.'

In spite of the biting wire, the white-blonde head drooped.

'Sorry about this, sweetheart,' Brad sighed, and kicked her feet out from under her.

He lost no time in taking her weight off her feet before she throttled. 'C'mon, sweetheart,' he growled, rolling her head from side to side, as blood oozed down the pale throat.

After a few moments, the unfocused eyes fluttered open. 'Just tell me who,' Brad whispered.

'Si – Sidorov.'

'And where.'

'Not far – the old – upholstery factory –'

Brad reckoned he'd have to settle for that. He wouldn't get any more from her, and it was time to get out of there anyway. 'OK, sweetheart,' he said, letting the girl slump for the last time. Her horrible gurgle lasted only a second.

Deftly, he unhooked the pathetic little corpse from the door, and let it fall. Mounting the step to the cab, Brad noticed a suspicious-looking swelling in the front of the young woman's jeans. Curious, he jumped down and undid the zipper, to be greeted by the sight of an erect penis. So little Helga was a trans-sexual, but only halfway there! What a hell of a way, Brad marvelled, to earn the money for the surgery!

28.

Brad spent the rest of the night in the truck, hidden in the edge of the thick woodland a couple of miles down the road. The timer on his watch vibrated to waken him at first light.The flat fields and trackless woodland were all grey in the chilly April dawn, and the air felt raw, almost icy. Summer would be a long time coming.

• • •

The truck's ancient engine spat and spluttered, and died a few times. Brad cursed, yanked out the choke and revved furiously. Reluctantly, the engine turned over, and within minutes he was on the road. Reckoning that Helga and her Russian friend had been heading in the direction of their final destination, he continued on down the same road. He translated 'Not far' as five miles, and decided that if by then he hadn't found anything that could be described as an old upholstery factory, he would go back and try another road. His instinct about which way to go proved right.

The village, which was too small to appear on his Hungarian map, had seen better days, and was now ramshackle and poverty-stricken. A couple of dispirited-looking shops were open for business, otherwise most of the buildings were actually derelict. Brad drove cautiously along the deserted main street, his eyes peeled for the upholstery factory. Leaving the town again on the far side, he caught sight of a dilapidated blocklike building, with a faded, barely-visible painting of a bedstead high up on one wall. He drove on a little way, and parked out of sight behind a tumble-down pile of rotting planks and corrugated iron. There was no one around, and he was able to double back unseen through a squalid wasteland of neglected vegetable plots and the remains of partly-demolished jerry-built houses.

He circled the factory with practised stealth. Every window was completely boarded up, and there was only one door, certain to be locked.

The drainpipes were hanging from the gutters, having long ago parted company from their rusted brackets. Brad patiently scanned the rear wall, to see if the rain-rotted brickwork would afford the narrow hand and footholds he needed. His gaze kept returning to an ugly vertical buttress which ran the height of the building. He took a chance, ran over to it, and tapped it gently with his knuckles. Damn, he was right! It wasn't part of the building at all!

It was a cleverly-disguised air-conditioning duct, its metal cladding painted to look like the rest of the rotting exterior. And it was held firmly to the wall with heavy, iron brackets. As he swarmed up the duct, Brad could hear a faint roar, which told him the air-conditioning was working. In under a minute, he had reached the roof.

Once there, it was clear that money had been spent on the building. The roof was covered with newish watertight asphalt, and the skylights had obviously been installed only recently. Brad inched over to one, and looked down. What he saw took his breath away.

Twenty feet below lay a stunning modern scientific laboratory, its gleaming work surfaces covered with every imaginable piece of equipment and gadgetry. Two men in white lab coats were checking figures on a computer; otherwise, the place appeared to be deserted. But Brad was taking no chances. The two men he could see, preoccupied as they were, could be easily dealt with, but there were bound to be others around, maybe even security guards.

Silently and swiftly, he climbed back down the metal duct. He took a small gas cylinder and a coil of nylon tubing from his backpack, and crept round to the door. As he'd thought, it was locked. But it was an old door, peeling and blistered, and so warped that there was a gap at the bottom. Only the lock, gleaming against the battered wood, looked new.

Brad swiftly inserted one end of the nylon tubing under the door; the other fitted neatly over a nozzle on the gas cylinder. He stuck a small timed explosive charge to the door near the lock. The whole procedure took less than ten seconds. He broke the seal over the valve switch, pressed it and, flattening himself back against the wall, quickly put on a mask with a short-term supply of compressed air.

Soon the silence of the building was shattered by shouts and running feet, and Brad could hear a furious banging at the boarded-up windows. It didn't last long. Whoever was inside the building succumbed quickly to the invisible nerve gas.

'C'mon, c'mon!' Brad whispered tensely. The timed explosive blew the lock. Flechette gun in hand, he kicked the door in, and ran into the lab. Just inside the door, he found a huddled, unconscious figure in a white coat. He turned it over with his foot; a squarish face with receding fair hair gazed blankly up at him. Not Volkov. Brad stuck a cyanide patch on the man's neck. Two men, both armed with machine pistols, lay unconscious in the aisle between the workbenches.

Brad ran up the stairs two at a time. Upstairs, the rooms had been turned into dormitories, with showers and a kitchenette, every window sealed with breezeblocks but plastered over and painted inside. The rooms were littered with unconscious people, some half-dressed, some sprawled across the beds. In one room, a pornographic video was playing; the guards had obviously been engrossed in it. On the stairs, Brad turned over a tall dark-haired figure wearing a white lab coat. He recognised the face he had been shown in photo briefings. The wide-staring eyes were unmistakeably green.

He stripped off Volkov's lab coat, hauled the man's inert weight as far as the door, applied an antidote patch to his neck and left him just out of sight inside the building, while he dashed back through the wreckage of the village outskirts to retrieve the truck. He was no more than halfway there when he felt, rather than heard, the familiar whump-whump-whump of helicopter rotors. He took cover, and watched.

All round him, the weeds and scrub were flattened in the downdraft as the helicopter hovered in the yard in front of the factory. Even before it touched down, Brad was running, crouched close to the ground like a hare; he was in position by the time the aircraft landed and the rotors slowed. The pilot had scarcely taken a couple of paces when a flechette found its target, and he crumpled to the ground.

The passenger, a heavily-built woman in a Burberry raincoat, had already started to walk purposefully towards the factory, apparently annoyed at the lack of a formal reception, and unaware of what was happening behind her. Brad followed her, waited until she had gone in through the door. As she stood there, amazed to find the lab silent, peopled only by the dead, her broad back presented a target Brad couldn't miss. In a couple of seconds, she too lay lifeless on the floor.

Scarcely able to believe his luck, Brad wasted no time in retrieving the hold-all from the truck, and threw it into the helicopter. Then he hauled the unconscious scientist across the yard, manhandled him into the passenger seat and buckled the safety belt. He risked one more minute, running back to the lab to wrench off the dead woman's Burberry raincoat.

He scrambled into the cockpit, and started the rotor blades. Just as the helicopter lifted from the ground, pitching slightly as it rose to avoid some overhead cables, he felt a sharp impact on the metal skin. Darting a swift glance downwards, he saw men running across the compound from the neighbouring buildings. Damn! He should have known those deserted-looking buildings would be occupied by guards! Some of the men were armed with AK-47s, which they fired at the swiftly-rising helicopter, hitting it a few times. One even tried vainly to fire at it with a heavy, outdated Nagant pistol. But, to his alarm, Brad realised that one of them was carrying a hand-held rocket-launcher. Even in the few seconds it took for the man to kneel, position the rocket-launcher on his shoulder and aim, Brad managed to force the helicopter a long way up, and fast.

He flinched as the rocket shot past the helicopter, leaving a black snake of vapour as it flew, and thanked his lucky stars that it wasn't a heat-seeking missile. If it had been, they wouldn't have stood a chance.

Far below them, the frantically-milling figures slowed down to watch them go, dwindling almost to invisibility among the match-box-sized houses. Safe for the time being, Brad swung the helicopter round and headed towards the Hungarian border.

• • •

As he flew, Brad kept an eye on the pale, motionless figure slumped against the door. After half an hour in the air, he put the helicopter on automatic pilot, leaned over and turned the man's head towards him, gently slapping his face. The effect of the paralysing gas hadn't quite worn off, so Brad busied himself concealing a transmitter in the collar of the Burberry raincoat.

After a few minutes, Boris started to come to; he muttered something in Russian. For a second, the green eyes struggled to focus, then closed again. Again Brad leaned over. Keeping a firm hold of Boris's shirt collar, he pushed his head forward, well over to one side. He was only just in time.The Russian threw up violently. Brad hauled him back to a sitting position. He waited a few minutes longer. Eventually Volkov groaned and opened his eyes. Again he mumbled in Russian.

'We'll have to talk in English,' Brad told him, handing him a fistful of Kleenex. 'I'm Colonel Brad Foster, US Special Forces.'

'Why – are you here?' Boris struggled, as he coughed and spat into the paper tissues.

'To find you.'

Dazed, Boris looked down at the flat Ukrainian landscape. 'Where is this?'

'We're about a half hour west of that place I just hauled you out of.'

'I never knew where it was. I was taken there, blindfold.'

'Can't say I know where it was either. Some half-assed place that's not even on the map. Someplace south-west of Kiev.' He jerked his head in the direction of the looming mountains ahead of them. 'See those? They're the Carpathians. Hungary's just the other side.'

'Is that where we're going?'

'Wait and see.'

Brad uncapped a bottle of water and held it out. Boris drained it greedily.

'There are so many questions,' he said at last.

Brad resumed control of the helicopter. 'I'm taking you back to the States,' he said curtly. A look of acute fear flickered in the Russian's eyes. 'Remember a dud formula you sold for twenty million bucks? Well, they're prepared to let bygones be bygones, so long as you can sort out a few problems.'

'Even here, I have heard of the problems. I knew a long time ago that the formula caused aggression in animals. But the other problems: I knew nothing about those. You must understand – I was forced to act as I did.'

'Just following orders, huh?'

'Exactly.' Boris's voice was bitter.

'What was that place back there, anyway?' Brad asked. 'And what's your involvement?'

Boris leaned back, his colour starting to return. 'It's a long story,' he sighed.

'Last we heard, you left the States with twenty million dollars of Pharmavax's money in cash. What happened after that?'

'I deposited the money in a bank in Vienna, as I had been instructed. Then I went back to Moscow. But when I got there, I found that my boss, Viktor Malakhin, had mysteriously disappeared. He knew that I was unhappy about taking the formula to sell to the Americans, but he was my friend. He'd always protected me. Well, he had been replaced by someone who wanted to get rid of me. He gave me a choice. I could be eliminated. Or I could spend the rest of my life in a labour camp somewhere I'd never heard of. Or I could come down here and work for his friend Sidorov.'

'And who exactly is this Sidorov?'

'Mafia. It was arranged that Sidorov could have access to the twenty million in Vienna whenever he wanted it. Some of it undoubtedly found its way to my new KGB boss. You could say I was sold into slavery. I lived in that place for months, never going out once. This is the first time I have seen what the world outside looks like.'

'You mean you slept there, ate there?'

'Yes. Upstairs there were bedrooms, and washrooms. We slept at night under armed guard. And we were told that if one of us tried to escape, the others would be shot. That is a strong inducement to stay.'

'Couldn't you have all banded together in some way? Overpowered the guards?'

Boris sighed. 'We had no money, not a rouble between us. They had confiscated all our papers. Even our clothes had been taken. Clean things were provided whenever we wanted them, but they didn't belong to us. Even if we'd managed to get out, we couldn't have got far. Most of the other buildings were converted into labs, or housing. There was even a barracks for the security men who patrolled the whole compound. For several months – I've lost count – I have known exactly what it was to live like a laboratory rat.'

'So what kind of work were you doing?'

'Designer drugs. You know – psycho-active agents, like second-generation crack cocaine, ecstasy. It's big business now.'

'So I've heard. But, as a serious scientist, how do you square that with your conscience? Or don't you KGB guys have any such thing?'

'Sure we do, but I have no taste for being a dead hero. At least this way I'm still alive. And I have not surrendered quite as passively as you might think. I've left a nice little time bomb there. I programmed the computers so that the files which contain the manufacturing details will self-destruct if I don't update them every week.'

'Cute,' Brad grinned.

'How did you get me out?' Boris asked suddenly. 'I hope no-one got hurt.'

'Course not. They're all fine. So, back to Sidorov and these Mafia guys. Where'd they all spring from?'

'Have you heard of the Uralmash group? They split off from that.'

'Means nothing to me.'

'The Uralmash had a lucrative scam going in rare metals. You know we used to have closed cities, like Chelyabinsk-65?'

'A sort of scientists' colony?'

Boris nodded. 'After 1989, there was no need for such places. So whole cities of scientists were just thrown out. Do you know how much a good researcher earns now? A hundred dollars a month. Which means life is pretty bleak. It's hard for them not to try to make a bit more money by selling strategic metals, such as osmium or boron or any of the others used in nuclear power plants, when they know that just one gram can fetch seventy thousand dollars from a Swedish company.'

'I can't believe the Swedes would buy their raw materials that way. They're squeaky clean.'

'Oh, they don't buy direct. Moscow is heavily involved.'

'Officially, or unofficially?'

'Both. But they disguise their involvement by shipping things through Eastern bloc countries. For instance, Moscow might set up a deal whereby a Western company puts up a loan to develop a new company here in Russia. By way of collateral, a certain amount of the requisite rare metal is deposited in a Swiss bank. Then the company that received the development loan goes bankrupt, and the Western company claims its collateral, having paid less than it would have had to on the open market. All legal and above board, and everybody's happy.'

'And the KGB has a hand in it all, I suppose?'

'Of course. When I first went to Pharmavax, I told them I wanted to get out of Russia because things were so bad. It was a lie at the time, but that was a year ago. It wouldn't be a lie now. One way and another, the whole country is effectively being run by the mob.'

'Don't the authorities clamp down?'

'What authorities?' the Russian sneered bitterly. 'The banks? The police? The mob own them. They're not stupid. Russia, my motherland, home of the Tsars, is up for grabs. There are places where the gangs own just about everything, and control all the natural resources. Every year scientific know-how is exported, indiscriminately, to anyone who'll pay the price. And as many as eight out of ten private companies pay protection money, sometimes as much as half their profits.'

'Why do they do it?'

'It's not just the threat of murder, or damage to their property, though that's bad enough. They don't want to get into the hands of the fiscal police and end up paying huge taxes. Effectively, the police are in the pay of the mob. And they have ex-KGB people working for them as well.'

'For someone who's been locked up for so long, you seem surprisingly up to date with what's been going on.'

'We had television, satellite channels, videos – hard porn, if we wanted. The guards used to watch it. And whenever a new person joined us, they brought news.'

'I read someplace that a lot of these scams are almost tribal.'

'That's true. In St Petersburg, the Chechens control all the counterfeiting. The Azeris run the markets and the small drug traders. In fact, the group who started that lab with the Uralmash are Azeri.'

'And they're just as bad down here in Ukraine, I guess.'

'Independence hasn't done much for the people here. They have to live,' Boris replied dully.

'Well, you'll soon be back in the States. We Americans may have our faults, but we haven't gotten that bad yet.'

'Where will you take me in the US?' The Russian's apprehension had returned.

'The CIA and the FBI will both want to spend a little time with you, I guess. Then they'll have to make sure you're all nice and legal. After that, I guess they'll send you over to Pharmavax to work on the antidote.'

'I thought, perhaps, I might work for your government. After all, they had the formula first.'

'You heard how they lost it?'

'I was responsible for that.'

'You?' Brad shouted. 'One of the great unsolved mysteries of our time, and the guy says, "I was responsible for that"!'

'I wasn't always a scientist. After I returned from MIT, I was trained in industrial espionage. I ran the government's industrial espionage unit for a while.'

'Was that as Boris Volkov? Or were you Ivan Kandinsky then?'

'I see you know all about that.'

'The guys in suits have been keeping tabs on you all the way, Boris. By the way, is Boris your real name?'

'Yes, Boris – Boris Volkov,' he said distractedly. 'The formula was never supposed to go to a government laboratory. It was always intended that it should go to an American pharmaceutical company. Trouble is that they don't have their own crack espionage units, so we had to get the military to steal it – and then get it into the right hands once it was in the US.

'You see, we knew the vaccine was flawed. The original research was all mine, and I warned the bosses how dangerous it was. But they took a gamble that a company like Pharmavax would work more quickly than a government lab, who would take years to develop the product. Of course, had NIH discovered what the flaws were, the vaccine would never have been marketed. And my bosses wouldn't be able to sell the antidote for hard currency, which was how they intended to recoup the money they had spent on the vaccine – and of course make a lot more. I was furious when I found out what they were going to do. But they own you. They can do what they like.'

'So when they found out their plan had gone wrong, they sent you in to wreck NIH's data, and then sell the formula to Pharmavax. Pretty damn cool!'

'It wasn't hard. NIH's security is good, but not impossible to get past. And Pharmavax just heard what they wanted to hear. Greed can do that.'

'It wasn't Montgomery's fault entirely. They were under a hell of a lot of pressure from our Administration to get results.'

'So perhaps your bosses aren't so very different from ours?' Boris observed wrily.

Brad's reply was drowned by the shrill crackle of the helicopter's radio. A man's peevish voice was asking the same question repeatedly in Russian. 'I don't speak Russian,' Brad hissed. 'What do they want?'

Boris grabbed the headset, and listened to the frantic conversation. 'The security guards at the lab have reported that their helicopter has been stolen. Also, they say everybody at the lab is dead.' He swung round, green eyes blazing. 'You lied to me!'

Brad shrugged. 'What did you expect?'

Boris turned back to the headset, and listened for a few more minutes, his face furrowed in concentration. Brad watched him sharply. 'What else are they saying?' he demanded.

'The bosses are furious. They've sent a helicopter gunship to track us down.' Boris struggled to concentrate on the shouted exchange through the static. 'Correction. To shoot us down, I should have said. It took off a few minutes ago and is heading towards the border, fast.'

'Do you know where it's coming from? How long do we have?'

'I've flown those big MI-24s – what you call a Hind. It's a clear day, flat terrain; they'll maintain their top speed easily. Some of the old military air-bases are now in private hands. There are several places it could come from.'

'Try and find out where it is, OK?' snapped Brad, and pushed the helicopter to its highest speed, scanning the forest beneath for somewhere to put down. He could see the railway line snaking east-west below them, and set a course to follow it.

'Best get out of this thing as soon as we can, then.'

'How will we go on, if we do that?'

'I have it all planned. I even brought along a raincoat for you.'

'Good. I'm freezing.' Boris was wearing only a garish man-made-fibre sweater over a check shirt, and lightweight polyester trousers. 'These disgusting clothes are not what I normally wear, you know.'

'They'll have to do for now. I want to put down someplace this side of the border, then get to a train and travel to Budapest. Then we'll fly to the States.'

'Just like that?'

'Sure. I have all the documentation you'll need, and an American Express Gold Card. To say nothing of half a million bucks in cash. Come to think of it, the mob'll be sore about that too.'

'So you met Helga and Kolya?'

'Briefly.'

There was silence for a few minutes. They were flying over dense forest now. Brad was looking for somewhere, not too far from the railway, to land.

Boris said, 'Helga and Kolya – did you kill them?'

Brad shrugged. 'It happens,' he said.

'Helga – she used to be Holger – was ex-Stasi. He – she – knew what to expect. But Kolya was just a driver, a decent sort. He had a wife and a child, a little girl. He used to bring her sometimes, in the truck. You shouldn't have killed him.'

'You're not so squeaky clean yourself, Volkov,' Brad snapped, annoyed at the Russian's display of sentiment. 'If you hadn't done that dud research in the first place and let your bosses make it available to us, and if you hadn't then sold it to Morton Montgomery, you'd have saved everybody a hell of a lot of grief, me included. Did you know some cowboy outfit somewhere's found a way to replicate the stuff? Your vaccine's out on the streets!'

Boris leaned back in his seat and sighed, his eyes closed. 'That was my worst fear. That it would somehow find its way out in to the world.' He pulled himself together. 'Has there been much violence?'

'I haven't paid too much attention just recently. There was a TV special in Austria about the increase in rape and domestic violence this year alone. And I guess there've been other pieces in the media in other countries. You'll get the full story on that from Pharmavax when we get back to Washington. And on the burn-out, of course.'

'Burn-out? What sort of burn-out?'

'Sexual. After a few months, your wonder drug turns guys off sex. Did you know that? Might even make them impotent for life.'

Boris laughed bitterly. 'Now I understand! I've been caged up with a dozen people, half of them women, and I haven't felt the slightest interest. And I thought it was because I didn't fancy them. Russian women aren't like American women; after a certain age, they lose their looks. Raisa Gorbacheva is an exception. But even if I had been locked up with Julia Roberts or Michelle Pfeiffer, now I think about it, I couldn't have done anything! I'd put it down to the strain and stress of being held prisoner, and worrying if I'd ever be free.'

'So you took it too, huh? Wasn't that kinda stupid?'

'I was arrogant. I had such faith in my ability as a scientist that I gave myself a shot. All through medical history, you'll find that almost every real advance has been tried out first by its inventor. But if I had waited until I saw the results of the long-term animal testing, I would have destroyed every drop of the vaccine, all my records, everything, rather than let such a plague loose in the world. There is nothing you can imagine that my government could have done to me that would have made me obey them. If I'd only known,' he finished grimly.

'Well, back in the States, you'll have your chance to set things right. I had a shot not so long ago, so I have a personal interest in seeing you succeed,' Brad said drily.

'I can only apologise,' was all Boris said.

Brad took the helicopter down low and skimmed the tops of the trees. Every minute or so he scanned the skies, as well as relying on the formidable array of instruments and radar with which the Russian helicopter was equipped.

'Looks like your friends have found us,' he observed.

Boris twisted round in his seat. High above, a massive MI-24 gunship, gleaming evilly in the cold morning sunlight, was gaining on them rapidly.

'What range do their rockets have?' Brad snapped.

'Let's just say we're well within it,' the Russian answered drily. 'They'll have heat-seeking missiles and laser targeting. Time to say your prayers, colonel.'

'No way!' Brad grunted, and took the helicopter, dangerously, lower still. A sharp intake of breath was the only indication that Boris was nervous, as they practically brushed the treetops. 'If they can hit us so easily,' Brad muttered, 'why the fuck don't they shoot?'

'Because they may not actually have seen us,' Boris answered. 'The pilot may well be relying on radar, rather than using his eyes. And we are flying very low.'

'Not low enough. I want to ditch this baby.'

In the midst of the trackless mass of woodland, dense even though it was still leafless, Brad caught sight of a squarish clearing; it looked as though it was less than a mile from the railway track. Ahead of them – some distance away over rough terrain – he could just see a small town, where sooner or later a train was bound to stop.

No sooner had he seen the clearing than they had overshot it; Brad swung the helicopter in a wide circle, always keeping a wary eye on the great MI-24 overhead, and approached the tiny clearing a second time. The place was deserted, the only sign of human activity a few vehicle tracks in the lumpy grass. Within minutes, Brad had skilfully and neatly set the helicopter down. He grabbed his backpack, the hold-all and the Burberry raincoat.

'C'mon, Volkov! Get moving!'

'Where are we going?' the KGB man stuttered.

'No questions! Just haul ass!'

He hustled the reluctant Boris out of the helicopter, across the open ground and into the cover of the trees. The Russian stumbled clumsily over the tussocky grass.

'Don't they train you guys in the KGB? Run, dammit!'

'I'm not as fit as I was,' Boris panted. 'I haven't taken any proper exercise for months. I'm not up to this!' As they gained the shelter of the trees, he gasped, 'I must rest. Please!'

And this was the guy Jill had said was so damned 'drop-dead gorgeous'? She should see him now! 'No time,' Brad snapped. 'If they have heat-sensing targeting devices, we're just as vulnerable down here as up there. Move it!'

Brad walked at a swift lope through the undergrowth, pausing every few hundred yards to wait for the breathless Russian, who crashed along panting behind him in an ungainly fashion.

Their path ran diagonally towards the railway line.

The enormous gunship swooped low, hovered over the clearing and made several wide swings over the surrounding forest. After what felt like an eternity, it rose into the sky, and sped off back the way it had come.

'So how do you account for that, Volkov?'

Boris laughed grimly. 'I can only think that the Mafia bosses are being ripped off by their own pilots. They could easily have sold the radar and the targeting devices for hard currency. I wouldn't want to be in that pilot's shoes when he's found out.'

'A bullet through the back of the head, huh?'

'Very probably.'

The two men made their way onwards, always bearing west, and occasionally veering slightly to the south. As before, every few hundred yards, Brad had to wait for Boris to catch up with him. Suddenly, they were brought up short by a wire fence, twelve feet high, which stretched away into the forest in both directions as far as they could see. Every alternate concrete upright carried a steel plate with the international sign for "High voltage", a red lightning-flash, and – for added emphasis – a crudely-stencilled skull and crossbones.

'What do we do now?' Boris asked apprehensively.

'We call their bluff. You don't believe everything you read, do you?'

For a moment, Brad listened carefully, his ear close to one of the fence supports. There was no faint hum of electrical current that he could hear. Then he took a coil of fine nylon rope and a bottle of drinking water out of his backpack, soaked the cord, secured one end to a fallen branch and threw the other end, weighted with a short but heavy stick, high over the fence. The expected crackle, as the cord hit the fence, never came. Calmly, Brad pulled the wet line down from the fence, rolled it up and put it away.

'I guess they never paid their electricity bills,' he remarked drily, heaving on the wire fence with his bare hands to test it for strength. 'After you.'

'No,' Boris protested. 'I'll never make it. It's too high.'

'Tell you what. Rather than sit here all day arguing about it, why don't I just shoot you now and have done with it? I'll say you tried to escape. A helluva lot of people would be only too happy to thank me for a job well done.' Brad levelled his gun at Boris. 'Now, are you going to move?'

'OK, OK. You don't have to shoot me.' It took an age, but somehow Boris hauled himself up the concrete fence post, over the top wire and down the other side.

'Christ, Volkov, you wouldn't last thirty seconds at Quantico!' Brad was over and down the other side in seconds.

The two men set off again, always bearing towards the railway track. Boris seemed to be managing better now; he was walking more quietly and less clumsily, not complaining, and keeping up with Brad.

Suddenly, Brad froze. A few yards behind him, Boris dropped out of sight into the undergrowth. Barely fifty yards ahead, two armed guards were lighting cigarettes and chatting.

For ten minutes, Brad and Boris crouched unseen, and eventually the guards wandered off. Brad stood, warily, and beckoned to Boris to catch him up. 'Think you can manage not to fall over your own feet?' he asked. Boris nodded. They moved on quietly but encountered no more guards. A few minutes later, Brad froze again.

'Do you see what I see?' he whispered.

'Yes. It's a T-72,' Boris answered. 'In fact, it's a great many T-72s.'

From the air they would have been invisible. Even at a range of a hundred yards or so, it wasn't easy to see them. Lined up as precisely as apple trees in an orchard, ranged in perfect lines as far as they could see, were hundreds of Soviet tanks, their barrels all precisely angled like the swords of a guard of honour at a military wedding.

'What sort of place is this? What have you dragged me into?' Boris whispered fearfully.

'What I think it is, is a storage compound for ex-Warsaw Pact weapons.'

'But I thought we were supposed to have got rid of all those.'

'Sure. But you didn't think the bosses would really do that, did you? Look, you remember the CFE Treaty – Conventional Forces in Europe? It limited the amount of hardware each of the old Cold War enemies was allowed to have. The Soviet bloc had vastly more than the West, so they had more to get rid of. OK, some got scrapped. Some got shipped so far east not even Zhirinovsky and his crazy friends could get their hands on it. But my guess is some got sold off. And what we're looking at is what your Mafia friends are spending their ill-gotten gains on. What's the betting they've got stockpiles of ammunition as well?'

'How do you know all this?' Boris asked in wonderment.

'Right at the end of the Cold War, a whole crowd of us at the Pentagon were asked to take a look at some of the maps and other stuff the East Germans didn't manage to destroy – about 25,000 pieces. All of which proved that the Warsaw Pact countries were armed to the teeth for a first strike with nuclear weapons, despite all their public declarations to the contrary. Caused quite a flurry among the top brass, who'd always believed there'd be a slow build-up to any hostilities in Europe.'

'We, too, in Moscow believed that war would come slowly, in weeks rather than hours,' Boris said gravely. 'OK, military planning was not my line of business, but, even so, we all believed that war would start with conventional weapons, conventional tactics, and that any strategic advantage would be gained at the conference table, before the war escalated to nuclear weapons.' He shivered suddenly. 'Obviously, we were misled.'

'Looks like it,' Brad said drily. 'Well, we have nothing to gain by sitting here in a thorn bush waiting for the Mafia to declare World War Three. I say we get out of here.'

Always bearing slightly to the left, Brad and Boris came eventually to the further perimeter fence. This time Boris scaled it less clumsily. Brad noted with relief that he seemed to have stopped crashing around quite so much. But the improvement didn't last. By the time they had put a few hundred yards between themselves and the arms dump, Boris was making heavy going of the journey once more.

'Can we rest, please?' he panted, his face pale and his eyes sunken with fatigue.

'Not till we get to the railroad,' Brad said, hauling him roughly to his feet.

At last they came to the track. A small road ran alongside it. Brad judged they were getting near a town. He stopped, and handed Boris the dead Mafia boss's Burberry. 'Put this on,' he said. It fitted quite well, being a large size, and with the belt done up Boris looked like a reasonably typical Russian who'd had a stroke of luck. He turned the collar up, glad of the warm woollen lining. Brad handed him the hold-all, since, he reasoned, it would look odd if anyone saw them together and one man was carrying two bags.

It was mid-afternoon by the time they reached Cop. They simply walked through the town to the train station, keeping a few yards between them as though they were complete strangers. At the station, Brad said to Boris, 'You go in first, and look at the rail timetable nearest the ticket window. Don't move from there till I tell you.'

Brad spent several minutes as a bemused tourist with an American Express Gold Card and a passport showing he had spent three weeks in Russia, buying a train ticket. Then he picked up his backpack and sauntered over to consult the same framed timetable as Boris.

'Get a return ticket to Budapest, the 16.40 train,' he whispered. Unseen, he slipped a Hungarian passport and a wad of roubles and forints to Boris. He also handed him a cheap, mass-produced cigarette lighter. 'Put that in your pocket,' he said. 'It'll come in handy later.'

Then he moved along to study another frame, before wandering outside. From the platform he kept an eye on the queue, until Boris turned away from the ticket window, carefully folding his ticket into his passport at the page with the Russian entry stamp, before putting it away in the pocket of his raincoat.

For the next half hour, the two men waited on the same bench, looking for all the world as though they had nothing to do with each other. At last a raucously incomprehensible loudspeaker announced the arrival of the Kiev-Budapest train, and they got on. They found two facing seats in a smoking compartment, stowed their bags and settled down. The train pulled out of the station.

Brad waited until they were well over the border before pulling out a pack of Camels, ostentatiously searching for a lighter. Boris obligingly produced the lighter from the pocket of the Burberry. As he leaned forward to light Brad's cigarette, he whispered, 'You haven't told me what we do when we get to Budapest.'

‘We fly out. I have documentation for you,’ Brad answered, exaggeratedly smiling his thanks for the benefit of anyone who was watching. He drew on the cigarette, which he had no wish to smoke, and offered one to Boris. This little charade meant they could now safely talk if they wanted to.

Once through the mountains the landscape became flat and monotonous again. The afternoon was beginning to darken, and Brad suddenly started to feel the after-effects of a strenuous twenty-four-hour operation with only a few hours’ uneasy sleep. Opposite him Boris, obviously exhausted by the events of the day, was huddled up in his newly-acquired Burberry, sleeping like a dog.The transmitter was securely inside the collar of the raincoat, so if the Russian moved so much as a yard, he would know. He set the Sony Watchman upright on the table in front of him, and made sure the earpiece was working. Then he yielded to the stuffy atmosphere in the train, and fell asleep.

Whenever the train stopped, Brad forced himself to wake up for a few seconds, and make sure that Boris was still asleep in the seat opposite. The Russian never moved. The evening dimmed into darkness, and the lights came on, as the train hurtled westwards across the endless plains of Hungary.

• • •

Brad was woken by a hand shaking his arm. The ticket inspector was standing beside him. He handed over his ticket and passport, and forced himself to stay calm, as he saw that Boris’s seat was empty. A swift glance at the Watchman showed no reassuring green dot. A second later, Brad realised his earpiece was dead.

In a cold fury, he strode to the carriage nearest the engine and, retracing his steps, checked every passenger the whole length of the train. There was no sign of Volkov. Only an open door near the freight van, crashing open and shut with the motion of the train, gave any indication of what might have happened.

Brad returned to his seat, almost sick with rage. All that dopey clumsiness had been no more than a clever act, and Colonel Brad Foster of the A10 Task Force had fallen for it! Even if the guy had been locked up like a rat in a cage for the best part of a year, he had still been trained by the KGB. And they never forgot a trick.

Within twenty four hours, Brad was going to have some hard questions to answer. Not least, how he had managed to lose Boris Volkov, former head of the KGB's Industrial Espionage Unit, first on the FBI and CIA's Most Wanted list, in Eastern Europe with a specially-provided Hungarian passport. And half a million dollars in cash!

29.

'Pharmavax's time is up. We've laid it on the line for them: develop an antidote, with or without Volkov, or we seize your assets and close you down. We've told them to call a strategy meeting first thing Monday March thirty-one. We want you there, Foster. Nine a.m.'

Jill was almost asleep when the telephone rang.

'I'm back,' Brad said.

'How'd it go?'

There was a heavy sigh, followed by silence. Jill hauled herself up on one elbow and brushed the hair back from her face.

'Brad? What happened?'

'I screwed up. First time ever. And the last. They won't give me another chance.'

'I know you can't tell me what you were up to –'

'Don't see why not. Can I come over for an hour or so? I won't stay, though. I'm bushed.'

'OK.'

• • •

Jill had never known Brad tired or dispirited, and was shocked to see him looking so drawn. Clearly, there was more involved here than just a demanding mission. She quickly poured him a drink, and curled up at one end of the couch, as he started to talk. But within seconds she was sitting bolt upright, amazed at what she was hearing.

'They sent you in to kidnap Boris Volkov? I don't believe it!'

'You'd better. Because I found him. Damn it, I had him! Then I lost him.'

For the first time, as Brad told Jill about his three weeks in Austria, she began to have an inkling of just how he operated. She could sense that he was leaving out a lot, but decided that if he wasn't going to tell her, she didn't want to hear it anyway.

'So tell me about Volkov,' she insisted. 'What did you make of him?'

'The guy's good. And that's what I forgot for a moment, that he'd been KGB trained, one of their top operatives. I'm so damned angry with myself!' Brad drained his glass, scowling.

'How did he get away?'

'Same way the ex-Stasi courier almost did. I wasn't about to let that happen again, so I'd covered all the angles. I'd wired him, but he must have guessed. Whenever the train stopped at a station, I was awake and watching him the whole time. But – and I'd really like to know how he did it – he managed to find and disarm the transmitter in the raincoat while I was asleep, and jumped the train. With five hundred thousand bucks, in cash. I just came from the Pentagon, and I have to tell you Colonel Foster is not exactly flavour of the month.'

'What can they do to you?'

'Retire me on full pension, if I'm lucky. Or they could give me the most boring, soul-destroying jobs in the most god-awful places, until I lose patience and quit. Or they might send me off on some suicidally dangerous operation, hoping I never come back.' Brad got up and poured himself another Scotch.

'What I don't understand,' he went on, 'is why he did it. I told him I was bringing him back here, and that he'd probably be working with Pharmavax on an antidote. He didn't seem exactly enthusiastic about the idea; probably reckoned he'd have to survive a whole lot of flak before he got to work, but even so –'

'Did Mort know he was going to have Volkov actually working for him?'

'Maybe. Nobody told me,' he grunted. 'How's everything been here? Did I miss anything exciting?'

'You were well out of it. All the things we were worried about with Seminon, and the pirated version, are coming to a head. The media have been really digging their knives in, and the press have set themselves up as moral crusaders against the pharmaceutical industry in general. You'd think Pharmavax had put cyanide in the water supply on purpose, the way they're carrying on.'

'So your phone hasn't stopped ringing, huh?'

Jill nodded tiredly. 'I could do with a drink myself,' she said, pointing to the Scotch. 'Even NIH has been in a state of siege this last week. *Time* magazine did a huge piece on the worldwide escalation in domestic violence, which just stopped short of saying that Seminon was directly responsible.'

'Guess they took legal advice. There was an hour-long special on Austrian TV. I didn't understand all of it, but the presenter seemed to be getting fairly steamed about American pharmaceutical companies being the rogues of the world.'

'There was a special two-hour television feature shown nationwide on ABC, just last week, about the impotence Seminon causes. The numbers were just unbelievable. Mort and I thought there might be a few hundred people affected in the States, and another few thousand scattered round the rest of the world. Turns out there are thousands and thousands in every country in the world, and hundreds of thousands here. And that's just the reported cases.'

'Looks like it's blown up faster than you expected.'

'Normally, things take years to escalate to this point. Now, every time you turn on the news, there are statisticians and epidemiologists spouting figures; none of them knows anything.'

'People are getting real angry, I guess,' Brad observed darkly.

'They're entitled to, don't you think? The latest scare is that birth rates will plummet within twenty years, causing worldwide economic disaster. Mort's had to go into hiding. Even I don't know where he is. He was really worried for his own personal safety plus, of course, the media wouldn't leave him alone. They've even had to station armed guards round the clock at Pharmavax to protect the employees.'

'Ever think it might be neat to run away to a little desert island someplace? We could take several cases of Scotch, some decent books, a stack of videos –'

'A good sound system and all my cds. Lots of wine. Your cookbooks –'

'– and just lie in the sun all day and catch fish for dinner.'

'And never watch the news or read a paper. Oh, Brad, when do we leave?'

He put his arm round her and kissed the top of her head. 'I'd go tomorrow, angel, believe me. But the guys at the Pentagon want a bit more of me yet. They've told Mort he has to come up with an antidote pretty damn soon, or they'll close him down for sure. He's been told to get all his people together for a meeting first thing Monday, and, for God knows what reason, they want me there as well.'

'I haven't talked with Mort for a while now. You'll see him before I do. Will you say to him – tell him – I –' she stammered, unsure of what she did want to say to Mort.

Brad nodded. 'Sure,' he said curtly. He leaned back, his eyes closed. He looked relaxed, but Jill could see the tension just under the skin. She stroked his close-cropped hair.

'I've never seen you down like this before,' she said softly.

'That's because I never failed like this before.'

'You haven't *failed*. You said yourself Volkov was the KGB's best. Being outwitted by someone like him is no disgrace –'

'Angel, just stop trying to stick some sort of goddam bandaid over everything, OK? I screwed up, that's all there is to it. Story of my life these past few months. The two things I've always relied on, which made me what I think I am, are being good at sex, and being good at my job. And now – guess what? I can't get it up for the military, can't get it up for you – what the fuck good am I?'

Furiously, he hurled the whisky tumbler across the room. Fortunately, it was one of Jill's unbreakable French glasses, and it bounced back off the far wall, and rolled to a halt on the carpet.

Brad sighed heavily. 'I apologise,' he said.

'It doesn't matter.' Jill was kneeling on the sofa beside him.

'Look at me,' she demanded, still not touching him. 'Brad, I am not the enemy.'

He reached for her hand. 'I know that. It's not you I'm angry at; it's myself.'

'It's Mort and Volkov you should be angry at, not yourself. If it weren't for Seminon –'

'I wouldn't be in the same situation as God knows how many other poor schmucks. But as far as I know, there isn't a single case yet of Seminon preventing anyone being a certified public accountant, or a lawyer, or a farm-hand. Whereas I'd bet good money that that shot I had is what made me screw up.'

Jill leaned forward to put her arms round him. She rested her face against his shoulder for a long minute. Then she said, 'Don't go home.'

'Stay here, you mean? But I never stay here.'

'Well, tonight I want you to. Please.'

'Even though I'll be about as much use as a goddam teddy bear?'

'I'm not going to beg.' She stood up and held out her hand. 'Are you coming to bed, or aren't you?'

Brad heaved himself up wearily. Jill held him close for a moment.

'Look,' she said, 'there are more things to do in bed than just screw. We smart lady scientists have inventive minds, you know!'

He managed a faint smile. 'Looks like I'm entirely in your hands, ma'am.'

She grinned wickedly. 'That's right.'

30.

'Dr Peters? This is Heidi Weissman calling. I'm assistant to Roxanne Delgado, of *WorldView.* We're doing a special, live this coming Saturday night, on the whole Seminon thing, and we'd really like to have you on the show. Of course, we'd fly you to New York ... Well, everyone says you're the most distinguished scientist in the field, and we need someone who can speak with authority but who isn't involved with Seminon in any way ... Oh no, we're not going to sensationalise anything, anything at all ... We want to introduce some balance here, like – some sanity, you know? We feel you'd be the very person to do that. ...'

Pia Tarantini, at thirty-five, was reckoned to be one of the Pentagon's brightest psychiatrists. Not only was she possessed of almost chilling professional detachment and objectivity, she had an exceptional understanding of the military mind. Over the past two years she had been carrying out a special study of Colonel Bradley Foster in addition to his regular assessment interviews and today, maybe, she was going to find out why and for whom.

'In all the years I've been working for the Pentagon, there haven't been too many occasions when I've been asked to come in and talk over a subject's assessment,' she said, shedding her winter overcoat, scarf and leather gloves. Ben Schwartz, the Vice President's personal aide, drew up a chair for her on the far side of his desk, and they both sat down. Pia placed a thick folder in front of her.

'So what's with this guy?' Schwartz asked, jerking his head at the file of summaries.

'Well,' Pia said deliberately, refusing to be fazed, 'I have to say I'm not exactly one hundred per cent sure. I could give you much more useful answers to your questions if I knew why you were asking.'

'Just tell us as much as you can.' Pia was briefly amused by the aide referring to himself as "us", although there was no one else in the room with them. Schwartz went on, 'You assured me, at our last meeting, that this man was some sort of a robot, hard, tight as a nut, reliable. A supreme professional.'

'That's right, I did. Because he was. Had been for years.'

'Why the past tense?'

Pia took her time, leaned back in the chair and maddeningly slowly crossed her legs. Two can play at this game, she thought; if you won't tell me why you want to know, then you can damn well ask me for every scrap of information you get!

'Well, there have been – let's say, changes.'

Uh-oh, the bitch was going to be difficult, Schwartz thought to himself. He was going to have to beg pretty-please for every answer. Well, OK, if that was the way she wanted it. But he still wasn't going to tell her why.

'Can you be a little more specific? What do you mean by "changes"?'

'We both know that the reason Colonel Foster has headed the Special Ops team for some years is that he was quite simply the best. There was no one better.'

'Are you saying that that is no longer the case?'

'Ben, if you know of a better soldier than Colonel Foster, I'd be *very* interested to meet him!'

'Pia,' Schwartz said in a warning voice, his patience beginning to fray, 'are you saying that Colonel Foster is, like, maybe losing his edge or something?'

'That's a very good way of putting it, Ben,' she said flatteringly. 'Losing his edge is exactly what he's doing.'

'But less than a year back, he led that raid into Russia which, in military terms, was judged a success, even if he did lose a valuable member of his team.' Schwartz didn't think Pia Tarantini knew about Foster's latest foray into Eastern Europe, and wasn't about to enlighten her. 'How do you measure whether he's losing his edge or not?'

Pia smiled sweetly. 'I spend time with him every two weeks, Ben. Getting people to tell me things is my business. Most of the time they don't know the half of what they tell me. They think if they don't say it, I won't know.'

'Such as?' Schwartz's rimless glasses fixed Pia in a cold gaze.

Pia shrugged. 'Oh, stuff about childhood, life, relationships.

You'd have to be more specific.' Schwartz waited. 'Put it like this: if there was something Brad Foster wasn't going to tell me, I'd never even know it existed.'

'Ah. I see.'

No, you don't, Pia said mentally; you haven't the first idea what makes a man like Brad Foster tick. 'What is it you really want to know?' she asked.

'Why don't you just tell me some fairly general stuff, and what you think about it?'

'OK. Let's throw you in the deep end. Do you know what's meant by the drama triangle?'

Ben shook his head slightly, but said nothing.

'Well, Brad Foster was abandoned at birth, and grew up in a variety of institutions. He was abused, and deprived of even the rudiments of affection. In other words, he was a classic victim.'

Still Ben Schwartz said nothing, not betraying by so much as a flicker of an eye that he had heard any of this before.

'When someone who's had that sort of a childhood grows up, they deal with their internal pain by unconsciously adopting one of two coping mechanisms. They become either a rescuer or a tyrant. Now, a rescuer focuses on the pains of others, so as not to have to confront his own, which are unbearable. The tyrant is really a victim, someone who beats up on themselves or others, physically or emotionally repeating what they came to accept as normal in their own childhood.'

'And you're saying Brad Foster is – which?'

'Well, he had a hard time. And like most abused kids he identified with his abusers, and sort of internalised a model of aggression as a defence against his inner pain. But at the same time, he displays elements of the rescuer in that he is serving the State in a very specialised capacity – helping it to solve its problems, if you like.'

'So he's in the right job?'

'Absolutely. I've always found the most remarkable thing about him to be his self-control. It's almost inhuman. But that's what makes him so useful to us in the military. He sailed through counter-interrogation training, and has always had about as much compunction about the taking of human life as a robot.'

Still the cold stare from behind the rimless glasses never changed.

'Can you account for that?'

'Well, his history of abuse, coupled with his extreme self-control, means he has a whole bunch of highly sadistic behaviour patterns. Doing the job he does legitimises them, makes them seem natural, even acceptable. Hell, he gets a decent salary and a fistful of medals for doing things that if he weren't working for us would get him jailed for life.'

'But in civilian life – what does a man like Foster do about human relationships? I mean, with women. Or with – uh – men. Would you say he was gay?'

'That's an interesting question. Why do you ask?'

'I just like to have an overall picture.'

'Well, I'd say he's a classic example – an extreme example, even – of an anal-sadistic personality. Men like him get stuck, way back in the pre-genital phase of their sexual development. Which means that, while he *could* be gay, he needn't necessarily be. And any woman he became sexually involved with could easily find the fun and games going rather further than she bargained for.'

'Are you saying he's a danger to women?'

'Not entirely. This is a very bright man, not a thug who goes around beating and raping women. But in a relationship, with someone he actually knew, and knew well, he'd be likely to get off on control and manipulation. It could be "games people play" or he could physically act out his women-hating fantasies, probably quite sadistic ones. It's quite common for a man like Brad, abandoned at birth, to have very confused ideas about his mother. On the one hand he idealises her, and projects that ideal on to his sexual partner. On the other hand, it was she who betrayed him, abandoned him – sort of handed him over as a baby to others who abused him. So if he can control women, he can control her.'

'I've read enough to know that a sadistic personality can often have a masochistic side as well. Would you say that applied to Colonel Foster?'

'Yes, I would,' Pia answered seriously. 'Obvious sadism can mask a far greater unconscious need to be on the receiving end of pain – physical, sexual or mental. It all relates to his childhood.'

'Would you say there was more to it than that?'

'I'm not sure I understand –'

'Well, it seems to me that if someone gets off on the whole idea of pain, then the logical endpoint has to be a deathwish. Is that what you call it?'

The tentative grin didn't fool Pia. Schwartz knew exactly what he was talking about!

'Not exactly,' she answered. 'Danger is undoubtedly attractive to him, almost addictive. But people like him get their highs out of *cheating* danger. Less pronounced types get kicks from driving dangerously, smoking themselves to death, doing drugs, whatever. But Foster has a PhD in survival. He may like living on the edge, but I mean *on*, not over the far side!'

'So you'd say he was more likely to come to an untimely end by accident rather than because he was out looking for it?'

'Let's just say you don't meet too many like him in retirement homes,' Pia temporised, thinking: we're getting there! Soon he's going to get around to asking me what he really wants to know.

'The change you mentioned,' Schwartz said, deceptively softly, 'the softening of the edge – is that likely to blunt his judgement?'

What you mean, Pia thought, is: will Brad Foster's love affair with danger lead him to go all the way – and kazoom! – no more Colonel Foster? C'mon, Schwartz, time you came clean.

Again, she leaned back in the chair, her head tilted to one side and her professional face, an interested half-smile, in place for Ben Schwartz's benefit. The surest way to get someone else to say something, she always found, was to say nothing herself, but wait for the other person to find the unfilled silence unbearable. It nearly always worked.

Sure enough, Schwartz said something, but not what she was expecting.

'We value your opinion, Pia,' he said silkily. 'It's what we've been paying you for.'

Pia could hardly fail to pick up the use of the past tense. She was employed on a series of three-month renewable contracts, and Schwartz was reminding her that renewal was by no means a foregone conclusion. Job-on-the-line time!

'How much do you know about Seminon?' she asked.

'Only what I hear around, and read in the newspapers. I'm certainly no expert. Are you saying Colonel Foster has had a shot of it?'

'Yes, about four-five months ago. He bought it illicitly in a street deal back in early November. There'd been a mix-up over a blood test and he thought he was HIV-positive. Turns out he wasn't, so he need never have taken it.'

'But he did. I thought the side-effects normally took six months, maybe more, to become apparent.'

'There are a whole lot of side-effects – the improved sexual performance and the increased aggression – which kick in earlier. But yes, it seems to take about six months for testicular burn-out to occur.'

'And in Colonel Foster's case?'

'It's as though everything had been speeded up. You'd have to run tests to be absolutely sure, but I'd say that all the drugs he's had pumped into him for his military duties – you know, all those nerve-gas and germ-warfare antidotes the guys who went to the Gulf had – have affected it somehow. Whatever, in his case everything's taken half the time it seems to be taking with everyone else.'

'And as a psychiatrist, how would you expect it to affect him?'

Damn Schwartz; he knew all along that Brad had had a shot! But how did he know? Unless they'd actually been *looking* for it –.

For a further second, she wondered which of them, Brad or Schwartz, she owed her loyalty to. Neither, she decided in the end. The only thing she could do was tell the truth, and let them make what they wanted of it.

'He already has in him a latent tendency towards passivity and masochism. In the absence of testosterone, that tendency will simply become more marked.'

'So he'll lose his edge over time, maybe totally?'

Pia nodded. 'It wouldn't surprise me,' she said.

Schwartz stood up, holding her summary folder. The conversation was obviously at an end, so she stood up too.

'There are thousands of men out there who've taken the stuff, but none of them's under the tight psychological supervision that he is,' she observed, more relaxed now. 'His case is really interesting. I'm going to get one hell of a paper out of all this, I can tell you.'

She stretched out her hand, expecting Schwartz to hand over her folder. It was the only record of Brad's professional history – nothing involving Special Ops personnel was ever put on the Pentagon's computers, in case a determined hacker succeeded in blowing their security operations wide open. But instead of giving the folder back, Schwartz held it well out of her reach, tucked under his arm.

'No, Pia,' he smiled thinly. 'I think not.'

31.

'Mort? This is Hari Rajananda calling you from Delhi.I know you will forgive me for calling you at the weekend, because a most terrible thing has happened. You may see it on CNN quite shortly. We can be thankful that it is not our own drug which has caused this terrible thing, but I fear we will be blamed for it all the same ...'

Roxanne Delgado knew perfectly well that her production team referred to her behind her back as the Drag Queen From Hell, and took it as a compliment. Long after they'd gone out of fashion, she still wore power shoulders, big hair and massive gaudy jewellery, and it had been suggested that her fearsome false fingernails were actually razor-edged. A rival presenter once risked a major lawsuit by saying, live on prime-time TV, 'The most disconcerting thing about la Delgado is that when she smiles, all you see is expensively capped white teeth. You expect to see steel.' But no lawsuit was forthcoming. That was just the reputation Roxanne Delgado wanted; living up to it came naturally. The station paid her four hundred thousand a year to anchor the late-night live slot, and she earned every cent as the hard-to-please channel surfers stuck with her, knocking David Letterman into second place night after night.

The last few minutes before the show went on air were always a war of nerves, as Delgado psyched herself and her team into a state of hair-trigger readiness. Tonight was no exception.

Jill was used to appearing on live television, and as a rule could handle any nervousness she might feel. Tonight was different. Sitting next to Delgado on the set, she shifted uneasily in her chair, as the sound levels and lighting were minutely adjusted and the studio audience given its last-minute instructions.

'Run the damn autocue *slower*, I said!' Delgado snapped. In fact, it was running at its usual speed, but the hapless operator pretended to adjust it, to keep the Dragon Lady happy.

'Bitch could make medical history,' she muttered to her colleague over her link to the control box. 'Pre-menstrual every day!'

'Born that way,' the satellite-link technician replied.

'Delhi and Tokyo in place, Louise?' Delgado demanded.

'Sure. We have everything lined up,' the technician answered calmly.

'Sixty seconds, Roxanne,' came the producer's voice through her earpiece. Ray Lennan had been *WorldView's* producer for three years, and knew Roxanne Delgado's psyching-up routine backwards.

Delgado snapped her fingers for the make-up girl to give her a final checking-over and, with seconds to go, sat poised and motionless, ready for the cameras to go live.

On a signal from Ray, the floor manager raised his hand and counted down the last five seconds on his fingers, ' ... three ... two ... one ... zero!' A swipe of his index finger cued the nationally-recognised theme music, which burst through the studio speakers. The monitors sprang to life as the title sequence rolled.

'Good evening, and welcome to *WorldView*!' Delgado flashed her dazzling dental work at forty million US viewers and probably as many as sixty million more worldwide. For the next fifty minutes, she would push, pull, press and probe, manipulate facts, rumours and people, to bring the most hard-hitting investigative TV viewing to her audience.

'Tonight, we're going to be taking a look at Seminon!' she announced, reading effortlessly from the autocue, and relaxing into her habitual on-screen mode. 'Introduced less than a year ago, Seminon has already become part of our history. Welcomed at first as every couple's dream contraceptive, it soon turned into their worst nightmare. This disaster threatens to dwarf every other medical scandal there's ever been –'

Any moment now, Jill told herself, I'm going to find myself pinned down, out here under the lights, with nowhere to run. The hard-edged phrases, which only minutes before were still being honed by the writers, the earnest look of concern, and the cool professionalism, all impressed Jill in spite of her feeling of chill dread. She could feel her own hands sweating, her heart pounding sickeningly. She hated being unprepared, as she was now. Delgado had refused to give her any idea what sort of questions to expect. The producer had assured her that Roxanne always liked to take her guests by surprise – it made for a zappy start – but at that precise moment, Jill could have done without the histrionics of global television.

'– with me in the studio here in New York is Dr Jillian Peters of NIH. Dr Peters has been involved in research in this area for nearly fifteen years, and has seen the Seminon saga unfold from Day One. Dr Peters, what's your opinion of multinationals who put untested drugs on the market?'

Jill nearly died. Of all the god-awful questions to start with! Pharmavax hadn't got as far as putting Seminon on the market and the bitch knew it! Don't rush it, she told herself, taking a deep breath.

'Pharmavax were in a very difficult position, right from the start,' she began. 'They came by what seemed like a perfectly good contraceptive vaccine, the result of some excellent and very innovative Russian research –'

'Which as we now know wasn't all it claimed to be.'

'Indeed. As you say, we now know. But we shouldn't forget that at the time Pharmavax was encouraged by the authorities to get moving as fast as they could –'

'Mainly on the understanding that Seminon also gave protection against HIV.'

'Exactly.'

'Which it didn't,' Delgado needled.

'To start with, it did. To that extent, Pharmavax acted in good faith, with no intent to deceive the FDA. It wasn't until later that it was discovered that the HIV protection was only temporary.'

Damn it, she thought. I wasn't even involved. So why am I being made to defend Pharmavax? It's not as if I even want to defend what they did!

'Pharmavax is one of the most respected pharmaceutical companies in the country. So why do *you* think they got it so wrong?'

'I really don't know,' Jill replied blandly. 'You'd have to ask them.' Chew on *that* with your twenty-thousand dollar dental work!

'We did,' Delgado rejoined with poisonous sweetness. 'But

they said – and I quote – "There is no one available to speak with you at this time".' She turned to face camera one, which had her in big close-up. 'I think we can all draw our own conclusions from that!'

'That's not exactly fair!' Jill jumped in, mentally cursing herself for not sitting mute so as to give Delgado as little as possible to work with. 'There are other people who also have some explaining to do.'

'Could you give us a for-instance?' Delgado sounded almost charming.

Careful, Jill, don't go pointing the finger at the government until you know a whole lot more, a little voice whispered inside her skull. 'Well, have you talked with anyone at the FDA?' she enquired carefully, reluctant to name Frank Osborne. While she had no reason to believe that he'd behaved other than completely properly, she didn't want to be responsible for subjecting him to this sort of exposure.

'As it happens,' Delgado announced triumphantly to the audience, 'earlier today I spoke with Commissioner Frank Osborne of the Food and Drug Administration, in Denmark for a conference, from his hotel room. This is what he had to say.'

Frank Osborne's thoughtful, dignified face filled the on-set screen.

'We at the FDA have always tried to do the very best we can for people with life-threatening illnesses. Cancer and AIDS are, of course, high on our list. Over the years, we've tried to balance the needs of patients who require potentially useful drugs but can't wait the requisite length of time for them, with the need for safeguards. Our system of what we call 'conditional approval' has, on the whole, worked well. Our only requirement is that the companies who supply such drugs continue to carry out the full range of tests, even though the drug is actually being used.'

'Commissioner, would you say Pharmavax adhered to the law on this?'

'Yes, I would,' he replied. 'It was not Pharmavax's fault that some of their employees took the vaccine outside the labs during the early stages of its development, still less that certain unscrupulous individuals then attempted to replicate it.'

'So what would you say to critics who claim that the FDA has been sitting on its hands all this time?'

'I would understand their concern,' Osborne replied calmly. 'But I'd ask them to take a compassionate view. After all, if they or a member of their family were HIV positive, I'm sure those very same critics would want us to make such a choice available to them.'

'That was Commissioner Frank Osborne of the FDA,' Delgado said, as the VT insert came to an end. Such apologies and justification were not what she wanted on her show. She turned to Jill, as Frank Osborne's face disappeared from the studio monitor to be replaced by the *WorldView* logo. 'Dr Peters, increasing numbers of men in this country and worldwide are becoming impotent. How do you see things going?'

'I can't say what the future will hold. All I can say is that I and my colleagues at NIH, and many other scientists in labs around the world, are doing all we can to find an antidote to the impotence problem. And others are working on perfecting a variant of the vaccine that will be an effective contraceptive, but without any of the side-effects.'

'So how long will all this take, doctor?'

'I really can't say.'

'Weeks? Years?' Delgado prompted.

'It's impossible to tell,' Jill insisted quietly. Of course it was likely to be years - a great many years - rather than months, but there was no way she could say that.

'Well,' Delgado said brightly to camera one, 'while the western medical establishment tries to find ways to heal this self-inflicted wound, let's take a look at the rest of the world. We'll be going live to our India correspondent to see what's happening out there, after the break.'

'Nice pacy start, Roxanne,' Ray assured her via her earpiece. 'Eighty seconds, we go over to Amy in Delhi, OK?'

'Sure,' Delgado replied dismissively. 'You all right, doctor?' she asked Jill, but not as though she really expected an answer.

'Yes, thank you,' Jill said as graciously as she could bring herself to. 'But I think it's only fair to -'

'One moment!' Delgado interrupted her. She frowned as Ray's voice came through her earpiece. 'You're kidding me! You haven't ... but why would he? ... I mean, now? OK, straight after the Delhi insert. Sure, I won't tell her ...'

Jill froze in her seat. What was Delgado going to throw at her now? She prayed the Indian coverage would last a good few minutes, so she could collect her thoughts.

Once more, the floor manager was counting down the last five seconds to air.

'Welcome back to *WorldView*. We all know what's happening as a result of Seminon here in the States, but what about the rest of the world? Next, we're going live to Delhi, where our Asia correspondent, Amy Larsen, has this report –'

'Thank you, Roxanne. Here in India, Seminon has caused havoc on a scale Americans can only dream about in their worst nightmares. Entrepreneurs have replicated the vaccine, and hundreds of thousands of men have taken it in the past few months. Early signs of increased libido were welcomed in a culture where a high value has traditionally been placed on sexual prowess –' The screen displayed a close-up of the famous temple carvings showing men and women engaged in every imaginable form of sexual intercourse. ' – and where there is a long history of drugs and love potions being used to enhance sexual activity. This almost certainly accounts for Seminon taking off so fast here. But, as happened in the States, the initial improvement in sexual drive proved to be a cruel deception. I have with me Dr Anwar Banerjee, Director of the World Health Organisation's Epidemiology Unit in Delhi ... Dr Banerjee, can you describe, for our viewers back home, the effect Seminon has had in the Indian subcontinent?'

The camera zoomed slowly to a close-up of Dr Banerjee's face. 'At first,' he said, 'it seemed like a blessing. Millions of men wanted to have a shot of this magic drug, not only because it promised them a better sex life, as you suggested in your opening remarks, but because of the anti-HIV effect.'

'But the Indian government hadn't licensed it, isn't that right?'

'Indeed. But here in India, we have so many new multi-millionaire entrepreneurs now that if something can be done, it usually *is* done, whether it should be or not. And please do not forget that although AIDS is less of a problem now for you in the

West than it was, here in India it is only just beginning. We are forecasting many millions of cases in India alone, in the next two years. Here and in Southeast Asia, it will run away like wildfire. People will try anything, take any risks, to escape the disease.'

'Isn't it a fact that your government has had to create special prisons solely for men who have become violent as a result of taking Seminon?'

'Yes, that is true,' Dr Banerjee said, his fine-boned face and gentle voice becoming grave. 'And it is not only women who are at risk, but men too.'

'Here is some footage we shot earlier today,' Amy Larsen took over. 'Viewers are warned that what they are about to see is extremely violent.' The picture changed to a primitive rural prison. Several men, handcuffed and wild-eyed, were being beaten by warders with lathis and herded into an already-crowded cell. The picture cut to show a large, raggedly-dressed man, with bared teeth, rampaging back and forth behind bars, dragging the corpse of another, smaller, man by its hair. A cry of horror rose from Roxanne Delgado's studio audience.

'In the States,' Amy said in voice-over, 'men who took Seminon in the early days are now past this stage of uncontrollable violence. But in India, because so many more men have taken it, and all in the past few months, the problem is rapidly becoming uncontainable. Women rarely leave their homes, and those who have to go out do so only in the company of a male relative. But even that is not sufficient protection, as the following footage shows. Once again, viewers are warned that they may find it distressing.'

Jill couldn't bear to watch. She broke out in an ice-cold sweat as the memory of Art, raining blows on her and screaming, 'Bitch! Bitch!', threatened to overwhelm her. She shut her eyes to the appalling scenes on the screen, but the shrieks and screams of the women being beaten on the streets of Delhi would haunt her as long as she lived.

'This rampage alone left twenty-three women dead,' Amy Larsen's voice continued. 'Many more were badly injured, and four have since committed suicide, unable to bear the disgrace of being publicly raped and disowned by their families. As many as twenty men are also thought to have been killed, some by the police. Others were the husbands, fathers, sons and brothers of the women who were attacked, who died trying to protect them. Sami Desai was eleven years old. He died trying to save his grandmother, who was also killed.'

Jill opened her eyes. On the screen she saw a little boy, scrawny as a sparrow, lying in a pool of blood. Silently, the camera panned back, to show dozens of bodies scattered in the deserted street, the only movement the hem of a sari caught by the breeze.

Thankful that everyone's attention was diverted away from her, she brushed the tears from her face with her hand. Behind her, she could hear some of the studio audience pushing their way towards the exits.

Mercifully, the footage came to an end, and once again Amy Larsen was in conversation with Dr Banerjee.

'Would you say that this level of violence was typical, Dr Banerjee?' she asked.

'I am sorry to say that it is,' he replied gravely. 'I believe that the vaccine that was pirated in the States from the original Pharmavax formula was probably much purer than ours. Here in India, we have not the same equipment you have; we cannot afford to buy good raw materials. This is what happens when a sophisticated technology falls into the wrong hands. And I fear our troubles will not end for quite some time.'

'Thank you, Dr Banerjee,' Amy said quietly, clearly shaken by the footage, even though she must have seen it several times already. 'Well, as you can see, Roxanne, it's pretty dangerous out here. I'm afraid even for my own personal safety. But the women most at risk are those whose menfolk have had a shot of Seminon. For many of them, there's no place else to go.'

'Well, you take care now, Amy,' Delgado said, her voice uncharacteristically gentle.

Then, resuming her Dragon Lady persona, she turned back to camera one. 'Still in the studio, we have Dr Jillian Peters of NIH. Dr Peters, what did you make of all that?'

What do you *expect* me to make of it? Jill thought savagely. But she said, as collectedly as she could, 'It was horrific.'

'This is clearly very dangerous technology, wouldn't you say?' Delgado went on, her voice edged with aggression. 'Do you think Phamaco really did everything they could to make sure samples couldn't get out of their R and D lab?'

'I'm not in a position to speak for Pharmavax. But I'm sure that –'

Delgado's head turned sharply towards a commotion on the studio floor. 'Ladies and gentlemen,' she interrupted Jill, 'we have a dramatic development on this story, right here in the studio!'

Jill's heart missed a beat as Mort pounded on to the stage. As he caught sight of her, he shot her a look of amazement, as if to say: What the hell are *you* doing here?

'Camera three, get him in close up!' the producer barked. 'And stay with him. I want to see every expression even before he knows he's making it!'

'Dr Montgomery, welcome to *WorldView*!' Delgado beamed, in her element. This was better television than even she had hoped for! To her close-up camera, she said, 'Dr Morton Montgomery is the CEO of Pharmavax, the company which originally developed Seminon for the US market, before it was pirated all over the world with the results we've just seen. Dr Montgomery, how do you feel about all this? I expect you were watching the Delhi footage on the monitor backstage.'

'That's right,' Mort said tersely. 'In fact I had word from our Delhi office just this afternoon that this most recent appalling violence had taken place, and that's why I decided after all to come on your show.'

'Now, I think I'm right in saying that this is the first time you've spoken publicly about Seminon for some months.'

'It is. But I felt it was time to set the record straight. Pharmavax has been unjustly blamed for everything that has gone wrong with Seminon. Many people assume that it was Pharmavax's own vaccine which caused the side-effects such as that dreadful violence we just saw. But it just isn't so. It's my belief that whichever company had chosen to develop it, they would have run into the exact same problems we did. Even in an organisation like Pharmavax, if someone chooses to act in a dishonest way and smuggle stuff out, there's no way we can stop it. We don't treat our employees like criminals, with routine searches and such. For one thing, it would be an infringement of their civil rights. Secondly, these are skilled graduates, not idiots, and many of them have given years of loyal service to Pharmavax. Of course we have to trust them. Which means they have a responsibility to justify that trust. If someone abuses it – well, frankly, Ms Delgado, there's nothing we can do to prevent that.'

Jill had to admire the way Mort stood up to the ruthless TV chat-show host. In all her many public appearances, she herself had never been personally attacked, but she knew how hard it was to stay cool under such public pressure as this. Mort seemed to be handling it so well, she allowed herself to relax slightly.

That was a mistake. Without warning, Delgado turned to her and demanded, 'Dr Peters, isn't it a fact that the vaccine was originally intended to be developed at NIH?'

'Yes, that is true,' Jill said evenly, determined to give away as little as possible.

'So why didn't you go ahead with it? Surely this whole disaster would never have happened if the vaccine had stayed in the safe hands of a respected government laboratory?'

'There were reasons, very good reasons, why we didn't go ahead with it.'

'Isn't it true that the computer files containing the data on the vaccine were stolen from NIH?'

'No,' Jill said, thankful to be able to give a straight answer at last.

'The computer data wasn't stolen. So you're saying you still have that information at NIH?' Oh Lord, that straight answer wasn't such a good idea after all.

'No, we no longer have the information.'

'Well, I wonder if we can guess why that might be.'

To Jill's horror, a series of stills flashed up on the screen – she and Mort laughing together at a charity dinner, both of them standing suspiciously close together at a gallery opening, Jill looking admiringly up at Mort as he addressed a conference in Santa Fe. All had appeared in newspapers or magazines over the past ten years.

Seen in this context the body language said sex, lovers, much more than just good friends.

'It's no secret, is it, that you and Dr Montgomery have been close friends these past ten years?'

Damn, but the bitch was being careful what she said! Nothing offensive, nothing actionable. But it all *looked* so damning!

'No, that's never been a secret –' she forced herself to say, while thinking: I have done absolutely nothing wrong, and there's no way she can make me say I have.

Jill had never been put through anything like this. She was used to being courted by the media; interviewers all but grovelled to her for her expertise; magazines quoted her with something approaching reverence. Now here she was, being practically stripped bare in front of a hundred million viewers! '– and it has absolutely nothing to do with the Seminon issue,' she finished firmly.

But no one took control on air from Roxanne Delgado. Like a shark, she homed in for the kill.

'But, Dr Peters, suppose it were alleged that you stole the data, or arranged for it to be stolen, so that Dr Montgomery could take commercial advantage of a government department's confidential information, wouldn't you think the people of America had a right to –'

Mort leapt to his feet, shaking with anger. 'That is a damn lie!' he shouted. 'At no time has Dr Peters behaved improperly. If anyone has, it's the government of this country, who put pressure you can't begin to imagine on me and my company to get the vaccine on the market before anyone else. And they damn near suborned the FDA into licensing it before it was properly tested. Compared with that, Ms Delgado, the flaws in our own security don't seem too significant, do they? And I would just like to make one more thing crystal clear. Dr Peters has had no involvement of any kind with Seminon for close on twelve months. Oh yes, I know you've stopped short of actually declaring that she's in some way to blame, but you've suggested it, and that's enough! So I hope you've got some damn good lawyers, Ms Delgado, because they're going to be hearing from mine in the morning!'

Mort stormed off the set, jostling camera one as he pushed past and knocking it off its line-up on Roxanne Delgado.

'Go for a break, guys, for fuck's sake! *Now*!' the producer yelled at his vision mixer.

Not caring whether she was still on camera or not, Jill fled the stage. Mort was nowhere to be seen.

32.

'They're all in it together! He actually said it; didn't you hear the guy? This is the moment we've been waiting for, and is it ever going to be sweet! We can nail Pharmavax now! But we have to get everyone on the streets, or we'll miss our chance. Look, I know a coupla hundred guys who'd rise from the grave to be there, plus they have friends, families. I reckon I could guarantee you five hundred, no problem. The guy on the *Post* – sure, I'll talk to him right away. Yeah, I just talked with the Seminon Survivors people too – man, they can't wait! Meet at eight, march at nine, they say. Sounds good to me ...'

Long before his wake-up call, Mort abandoned all attempts to sleep, and got up. He filled the coffee-percolator, went over to the huge window of his penthouse apartment, and drew back the blinds. The wan grey light of dawn was just creeping over the city, and the street lights were still on. Even at this early hour there was already a build-up of commuter traffic. From his window, Mort could see right across to the wide Potomac. He remembered how Jill had always loved to turn the lights off and look at the city by night. For how much longer, he wondered, would he have this apartment, and the antique European furniture and Hudson Valley School oil paintings that graced it? For three weeks he had been sequestered in a comfortable hotel, but the temporary, impersonal atmosphere, the constant attendance of armed guards, had finally got to him, and at his own risk he had returned home. Surprisingly, none of the media appeared to have noticed.

His eye fell on a set of English hunting prints that Jill had given him – how many years ago now? They'd always meant to take a holiday in England – explore Hampshire, where Jill had grown up, see the cathedral cities and the beautiful countryside. Now they never would.

There were so many things he was never going to do. His

whole life had narrowed down to one thought – that he was about to run out of time. Even the impending collapse of Pharmavax, and the all-too-possible prospect of Congressional committee hearings and legal proceedings against him personally, as well as the whole board of Pharmavax, suddenly seemed surprisingly unimportant, just one more inconvenience to be surmounted.

The expensive Arabica blend coffee tasted bitter and gritty this morning. He threw it down the sink and forced himself to eat a rudimentary breakfast before taking a shower, shaving and getting dressed.

'Good morning, Dr Montgomery, sir,' the janitor called cheerily, as Mort made his way down to the garage in the basement of his apartment block.

'Good morning, Patrick,' Mort answered, thinking: I must remember to give him his annual bonus in good time, while I still have the cash. But as he drove up the ramp, out of the dim artificial light into the early morning sun, he mentally pulled himself together. Now was no time for maudlin thoughts or self-pity. He had a multinational pharmaceutical company to save and a hard deal to drive with the government. Plus, he owed it to Randy and Phil and the other members of his board to get them off the hook if he possibly could. As he joined the slow-moving traffic on the freeway, he sighed heavily and thought: Just how the hell am I supposed to achieve all that?

• • •

Jill had been up only a few minutes when the phone rang. She picked up her mug of freshly-brewed coffee, and padded over to answer it. It was the personnel director at NIH.

'We're calling everybody to say don't bother coming in today,' she told Jill. 'You can hardly get through to the building for TV cameras, and we're not sure how secure the phone lines are. What it comes down to is that we can't guarantee your safety, not after your appearance on *WorldView*. Actually, you were good, but that Delgado – what a witch! I cheered when Mort told her where she got off! The thing is, for the rest of the week, can you work from home?'

'I guess so,' Jill said, thinking: is this where my job starts to cease to exist? 'I have plenty I can catch up with on my pc. And of course I could always tidy my closet.'

'Enjoy, enjoy,' the personnel director laughed, and Jill felt a sudden stab to the heart. That was what Mira always used to say. 'I'll call you when the excitement's died down. 'Bye for now.'

• • •

Looking at her watch, Jill wondered whether Mort would have left home yet. She wanted to call and thank him for standing up for her so publicly, possibly to his own detriment. All Sunday, after her return from New York, she'd tried his number, but only got the answering machine. She'd call him in the evening, she promised herself; they would talk at length then, and she would hear what transpired at his strategy meeting.

She poured some more coffee, and sat down in her bathrobe to sort out exactly what she had to catch up with. In fact, there was less than she had thought; it certainly wasn't going to take all day. Although she had meant the comment about tidying her closets as a joke, nevertheless she opened the sliding doors and looked critically at her wardrobe. Everything was hung up neatly, all the coathangers facing the same way, and her shoes were all lined up tidily and – for once – freshly shined. Nothing to do there.

Her kitchen storecupboards looked pretty much the same as they had a year earlier. Not surprising, as she hardly ever cooked a meal.

Her personal papers were all in order, everything up to date and filed away. So nothing to do there either.

What was she going to do with the gift of a few free hours? She could go out and buy a paper and see what was on in Washington – she couldn't remember when she last visited any of the city's museums or galleries. Or she could ring up the stables, see if they had a horse free at short notice. Maybe Jim could come too. She couldn't remember exactly when his school would finish for the spring vacation, but he might be at a loose end. So she called him.

Even though she had called many times since Art had attacked her so savagely, and even though Art, clearly distressed and overwhelmed by his own behaviour, had clumsily apologised, she still prayed every time that Jim or Shirlene would pick up the phone instead.

This time it was Jim who answered. She vaguely registered that his voice sounded slightly odd, as she said gaily, 'How'd you like to be taken out for a hamburger by your mom? Then you could come riding with me this afternoon, if I can get Jasper at short notice. Or we could go bowling, or –'

She was cut off in mid-sentence by Jim, almost shouting, 'Mom! I can't!' She could hear him gulping back sobs.

'Jim, what is it! What's wrong?'

'It's Shirlene. They took her to the hospital in the night. Dad's there now.'

'Oh, Jim, I'm so sorry. Do you want me to come over? Is there anything I can do?'

Jim was crying openly now; it took a few moments for him to get control of his voice. 'Uh, I don't know, Mom. I'm waiting for Dad to call, tell me if I can go over. Or he might come back home. I really don't know. See, she was in real bad pain, and the pills weren't doing any good, and Dad didn't know what to do –'

Tears got the better of him, and Jill had to hang on helplessly while she listened to her son weeping uncontrollably like a little child.

Eventually she said, 'Look, if you want me to come over, I will. Or you could come here. Whichever. If you want to wait till you've talked to Dad, fine. Will one of you call me anyway, as soon as you can? Just to tell me how –'

'Sure, Mom,' Jim hiccuped. 'But there's nothing you can do right now. Me neither. We just have to wait, I guess.'

'Tell me which hospital she's in. I could go and see her, send flowers –'

As she hung up, Jill was seized by a feeling of utter despair and hopelessness. Even when everything had been darkest and most confusing over the past year, Shirlene's strength and understanding had always been there. In Jill's turbulent life, one part of it – her family – had been in the care of a woman she respected, trusted and loved, a woman who seemed to regard even her husband's ex-wife as a candidate for her boundless generosity and affection. Now that prop, too, seemed about to crumble.

Jill sat down at her computer, the screen wavering before her eyes as she struggled to fight back the tears. All those closest to her, every single person she loved, had suffered, or was about to suffer, violent change. Mira had been killed, viciously and unexpectedly; her body still lay in a police morgue. Mort's life was in ruins, the company he had striven to build about to be destroyed. Brad was on the very brink of disgrace, his job, and possibly his life, in jeopardy. Jim was facing yet another challenge – and he'd been through more than most kids his age – the loss of his beloved stepmother. And poor Shirlene, who had been fading visibly over the past few months, was almost certainly going to die soon.

And what about you? a little voice niggled inside her. Where do you feature in all this? What are you going to do about it?

Jill gazed blankly at the screen, realising that she really didn't feature in any of it at all.

The Seminon vaccine would have been stolen from Russia even if she had refused to give Brad the information he needed. The computers at NIH would have been contaminated with the virus in any case. Mort would have bought the formula when it was offered to him – no way she could have stopped that. The trial batches of the vaccine would have found their way past Pharmavax's security regardless of anything Jill had or hadn't done. And now, when all the most important people in her life were facing crises, there was no place for her, no role to play. There was nothing she could do to help any of them.

Useless, the little voice nagged; you're useless.

Mentally, Jill shook herself, poured another mug of coffee. You may not be able to save the world today, she told herself, but at least you can get all your references for the *Nature* paper in order. Determined to achieve something at least, she settled down again at her pc.

• • •

The moment Mort walked in through the electronic glass doors of the imposing Pharmavax building, he recognised a difference in the atmosphere. The usual hum and clatter of the day's work getting under way was missing; people were standing glumly in clusters, talking quietly in the corridors, as if unable to get down to the tasks in hand. Only Sandi Sidell seemed to be in her element, fielding several calls at once, barking instructions at her harassed assistants, parrying all enquiries with a skillful smokescreen of meaningless assurances.

Randall Church looked grave. He had dressed in the most Ivy League suit, shirt and tie he owned, in an effort to appear irreproachably respectable. Even Phil Zuckerman was subdued, his usual barrage of gritty wisecracks silenced.

'Jane, have them bring coffee to the boardroom in a half hour, would you?' Mort snapped as he strode through his secretary's office. Jane immediately buzzed down to the canteen.

Shortly before nine, Brad arrived. By this time, a phalanx of TV crews had gathered in the street outside the expensively-landscaped plaza, and rather than run a gauntlet of camera technicians, TV reporters and journalists with cellular phones, he asked the cops to bring him in the back entrance.

'I hope you've come up with something to throw to those guys,' he said to Mort, as they met in the boardroom, way up on the twentieth floor. 'Looks like they're hungry.'

'I guess the suits are as well,' Mort responded drily.

At that moment, one of the canteen staff brought in the coffee. Mort poured a cup and handed it to Brad, before helping himself. The two men walked over to the huge plate-glass window.

'Christ, look at them!' Mort growled. 'There's a Japanese team. The Germans have sent their guys over. And the BBC are down there as well. Looks like the eyes of the world are upon us, doesn't it?'

'Sure does,' Brad agreed laconically.

Phil, Randall Church and several other board members came in together. Last to arrive was Frank Osborne of the FDA, patriarchal and courteous as ever.

'I dare say you'll be glad when this is all over, Mort,' he said in an almost fatherly voice, as Mort poured him some coffee. 'You're looking tired.'

'I am, Frank; I am,' Mort smiled wearily. 'And you don't know the half of it. You wouldn't believe it if I told you.'

The FDA Commissioner merely raised an eyebrow, but said nothing. Mort thought to himself with grim hilarity that one way to crack Osborne's veneer of unflappable urbanity would be to tell him that Dr Morton Montgomery, CEO of Pharmavax, whom he had known for twenty years, was HIV-positive!

A few minutes later, as if by common consent, everybody put

down their coffee-cups and took their places round the boardroom table.

•   •   •

After an hour at the computer, Jill stretched, feeling the tendons in her neck and shoulders snap back into place. Time for a break. She reached absent-mindedly for the TV remote control, while still scanning the computer screen, and turned on the television.

'– are out in force here at the Pharmavax building. Police Commissioner Franklin this morning called for extra support from neighbouring precincts to help control the crowds. With little prospect of any word from the Pharmavax board before midday, this corner of the city looks like becoming more congested still, as more and more demonstrators and special-interest groups arrive. Stay tuned for up-to-the-minute –'

Jill killed the reporter's annoyingly high-pitched voice. The camera panned over the crowd, as Jill continued to watch with the sound off. Except for the cordoned-off area directly in front of the huge plate-glass doors, and the plaza itself, all the space around the Pharmavax building was a seething mass of angry people. Some were brandishing crudely-painted placards – she could see 'Pharmavax Guilty of Genocide' waving over the heads of the crowd. Occasional close-up shots showed waving fists and shouting faces contorted with rage, while the wide-angle shots revealed alarmingly concerted movement among some sections of the crowd.

Keeping the sound off, Jill zapped through a few other news channels, but the pictures were much the same. One reporter was interviewing a police officer in full riot-control gear. Jill didn't much want to hear what he had to say; his sombre face said it all. Pharmavax was in bad trouble.

For a moment she considered calling Mort, but instantly dismissed the idea. He had enough on his plate. Still keeping an eye on the silent television screen, she turned back to the computer.

•   •   •

'OK, say you *had* succeeded in dragging Volkov back here, do you think he would have co-operated, come up with an antidote?' Phil snarled at Brad.

Brad just about hung on to his temper. 'I'm no scientist, you know that,' he answered evenly. 'I understood him to say that he had reached a certain point with his original research, and had then been forced by the Russian administration to abandon it. We never discussed the work he had managed to do toward developing an antidote. Not that it would have made too much sense to me if we had. Anyway, most of the time we had other things on our minds.'

Frank Osborne cleared his throat. 'It is, of course, regrettable that Colonel Foster was unable to bring Dr Volkov back to help Pharmavax develop the antidote. But I see no point in continuing this line of discussion. It is not germane to the problem at hand. The question is: can Pharmavax develop an antidote without his help? And how soon?'

'Depends whether your people are going to make us run the usual range of tests,' Mort said brusquely. 'We don't need Volkov. We can do it. You just have to give us time, Frank. Maybe work out some special accelerated schedule for the testing –'

'Mort, time is the one thing you don't have,' Frank Osborne said gently. 'I have no idea how many liability suits you have pending. And I have only the haziest notion of the latest figures for the number of people afflicted by Seminon's side-effects throughout the world. But one thing I do know – time has run out.'

'So what do you want me to do?' Mort lashed back. 'Liquidate Pharmavax and use all our assets to settle liability suits?'

At that moment, the shouting of the crowd reached an ugly crescendo, audible even twenty floors up. Mort leapt to his feet, and strode over to the window. 'Turn on the news, Jane!' he barked.

Jane reached for the remote control. All those present turned to look at the huge TV screen set in the wall of the boardroom. A shrill-voiced activist was screaming into a mike held close to his face.

' – don't care about the way it's ruined people's lives, the way it's wrecked society, just so long as they get rich. We say, these guys are guilty as hell, and they're gonna be made to pay!'

'Christ!' Mort swore. 'Those guys want blood!'

• • •

Unable to concentrate on her work, Jill turned, distracted, to the

TV. CNN's industry reporter, Barton DeWitt, was flicking his improbably luxuriant hair at the cameras. Jill had never been able to stand his self-satisfied smirk, but he was damned good at his job. He was interviewing a fiery-eyed demonstrator. Just as she turned the sound back on, the man was ranting, '– guilty as hell, and they're gonna be made to pay!'

Suddenly, a deafening roar of human rage off-camera made Barton DeWitt swing round, almost ripping the mike away in mid-sentence. The camera panned dizzyingly over the blur of faces, and focused on a horrifying scene.

The demonstrators were heaving at a length of ironwork that fenced off the plaza from the street; it was only a matter of time before the struts snapped under the relentless back-and-forth pressure. Others were ripping up paving stones, wrenching the concrete surrounds out of the earth around the young trees. The picture on the screen jerked and jiggled as the cameraman was jostled by the crowd.

Barton DeWitt's voice had long since lost the smooth, affectedly Ivy League tone that had always irritated Jill. '– are donning their riot gear. I can see some cops moving out in front of the Pharmavax building. They appear to be carrying riot shields. But the view from here is that the fence out front can't last long. This is Barton –'

The picture heaved and pitched, the sound died, and the screen went blank. Frenziedly, Jill grabbed the remote control and quickly found another news channel. Their reporter, too, sounded on the verge of hysteria as she chronicled the crowd's every move.

Things were quickly going from bad to worse. The roaring became uglier still, more hate-filled, and missiles started to fly. Jill sat, hunched and rigid in her chair, unable even to blink. 'Oh, my God!' she moaned helplessly, as the appalling violence unfolded on the screen.

• • •

Randall Church handed the telephone to Mort. 'The guys on Capitol Hill,' he said bleakly.

'We want you to go out there and talk to them, Mort. We didn't ask for this, but it never would have happened if you hadn't lost control on prime-time television. So you owe it to us to go out there, refute your allegations and tell them what you propose to do. Put it this way: if you don't, two things will happen. One: as of mid-day today Pharmavax will cease to exist. And two: the way things are going, we're going to have to give orders to use tear gas – maybe more. It's in your hands.'

• • •

'– and it looks like the doors of the Pharmavax building are opening. I'd say one of those men is Morton Montgomery, CEO of Pharmavax. We have no information for you at this time as to the identity of the other man. It looks like the cops are advising them not to proceed further – uh, a reasonable suggestion in view of the – uh, temper of the crowd –'

Horrified, Jill watched, knuckles rammed into her mouth, biting almost to the bone, as Mort and Brad appeared on the wide steps in front of the Pharmavax building. Behind them the huge glass doors slid silently shut.

'I guess Morton Montgomery is about to make a public statement. We'll do our best to bring it to you live –'

Once more the picture on the screen shook – this time as a deafening explosion, followed by a burning roar, momentarily silenced the crowd. Again the camera panned crazily. A whole wing of the Pharmavax building had simply disappeared. In the gap where it had been, pieces of wreckage were drifting earthwards in balletic slow motion while, high above, a raging fireball rose fiercely into the heavens, trailing a billowing pall of oily black smoke.

After a few seconds' shocked silence, the TV reporter resumed her incoherent raving. The crowd, spurred to sudden hysteria, charged like rabid animals through the iron fence, flattening the police cordon in their path. Mort and Brad turned and ran for the refuge of the Pharmavax building.

• • •

'For some reason I don't understand, the doors of the Pharmavax building have failed to open. It doesn't look like they stand a chance! They're hammering on the door; I can see – uh, people inside – uh, but I can't tell whether they're trying to get the doors open. Oh, my God! The police line has given way! I can't see what's happening – this is the most awful – uh, it looks like they're being attacked – Oh, my God! I can see blood! It looks from here like they're being torn in pieces! We'll try to bring you a closer view –'

If the long-suffering cameraman ever managed to bring his audience a closer view of the carnage, Jill never saw it. Grey, choking horror swirled through her, all around her, cutting off air, light, hope.

She was out cold before she hit the floor.

PART FOUR

Florida, July 2001

33.

Jill often managed to complete an hour's work even before her colleagues made it into work. When they appeared, she would break for a mug of instant coffee, and spend fifteen minutes or so gossiping and catching up with their news before returning to the workbench. Her colleague Susie Freeberg, with whom she ran the lab, worked almost as hard. The two women had met soon after Jill arrived in Florida, liked each other immediately, and had both found jobs with a private commercial laboratory doing routine analyses for local private hospitals, something Jill would have found unthinkable only a few years before. The lab employed seven junior technicians and the owners, who had struck gold when they took on two such formidably over-qualified women, more or less left Jill and Susie to run the business the way they wanted. Jill looked after the technical side, and Susie ran the administration.

Susie knew all about her friend Jill Farleigh's previous identity as Dr Jillian Peters of NIH, but after their first few intense conversations on the subject, she never referred to it again, something for which Jill was profoundly grateful.

This morning, Susie arrived a little earlier than usual, so the two women had a rare opportunity to talk uninterrupted before the day began.

'I was planning to take off early this coming Friday,' Jill said. 'That OK with you?'

'Sure,' Susie answered, picking through the morning mail. 'What do you have planned?'

'I have these friends up in Palm Beach, and they've been asking me for so long to go and visit. Well, at last I'm going.'

'You're allowed to sneak off early once in a while,' Susie teased. 'Just so long as you return the favour. Hey, you could try that new Pleasure Center up there. It's supposed to be the best there is. I heard they improved the VR technology way beyond anything that's available round here.'

'Susie!' Jill spluttered into her coffee. 'I wouldn't go to a place like that!'

'Why on earth not?' the younger woman asked, amazed. 'You have your hair done, you have your legs waxed, you go for massages and work-outs. What's the difference?'

'I think there's a lot of difference.'

'Look, it's not like you're doing anything disgusting, or illegal. It's loads of fun. I go to a local one most weeks.'

'It just seems so – so artificial. Mechanical. Sterile, in every sense.'

'You should be thankful – sterile in every sense is exactly what it is. You can't get pregnant, or AIDS. You have one hell of a good time, though. What more do you want?' Susie called over her shoulder as she headed off to her own workstation.

Jill suddenly felt much older than her forty-three years. Were women who remembered what it was to have real sex, real love, with real men, such freaks? When Jim was four, he had asked her, in all seriousness, 'Mom, when you were a kid, did you ever see a dinosaur?', and at the time she had laughed. Now she began to feel it wasn't so far from the truth. Maybe Susie was right, and she should try out this new Pleasure Center. After all, if she didn't like it, she need never go back. And it had been four long, lonely years since she had had a sexual experience of any kind with a man. Not that she had been able even to contemplate it after what had happened to Brad and Mort. Oh well, she had nothing to lose by finding out a bit more.

She went over to Susie's workstation. 'Have you actually been to the one in Palm Beach?' she asked.

'Not yet,' Susie replied, smiling at the computer screen. 'But as soon as I can make the time, I'll go. It's not like some of these places downtown you hear about, real dives some of them. It's like a top health club. You can swim, have a manicure or a massage, have your hair cut. OK, the first time I went to the one here, I took a girlfriend with me. She didn't want to go on her own either, so we went together. It was great, not as scary as we'd expected.'

'Did you actually go on a sex machine?'

Susie laughed out loud. 'Oh, Jill, you make it sound like the Big Wheel at a fairground! Of course we did! You don't think we went just to get our nails filed!'

'And it was OK?'

'What do you mean, OK? No, they didn't offer add-on services, if that's what you're thinking. And I'm sure they don't at the one in Palm Beach either.'

'Add-on services? What the hell's that?'

Susie tore her attention away from the computer screen. 'Jill, dear,' she said in mock exasperation, 'four years down here in the boonies have addled your fine intelligence. Add-on services is when they provide men – you know, to do things to you.'

'Do they really do that?' Jill asked, aghast. 'If anything like that happened, I'd never go again!'

'I just said – they don't. We're not talking sleaze here. It's a highly respectable place. All the staff are women – not one of them over twenty-two or larger than a size eight, according to my friend Lulu Lamarque, and all infuriatingly charming. Look, like you, I'd rather have a regular guy. But regular guys who can come up with the goods are a little thin on the ground right now, so a girl has to do what she can. I tell you, if you don't go, you'll be missing out.'

'I'll think about it,' Jill conceded. 'Maybe it is time I broke out of my self-imposed purdah.'

Knowingly, Susie half-scowled, half-smiled, and reached for her purse. She fished for a small card, and handed it to Jill. 'There's the number. Better call soon; a place like that'll get booked up well ahead of time.'

'Thanks.'

'And let me know how you get on!' Susie called after her friend, as Jill went back to her own workstation, and carefully put the card away in her purse.

• • •

Jill was glad to have DeeDee Felker around to help. The girl was keen, anxious to please and almost painfully careful, checking everything over and over. She was doing a Master's on the psycho-sexual effects of Seminon at the University of Florida at Talahassee and was earning money and gaining experience during her summer vacation, doing routine jobs around the lab.

'Once you gain confidence in your own abilities, you'll be good,' Jill assured her. 'You just have to learn how to use your energies most efficiently. Trust your instincts. If your instinct tells you something needs re-checking, listen to it. Better spend time checking something and finding it was right all along, than assume it's OK and run into trouble. You're an intelligent woman, DeeDee. Trust your own intelligence as well as your instincts. At the moment, you're wasting time and energy because you don't trust yourself. Believe me, I've been den mother to a lot of summer students, and you're the brightest I've had yet.'

DeeDee nervously scraped her long brown hair back behind her ears. 'Really?' she asked.

'Yes,' Jill said firmly. 'Look, I don't dish out empty compliments, particularly to students who have their way to make in the world. But you're being a real help to me this summer. With two hundred and forty blood tests to get through every hour, we can really use someone like you. And you're doing well.'

Jill pushed the wheeled chair back from her Kone Delta workstation. The fully automated benchtop analyser enabled her and her technical staff to get through a huge number of blood tests, from routine blood chemistry to specialist immunology studies, but even so, the sheer volume of work was enough to defeat any but the most organised team. She looked at her watch.

'We've done enough for today.' she said. 'Look, you've been here – what, three weeks? – and all we've ever talked about is work. How about coming over to the wine-bar across the street, unless you have to rush off?'

'Thank you. That'd be great.'

'OK. Meet you outside the main entrance in five minutes.'

• • •

'Do you mind if I ask you something?'

'You can ask,' Jill grinned, pouring a glass of wine for DeeDee. 'You may not get an answer. What is it?'

Again DeeDee pushed her hair back behind her ears, something she always did when she was nervous, which was nearly all the time. 'I had a summer vacation job last year, cleaning out the cages at NIH, up in DC. They were always talking about a Dr Jill Peters. Was that you by any chance?'

Jill watched as the level of wine in her own glass rose, then carefully set the bottle back on the table. Of course, this had to happen sooner or later. Ever since DeeDee had mentioned the degree she was doing, Jill had dreaded the moment when the girl would put two and two together, ask this very question. 'Yes,' she said. 'I used to be there. But that was four years ago.'

Oh God, she thought. I disappear without trace, revert to my maiden name, bury myself in the back of beyond, and even now, they're still talking about me. Still talking about the woman who saw her lover and her ex-lover ripped to shreds on live television; the woman who fled a distinguished career in human reproductive biology, to hide out someplace, nobody knew where. The woman who couldn't bear to watch anything on television for a whole year. The woman who even now has to turn off her set every time a documentary about urban civil violence or award-winning reportage is shown, because she can't bear to hear or see the so-called classic coverage. And, damn them: they show it over and over. Like the Kent State shootings, or Kennedy's assassination in Dallas – Christ! nearly forty years ago now! – or the Los Angeles riots, the tanks in Tiananmen Square, that Protestant lunatic from Belfast taking a shot at Bill Clinton – all classic footage. And all shown every few months, one way or another, on nationwide television over the past four years!

DeeDee was looking slightly harassed. 'They still talk about you,' she persisted.

Jill took a fortifying mouthful of wine. Nothing for it. 'Did they tell you why I left, exactly?' she asked.

DeeDee sipped at her wine like a small bird at a bird-bath. 'Well, I kinda understood that something bad happened –'

'DeeDee,' Jill broke in. 'My lover of ten years, with whom I had broken up some months previously but with whom I still maintained an affectionate friendship, and my current lover, were both beaten and torn to pieces by an enraged mob, and I saw the whole thing happen on live television. Is that what they told you?'

DeeDee was shocked into silence. 'I'm sorry,' she whispered at last. 'I never should have said anything.'

'That's OK,' Jill reassured her. 'It's nothing to what I've had to handle over the years. You might as well know.'

'But how could you *live* through something like that?' DeeDee asked, her eyes wide with horror.

Jill sighed, and folded her arms on the table. 'Short of suicide,' she told the girl, 'you just do. I had some professional counselling, of course. But in the end, the only person who can get you through it is yourself. What the coverage at the time failed to mention, thank God, is that I had also some months earlier lost my oldest, dearest friend –'

'Was that Dr Harman?' DeeDee interrupted.

Jill nodded. 'Yes. So they're still talking about that too?'

DeeDee nodded.

'And just after Dr Montgomery and Colonel Foster were killed,' Jill said, marvelling to herself at the fluency with which she managed to say it, 'my ex-husband's second wife, whom I loved very dearly, died of uterine cancer. That meant that Art was able to move down here to Florida, which he'd always wanted to do. It's worked out rather well actually, him being so close. We see each other quite a bit.'

'Do you have kids?'

Jill nodded as she took a mouthful of wine. 'Yes,' she replied. 'Art and I have a son, Jim. He's starting college next month. So when they came down here, there was no reason at all for me to stay in Washington.'

'You mean you threw up the job at NIH?'

'DeeDee, is a career at NIH what you're shooting for? If so, I hope you get it. It's a good place to work. I was there a long time. Don't let anything you hear about my experiences there put you off. It's just that I'd had enough of the corruption of Washington. You're probably more up to date with the Seminon business now than I am, because of your Master's degree. All the deceit, skulduggery and double-dealing – it got to me in the end. And I'd had four major personal losses to deal with. There was nothing – *nothing* – to keep me there. I just needed to get away.'

'But they said you were going to do all the work on developing an antidote to the side-effects of Seminon,' DeeDee insisted.

'They *told* me to do it, as though I should be grateful for the chance to sort out their mess. But I couldn't stand it any more. So I told them they could take their job, and shove it. And I walked out.'

'You walked? Just like that?'

Jill emptied her glass and scrutinised the amount left in the bottle. 'I don't think we'd better have another,' she laughed. 'Or neither of us will be fit to drive. So, a half glass for you,' she poured some for DeeDee, 'and a half for me. Yes, I walked out. It was only when I got as far as the subway that I remembered I'd left a calculator and four pairs of Dior panty-hose in my desk drawer. I hope the guy who replaced me found a use for them!'

'Do you think you would have found an antidote, if you'd stayed on?' DeeDee asked intensely.

'Who can say?' Jill answered. 'All I know is that I spent almost the whole of my career searching for the ultimate contraceptive, which Seminon purported to be. I guess at some point in my researches, I must have come very close to something which could have acted as an antidote, if only I could've identified it, developed it, made it work.'

'But they haven't, have they? Nobody has,' DeeDee said. 'Would you mind if I asked you something else? I mean, you may feel I'm going too far here –'

'Ask all you want, DeeDee. Like I said, I reserve the right not to guarantee you an answer.'

'OK, thanks. It's just that – coming from a Southern Baptist family and all – I never had sex. Nice girls don't, back where I come from. I'm not sure even bad girls do, come to that. Anyway, by the time I was old enough to realise that making out wasn't a mortal sin, it was too late. Nobody was doing it any more. They couldn't.'

'All the oh-so-moral Southern Baptists had rushed to take Seminon at the earliest possible moment, is that it?'

DeeDee nodded. 'They either took it to perform better or because they were terrified of AIDS. See, they didn't know–'

'Of course not. No one did. So what is it you want me to tell you?'

DeeDee ran her finger round the rim of her glass. 'What it was like, I guess,' she said wistfully. 'I mean, was it that great?'

Jill smiled ruefully. 'It could be, sometimes. On the other hand, it could be a bad experience. I'm sorry, but it doesn't look as though you're about to find out either way. Is there someone you care about?'

'Well, there's this guy. We share an apartment, and we love each other. My mom and dad think it's just kind of a brother and sister thing. And I guess it is – in a way. But it's something more as well. I mean, I don't know anyone else I'd want as that kind of a brother.'

'I understand,' Jill said quietly. 'You mean you find other ways of – how shall I say this? – showing your love for each other?'

DeeDee blushed violently. 'Yeah,' she nodded. 'I guess what I mean is, if we have kids – I mean, if I have a kid – I'd like it to be his. But it won't.'

'Of course not. It'll be a Caucasian, fair-skinned, blond-to-brown-haired, medium height, gender of your choice, sign-here-and-ten-thousand-dollars-please kind of kid.'

'Exactly,' DeeDee nodded, her flushed face starting to return to normal. 'We've sort of discussed it once or twice, and I get the idea he feels – well, disposable. Like he doesn't have a purpose. That's what's so cruel; not that people can't have sex, but that men can't father kids any more. It must be real nice to love someone, and have a kid with them. Properly, I mean. Not by some – mechanical *procedure*.'

Jill laid her hand over DeeDee's tightly clenched fist. 'Sure,' she said gently. 'But it isn't always as simple as that. Jim's dad and I broke up when Jim was only a little kid, and after several years of total misery. We get along better now than we ever did back then. And there was never any question of having kids with – either of the other two lovers I've had.'

'You could still have more kids!' DeeDee exclaimed. 'You're not that old. I mean, you're not as old as my mom, or anything!'

'And your mom is a little old lady of forty eight, I guess?' Jill smiled at the excited student. 'It's sweet of you to think that way, DeeDee. But believe me, there are days when I feel anything but young. And I can't imagine meeting anyone I'd want to start all over with – not now. Anyway, I have Jim.'

DeeDee smiled back. 'I feel like I ought to apologise,' she said. 'I never should have asked you all those things.'

'That's OK,' Jill assured her. 'If I were you, I'd have asked. And if you're going to be a good scientist, you must never stop asking. Never!'

• • •

After her drink with DeeDee, Jill returned to the lab to put in another hour or two. Towards the end of the evening, the mobile phone on her desk gave out yet another warble. Still concentrating on something else, she reached for it.

'Oh, hi, Art!' she said, on hearing his voice. They saw each other frequently now, and had become better friends than they had ever been.

'I just had a call from someone who wants to meet with you.'

'Oh, yes? Who?' Jill enquired, still half concentrating on an analysis print-out.

'Does the name Boris Volkov mean anything to you?'

'Boris Volkov?' Jill's attention snapped completely to what Art was saying. 'You sure? It certainly *does*!'

Art laughed. 'I thought it might. Wasn't he the guy who sold that dud formula to Pharmavax and started all the trouble? Hey, we could write our own terms for life if we handed the guy over to –'

'Art, don't even think it!' Jill implored. 'Tell me more. Where is he? Why does he want to meet with me, after all these years? And where's he been?'

'Hey, wait a minute! We didn't talk all day. You'll have to ask him all that stuff when you meet with him. Which he is very anxious for you to do. He sounds kinda desperate. He said it took weeks for him to find me, and even then he didn't know if I had any contact with you. Looks like changing your name worked.'

'Art, you said you understood about all that. You know I didn't do it to reject you or Jim.'

'Sure, sure. I understood right from the start. I even thought of changing my own name, the amount of hassle I was taking from the media. Anyway, this Volkov guy asked me to set up a meeting for him, with you.'

'Did he say what he wanted?' Jill asked warily.

'I asked. Who wouldn't? But there was no way he was going to tell me. Only you. He's calling back in a half hour. What do I tell him?'

Jill thought for a moment. 'I don't want him to come here,' she said carefully. 'And I feel it would be better if he didn't come to the house. We could meet in some public place, if he likes. I have to work late tonight. But tomorrow would be OK.'

'I'll tell him. Look, if you want to talk someplace that's

totally secure and private, you could come here. OK, OK, I know what you're thinking: that I want to listen in. But what I'm suggesting is that you spend as long as you like in Jim's den down the end of the yard. He's made it real nice in there; I'll even stand you a bottle of wine and some nuts. How's that?'

Jill forced herself to relax. Even after four years, she still found it difficult to take Art's jokey good-naturedness at face value, to understand that all his bitterness and rages really were in the past. It was as though Shirlene's death had taught him something that even her life hadn't been able to.

'It sounds perfect. I'll be there as soon as I can tomorrow after I leave the lab, but it won't be before seven. Can you tell him that?'

'Sure. See you then.'

'I'll look forward to it. And, Art – thanks.'

34.

For an ordinary tract property, Art's home had more than the usual amount of land. He'd done a deal with his neighbour to buy half her lot, which suited her because she was too old to manage it herself, and also meant that there was a large secluded space at the end of the yard where Art and Jim had been able to put up a log cabin for Jim to use as a den.

At eighteen, Jim was dreamy, creative, something of a loner. At first, Art had worried that the boy was reacting badly to Shirlene dying, but it was soon clear that he was mourning the loss of his beloved stepmother quite healthily, and simply wanted to be alone much of the time. He would spend hours painting, and the walls of the den were liberally covered with posters, and examples of his own work.

Art made his way down the garden to call Jim in for the evening meal. He always did his son the courtesy of knocking before opening the cabin door – one of the many things he had learned from Shirlene.

'C'mon in, Dad.'

Art seated himself on the long pine bench and leaned up against the planking of the cabin wall.

'Can I see what you're working on?' he asked.

'Sure,' Jim waved offhandedly at a canvas propped up on a workbench. It was abstract, highly-coloured and dramatic, and Art couldn't tell if it was any good or not. But he had learned to find positive things to say about Jim's work, which camouflaged any opinion he might have.

'Your mom would be interested to see that,' he said.

'Maybe,' Jim shrugged. Art had also learned that taciturnity on the part of an eighteen-year-old didn't indicate rudeness, just a temporary unwillingness to talk.

'The meatloaf's about done,' he said. 'We can eat any time.'

'Uh, Dad, I'm sorry. I should have said. Me and Chet made a plan that I'd go over to his place – like about now – and we'd take in a movie. I'm sorry, Dad. I forgot to say.'

Art felt justifiably annoyed. Shirlene would have had something to say to young Jim about being inconsiderate, so he reckoned he could build on her good work.

'Why is it,' he started, 'that you're always off out with Chet? You're never home. I never see you –'

'I'm sorry, Dad. It's just that – well, Chet's my friend, and –'

'Yeah, well, I wish you'd chosen some other friend –'

Art instantly regretted his words. He had vowed he wouldn't criticise Jim's choice of friends, but Chet was one about whom he had grave misgivings. Chet came from a broken home and never saw his mother, who had disappeared when he was very young. Since then a crowd of women, of varying ages and degrees of respectability, had trooped in and out of his father's life, none of them staying for long. Having himself had a less-than-useless mother, crippled with depression since he was born, Art mistrusted the idea of a family without a good woman in it, and Chet was the product of just such a home. However, Art told himself not to get mad, just to play it cool. 'I'm sorry,' he amended. 'It's OK. The meatloaf'll keep. You go on out. I just wish you'd told me in time, that's all.'

'Dad, the movie'll keep too. We can see it some other time. I'll stay home, if you like.'

Art looked at his son, an astounding mixture of his own touchy sensitivity and stubbornness, and Jill's self-driving intelligence. Plus he had a few qualities of his own, which seemed to come from nowhere. With any luck, he'd be able to achieve all the things Art had longed for, but hadn't brought off.

'That's OK,' he sighed, getting up to return to the house.

'No, really, Dad. I'll stay.' Jim reached out to take his father's hand. Art paused.

'I'd like to stay. I mean it. I need to talk with you any way. There's something I have to tell you.'

'OK,' Art sat down again. 'What is it?' he asked good-naturedly.

Jim fiddled with some brushes and tubes of paint, ranging them neatly on the narrow shelf above the workbench.

'Dad, do you still miss Shirlene?'

'Sure I do. Why?'

'It's just that – that – well, I miss her. All the time.'

Art leaned forward, his elbows on his knees and his head buried in his hands.

'Son,' he sighed. 'Let me tell you, I miss that woman every minute of every day. The best thing I ever did was marry her. Look, your mom is a fine person, and a good scientist. But Shirlene – Jim, I cry myself to sleep nights sometimes, even after all this time –'

'Me too, Dad,' Jim said quietly. He left the tidying of the shelf and came to sit down next to his father. 'Dad, how'd you feel if I didn't live here any more?'

Art sat upright, his face suffused with shocked surprise. 'What d'you mean, not live here?' he demanded. 'Where you planning on going?'

Jim shuffled on the bench trying to find words. 'Dad, will you promise not to get mad at me?'

'Look, if you want go and live with your mom, that's fine by –'

'It's not Mom I want to live with, Dad.'

'OK, I get it! You picked up some cute little piece of ass, and now she wants to play house –'

'Dad, I asked you please not to get mad!'

Art made a conscious effort to calm down. 'OK, OK,' he said at length. 'So where is it you want to live if you don't want to live with your mom?'

'Chet wants to move out from his dad's house. Says he's had enough. He says he can find an apartment someplace and it won't cost much –'

'So you'd rather go and live in some – some *tenement* block-with this guy Chet, than live with your mom or dad, is that it?'

'Dad, please!' Jim was very near to tears. 'You're not making this easy for me. I'm finding this real hard, you know!'

'OK, I'm listening. You tell me exactly why you want to leave home and share an apartment with Chet.' A trace of the old belligerence was back in Art's voice. He could hear it, and knew perfectly well it was only covering up the agitation he could feel churning in his stomach at even the thought of losing his son.

Jim was trying hard. 'It's just that – me and Chet – we want to live together.'

'Live together, huh? And what does that mean, precisely?'

'*Dad*!'

'The way you put it, it sounds like you're thinking of setting up home with some *girl*!'

'Dad! *Please*! I'm trying to tell you something here!'

Memories of Shirlene's calming counsel echoed in Art's mind. Once more, he made an effort to control himself and listen.

'All right,' he said finally. 'I promise not to interrupt, not to get mad. Just say whatever it is you want to say.'

Jim took a little while to formulate what he wanted to tell his father. 'You know how you always get on my case about the girls at school? Like you wanted me to get married practically in high school, or something?'

'I don't do that, son.'

'Dad, I'm sorry. You do. It's OK. I mean, I don't mind or anything. I guess it's what all dads do. It's just that - while there's a lot of girls I really like, as people - I don't feel I want to date any of them. Do you understand?'

'Are you trying to tell me you're some kind of a faggot?' Art glared at his son. 'That Chet's a fucking, limp-wristed -'

'Dad!' Jim almost shouted. 'You can say it like that if you want. But yes! OK! I *am* gay! I know how you feel about the whole thing. And if it could be different - if *I* could be different - I would. I'm sorry!'

Art sighed heavily. The silence hung heavily between them. 'I guess I always knew it. I just didn't want to admit it, that's all,' he said at last. 'So - you and Chet. You have sex and everything?'

Jim winced. 'Uh, Dad, I don't want to talk about that. It doesn't feel right.'

'Look, I'm not going to get mad at you. I just want to know.'

'You mean, in case it's only something I'll grow out of?' Jim said, with a sour edge to his voice. 'I'm sorry, Dad. I don't think it is. Right from when I was just a little kid, you know? - Shirlene used to tell me to ask all those girls over, like she wanted me to date them, or like having girls around would make me *not* gay. But even then, I knew how I felt.'

'OK, just answer my question,' Art said relentlessly.

'Look, Dad,' Jim said desperately. 'We have a lot going for us. We like the same things; we like being together. I have to tell you, I'm real relaxed about it. I'd like it if you could be too.'

'You still haven't told me. Do you and Chet sleep together?'

'No. We can't. Chet knew this guy before, and got scared that he might have gotten infected with HIV. He wasn't, but it was too late; he'd taken the vaccine. You know what it does to straight guys? Well, it did it to him too.'

Deep down, Art felt a surge of relief. It was hard enough for him to accept that his son was in love with another man, but he felt a small glow almost of triumph that, after all, they weren't actually having sex. However, he felt impelled to ask, 'So you're telling me that if one day they come up with an antidote, you and Chet'd have a full relationship. That it?'

'Yeah, I guess so.' Jim stood up, his hands in his pockets. He grinned uncertainly at his father. 'I'll go call Chet. Tell him I had a better invitation – from a meatloaf! That is – if you still want me to stay.'

Art heaved himself to his feet, put his arms round his son, and hugged him close. He held him hard to his own body for some time before saying, 'Faggot or not, you're the only kid I've got. Of course I want you to stay. You think I can get through a whole meatloaf on my own? Just tell me one last thing. Does your mom know?'

'I never said anything to her. But then she never asks who I'm dating, or anything like that. So I guess she must. I'll tell her properly next time I see her.'

'You'll have your chance soon enough. She's coming over tomorrow. I said she could use this place for a meeting with someone she needs to see in private. I know, I shouldn't have offered it without asking you, but you weren't around.'

'That's OK, Dad,' Jim said. He put his arm over his father's shoulders. 'Dad, I'm sorry. I know a gay son is the last thing you want. I know how much you and Shirlene would've liked kids. Now you won't even be a grandfather. I feel like I've kinda stolen something from you. And from Mom too.'

Art ruffled his son's hair roughly. 'Yeah, well, if that's the way it is, then that's the way it is. You coulda turned out a whole lot worse! Look, they have late showings at the movies, don't they? Why don't you call Chet, say your old man made too much meatloaf again, and have him come over and help us out?'

35.

Art threw a handful of weeds on to the smouldering fire. As he straightened up, his face creased for a second as a twinge shot through his lower spine. Damn! His back was acting up again! It hadn't been right for weeks, ever since he'd played a frisky twenty-pound fish for a whole hour before it somehow wrenched itself off the hook, and was lost. Enough gardening for one day, he told himself; time for a drink. He dusted the dry soil off his hands and contemplated the thickly-smoking fire for a moment. Better put it out before Jill turned up, he decided, and started to kick the embers apart. Even so, the weeds were still producing smoke, so he started for the house to fetch the hose.

Jill came out of the patio door, and waved. She was looking well, less groomed but more relaxed than she had in Washington. She skirted a small group of palmettos and met Art halfway down the yard.

'Hi,' he greeted her with a peck on the cheek. 'You're a little early. It's only six forty-five.'

'One of the fringe benefits of only having to work an eight to five day is that you get to places on time,' she grinned. 'When I think how I had to practically kill myself not to be late, back in the old days!'

'Yeah,' Art grunted, turning on the water. 'Stand back a moment. I just have to put out the fire. We don't want to asphyxiate your elusive Russian scientist.'

'After all these years, I should hope not!' she laughed. 'Is Jim around?'

'Uh, no,' Art said. 'He said to say hi, though. He's over at Chet's place.'

'He seems to spend a lot of time there,' Jill observed.

'Uh,' Art started uncertainly. 'Has he ever talked to you – about Chet, I mean?'

'Sure, from time to time,' Jill answered non-committally. She watched Art closely, but he was concentrating on saturating the hissing, steaming bonfire, and wouldn't meet her eye. She had a shrewd suspicion what he was trying to tell her, but wanted him to be the one to voice it. So she waited while he turned the water off, wound the hosepipe back on to its reel and put it away in the storage space under the patio.

'Has he told you he wants to – uh – share an apartment with the guy?'

'No. But it doesn't surprise me.'

'It doesn't?' Art replied, taken aback. He ran his hand through his thinning hair. 'Look, when I say share an apartment, I mean – Christ, what do I mean?'

'You mean they want to live together,' Jill said mildly.

'Yeah,' Art sighed. 'Did you know about all this?'

'I suppose so.' Jill sat down on the bottom step. Art joined her.

'He never said anything, but you watch the signs over the years. Did he tell you himself?'

Art nodded.

'That was brave of him. There was a time –'

' – when I'd've flayed the hide off him. I know. And of course he knew that too. I guess Shirlene changed all that for me. Thing is, since she's been gone, I need Jim all the more, gay or not. Sure, I wish he wasn't gay – any father would. And I wish he'd found someone better than that Chet. But he's a big boy; he can make his own decisions.'

'Yes,' Jill agreed soberly. Then she smiled at Art. 'This explains something. He said last week he was going to take me out to dinner. He's banked all the money he made stacking shelves at the supermarket, and he feels rich. I guess he wants to tell me himself, so I won't let on you've said anything. And I'll also insist that I want a pizza more than anything, so as not to bankrupt him.'

'Yeah, he mentioned that to me. I said I'd pay for the wine. Speaking of which –' Art got up – 'that Russian'll be here any minute. I hope he likes chilled Chardonnay.'

Jill followed Art into the house. He put two glasses on a tray and emptied a pack of mixed nuts into a dish Jim had made at pottery class in fifth grade, and which Shirlene had insisted on using every day. Then he took a bottle of wine from the refrigerator, opened it and set it on the tray, which he handed to Jill.

'You go on down to the cabin; I'll send him along when he comes, OK?'

Jill rested the tray on the worktop for a moment. 'You know, I'm feeling really nervous about this whole thing,' she confessed.

'You, nervous? C'mon! Surely not!'

'I mean it. I don't know why, but I am. I only met him once, at a conference in London back in 97. I thought at the time that he was straight. You know, honest. But since then, everything he's touched has turned to disaster. I really don't think I have the strength left to get involved in any more schemes or scams. I've left all that behind me, or so I thought.'

'You don't have to get involved in anything,' Art reassured her. 'All you have to do is listen to what the guy has to say. Want me to come on down after half an hour, see if you're OK?'

Jill grinned wearily, and hefted the tray in both hands. 'Thanks for the thought. But I'll be OK.'

Unlike Art, Jill could see real merit in her son's work. It had force and energy, and his use of colour was daring and challenging. Of course, it was still immature, but Jim was young; with proper tuition and training, she could tell, he was going to be good. Not for the first time, she wondered where Jim had inherited his gift from. Certainly not from either of his parents. Art couldn't tell a Titian from a Tretchikoff, and Jill freely admitted she couldn't draw so much as a straight line. Her parents-in-law showed no interest in the creative world, and her own father thought all artistic effort a waste of time. Maybe her mother had had some yearning to draw and paint, and had never been allowed to express it. Jill would never know. She could only hope and pray that Jim's gift would bring him success and happiness.

A soft knock startled her out of her musings. She opened the door.

Boris Volkov looked older, more worn, than she was expecting. The glossy black hair was turning pewter-grey at the temples, and his face was thinner. But when he smiled, and the green eyes lit up, the force of his charm hit her just as it had all those years ago. Yes, she'd been right first time. In spite of the tired lines round the eyes, this man was still seriously attractive! Calm down, she told herself. This is business!

'Dr Peters?' Boris said, extending his hand as he came into the cabin. 'Or should I call you Dr Farleigh?'

'Jill will do. I'm sure you understand why I had to change back to my maiden name.'

'Of course. The media must have made your life unbearable.'

'My life was unbearable in any case,' Jill replied, more crisply than she had intended. 'You may remember, two men I knew very well were torn to pieces by a deranged mob, on live television. And in addition –'

'Yes, I know,' Boris said softly. 'I know everything that happened. I would quite understand if you refused to have anything to do with me. It must seem as though everything happened because of me.'

'Didn't it?' she asked challengingly.

'To a certain extent. But you cannot imagine my own situation at the time, if you have never lived in Russia. I was in a stranglehold.'

'I'm sure.'

'It's true, and one day I will answer every question you put to me. But not now. We have very little time. First, I must ask you a question. It is about American etiquette. If two people meet, and neither is in their own home, which of them should pour the wine?'

In spite of herself Jill relaxed, smiled weakly and picked up the wine bottle. 'I'm sorry,' she said, pouring a glass and handing it to Boris. 'Of course there must be more to it than I'm aware of. And there are a lot of questions. I'd more or less resigned myself to never knowing the whole truth.'

'One day soon, you will. I promise.'

Jill sat down at the paint-spattered table. 'Sit where you like,' she motioned. Boris settled himself on the bench, long legs stretched out in front of him. 'I feel entitled to a few answers straight away, though. Last anyone saw of you, you'd jumped a train somewhere in eastern Hungary.'

Boris looked up, his eyes alight. 'You really think I jumped that train?'

'Didn't you? There was a door open and no sign of you. Brad Foster told me.'

'Not even the best KGB people can fling themselves out of

trains going that fast. In fact, we were discouraged from doing so. Highly-trained people are expensive to replace. No, I stayed on it until Budapest.'

'And Brad Foster never saw you?'

'Yes, he saw me, more than once. But he didn't recognise me. To disguise yourself, you don't need to put on a false beard and a wig. You simply become somebody else. I don't think the CIA is trained in quite the same way.'

'It seems hard to believe that you could just be there, in plain sight, and get away with it.'

Boris shrugged. 'There was something strange about Foster, during that time we were together. One professional can judge another fairly accurately, and there is no doubt that he was very, very good. But there was something about him that puzzled me, as though he had to work too hard at being professional. It seemed not to come naturally to him, as though he had – gone soft, do you say?'

'If I told you he'd had a shot of Seminon, would that explain it?'

'I knew he had. He told me. And yes, it does explain a lot. I had a shot too, you know. In fact, I was one of the first guinea pigs in the world.'

A pang of disappointment shot through Jill. So the most attractive man she'd met in years had just ruled himself out of the game! Oh well, she sighed to herself. 'So you know what it does better than anyone.'

'Indeed. Now, there are two other questions that you haven't asked me.'

'Two!' she exclaimed. 'There are a hell of a lot more than two, I can assure you. But let's start with just two, if you like. One: where have you been since you got off the train at Budapest? And two: why are you here?'

'When I found myself in Budapest, with half a million dollars and a Hungarian passport, I realised I had almost complete freedom. I could do anything I wanted. But I didn't *know* what I wanted. I stayed in a hotel for a few days and drank far too much vodka. And I did a lot of thinking. I soon concluded that the one thing I had to do was to atone for the way I helped cause this disaster. Obviously, America was not the place to do this. And I couldn't go back to Russia; too many people wanted my blood, including the mafia bosses whose computers I messed up with a time-bomb virus. Of course, there are labs operating outside the law in many countries, but in most cases they don't have the money that the big multinationals have. There seemed only one answer: Colombia.'

Jill looked up from her glass and fixed him with an incredulous stare.

'Yes, I knew you would be horrified. You're thinking: the bastard is into crack cocaine now. But the cocaine barons also want to develop designer drugs, miracle cures. There's huge money to be made, just as much as with heroin and cocaine. They are prepared to spend enormous amounts, millions, to get it right. And for me, getting it right is the most important thing. So that is where I went.'

'And the answer to my second question is –?'

'That I want you to come with me back to Colombia.'

'No way,' Jill said dismissively. 'I left all that behind, and anyway I don't believe in it any more.'

'But I do. And I have good reason to. Listen, the people I work for have so much money, they don't know where it is half the time. They don't even know how rich they are. So for four years I have had everything I asked for provided without question, the best facilities money can buy, the best scientists. I really think I have found an effective reversal agent *and* a viable delivery system. And I have come close, so close, to finding the vaccine as well. But I have hit a problem, and now I need you. You're the only person I know who could come up with the solutions. I know that with your help, I can do it. *We* can do it.'

'Are you crazy? If you think I'm just going to throw up everything here, take my life in my hands and go off to work for some Medellin drug baron, you can think again. I have a job here – not much of one, I agree – but it's a job, and I owe some loyalty to my employers and colleagues. And I have my son to think of –'

'I apologise,' Boris broke in gently. 'I did not make myself clear. I'm not talking about a lifetime commitment, only a matter of a few weeks. Two, perhaps three. My employers would pay you generously for your time; you would live in complete luxury while you were there. And if we succeeded, you could ask for any amount of money you wanted.'

'None of that's important,' Jill said impatiently. 'I didn't go into research to get rich.' But inside, she felt a tingle of excitement. Boris had touched on the part of her she'd kept hidden for the last four years.There were so many loose ends she'd wanted to tie up. Her intellectual curiosity started to get the better of her. 'But tell me more.'

'Well, we've set up our own vaccine production plant. We have the best fermenter that can be bought, and the highest quality raw materials. Our yields could be formidable. I believe we're on the verge of finding a vaccine that will give protection against pregnancy without affecting the testes. And, more important still, we're well on the way to finding an antidote that will reverse the existing side-effects in men who took Seminon. But I need you to help with the end-stage production processes.'

'So what's this problem you've run into?' Jill reached for the wine bottle and poured them each another glass.

'We can't seem to get the culture medium quite right. The way we're doing it now, the yields just aren't high enough. And we're getting too much degradation in the final stages of the process. The cells aren't doing their job properly.'

'Why ask me? I'm not a process engineer,' Jill interrupted.

'I know. But you know all there is to know about CHO cells. Look, we have technicians, dozens of them. But they can't make the monkey cells do what we want, and it's holding us up. And the guy who owns us – and I can tell you he is just like the old serf-masters of Russia before 1917 – is becoming understandably impatient.Trouble is that when men like him get impatient, their trigger fingers start to twitch; it's the only way they know.'

'Are you telling me your life's in danger if you don't come up with the goods?'

'I wouldn't want to put it to the test,' Boris replied wrily. 'I know I'm dispensible – I'm living on borrowed time anyway. But please don't think that I'm asking for your help only in order to save my own skin. I really do want to find the solution.'

'Boris,' Jill leaned forward earnestly. 'If you were me, and some Russian scientist whom you had no reason to trust, turned up one day and asked you to go to Colombia to work for a trigger-happy cocaine baron, would you trust him?'

'Of course not.' There was a gentle twinkle in the mesmerising green eyes.

'But you expect me to trust you?'

'Not really. But I hope you will.'

'Before I make any decision at all, I'm going to ask you a few questions to which I've always needed answers.'

Boris spread his hands, palm upwards, and nodded. 'Feel free,' he said.

'There's something I still haven't understood. Why, if you wanted the original formula stolen so it could be developed in America, did you then steal it from NIH and sow that damn virus in our computer system? And why did you go and sell the formula to Pharmavax? It looked as though you were playing on your own, and for greed.'

'Of course it did. But it wasn't like that at all. My bosses hoped that a company like Pharmavax would steal it, knowing that such companies can be – less than meticulous, let's say – in observing safety regulations. But with a government lab, every rule would have to be observed, and it would have taken far too long; longer than we had, anyway. You don't understand how desperate the Russian government was for dollars. And the only way we were going to make money was from selling the antidote.'

'I know how much you needed the foreign curency, but were you really desperate enough to cause the appalling –?'

Boris sprang to his feet, and leaned towards her, his palms flat on the table, a look of near-agony on his face.

'No!' he almost shouted. 'No matter what you think, we Russians are not monsters. Even the bosses have some shreds of decency left. They would never have devised this plan if they had known of the eventual side-effects, the burn-out and the impotence. Yes, they took a calculated risk that the aggression it caused in monkeys wouldn't manifest itself in humans. In that, I agree, they are to blame. But they put me under huge pressure, blackmailed me, threatened me with all kinds of things. Not just to hurt me but others too. And we were to start on an antidote. If I thought there was no possible antidote, I would go mad with guilt and shame. That is why I have spent four years working, struggling to find it. Please, Jill, I need your help.'

Jill forced her mind away from the thought of her purloined research data, snug in among a box of floppies at the very back of her desk, and asked, levelly, 'As a matter of interest, if you had chosen to disbelieve them, what could you have done?'

Boris sat down again. 'I think you already know the answer to that. There would have been nothing I could do. You can be the best industrial espionage expert in all Russia, with a fancy Moscow apartment, cars, dacha, privileges of every kind, the Government's darling. But if they choose, overnight you have nothing, certainly no power. You can easily end up dead, too.'

'OK, but why Pharmavax?' Jill grilled him mercilessly.

'I know I said I would answer all your questions, but I hoped you would let me do it later; we really don't have much time. We'd been watching Montgomery for some time; we were pretty certain he wouldn't be able to resist the chance to become involved, and that he would shortcut some of the testing. As it happened, we were proved right.'

'And what about Mira Harman?' Jill went on implacably. 'Did you kill her? Don't lie to me. I have to know.'

'No,' said Boris, gazing at her steadily. 'I heard she was killed, but I swear her death was nothing to do with me, or my bosses. In any case, why would we want to kill her? She was no threat to us. She had good reason to hate Russians, from what I learned of her, but we don't kill people just because they hate us. She was your friend. I'm sorry.'

'It's been difficult, not knowing why she died. Do you know, I still haven't buried her yet? The case is still open, and the police won't release the body. I keep asking and asking. She was born Jewish, you know, and Jewish law stipulates that a body must be buried very soon after death. She would be deeply offended at being kept all this time in a – a freezer! I'm sorry, it still upsets me.'

'That's a mystery I cannot help you solve; I'm sorry. One day, I'm sure, you will be able to bury her.'

Her grief for Mira was none of his business, Jill felt. So she said nothing. Boris leaned forward, elbows on knees. 'I'm sure you have a thousand other things to ask, but there's only one question I want you to answer. Will you come to Colombia and work with me, soon?'

'I'll have to think about it. I couldn't come right away, in any case. I'd have to clear it with my bosses, and with my colleague Susie Freeberg.'

Thank God, she thought, Boris had the grace not to give her the devastating green-eyed treatment, as though her agreement were a foregone conclusion. But she had to admit that the idea of working in her own field again, using all her hard-won research, and alongside the charming Russian, was the most exciting prospect she had contemplated since leaving Washington. 'I'm sure I have some vacation due,' she told him. 'I promise to let you know definitely, one way or the other, tomorrow afternoon. Give me a number where I can call you.'

He scribbled a local number on a scrap of paper from Jim's pad and handed it to her. This time he did flash that disarming smile, damn him! 'I look forward to a very profitable and enjoyable partnership,' he said, as he got up to go.

'Me too,' she blurted out, before she realised what she was saying. But Boris had already disappeared into the darkness outside.

36.

Jill cautiously made her way round the workmen busy on the floor of the lobby. The room she entered, with its deep-pile carpet, spotlit limited edition prints and silk wallcovering, could have belonged to any top medical or legal practice in any major city in the States. She felt reassured. In spite of Susie Freeberg's insistence that this was no sleazy dive, but a classy, upmarket establishment on which no expense had been spared, she had had her doubts. She couldn't help being amused that the receptionist conformed exactly to Susie's description of the staff. Hair, body, nails and smile had cost thousands of dollars and the result, even if slightly predictable, was certainly worth looking at.

'Hi!' the girl grinned dazzlingly. 'I'm LouAnne. How may I help you?'

Jill was beginning to feel untidy, flabby, out of her depth. But she was here now, and there was no going back. 'I'm Jill Farleigh,' she answered. 'I have an appointment for two-thirty.'

The Spandex-clad receptionist scanned the computer screen, and tapped it with a flawlessly-manicured finger. 'Here we are,' she said brightly. 'This is your first time with us, isn't it?'

'That's right.'

'I expect you're a little nervous. Don't worry; everybody is, their first time. Can I just take some details, for billing purposes? How will you be paying?'

'Amex OK?'

'That's fine. Now, your personal attendant will be with you momentarily. Would you like to take a seat?'

Jill sat down on the sumptuous leather couch. One glance at the titles of the magazines neatly fanned out on the low travertine table was enough to remind her exactly why this wasn't quite like a doctor's or dentist's consulting rooms. She looked around, still feeling slightly nervous. LouAnne was busy methodically entering items into her computer via the touch-screen icons, and occasionally using the keyboard. The air of quiet calm was slightly eerie. Jill picked up a magazine, but felt so tense she realised she was hardly reading it. The pictures of naked men, many with full erections, slid under her gaze and had little effect on her.

Why on earth am I in such a state?, she demanded of herself angrily. Here I am, age forty-three, a former top government research scientist with a staff of nearly eighty, and I'm as jittery as a schoolgirl on a first date.

'Ms Farleigh? I'm Anna, your personal attendant. Will you come this way, please?' For a moment, Jill thought it was LouAnne who was speaking to her. But no, it was another lookalike leggy blonde, clad in aquamarine Spandex and flashing a welcoming smile. Jill stood up and took the proffered hand, uneasily aware that Anna would guess from the clamminess of Jill's own hand how anxious she was. But the girl was a pro, Jill reasoned; she must deal with nervous customers all the time. So what the hell?

'Come on through, Jill,' Anna invited, holding the pale oak door open for her. The two women stepped through into a spacious corridor. 'Have you been to other pleasure centers before?'

'No. To be honest, I never much liked the idea. That's why I'm slightly uneasy. But a friend talked me into it.'

'You won't be disappointed, Jill,' said Anna. 'I can guarantee it.'

Jill wondered what Anna and LouAnne had looked like before their metamorphosis into smiling taut-bodied blondes, but conceded that both girls were immaculately and professionally presented. She was only too aware of the narrow line that divides the classy from the tacky, and realised that there was nothing tacky about this place. Even the Spandex leotards were well cut and clearly expensive.

The room Anna showed Jill into was small, but stylishly furnished. One wall was completely covered with mirror glass, and the low table, also made of travertine marble, held a florist's bouquet of real flowers. A computer terminal stood on a small desk, and one corner was curtained off, rather like the changing area in an upmarket clothing store. The air was deliciously scented with something herbal and heavy which Jill couldn't for the moment identify.

'Coffee?' Anna indicated the percolator.

'Thank you, I'd love some.'

'Now, since this is your first time with us, I'll be staying with you nearly all the way through. Of course, on subsequent visits you won't need me at all, but I'll always be around the place anyway. First, I'll need you to fill out some personal details about yourself on our computer. And in case you're worried, I can assure you that everything you enter will be absolutely confidential. First thing you do, you create your own security code. You can keep it private if you want, though some of my ladies do tell me their codes, so we can help them better. When you're all through, would you undress, and ring for me when you're ready?'

Anna indicated a small push-button beside the computer. Jill settled herself at the screen as Anna left the room, her initial attack of nerves already somewhat reduced by Anna's serene, business-like manner. She clicked the mouse to start the routine, and was immediately offered a choice of English or Spanish. She chose English.

'Welcome to Palm Beach Pleasure Center.' The computer spoke in soft, feminine tones, totally unlike the way computers spoke even five years earlier, which had sounded like Mickey Mouse with adenoids.

'Please use the icons on the screen to create your own security code,' the voice invited her. Jill did as she was bidden.

'If you'd prefer to turn off my voice, please do so now.' Jill was slightly thrown by this. Did she want to go through the program alone and in silence, or would she rather have the company of her so-nearly human electronic guide? Quickly, she touched the 'voice' icon on the screen.

'Thank you. Now enter the name by which you wish to be called.'

Obediently, Jill keyed in J.I.L.L.

'Thank you, Jill,' the voice cooed. 'Please continue with the questionnaire. If you need assistance, please call your attendant. Have you ever had sex with a man?' Jill touched the 'yes' icon.

'How long ago was that?' 'Four years' she chose from the grid of boxes offered on the screen.

'When you had sex with a man, what were your favourite sexual pastimes?' I hope to God this is confidential, Jill thought, as she scanned the list of options. However, clearly the Pleasure Center wasn't about to be surprised by anything their clients did;

the range of activities was almost hair-raising. Jill was relieved that her choices, by their standards, were probably fairly modest.

Sipping her coffee, she worked her way methodically through the questions, intrigued to find she was actually quite enjoying it. For four years, she had buried herself in her work, hadn't even been out on a date. She had forced herself to forget her ten satisfying years with Mort – satisfying, at least, until he had tried to manipulate her life more than she felt was right – and the voraciously sexual, game-playing creature she had become with Brad Foster. Now she realised that she had shut off a whole part of herself which had once been alive and important. Even in a world where men were violent, impotent and sterile, women were still – it seemed – having a good time, probably a better time than before. After all, you could live out your wildest fantasies on a machine, and there would be no come-back, no morning-after regrets. Once you walked out the door, that was that.

The voice went on caressingly, 'What are your favourite fantasy themes? Please select as many as you wish.' Again, the range of choices was illuminating. Jill read the list, amazed that people would actually have such thoughts. She surprised herself by choosing fantasies so intimate she had never told anybody, not even Brad, about them.

Then the screen flashed up lists of physical characteristics such as height, build, colour of hair and eyes. The voice said, 'Please use the physical descriptions on the screen to describe the person with whom you wish to share your fantasy.'

Jill thought carefully about that one. Did she want to share her fantasy with a man she already knew? Certainly not Mort or Brad; it had taken her too long to sleep peacefully at night without being woken by nightmares about the way they had both been killed; she didn't want to start all that again. And, anyway, both men were part of a past she had left behind when she had fled Washington.

Instead, a recent memory flashed into her mind, of a lean body, long legs and a mocking green-eyed smile. So, he was out of the question, but what the hell, she thought. A girl can dream, can't she? And Boris Volkov was never going to know.

Almost furtively, she programmed his description on to the computer.

A few more questions, and she was done.

'Thank you for your time,' the electronic voice concluded. 'Now, please undress, and call for your attendant.'

By this time, Jill was beginning to quite enjoy the whole thing. It was a novel experience, and appealed to her love of hi-tech gadgetry, something she always enjoyed in her professional work. She quickly undressed and hung up her clothes. Even the quilted hangers were expensive, and bore the designer's name in a fussy repetitious print too small to read.

As she walked out of the changing area, she inspected herself critically in the mirror. So she was forty-three, twice the age of the Spandex-clad beauties who staffed the Pleasure Center. And she'd had a child. Even so, she reassured herself, she didn't look so bad. She certainly had nothing to be ashamed of. Everything was where it ought to be – gravity hadn't done its worst – and there wasn't too much of anything. Hours spent jogging, or working out in the health club, had paid off. She laughed to herself. Anna and LouAnne should look so good at her age! She rang for Anna.

'How'd you get on?'

'OK, thank you. Nothing to be nervous about at all.'

'Sure. It's the only way we know how to program the equipment so everything's right for you. Now, first thing we do is get you completely relaxed.'

Anna pressed a button in the wall, and, with a soft hum, a couch descended from a vertical niche in the wall, its legs extending automatically to settle into the thick carpet. Anna spread a luxuriously soft towel over the couch.

'Come and lie down, will you?'

Jill was used to massages at her health club, and didn't need to be asked twice. She lay face down on the couch, and Anna spread some warm scented oil over her back.

'That smells so nice,' she remarked.

'We have it specially made in the Middle East. They say it's based on some ancient recipe. Just wait and see what it does for you; that's even better than the fragrance.'

Anna soothed away the remaining anxiety and tension locked in Jill's body. Her shoulders were still tense after the long drive from Miami, but Anna's firm hands soothed away the stiffness within seconds.

'How's that feel?' she asked.

'Great,' Jill answered sleepily. 'Can you come home with me so I can have this all day?'

Anna just smiled and went on with her rhythmic caresses. Jill felt lulled almost to sleep by the warmth of the room and the heavy, musky aroma of the scented oil.

After about fifteen minutes, Anna gently commanded, 'Now let your legs open a bit.' Jill did so without any embarrassment or shyness. Anna's fingers caressed the base of Jill's spine, teasing the magic spot that had always been an arousal centre for her. It also brought back memories of Brad, and how he used to stimulate her in the same way, with scented oils and strong hands. It all felt familiar enough, yet her recall seemed to come from a great distance, as though her body was yielding lost memories that her mind had long forgotten.

Gently, Anna's fingers started to explore the crease between Jill's buttocks, slipping teasingly down her crack but tantalisingly retracing their path before reaching her moist darkness. Slowly, the young woman's hands circled the firm muscles, kneading them in such a way as to produce total relaxation tinged with intense erotic desire. For the first time, Jill admitted to herself exactly why she was there.

Then Anna started on Jill's thighs. The long overlapping strokes, with first one hand then the other, brought Jill to increasing heights of both relaxation and arousal. Her whole body was almost aching with the delicious sensations she knew would eventually bring her to the reason for her visit.

'Roll over now, Jill,' Anna ordered softly. 'I expect the front of you wants the same sort of attention.' Jill obeyed, feeling a delicious languor in every limb. Starting with her face, Anna worked her way down the length of Jill's glowing body, seeking out all the nooks and crannies that experience told her was what women really enjoyed. As the oil found its way on to Jill's breasts, Anna rolled her nipples firmly between her fingers and Jill realised that this was no ordinary massage oil. Her breasts started to throb and her nipples felt as if they would burst.

'I don't know what's in this stuff, but it's certainly having an amazing effect,' she gasped.

'It's meant to,' Anna grinned. 'Just wait till I get going lower down.'

Jill smiled contentedly. Not so long ago, she'd have been shocked to find herself enjoying such pleasure at the hands of another woman, would have tormented herself with agonised doubts about whether or not she was gay. But in those days, there were still men around. Now, women had to take their pleasure when and how they could, and were making the discovery that few men knew how to arouse a woman as well as another woman did.

Now Jill's belly was feeling the heat of Anna's touch, as the girl's hands moved in ever increasing circles centred round Jill's navel. Then, with deeply probing fingertips of both hands, Anna massaged her way down to Jill's thighs.

'Open your legs now,' she ordered. Jill did so unquestioningly, in a daze of sweet-smelling pleasure and hypnotic delight, as Anna wrapped each thigh in loving caresses, paying special attention to the backs of her knees, and lingering on the soft skin of her inner thighs.

Jill jumped a little with surprise as Anna's confident fingers teasingly skimmed her parted lips, even though it was exactly what she wanted. The exploring fingers gentled the mystical oil into her lips and secret opening, and slid over the inner surface of the delicate folds. Jill shuddered with excitement as the oil started to work its magic, and her whole body strained in sensual and erotic expectation.

'You're about ready now,' Anna said softly, taking Jill's hand and gently helping her off the couch.

Jill could hardly walk. Her head was swimming, and her body ached with excitement, her skin alive in a way she'd never known before, even in her best days with men. Anna led her through to a darkened room.

'This is our latest model Orgasmotron,' she said proudly. The machine stood about eight feet high; it was a kind of near-vertical bed quilted with numerous padded pockets, each about two inches square. 'You just lie back on it, like it was a bed, and let your feet rest on the supports at the bottom.'

Jill followed the instructions without question.

'Now, let's put the headset on.'

It was a standard virtual-reality kit. As Anna lowered the white helmet gently over Jill's head, Jill said, 'I learned to play golf on something like this.'

'Sure,' said Anna. 'It's just like the things the kids play games on, down at the mall.'

In a few seconds, it was strapped in place, the screen still blank. Jill's imagination started to race.

'Now, I'm just going to place these cups over your breasts – like this. There, how does that feel?'

'Fine.'

'OK, now, you'll feel a little suction as I apply the vacuum to them. When your boobs feel good and tight inside the cups, let me know.'

Jill felt the cups gradually tightening on her breasts, drawing them deeper and deeper into the warm cavities. When they were firmly tight, and she sensed her nipples being touched by something at the apex of each cup, she signalled to Anna to stop.

'For the best effect, they should feel pretty tight to start with. Is that OK?'

'It feels great,' Jill said sleepily.

Anna tore open a plastic vacuum pack. 'Now, I'm just going to slip this inside you, so you'll need to relax.'

Jill was so relaxed already that she scarcely felt Anna insert into her a warm, slippery object that felt for all the world like her favourite dildo. It was only when she felt it nudge the neck of her womb deep inside that she caught her breath, and uttered an involuntary cry of pleasure.

'I'll just take it up to size, so you tell me when it feels nice and snug.'

Jill heard a slight hiss as Anna let compressed air fill the inflatable organ. As it enlarged, she became even more aware of her breasts in their vacuum cups, and her whole body started to take on a new reality, as though it were beyond her own control.

For a second, she felt a rising surge of panic. Here she was, every inch of her, inside and out, in the literal grip of a machine that had the power to stimulate and control her every sensation and satisfy her most extreme fantasy. Yet at the same time Jill felt seduced by curiosity into going forward, to see just what would happen, rather than calling a halt there and then. 'That's getting a bit tight now,' she told Anna.

'OK, we'll stop for now. But don't worry, it'll adjust itself automatically to be as thick as you want it at any stage of your arousal. As you get bigger inside, it reads it and keeps in step with you. And it'll move in and out at any speed you choose. You regulate it with this hand control, here.'

Jill felt a control, rather like a gear-shift, being placed in her hand. Anna showed her how to operate it, since Jill couldn't see anything except the blank screen inside the VR visor. It was much like changing gear in her previous car that had a stick-shift.

'This direction starts the machine, OK? This one stops the whole thing, should you want to at any time. This one alters the depth of the thrusting, very gradually, and this one here changes the speed faster or slower, as you choose. Everything else has already been set by the computer so that what you described in the questionnaire will happen, just the way you like it.'

'Anything else I ought to know?' Jill laughed.

'I just have to warn you that the whole Orgasmotron revolves through 360 degrees, just like a flight simulator, so it actually puts your body into positions that feel right with gravity. Whatever positions gives you the best orgasms, the machine will put you right there, and it won't stop till you've had all the orgasms you want. But don't forget, you can stop it yourself any time you want to. Now, are you ready?'

Jill nodded, and Anna closed the front of the machine firmly and locked its sides together.

Jill's heart was thumping as though it would leave her chest. Her breasts were tightly encased in their cups, the inflatable organ felt enormous inside her, and her skin was glowing all over with the tingling warmth of the massage oil.

After a few seconds, the screen flickered into life, and the machine started to hum. The familiar scent of male sweat, something she'd almost forgotten, began to pervade the room. Second by second, the scientist in Jill was switching off as her primitive brain responded to the pheromones. A couple appeared on the screen, making love. The woman was Jill, and the man was – yes it was! – Boris Volkov. It was almost as though the computer had been able to read Jill's mind beyond the bare physical details she had chosen; it had matched up her memory of him astoundingly accurately.

A rippling ran through all the little inflatable pockets that surrounded and caressed her skin, stroking every inch of her from top to toe with warm, smoothing fingers. She let out a sigh of pure pleasure as the sensuality of it all began to overtake her. It was if a dozen men were all caressing her at once. How on earth could a real man ever hope to compete with this?

Her nipples began to feel a delicious sensation at the tip of each cup, as though little tongues were teasing them. The scene before her eyes was so real, so alive, that she was beginning to feel that she was actually in it. The man turned to her, and she thought he kissed her – at least, that was what it felt like, his lips and tongue gently exploring hers.

Now the whole machine started to move her body in space.The bottom half of the couch tilted upwards, bending her legs back towards her belly, and forcing the dildo deeper still inside her. The man on the screen moved closer still until his body seemed to cover hers. Jill reached for the control near her right hand. At her command the penis inside her thrust deeper than ever, and Jill groaned as it seemed to reach into the very depths of her. Her finger pushed the lever as Anna had shown her, and the organ did her bidding and went faster, compressed air increasing its size as she made more space for it. She could hear her own moans reverberating inside the headset. The nipple tongues also speeded up their insistent caresses until her breasts ached with the pressure of her own lust. Daringly, she increased the depth and speed of her pelvic thriller further still, and gave herself up to the overwhelming pleasure.

The whole machine began to move again, and she felt herself turned, as if by an enormous but gentle hand, until she felt herself suspended face down, with her legs drawn up as though she were kneeling on all fours. The screen showed her all this, as her fantasy man crouched behind her, his penis erect. As he came into her, the computer program took over from her hand control. The electric tongues swirled frenziedly round her nipples, and Jill felt she was riding on a wave of intense and overwhelming bliss. Just as she was thinking: I don't want this to end, ever, a tiny vibrator softly buzzed on her clitoris. As though it were the signal her whole body had been straining for, Jill abandoned herself to a crashing orgasm, her own screams of delight and release almost deafening her as the screen went blank.

An eternity later, Jill felt the nipple tongues slowing down, ceasing their erotic teasing; dimly, she heard the soft hiss of escaping compressed air, and became aware that she was slowly and gently being returned to her original position. She felt dazed and limp in the grip of the powerful machine, and could do no more than lie there, her eyes closed. She had told the computer that she liked to have one really big orgasm, and it had obeyed her.

Had real men ever been as good as that? She felt so shattered by sheer pleasure that the effort of trying to remember what it had really been like was too much. She drifted off into a dreamlike state.

A few minutes later, she heard Anna flicking up the clamps along the flanks of the machine.

'How'd it go?' the girl enquired brightly. Jill couldn't summon up the energy to reply.

'I just love it,' Anna went on. 'We go on it after hours. But I guess it's nothing like as good as a real man, is it? See, I never had sex with a guy, and I really like talking with women who can remember what it was like back then.'

Poor Anna, Jill thought. And poor LouAnne. All those thousands of dollars and all that effort, to achieve those glossy smiles and whip-thin bodies, and for what? Both girls had moulded themselves into a male ideal of beauty, but no matter how many men found them desirable, there were pitifully few who could do anything about it. She forced herself to gather her wits, to find something to say to the girl.

'I have to tell you, most men would never take so much trouble,' she said. 'And of course they couldn't keep on and on, like this thing can.'

'Oh, sure,' Anna greed. 'This'll keep going all day and all night if that's what you want.'

Jill laughed. 'I don't think flesh and blood could stand it!'

'But wasn't that kind of annoying, that they couldn't keep going? I mean, did you ever have an orgasm properly?'

'I was lucky,' Jill answered. 'A lot of women didn't, but I had a very considerate lover for many years. Even he couldn't compete with this, though.'

'But it must have been great. I mean, if you loved someone, you could have sex with them all the time –'

Oh dear! this poor child was under the same impression DeeDee was: that the past was some kind of sexual Golden Age, populated with men who both wanted sex and were good at it. Jill said gently, 'Sure, sex could be good a lot of the time. But men are human beings, not machines. They don't come with any guarantees.'

'So, I guess all this electronic stuff has been real good for women of your age, then,' Anna said, hiding a certain wistfulness behind her professional bright façade.

'Yes, in a way. But let's just say it's different.' Jill felt a slight chill of regret and disappointment creep into the warm cocoon of pleasure that surrounded her and invaded her mind. 'Would you just let me rest for a while, Anna, nap maybe? Just for a few minutes?'

'Sure, no problem. I'll turn out the light. Sweet dreams.'

The room was plunged into silent darkness, and Jill surrendered to it.

37.

Jill was finding it an effort to keep her eyes open as she drove along the freeway. If it weren't so expensive, a visit to the Pleasure Center now and then would be better than any sleeping pill. On the way up to Palm Beach, she had been playing a tape of Schubert's Quintet in C, but now she felt she needed to play something louder, less elegiac, to wake her up and to dispel the chill that was nibbling at the edges of her feeling of wellbeing. She wondered whether she would go to the Pleasure Center another day. It had been the most stunning experience at the time; she'd never had an orgasm like it. But she wasn't convinced now that it was something she'd want to do again. It was, after all, emotionally soulless and empty.

Taking her eyes off the road for a second, she reached for another tape. She always carried a fairly eclectic selection of music for long trips, anything from Beethoven to the latest loudest rock as recommended by Jim, and it took her a minute or two to decide on Tina Turner. Not something she'd normally listen to, but right now all that shouting and wailing would shut out the doubts nicely. She pressed the 'Eject' button.

But the cassette that appeared wasn't Schubert. Curious, she turned it over to see what it was. It was a blank tape, the sort you get in multi-packs in shopping malls. The label had typed on it 'For the immediate attention of Dr Jill Peters.' How the hell did that come to be there? As an instinctive reaction, Jill pressed the central locking switch, and heard all four doors clunk reassuringly. Had her car been open all the time she was in the Pleasure Center? She was sure it would not have been; she always locked it without fail. Hardly taking her eyes off the road, she scanned the interior. All the windows were intact; there was no sign that anyone had tried to get in. But someone had, and had left no trace except for the mysterious tape.

Jill felt her hands trembling on the wheel. A blaring horn and the obscenely raised middle finger of a furious passing motorist made her realise that she wasn't driving well. She put the tape on the passenger seat, and forced herself to concentrate on the road until she could pull into a gas station.

She forced herself, too, to fill the tank with gas, check the tyres, and pay the cashier. She bought some black coffee in a styrofoam cup from a machine and pulled her car round to the back of the forecourt out of the glare of the floodlights.

Deliberately, she locked the doors once more, put the tape into the slot, pressed 'Play', and levered the plastic top off the coffee.

For a while there was nothing but crackles and static. When it came at last, the voice was a man's, old and tired and rattling with emphysema. The owner was clearly very sick, and spoke slowly, leaving agonising pauses between sentences. It took Jill a minute or two to be able to understand what he was saying.

'... no need to be frightened. I'm recording this just after Easter, and I've been told I don't have long to live. So if you're listening to this, you can be sure I'm dead.'

There followed half a minute of racking, gurgling coughing, painful to listen to. Then with an agonised indrawing of breath, the halting voice began again. 'I guess I should apologise if this has alarmed you. And I guess I should explain who I am. Mira Harman used to call me Abe. Not my real name, but no matter. She may have told you she had a friend who worked for the FBI. Well, that's me. Least, it was till the old chest got kinda waterlogged.'

Jill sat through another half minute of hoarse rasping, impatient for the speaker to regain what little breath he had. Her coffee sat on the dash, ignored.

'I knew Mira well, for a long time. Guess you did too, the way she used to talk about you. Fine woman. Now, listen hard, 'cause this is important, and I don't have the wind to say it more than once. She asked me to dig around, come up with the goods on this Russian Volkov, who turned out to be this guy Kandinsky that we already knew about but didn't know he was KGB. But you know about all that already. Mira'd have told you. What you don't know is that she asked me to look into an officer in the military, see what we had on him. Name of Foster. Well, we both had quite a shock. Turns out the guy was AC-DC. Not so serious, even in his job. But we discovered who he'd been AC-DC with.'

The man chose this precise point to go into another racking spasm of mushy coughing. Jill suddenly felt suffocated, and turned up the air-conditioning. She reached for her coffee, but it was bitter and tepid, so she clicked the top on again and put the cup back on the dash. Come on, come on, she whispered impatiently to the dying man.

'Don't see why I shouldn't tell you. It was the Vice-President. Squeaky-clean sonofabitch swung both ways. Turned out he always did. Married to a pretty woman, too. Betcha thought he was the answer to a nation's prayer. Church on Sundays. Never touched a dishonest deal in his life. Looked good for the cameras. All that. And all the time he had just enough guys on some kind of unofficial payroll that he never had any trouble from any of his sexual involvements. Why? They all fetched up dead, is why. But our guy stayed clean. Only one he couldn't touch was Foster. Not that he didn't try. Had him sent off on half-assed operations to get himself killed. Musta been mighty relieved when all those activists did it for him, back in 98.'

'Oh God!' Jill almost screamed, as the narrative was broken yet again by an eternity of what sounded like death-rattles. '*Get on with it, can't you*!'

'Anyways, one of the Vice-Prezz's poodle-dogs worked in my department, and knew Mira'd asked me to find out about Foster. Knew I'd told her, too. So he tells the Vice-Prezz, who tells him to have her taken out. Just like that. I blame myself, always have done. Mira was a good woman, didn't deserve to go like that. Guy did a real neat job. The cops had nothing to go on. Till now. I did another tape yesterday for them. Call Lieutenant Rafferty up in Washington, and he'll release Mira's body.

'Oh, and one more thing, I already covered all her funeral expenses. Rafferty knows which funeral home. I want Mira to have the best. Least I can do. Guess this all comes as a shock, eh? Like I said, I'm sorry. But from what Mira told me, you sound like the sort of woman who'd rather know the truth. No need to do anything except see Mira buried, though. Guess I'm lucky to have lasted as long as I have, the Vice-Prezz knowing that I know what I know. But I fixed the sonofabitch good and proper, and he knows it. He ever touches me or my family – hell, if he ever tries for the White House, it'll all come out, and he'll be finished. My own little revenge. Let him sweat. That's all I have to say.'

A last sandpaper breath was shut off in mid-gasp, and the tape continued to hiss quietly on to the end. Jill put it on to fast-forward, took the tape out of the deck with a shaking hand, and put it in her purse.

Of all the possible explanations for Mira's murder, the idea that she might have been killed by the Administration she had served so faithfully all her working life had never entered Jill's head. Like most people Jill believed that the government, while made up of people of all degrees of honesty and dishonesty, was not in itself a corrupt organisation. Incompetent most of the time, maybe; but not actually evil. Guilt flooded her, as she realised that Mira had been asking about Brad on her behalf, to protect her, and had put herself in the gravest danger as a result. She wondered why Mira had never told her what she knew about Brad, then laughed bitterly to herself; the Jill of four years ago would never have listened, never have believed it. Mira had known her better than she knew herself.

Jill put her head down on her hands, folded on the steering wheel, and felt hot tears scald her wrist. A few minutes later, she pulled herself together, combed her hair, and looked for the dog-eared, shabby address book she always carried. All the numbers she needed were in it. She reached for her cellular phone and cursed as she remembered she'd left it charging at home.

She got out of the car and strode back towards the gas-station, dropping the coffee in a bin on her way. There was a pay-phone on the far wall. She made six calls.

First, she called the friends she was going to stay with. 'I got held up,' she explained. 'I'll be about an hour later than I said.'

Then she called the lab. Susie Freeberg was out, so she talked to DeeDee Felker instead. 'Can you just say to Susie that I'll be back Tuesday instead of Monday? Some urgent personal business just came up. Also, can you tell her I'd like to take my three weeks' vacation next month some time? I'll discuss it with her first thing Monday, but I'd like to give her time to think about it, OK?'

Her next call was the most difficult. She had come to know Lieutenant Rafferty fairly well during the months following Mira's death, and had always been grateful for the weary patience he showed, even when she got frustrated and angry. He wasn't surprised to hear her voice.

'Hi, doc!' he greeted her cheerfully. 'I kinda guessed we'd be hearing from you. So you got one of those tapes too, huh? Damnedest thing!'

Jill established that the paperwork was through, which meant she could have Mira's body transferred to the funeral home whenever she liked.

'I'll make the arrangements, doc. Just let us have your authorisation in writing,' Rafferty said as he rang off. She would fax him from where she was staying.

After that, she rang the funeral home. She was amazed to find out how little time it would take to make the necessary arrangements. 'We can fix it all over the weekend, and book the cremation for Monday,' she was told. She hastily agreed and immediately called United. It took two minutes to book a flight to Washington first thing Monday morning, returning to Palm Beach the same night. Thank God for plastic, she thought.

She scrabbled through the pages of her book, looking for a scrap of sketchbook paper. As she made the sixth and last call, she could feel excitement churning inside. The five rings it took for the telephone to be answered seemed to go on for ever, but at last she heard a familiar voice answer.

'Boris!' she almost shouted. 'I've made up my mind! I'm coming with you to Colombia!'

38.

Jill had imagined that stepping out of the air-conditioned plane at Bogota airport would be almost like walking into a solid wall of heat and humidity. After all, she'd read enough about Colombia and seen the TV documentaries about steaming jungles. To her surprise, it was dry and warm but with a pleasant light wind.

The bus whisked the passengers across to the airport building in minutes. An attractive dark-haired young woman greeted her the moment she set foot inside the door.

'Dr Peters? Welcome to Bogota. My name is Catalina Pelaez, and I shall accompany you to your final destination.'

'Thank you,' Jill smiled, shaking the cool elegant hand. 'Do we take another plane from here?'

'Yes. Will you come with me, please?'

Jill followed her guide through the throng of arrivals waiting to clear passport control and customs, but instead of joining them, she found herself being escorted to a private lounge. Catalina showed a pass to every official on the way, and the two women were simply waved through. Once Jill's passport had been inspected and stamped, Catalina showed her to a seat, and told her, 'The plane is ready. I must leave you for one moment, while I settle things with the officials. Also, I must find your baggage.'

'No need,' Jill assured her. 'I hate waiting at airports, so I always travel light. This is all I have.' She indicated the neat carry-all which accompanied her all over the world.

'Oh, you are clever to be able to travel with so little!' Catalina exclaimed. 'I couldn't do that. I always take far too many clothes with me.'

'You'd be amazed what I can fit in,' Jill grinned. 'I was told I'd be here for three weeks, and as long as I don't have to get into full evening dress, I can manage with what I have.'

Boris had promised she would be met off the flight from Miami by someone who would look after her, and sure enough, Catalina Pelaez showed every sign of doing just that. The young woman was no more than thirty, tall and slender, with fine –

almost aristocratic – features and long, immaculately smooth hair. In her smart emerald-linen suit and heavy gold jewellery, she stood out from the drab mass of humanity around her like some rare, exotic bird. Clearly used to getting her own way, she dealt authoritatively with the airport officials, who obviously knew her and were unusually deferential and eager to oblige. Jill had had some hazy idea that her promised guide would be dour and monosyllabic, dressed in battle fatigues, ready for the rigours of the Amazonian jungle. She certainly hadn't expected this coolly elegant, imperious creature, who could easily have earned her living as a model in any capital city in Europe.

Her business done, Catalina returned to Jill. 'OK,' she smiled, 'we're ready to go. It will be a much smaller plane, only a twenty-seven seater Fokker.'

'Where are we going? Am I allowed to ask?'

'Of course. Our next stop is a town called Villavicencia. It's only a small place, you understand, but very busy, because it is the gateway to an area of Colombia called Los Llanos. From there we have to take a private helicopter, because there is no airstrip where we are going.'

'Sounds exciting. I have to travel all over the world, and after a while every airport and hotel starts to look the same. Sometimes I forget which country I'm in,' Jill laughed.

'In Colombia, you won't forget. It's not like anywhere else on earth,' Catalina assured her.

'Your English is amazing,' Jill complimented the young woman. 'Did you study in the States, or in England?'

'In the States,' Catalina replied. 'I spent three years doing management studies at UCLA, and during the vacations, here in Colombia, I acted as a tour guide for British and American tourists. To be fair, my English was already pretty good. My grandmother was American.'

Catalina led Jill outside to a waiting Daihatsu four-track. 'We'll get out to the airplane ahead of the others,' she explained, and within minutes they were aboard the small aircraft.

'I reserved all of the front section for us, so we won't be disturbed.'

Both women were comfortably settled long before the other passengers arrived to take their seats.

'I always imagined Bogota would be much hotter, more humid, than this,' Jill said.

'Most people think that,' Catalina answered. 'But they forget that we're so high. Here, we are more than two and half thousand metres above sea-level, nearly eight thousand feet. And the temperature is normally about fourteen degrees Centigrade all year round, which makes it really pleasant. But it'll be different where we're going. As we fly east you'll see how the terrain changes, from savannah to rainforest. There, the temperatures can reach the thirties, and we have four metres of rain a year.'

There were only about ten other people on the flight, all dressed with varying degrees of scruffiness. Catalina, however, was quite unself-conscious about looking like a princess by comparison. 'You'd better fasten your seat belt; we're about to take off,' she said.

'Buenos dias, señores y señoras,' came the captain's voice.

'We'll be landing in about forty minutes,' Catalina translated the flood of Spanish that came over the public address system.

'I'm glad you're with me,' Jill said. 'Even after living in Florida for four years, I don't speak much Spanish. And I imagine that, outside Bogota and Medellin, no-one speaks English.'

'That's right. But at the research facility there are plenty of people who speak English.'

'What do you do there?'

'You could call me a hostess, I suppose,' Catalina said. 'I see to the PR I look after guests and visiting experts, people like you. My boyfriend, Liborio, is the boss of the whole place. And because I speak good English – well,' she shrugged prettily, 'I was the natural choice.'

'I see,' Jill murmured, trying to get to grips with what exactly the words boyfriend, boss, and guests meant in this context. The place she was going to wouldn't be like any lab she had ever visited before, she knew that. Boris had been reluctant to tell her anything very much about it, even where it was. So why were the bosses content for her to fly there so openly? Weren't they even going to insist on her being taken there blindfold? She'd seen all the movies! But Boris had assured her that no one could possibly find the lab unless they knew exactly where it was. It was hidden deep in virgin forest, over two hours' flying time away, and after even ten minutes flying over the lush, never-changing jungle, each mile looked exactly like the last.

The plane took off at last. As Catalina had said, at first all Jill could see beneath them was an expanse of savannah.

'Is this what you expected?' Catalina asked, amused by Jill's fascination with the landscape.

'No. I don't know what I was expecting, really.'

'Most people don't. For many, Colombia is a place to travel through rather than to visit. Even our own people have changed round the name, and call it Locombia – the mad country.'

Jill smiled. 'But why should you be mad here, any more than anywhere else?'

'We have such an amazing ethnic mix here, like a mosaic. There are more than fifty different native tribes, each with its own distinctive culture. And we've had more than our fair share of civil war. I don't want to alarm you, but violence is still a problem –'

'And then there's the cocaine,' Jill nudged gently.

Catalina remained quite unperturbed. 'Of course, you are a medical scientist,' she said mildly. 'I can see why that would interest you.'

'I read somewhere that Colombia is still the biggest producer in the world,' Jill persisted.

'We produce more than 80 per cent of the world's supply,' Catalina replied with some pride.

'But I thought cocaine production was all controlled by the Mafia,' Jill said, playing the innocent abroad in an effort to find out all she could.

'Oh no,' Catalina laughed. 'My boss – my boyfriend – would never have anything to do with gangsters. Sure, he makes a lot of money, but he uses it only to do good.'

'I see,' Jill muttered. Like maybe he supports a whole load of orphan kids, because he just happens to have gunned down their parents? Then she asked, 'Catalina, how is it that someone like you – attractive, well-travelled, intelligent – is content to live out in the jungle, miles from anywhere?' In other words, what's in it for you, kid?

The pretty Colombian was not at all put out. 'I can imagine how it must look to you,' she said. 'But you see, we are cousins,

Liborio and I; our families have intermarried many times. It is unthinkable that I should marry outside a very small number of families.' Jill must have let a slightly quizzical look show on her face, because Catalina suddenly grew serious, and put her hand on Jill's arm. 'Of course, I'm worried about the spread of drug-taking in Europe and North America, but it's hardly our fault here in Colombia. Drug-taking is illegal here. Morally, this is still a very conservative country.'

'And Catholic too. That's what I find so hard to understand, that a country with such a strong religious tradition can produce a drug that causes death and destruction all over the world.'

'It's an industry, just like any other. And it supports the people. If the North Americans and the Europeans are prepared to pay –' Jill said nothing, but waited for Catalina to continue. For a moment, the lovely young woman looked gaunt, a lost, desperate look in her eyes. 'Look, whatever I think about it, I'm trapped. You can call it an accident of birth, but I promise you, they'd never let me out. I've always known that.'

So pretty Catalina had obviously long since computed the real cost of her emerald earrings, Armani suit and Manolo Blahnik shoes. Dear God, Jill thought, will they let *me* out? She judged it time to change the subject.

'So how did your bosses get into producing this vaccine then?' she asked.

'Think of what you just said about cocaine,' Catalina said, more relaxed now. 'Many people think as you do. So the bosses have tried to diversify into all sorts of legitimate projects – hotels, newspapers, community projects for the poor – in an effort to clear their name. Branching out into pharmaceuticals is a logical step for them. Also, many of them are devout Catholics. Liborio is a very religious man, and has a shrine to the Virgin in his office; he prays every day. He sees this vaccine as a way of helping the world.'

'But, Catalina, it's a contraceptive!' Jill whispered so as not to be overheard by the other passengers.

'That's OK,' Catalina answered blandly. 'Even quite devout Catholics don't believe in the Church's teachings about contraception any more. They see the reality every day, in the countryside, on the streets of our cities, in a way that the Vatican never can.

Liborio sees it as a way of making peace with God in this world. And as a commercial opportunity, of course. And, as you know, the most important part of the research and development will be the reversing of the effects of the original vaccine, the one that went wrong. The Church is very pleased for him to be doing that.'

'I see,' Jill murmured politely. She didn't doubt that there was a certain quid pro quo involved, that the Church would turn a blind eye to some of Liborio's other dealings, grant him absolution from all sorts of activities, if he somehow managed to restore the world's plummeting birth-rate. But there was no way she was going to voice such thoughts to Catalina. The girl was clearly from a powerful family, carefully brought-up as a good Catholic, intelligent enough to distinguish double-think and dogma from common-or-garden morality, but powerless to do anything about it for herself. Somewhere inside, she must have reached a compromise, and it would be cruel to unbalance it. She herself, Jill reflected, had struggled to a compromise somewhere along the way, and wouldn't welcome having her inner equilibrium – such as it was – disturbed.

'Señores y señoras,' the captain's voice barked.

'We're about to land,' Catalina told Jill. 'Vanguardia airport is tiny, not like Bogota.'

Jill gripped the arm-rests as the plane grounded and bounced along the uneven surface of the poorly-maintained airstrip. Even Catalina looked tense, though she must have made this same landing many times. She caught Jill's eye, betraying her own nervousness only by a swift flick of the eyebrows.

The two women were escorted off the plane before the other passengers. Jill's bag was magically already stowed in the Mercedes G wagon that awaited them only yards from the steps, and within minutes they found themselves being driven across the tarmac to a Sikorski, its rotors already in motion.

As they took off, Jill turned to Catalina to ask, amazed, 'How long did all that take?'

Catalina looked at her watch. 'Five minutes, perhaps? Sometimes it takes a little longer.'

'When I think of the hours I've spent queuing at international airports!' Jill laughed, feeling slightly light-headed.

'Yes,' said Catalina seriously. 'But this is not an international airport.'

Jill felt it prudent to keep her rising excitement to herself. In fact, she decided it might be prudent to use the two hours' flying time to catch up on some sleep.

• • •

The change in the monotonous tone of the engines wakened Jill two hours later. She blinked as the helicopter dived steeply and circled to find the clearing deep in the jungle. The savannah that had surrounded Villavicencia had been replaced by impenetrable jungle. As they flew in a wide arc, the tree canopy showed no sign of any break or clearing.

'Don't tell me we can land in that!' Jill exclaimed. 'Are you sure we've come to the right place?'

'Oh, yes,' Catalina smiled calmly. 'I know, it seems as though we are looking for what you English would call a needle in a haystack, but I promise you there is a place to land down there.'

Sure enough, the helicopter touched down softly in a clearing no larger than a football pitch, almost invisible from the air. When Jill stepped out she thought: now *this* is what I was expecting!

Here, the atmosphere was as hot, warm, and clinging as a jacuzzi, and the air heaved and gurgled with the sounds of the jungle. Insects, birds and animals were hissing, singing and howling all around them. Jill could feel her fair English skin becoming red and shiny, her hair clinging close to her scalp. Irritatingly, Catalina looked as cool and immaculate as ever. What was it about these Latin American women? If any Englishwoman had spent the day in a variety of aircraft wearing a linen suit, she would look like a bag of old laundry. But Catalina looked elegant and soignée. If she weren't so nice, Jill thought, I could hate her!

A guard with a holster on his hip retrieved Jill's bag from the helicopter, and set off in the direction of a small single-storey building. As she followed him, Jill managed to walk in a sort of 360-degree waltz, as if to reassure herself that there really was no skyline, nothing but jungle. Behind her, she was astounded to see, the helicopter was being towed down a ramp to a bunker below ground. Steel doors slid shut behind it, and the sheltering jungle did the rest. From the air, there would be no sign of a landing area.

At the door of the small building, the guard pressed a combination of buttons on the key pad. The doors hissed open, and they were faced by a very ordinary-looking elevator. Exactly the sort of thing you'd find in an out-of-town shopping mall, Jill thought.

'Is everything under the ground, then?' she asked Catalina.

'You saw the helicopter hangar? Everything is like that,' Catalina answered. 'You see, the Cartel has had bad experiences with DEA satellite reconnaissance. This way, there's nothing to see from the air.'

They entered the elevator and started a descent that felt as though it was going to take them to the very centre of the earth.

'How far down do we go?' Jill whispered.The air was cool, and it was impossible to tell how far they had come.

'About forty metres,' Catalina said. 'You see, we had to build well below the roots of the trees, or they would have died and the project would have been visible from the air.'

The elevator slowed, and stopped.

'Your room is on this level,' Catalina said brightly. 'Come with me. Later, we will have dinner in Liborio's suite, but first I expect you'd like to wash and brush up.'

That was an understatement, Jill thought. She was feeling grubby, sweaty and scruffy, though experience told her she probably looked perfectly all right.

Catalina pressed her hand to a palm recognition plate, and the door slid open to reveal a room that would not have been out of place in any country in the world.

'Good heavens!' Jill exclaimed. 'The Intercontintental!'

Catalina beamed. 'We had their designer handle all this,' she explained. 'Of course, he was slightly puzzled that there weren't any windows. But we paid him enough –'

'So how do I call you, when I'm ready? Jill asked, noticing that there was no way of opening the door from the inside.

'There's a keypad by the door,' Catalina showed her. 'We communicate by screens. My number is 512. Your security clearance will allow you to communicate only with certain parts of the facility. See, here is your directory. Everything is listed alphabetically.'

I might as well be back at NIH, Jill thought, only this is

worse. Never mind, it's only for three weeks, she reassured herself. For three weeks, I can stand anything.

Catalina left her to unpack her things. She realised she needn't have worried about what to bring. The air-conditioning was so efficient that she would need scarcely more than a silk T-shirt and a cotton skirt during the day.

She was both discomfited and annoyed to see that there was a closed-circuit TV camera slung from the ceiling in a corner of her room. She checked carefully to make sure there wasn't one in the bathroom as well before taking a shower and washing her hair. Oh well, she would just have to remember to dress and undress in there as well.

Clean and refreshed, Jill keyed in 512, and Catalina's face appeared on the screen alongside the keypad. 'Hi,' she smiled. 'You ready?'

'I think so,' Jill replied. She had chosen a rose-pink silk shirt and pewter-grey silk evening pants, and had clipped her hair back in a tortoiseshell clasp. For her fortieth birthday, Art and Jim had given her a pair of ruby earrings in a gold setting, which she had always liked and wore whenever she had to feel as well as look good, so she put them on now, as a sort of good luck charm. She had only just fixed them in her ears, and checked her appearance front and back in the carefully-angled mirrors, when Catalina appeared at her door.

'Is this OK?' Jill asked. 'I wasn't sure whether the dinner was to be formal or not.'

'You look lovely!' the girl exclaimed warmly, and immediately Jill felt better. She still hadn't completely faced up to the prospect of meeting Volkov again, but at least in such unfamiliar and exotic surroundings both would be on equal terms. Even if they could never be lovers, she still didn't want to look drab and middle-aged compared with the poised young Colombian.

Catalina led Jill down a short, carpeted corridor. There were security cameras at every corner, Jill noticed. Catalina stopped at a panelled teak door, and pressed her hand against a sensor plate. The door slid back.

Jill caught her breath. As a young girl she had seen the James Bond films, but this was the set of *Dr No* brought to life. The room was easily forty feet square, and one entire wall was filled from floor to ceiling with a huge, brightly-illuminated fish tank, in which fish of all sizes and colours swam mesmerisingly among columns of bubbles and swaying water plants.

The other three walls were hung with French masterpieces. Fleetingly, Jill registered a Cézanne, a singingly wonderful Rouault, and at least two by Dufy, but now was not the moment to rush over for a closer look. Catalina had taken Jill's arm gently, and was steering her across the expanse of polished hardwood floor.

'Jill, this is Liborio Ramirez,' she said. 'Liborio, here at last is Dr Peters.'

Jill's host took her hand and, correctly, kissed the air six inches above it. 'Dr Peters, I hope your journey was a pleasant one,' he greeted her warmly.

'Yes, thank you,' Jill said, slightly overwhelmed by the rather European ambience, and wondering whether she should call Liborio by his first name. She decided to take the plunge. 'Would you call me Jill?' she smiled. 'It makes me feel so old to be called Doctor.'

'Which you are not,' Ramirez bowed gallantly. 'And you will call me Liborio, please.'

He was in his late forties, squarely built without being actually fat, and handsome. His hair was thick and glossy without a trace of grey, and the Saddam Hussein moustache suited him well. Jill was slightly amused at the number of monograms that adorned him, one on the handmade silk shirt, another on the tie, a third on the belt buckle.

But Ramirez, to be fair, was graciousness itself as he led her across to a sunken area of the room and showed her to a seat opposite him on an opulently upholstered sofa.

'This is just like the set of a Bond film!' Jill told him admiringly.

It was exactly the right thing to say. Ramirez seemed almost to gleam with pride. 'You understand perfectly!' he exclaimed. 'I greatly admire James Bond – the books, the movie, the man – so I have created my own Bond world down here. For me, it is the realisation of a dream. There is a difference, of course. A movie set is only fantasy, but –' he waved expansively ' – this is the real thing.'

He went to busy himself at the drinks tray. Jill felt mesmerised by the wall of sauntering fish. 'Where did your fish come from?' she asked.

'You like my pets?' he asked with a flash of gleaming teeth. 'With a few exceptions, they're all local, you know. You see, I care very much about conservation, and when we excavated this place we had to dump the spoil into the Yari river. But first I had my people take every fish out of it for several miles downstream, and I saved the very best pieces for here.'

Quite consciously, Jill registered two things: that Liborio Ramirez regarded rare, live fish as 'pieces' in the same way as he regarded his collection of rare paintings, and that the ordinary, uninteresting fish had probably come to a swift and unpleasant end. But she accepted the proffered champagne and forced herself to smile sweetly.

'Dom Perignon,' Ramirez said, smiling unctuously. 'I'm sure you will appreciate my reasons.'

Oh Lord! What was she supposed to say? Ramirez clearly expected some kind of response. Why Dom Perignon, particularly? Why not Heidsieck, Roederer, Bollinger? Desperately, she trawled through her memory. Inspiration flashed.

'Of course! Bond's favourite champagne! And do you also smoke Morland's cigarettes?'

'Alas, no. They don't make them any more. So sad. Do you remember how elegant they were, oval not cylindrical? But I have some of the original red boxes in my Bond collection, which I am sure you would like to see.'

Jill nodded, feeling as though she had stumbled into some weird dream. 'Thank you; I'd be most interested,' she murmured. For a moment, she caught Catalina's eye. Did she imagine a split-second glint of amusement? What on earth did she make of Ramirez's odd mix of childlike delight and megalomania? Her bland, carefully-schooled smile gave nothing away.

Ramirez went over to a fine mahogany eighteenth century sofa table and picked up a small leather box. He said, 'Before we go any further, Dr Peters – Jill, I hope you will accept this as a personal gift from me, in return for your willingness to assist me.' Jill took the box, for a moment lost for words. Ramirez went on, 'I do not give this to you conditionally. It is yours whatever the outcome of your visit, a small token of our thanks that you have come at all. I hope you will accept it in the spirit in which it is given, as a souvenir of your visit to Colombia.'

'Thank you,' Jill stammered, in some embarrassment. Cautiously she opened the box. In the centre of the black velvet pad lay a huge emerald, polished but uncut, glinting with an ice-green flame. Jill's hands were shaking so much, she had to put the box and the fabulous gem down on the table beside the sofa, or she would have dropped them. 'I don't know what to say,' she said inadequately. 'It's astounding. But I can't accept it.'

'Of course you can,' Ramirez said smoothly. 'I insist. If you don't like it, any museum or jeweller would give you a good price for it. But we never discuss money here. I just want you to feel welcome, and happy to get on with your work for us.' He turned to Catalina. 'Querida, I have asked Boris to join us about now. Would you call him?'

Catalina stepped over to the screen to summon Boris, while Ramirez led Jill, awkwardly clasping the box containing the extraordinary emerald, to the palatial dining-room. The room was vast, but contained one carefully-lit picture, a Madonna and Child. 'Murillo,' Ramirez told her, seeing her gaze go to it immediately.

'It's lovely,' Jill said simply. Ramirez held Jill's chair for her as she sat down, and then went to the head of the table, while Catalina took her place at his right. Jill folded her hands to stop them shaking. Where was Boris? Half of her couldn't wait for him; the other half wished he would never arrive at all. What was taking him so long? To calm herself, she studied Liborio Ramirez carefully for the first time. She could see what Catalina found so attractive about him. His deep brown eyes were intelligent and, when they rested on Catalina, kind. This was not the sort of crude bandit she'd imagined might be the head of the production facility, but – in spite of his childish enthusiasm for Bond gadgetry – a civilised, cultured man who would have graced a corporate boardroom anywhere. The only difference was that he was far, far richer than any company director Jill had ever met.

'You must be miles from anywhere, out here,' she said, making small talk to fill the time until Boris arrived.

'Yes, we are,' Ramirez said off-handedly. 'But it gets boring after a while, so we try to get away as much as we can. We have an estate near my brother in Medellin, and several other houses around the world. I never like to stay too long in one place.'

I bet you don't, Jill thought, reminding herself that, charming and sophisticated though he might be, Ramirez was no benign industrialist but an internationally-wanted criminal. At that moment, Boris came into the room.

Her heart missed a beat. In the candlelight, those marvellous green eyes glinted with the same light as the emerald, now shrouded in its box, that Ramirez had just given her.

'Sit next to the beautiful Dr Peters, my friend,' Ramirez said expansively, waving to the only remaining place at the table. 'Of course, you are old friends.'

Boris half-bowed to Jill as he took his place. 'I hope your journey was comfortable,' he said in a low voice.

Jill nodded. 'Everything was perfect, thank you.'

Even that short exchange felt sufficient to enclose them both in a little circle of intimacy, to shut out everybody else. Ramirez's voice sounded strident as he broke in, 'Now, we will discuss no business this evening. Tomorrow we work. But tonight is for good conversation only.'

The evening passed in a daze for Jill. Afterwards, she could hardly remember what they ate or drank, except that it was all delicious. The conversation, as Ramirez required, was good. She suddenly felt tired, and knew that she was contributing little, but was happy to listen to the other three. All were dauntingly well-informed about world politics and the arts, even about the antics of the international jet-set, and the conversation rippled and occasionally snapped back and forth across the table. Jill was tactfully included, her opinion sought and listened to, but all the while she was mesmerised by Boris, who, looking tanned and rested, was more animated than she had ever suspected. Dear God! Working alongside this gorgeous man wasn't going to be easy if she couldn't control how she felt.

Eventually, the coffee and the liqueur brandy were finished, and they got up from the table. Boris said, 'Liborio, I think Jill must be very tired after so much travel.' And to Jill, 'Shall I show you back to your room?'

Jill smiled gratefully at him. 'Thank you for such a delightful evening,' she said to Ramirez.

'But you cannot possibly go to bed until I have shown you my Bond collection!' Ramirez exclaimed. 'I know you would like to see it. I insist!'

Boris shrugged imperceptibly; Catalina's elegant eyebrows went up a fraction. There was no hope for it. Jill, half dead with fatigue, decided to accept gracefully. Ramirez took her arm and ushered her into the next room. With great ceremony, he unlocked a walnut breakfront bookcase and spread the doors wide.

'There!' he said proudly, standing back.

Two shelves were loaded with books, hardback first editions. 'All signed by Ian Fleming!'

Below them, the next shelf was stacked with hand-labelled videotapes. 'I had them all transferred on to video,' Ramirez told her. 'But these are the uncut versions. There are some wonderful moments, which the rest of the world has never seen. One evening, we shall watch them all, you and I.'

Oh, please God, no! Jill thought weakly.

'And here, my dear Jill, are my three most precious possessions. Here is the very cocktail shaker used by James Bond himself –' Sean Connery, surely? Jill registered vaguely '– to make his medium-dry vodka martinis – shaken not stirred!'

Ramirez reverently put the cocktail shaker back among the carefully-displayed Bond ephemera on the plush-lined shelf. 'And this,' he said, taking down a camera, 'is – I wonder if you can guess what it is? No, not a Hasselblad camera – a gun! Designed by Q himself! They used it in the film *A Licence to Kill*.'

'Of course,' Jill murmured politely. 'I remember.'

'And this is the jewel of my collection!' On Ramirez's outstretched hand lay a gun, made of yellow metal.

'*The Man With the Golden Gun!*'

'I see you are a devotee like myself, my dear Jill,' Ramirez smiled delightedly. 'I shall enjoy your company while you are here.'

He took Jill's hand and kissed it, before carefully locking away his treasures. Then he took her arm again, and led her back to the others.

'Now I shall allow you to escort Jill to her room,' he said to Boris, as though handing Jill over.

Fighting a yawn, she forced herself to smile. 'Thank you for showing me your collection, Liborio. It was a great honour. And, Catalina, thank you for all your kindness today.'

Catalina took her hand, and smiled. 'Sleep well,' she said.

As Boris escorted her along the corridor, he said, 'I expect you find this a little strange.'

'Strange! Is that all you can say?' Jill laughed. 'Ramirez is a Bond freak, and this place is like a movie-set fantasy, but with added French masterpieces. Put it this way, it's a far cry from what I'm used to.'

'Or from anything I knew in Russia,' Boris agreed. 'I'm sorry if this has come as a shock. But I couldn't say anything to you at your husband's house. You can never be too careful when you're working with these people. It was only because I told the bosses about you that they allowed me to fly to Florida at all.'

'I understand. But I'm glad I came. I wouldn't have missed this for the world. The only snag is, no one will ever believe me.'

Boris stopped, and caught her arm. 'You must never tell anyone about this place, or that you have been here. You do understand that, don't you?' he said urgently. With the light behind him, and his face bent towards her and in shadow, his eyes became a deep, fathomless green – the colour of wine bottles, Jill thought irrelevantly.

'Of course not,' she said automatically. 'I'm used to keeping my mouth shut. Secret government projects and all that.'

He released her arm, and they walked the last few yards to the door of her room. There was no door handle, no key. 'How do I – ?'

'Like this.' Boris took her hand and held it up to a screen set into the wall beside the door, which slid open.

'How on earth did they do that?' Jill asked, amazed. 'I haven't been asked for a palm print!'

'One day, I'll explain it to you,' Boris grinned. 'Child's play, for the experts. May I come in for a few minutes?'

'Of course,' Jill said. There was, after all, no reason for her not to allow this man into her room, was there? Even so, she was glad she had left everything tidy, no underwear on the floor or make-up scattered about.

The room doubled as a sitting-room, and there was a group of armchairs and a sofa as well as a long, low table. They sat down. Boris leaned towards Jill urgently and reached for her hand.

'I'm so glad you came after all,' he said. 'I've been looking forward to seeing you again, very much.'

Jill was surprised at the genuine warmth of his words and gestures. In fact, all evening she had noticed subtle signs – a touch of the hand as he passed her something at the table, a particular warmth as they exchanged a swift glance during the ebb and flow of conversation – that had made her wonder.

Still holding her hand in both his, he said, 'There are only three people in the whole world who could have helped sort out our problems here, and you are one of them. But, for me, you are the only one I could work with.'

'Well, I hope I justify your faith in me,' Jill said, feeling as brittle as she sounded.

Boris let her hand go and stood up. 'I must leave you to get some sleep,' he said. She stood up as well. Suddenly, without knowing how, she found herself in his arms, and him in hers. As she felt the taut muscles under the thin silk of his shirt, she thought: God, it's been four years since I've done this. And it feels wonderful! For a few moments that stretched into an eternity, they stood there, neither of them caring about the ever-present security cameras. Finally, he stepped back, her face held in his hands, and looked deep into her eyes.

'I've wanted to do that ever since I saw you all those years ago, at that conference in London,' he said. 'I've dreamed of you. All the time I was alone in exile, I thought of no one but you.'

Jill gently took his hands away from her face and held them in her own. She felt so weak with desire, a desire which could never come to anything, that she couldn't find the words to say. He mistook her silence for something else.

'I'm sorry,' he said softly. 'I know you lost the only two men who meant anything to you. But if you only knew how my dreams of you kept me going, gave me something to live for! Seeing you here now, it's as if I have always known you.'

Trembling, Jill allowed herself to run her fingers through his wonderful dark, glossy hair – something she had always longed to do. 'There've been times,' she confessed, 'when I've felt the same way.'

Boris caught her wrist, and turned his head to kiss the palm of her hand.

Jill closed her eyes. The tiredness, the wine and the passion took their toll and she slipped gently into his supporting arms. As if she were a fragile and very precious doll, he settled her in the armchair and bent over her.

He kissed her once – a swift, light, almost-imagined kiss – on the lips. 'Good night,' he whispered. And, in a second, he was gone.

Early the next day, Boris showed Jill round the lab.

'I've been all over the world looking at labs, government and private, and I have *never* seen anything like this!' she exclaimed, gazing at the workstations, the unusually-spacious animal cages, and the gleaming expanse of worktops, all deserted so early in the morning.

'What you are looking at,' Boris answered, 'is the equivalent of the annual health-care budget for children under the age of five for – let's say – a small country in Africa, or one of the independent former Soviet states. Would you believe Liborio Ramirez is so rich that he and his brothers and his brothers-in-law, rather than bank their money just bury it in the jungle? When they want to buy another helicopter, or yet another apartment, they just go and dig some up. Sometimes they even forget where they've buried it.'

Jill shivered, even though the atmosphere was pleasantly air-conditioned. 'It seems immoral, somehow,' she whispered.

'That we should have everything provided for us on a plate when there are people dying for lack of this sort of money, you mean? Yes, I've thought that too,' Boris said sombrely. 'The only way I can make it right, in my own conscience, is to tell myself that when – and I mean *when*, not *if* – we find the antidote to the side-effects of Seminon, and create the new vaccine, then we shall have justified all this. Look, no government laboratory or multinational has been able to do it. I really do believe that, in this case, the end will justify the means.'

'And once they're available, they'll eventually be replicated by other labs, so Ramirez will only have a certain amount of time in which to clean up, unless of course he enforces his patents in ways that a multinational never could. I suppose you're right.'

Boris took her arm. 'Come and see the computer set-up,' he said. 'I expect it's one you're familiar with. Come this way.'

He led her down a short corridor to another spacious room, lavishly equipped with computer terminals and a substantial IBM mainframe.

'From here,' he explained, 'you can access almost any database worldwide. If the floppies that contain your original research aren't compatible, we can transcribe them. Whatever you want to do, that a computer can do, you can do it here.'

Jill propped herself against a desk, her arms folded defensively. 'I'm beginning to wish I hadn't come,' she said. 'The lab I help run in Miami has everything I need, but it's not like this. This whole place is like a movie set. I feel like some evil genius is going to march in and take control. And if we don't deliver the goods, we get thrown to the sharks.'

'As it happens, our friend Ramirez does keep a tank full of piranhas,' Boris replied calmly. 'Do you remember in the salon, there was a tank that ran along the wall at the end of the room? They are small and not very interesting to look at, so you may not have paid them much attention. It amuses him sometimes to throw in a chicken, or a T-bone steak with some meat still on it, and watch them fight for it. But as far as I know, he has never actually thrown a person to them.'

'Oh, thank you so much! Now I feel totally reassured! Boris, tell me something. Am I really going to be allowed to leave here after three weeks? You told me not to tell a single soul where I was coming to, so no-one knows where I am. If Ramirez chooses to kill me and dump me somewhere in the jungle, no-one's going to be any the wiser, are they?'

'It's OK,' he hastened to reassure her, resting a firm hand on her shoulder. 'We're both worth far more to him alive than dead. Don't forget, there are only two other people in the whole world who have anything like the same expertise. He's damn lucky to have us, and he knows it. He won't kill us.'

'But will he – can he – ever let us go home?'

'Yes,' Boris said firmly.

It wasn't a question he could answer with any certainty, Jill realised; she just had to believe him.

He went on, 'Of course, you have a home to go to. I have none. I have no family. My parents are dead, my wife is dead, and I have no children. My job is dead, my country is dead. And if I try to go back there, I shall be dead. So I might as well stay here anyway. I could probably make a good future for myself with these people. After all, they're very unlikely to stop at developing these things we're working on. There are huge fortunes to be made pirating and even innovating pharmaceuticals. So if I do well, I could have a job for life.'

Jill looked up at Boris sharply. 'I didn't know you'd been married,' she said, ignoring his other comments completely. 'I'm so sorry –'

'It was a long time ago,' he cut her off. 'We were very young, and we both had good government jobs. Then Yelena became pregnant. But there was no way we could start a family, not then. It would have been a disaster for us. So we agreed that – that –'

Jill reached out to cover his hand with hers. 'Don't talk about it if you don't want to.'

He pulled himself together. 'It's not as long ago as I thought,' he said ruefully. 'Even after twenty years, I still feel guilty. We agreed that she would have the pregnancy terminated. The hospital was an old-fashioned, filthy place. She died a week later of septicaemia. It happens too often, even now.'

'So that's why you were so dedicated to developing a reliable contraceptive vaccine. So that other women wouldn't die.'

'Exactly. And if you help me do it, you would do more than make Ramirez even richer than he already is. You would help heal a wound that has been open for twenty years.'

'I'll do everything I can, I promise,' Jill said solemnly.

'I know you will. But come over here; I must show you what I have already developed.' Boris crossed the room to a corner littered with journals and print-outs. 'Now, before I show you, you must promise not to laugh,' he said, picking up a tiny lucite box.

'All right, I won't laugh. What is it?'

She took the tiny box, which contained a small disk. 'It looks rather like an eighteenth-century beauty patch,' she said. 'What on earth is this?'

'Keep your promise, and I'll tell you. It's a self-adhesive testosterone patch – for men who've lost testicular function after Seminon. It should sort them out permanently, if we get the right ester.'

'And am I allowed to ask where or what it adheres to?' Jill enquired, with saucily-raised eyebrows.

'Where do you think?'

At that, she broke her promise and shrieked with laughter, as

Boris had known she would. 'Come on, Boris! It's grotesque! Can you really see that going down at all in the average bedroom?'

'Absolutely not,' Boris laughed. 'Which is why I'm taking it further. This is only the first crude prototype. The real thing will eventually be rather like a watch.'

Again, Jill snorted with uncontrollable laughter.

'Really, for a distinguished scientist, you have a disgusting mind!' Boris teased her. 'I don't know what you do in America, but most people in Russia wear their watches on their wrists. Which is where my particular watch will also be worn.'

Jill wiped the tears from her eyes with the back of her hand. 'I'm sorry,' she gasped. 'I know I shouldn't laugh. There's too much at stake. But this place is so unreal, it's starting to get to me.'

'That's OK. I like a woman with a sense of humour, even if she does pour scorn on four years of my painstaking research. Are you ready to hear about it?'

'Of course. And I promise not to laugh again.'

'Well, the watch, as I've said, will be worn on the man's wrist. But of course it's not just any old watch.'

'I didn't imagine it would be, go on.'

'Have you ever head of Gunter Hoffman's work on electroporation?'

'Can't say that I have,' Jill smiled, realising that he was probably teasing her about some extraordinarily erudite piece of research that only twenty people in the world understood.

'He's a Max-Planck physicist who has been working on the application of pulsed electrical fields in medicine for more than 15 years.'

'So you're going to get the drug through the skin using electrical pulses?'

'Exactly. In my new watch, based on Hoffman's system that he called electroporation, there's a battery-driven pulse generator that sort of punches a microscopic hole in the skin to let just the right amount of the drug through into the bloodstream.'

'Sounds impressive. And I suppose there's a reservoir of the stuff sitting there just waiting to be used day and night.'

'Not bad, eh?'

'And a lot better than skin patches, I should think.'

'We'll have to do rigorous tests to make absolutely sure that the testosterone ester we choose doesn't cause any local skin irritation. But if that's all OK, then I truly think this sort of device will be the way to go. I have a prototype in my office. I'll show you later.'

'Can I ask a silly question? Surely you've been working on the testosterone idea for ages –'

'Of course. But the problem has always been to get the right ester to work in combination with the delivery system.'

'I see. And have you thought of building in some sort of sensor to measure the man's natural testosterone level, so as not to overdose? We don't want any problems like that again!'

'Yes, I have,' Boris reassured her. 'This watch will deliver the hormone at timed intervals, just as the pituitary does.'

'You've obviously been working on this for some time,' Jill said admiringly. 'I'll soon catch up with you on the vaccine, though. I'd be interested to know what lines of research you've pursued, so I don't waste time looking at things you've already tried and rejected.'

At that point, some of the other lab workers came in. Boris introduced Jill to a whole United Nations of names and faces – there was a Cheng, she registered, and an Ibarruri, and a raw-boned Australian woman called MacIntyre – then hurried her out.

'You can meet them all properly later,' he muttered.

'Do they all live here?'

'Yes, and there are many others you haven't met yet.'

'So how many people are there in this place?' she demanded, whispering as Boris did although they were now alone in his office.

'Fifty, sixty, something like that. Don't forget, there's a whole team of pilots and maintenance people. They look after the lighting, the air-conditioning, the elevators, the water supply, the perimeter security. They feed the fish, stock the freezers, see to the laundry –'

'And go and dig up the odd million dollars from time to time. I get the message. Wasn't I in the middle of asking about your findings so far?'

'You were, but I can tell you now that none of them was of any use. After months of looking at the newer long-chain testosterone esters, I went back in the end to an old favourite.'

'Why?'

'Because it's predictable, which saves time and effort. And, so far, it hasn't caused skin irritation. All these floppies contain the data, if you want to see for yourself.' Boris indicated several plastic flip-top boxes of disks, neatly labelled in Russian and in English, on a shelf above the computer monitor.

'Thanks. Even though I'm sure you're right, I wouldn't mind spending a morning looking through them.' Jill took her own cardboard box of floppies from her shoulder bag, and held it out to Boris. 'Fair's fair,' she smiled. 'Let me know what you think.'

• • •

It took more than a morning simply to skip through the documentation of Boris's years of work on both the antidote to the testicular burn-out and the new vaccine itself. After two days, Jill had to agree with him that his most recent work was what they should concentrate on, particularly the disappointing yield of the vaccine. For the next few days, she hid herself away in the room that had been allocated for her to work in, leaving it only to go the bathroom, or to talk to the technicians manning various parts of the production plant. Every so often Boris would come in and put a tray of food on the desk beside her and, towards the end of the day, a glass of wine. If he tried to peer over her shoulder at her computer screen, she would say playfully, 'Boris, go away! The minute there's anything to show you, I'll show you, OK? Thanks for the wine. *Prosit!*'

Each night she would crash into bed, exhausted but with her mind churning so that she scarcely slept. After a week of staring at the screen, she was starting to feel light-headed, almost silly, certainly prepared to look at any possibility that presented itself.

It hadn't taken her long to recognise that the raw materials were the best that Ramirez's ill-gotten dollars could buy. So the fault, whatever it was, was not in them. She trawled with microscopic care through the production processes, discussed them at length with all the technicians and the research staff, and still couldn't find anything to explain the failure to produce a commercially viable yield.

So it only remained to look at external conditions, environmental triggers. 'Earth, air, fire and water,' she chanted, thinking of the conditions they were all working in.

Earth. They were forty metres below ground. It took scarcely an hour of enquiries to establish that there were no rare minerals lurking in the rock, no geological faults, no underground water courses, no sources of radiation in the ground, no unsuspected microfauna or flora that could account for the too-swift degradation of the culture.

Air. She tested the air of the lab, which came through the air-conditioning system. That too proved to be blameless.

Fire. The heating system? When the bemused head of the maintenance team showed her how it worked, she realised it was the most advanced and ecologically-sound system imaginable, and that there was no passage of air between it and the lab or any other room in the facility. They'd thought of everything when designing the place. So the fault couldn't lie there.

That left only water. Water! Of course! They washed in it, drank it, used it in the labs, and it came, filtered but unchlorinated, straight from the taps.

Once on the right track, it took so little time, it was laughable. Almost euphoric, Jill went to find Boris. She was dismayed to find Catalina, looking elegant and lovely as ever, perched on Boris's desk and chatting away animatedly. Boris, clearly, wasn't finding her company a drag.

'Sorry to disturb you,' she found herself saying rather primly. 'I've found out something that might interest you, Boris.'

'How wonderful!' Catalina exclaimed, her face alight as she jumped up off the desk.

'Boris has been telling me that you are one of the most respected scientists in the United States. Please, even though I probably won't understand a word of it, can I stay and hear what it is you have found out?'

The trouble with Catalina, Jill thought, was that she was so damn *nice* that you couldn't possibly resent her.

'What is it, Jill?' Boris asked gently.

Jill sat down. 'It's the water,' she said triumphantly.

'*What?*'

'I know it sounds unlikely, but that's what it is. I've found the most minute quantities of heavy metals – lead, arsenic, cadmium, that sort of stuff,' she explained for Catalina's benefit, 'in the water used to make up the culture medium.'

Boris leaned back in his chair, his eyes closed and his faced twisted in near-anguish. 'I'm so angry with myself,' he declared. 'Of course. It makes perfect sense. Such a simple thing. You know we've been importing the hamster ovarian cells from China? They're exceptionally sensitive. Trouble is they mutate with the slightest impurities in their environment.'

'But,' Catalina protested, 'Liborio insisted on importing only the best. He was told that the best culture cells came from this particular outfit in China. So he spent a great deal of money to get them.'

'Of course,' Jill hastened to reassure her. 'They *are* the best. But it doesn't matter how good the raw materials are, if the water supply you use is tainted. Look, Catalina, if the impurities in the water here cause one gene in the hamster cells to mutate, then that gene develops very rapidly, and it sort of swamps the other cell clones.'

'So you end up with a completely new protein, not the real vaccine,' Boris added.

'How did you find this out?' Catalina asked, completely overawed.

'I measured the molecular mass of the protein the cells were producing, and it was completely different from that of the original vaccine. I'd bet quite a lot of money that if you were to inject some of the new stuff into your monkeys, they'd remain fertile.'

'It looks as if there's only one way to find out. However, I don't think I shall risk my money by taking on your bet. I expect you're right.'

'I'm sorry if I sound really stupid,' Catalina interrupted. 'But surely, these chemicals and cells and stuff, don't they come already mixed? Why do you have to put water with them?'

'They come dry, as a powder,' Jill explained. 'They have to be mixed with absolutely pure water.'

'You mean distilled water?'

'No, that wouldn't be anything like pure enough. The water we use has to be passed through tanks of ion exchange resins to remove absolutely everything.'

'Or not, as the case may be,' Boris rejoined gravely.

'Exactly.'

• • •

'So the water you use has to go through an ion exchanger, is that right?' Catalina asked, as they made their way through the apparently-endless corridors to the water-purification tanks. 'Could you use our own river water, for example?'

'Oh, yes,' Jill explained. 'The local water here is purer than most, but it still contains all sorts of natural salts and minerals which have to be removed before it's pure enough to use for a sophisticated pharmaceutical process such as this.'

'Do you really want a physics lesson, Catalina?' Boris enquired.

'I'd like you to explain,' Catalina said seriously. 'You see, I know how much this means to Liborio. And to you and Jill. So, yes, I would like to know.'

'All right. When salts and minerals dissolve they break down into electrically charged particles, called ions. The positively charged ones are called cations – calcium and magnesium are cations, for example – and the negative ones are called anions.'

'Silica and chloride, among others,' Jill put in.

'So, these filters,' Boris said, indicating the cylindrical four-foot-high stainless-steel tanks that held the ion exchange resins, 'take natural water and put it through beds of resin beads which have been charged with hydrogen and hydroxyl ions. As the water flows through, the contaminant ions change places with the more desirable hydrogen and hydroxyl ions so that they're released into the fresh water.'

'But, surely, after a while the tanks of resin just fill up with the contaminating ions?' Catalina observed practically.

'Exactly. So then they're sent back to the manufacturers and "rejuvenated".'

'No, tell me what *really* happens,' Catalina insisted.

'That is what really happens. The manufacturing company washes through the resin with caustic soda and hydrochloric acid.'

'And –'

Jill took over. 'Sometimes, the washing just isn't adequate, and traces of heavy metals are left in the supposedly purified resin. To make things worse, the resin you send back to the manufacturers isn't necessarily the resin they return to you. Everyone's contaminated resin gets tipped in together, so that another company, making – say – printed circuit boards, could have returned resin beads charged with heavy metal ions, which then got transferred across the whole batch being washed.'

'We must go and tell Liborio immediately!' Catalina declared.

• • •

Liborio Ramirez was one of those men who could hide absolute fury behind a controlled mask of urbane imperturbability. 'So,' he asked, his level gaze betraying absolutely nothing, 'do you think, Jill, that this contamination is due to dishonesty or incompetence?'

'I couldn't say,' Jill answered carefully. 'All I know is what I have found in the filtered water.'

'Are you telling me that there were more of these contaminating heavy metals in the water after it had been through the resin tanks than when it originally came out of the river?'

Jill sighed. 'I'm afraid so.'

Ramirez nodded, and remained silent for a few moments, deep in thought. Then he smiled graciously. 'It seems I owe a debt of gratitude to my friend Boris for suggesting we invite you to work with us. If it had not been for your careful research, Jill, we still would not have solved this problem. But now, I am sure, we will be able to proceed very quickly. How soon do you think it will be before you have a trial sample of the vaccine ready for testing?'

'That will depend on how soon we can obtain some new resin for the tanks.'

Ramirez picked up a cellular phone. Jill was quite unable to follow the sharp, barked conversation. Clearly, this was a man who expected his every command to be obeyed immediately and without question.

'In two days you will have your resin,' he told Jill. 'So, how long?'

Jill glanced at Boris. 'Ten days?' she asked. They both knew it would take nothing like as long as that, but it did no harm to have time in hand.

Fortunately, Boris understood. 'Yes, I'd say so. Ten days,' he agreed.

'Good.' The conversation was obviously at an end.

Boris, Jill and Catalina left the room. Outside in the corridor, Catalina said, 'Why don't you join me for a drink?'

'I'd love to, but could I just take a shower first? I've been in these clothes all day, and I'd like to change.'

'Of course. Shall we say, in the salon in half an hour?'

When she had gone, Jill whispered to Boris, 'Oh dear, someone's head is going to roll for this, isn't it?'

'It looks very much like it,' Boris replied darkly.

• • •

In his office, Ramirez picked up his phone once more. Slowly, deliberately, and with care, he punched out a number.

'Juan! Mi amigo!' he shouted expansively. 'How goes it?'

For a few minutes, the conversation involved social chit-chat, and also confirmed the earlier transaction between Ramirez and the resin-tank manufacturer's sales manager. Then Ramirez said, 'My friend, you have never seen what I am pleased to call my little place in the country. It would give me great pleasure to invite you here as my guest. Of course, Señora Gutierrez would be welcome too, but I think perhaps you would find it easier to talk to all the pretty girls I have here if Señora Gutierrez were to stay at home. Oh no, my friend, I insist – I will send my own helicopter to fly you down here. It will be a pleasure, an honour. The weekend after next? Perfect. Catalina will make the arrangements. Adios, my friend.'

Ramirez then made his way to the salon. He ignored the various strange-looking fish in the larger part of the tank, and went to gaze instead at the smaller partitioned-off section which held just one species of fish, the small, ordinary-looking, but deadly piranhas.

'Soon, my pretty darlings,' he cooed, 'soon, you will have a dinner – a *banquet* – such as you have never had before.'

40.

'Well, our friend Liborio is certainly impressed with you,' Boris said, letting down the weighted bar of the Nautilus.

'But very unimpressed with the de-ionisation people, I'd say.' Jill slung a towel round her neck and sat down on the floor beside Boris.

'I simply can't believe they'd be so stupid as to send back contaminated resin – to him, of all people!'

'I don't suppose they'll make the same mistake again,' Boris said drily.

Jill looked up, horrified. 'You mean he'd have them killed?'

'Probably. But there's nothing you can do about it. It isn't your problem. If you work for someone like Ramirez, you learn to get on with your job and turn a blind eye. He doesn't tolerate interference.'

'But Catalina is supposed to be marrying him!'

'The beautiful Catalina knows what she's getting into. She'll be kept in comfort, and will probably spend a great deal of time alone. She'll also probably spend rather a lot of money. Every year for the near future, Liborio will present her with another piece of jewellery and a baby, and, in return, Catalina will cause no trouble. She knows what's expected of her.'

Jill shivered. 'She deserves better, don't you think?'

'Of course. But where is this "better"? Ramirez has one undeniable advantage, for all his faults. He never took Seminon. So Catalina will have lots of little niños to keep her busy.'

'What if she decided she wanted to marry someone else?'

'She knows it's out of the question. That's all there is to it.'

'Poor Catalina!' Jill sighed, towelling the sweat from her face and hairline. She got to her feet, and went over to the water fountain. She held out a paper cone of ice-cold water to Boris. 'Want some?'

'Thanks,' he grunted, as he got off the Nautilus and came over to take it.

Jill went on, 'Sometimes I wonder whether we'll ever both get out of here alive.'

'One thing is certain. There is no way out of here unless Ramirez says so. It's hell out there in the jungle. There are insects of every kind, flesh-eating ants, snakes, and it's rife with disease. Worst of all, you'd be hopelessly lost and wandering in circles in under an hour. Even with all my training, I wouldn't risk it.'

'So it looks as if we'd better get on with developing those trial batches if we ever want to go home.'

'You'll be free to go, whatever happens.'

'How come?'

'I wouldn't have asked you to come to this godforsaken place without first getting Ramirez to agree in writing that you would be safely returned at the end of the project.'

Jill smiled warmly at him. 'I'm not going anywhere without you,' she reassured him, 'but there's just one small problem, of course.'

'Only one!'

'A very serious one. Who do we test the first batch of reversal agent on?'

'Ramirez will have lined up something, surely?'

'I don't think so. Not long ago he was boasting that he was offering a lot of money to anyone who wanted to volunteer, but he hasn't mentioned it since. I don't think anyone has come forward.'

'Even in such a poor place as this? But even if no one offered themselves as guinea-pigs, surely he's the sort of man who'd just round up a planeload of men from the streets of Bogota or Medellin, at gunpoint probably. I mean, for Christ's sake, this is a country where three and a half thousand people simply disappeared last year alone. Why should Liborio Ramirez suddenly draw the line at behaving in more or less the same way?'

'The first reason is very simple. Although the vaccine was intended to help "the wretched of the earth", in Colombia they were the very last people to try it, either because they were too poor, or because the Church had too strong a hold over them. There just aren't enough men here who took the stuff originally, so they aren't impotent. And second, he doesn't want anyone coming here who doesn't absolutely have to. Imagine a whole planeload of people talking about this place in the slums of Bogota.'

'If they ever made it back there.'

'Precisely. And don't forget, Ramirez is highly intelligent. Even if he were prepared to dispose of his human guinea-pigs once the tests were done, don't forget the sort of people who staff this place. Maureen Cheng and Shona MacIntyre are the best scientists money can buy anywhere in the world. Raul Ibarruri was the most brilliant postgraduate of his year at the university of Toulouse. These are not people who can just disappear. Neither are they the sort of people who would accept the disposal of several dozen peasants. No, Ramirez wouldn't risk it.'

'But surely he's not going to risk letting all his scientists go back to wherever they came from, knowing about this place. How can he guarantee their silence?'

'You think he's bought yours with that emerald, don't you, Jill? That's not enough for him. If you, or I, or anyone working in this place, ever uttered a word about what goes on here, and Ramirez heard about it, they'd be dead within a week. Men like Liborio Ramirez have people all over the world to do their dirty work. He would only have to pick up his cellular phone, and the job would be as good as done.'

'I feel so stupid. Angry with myself. If I'd known what I was getting into –'

'You would never have come,' Boris said quietly. 'You can be angry with me, if you like, for bringing you here. But I truly do not believe you are in any danger.'

'I'm in serious danger of going stark, staring mad if I don't get out of this place, luxurious as it is. Do you realise I haven't seen daylight or breathed fresh air since I arrived here?'

'Only too well,' Boris answered. 'When I first came here, I spent several months underground without once going up to the outside world. And, before that, as I told you, I was locked up in a similar sort of gulag in the Ukraine. It wasn't as comfortable as this place, of course.'

'So how long is it since you've been really free?'

'Really free!' Boris laughed bitterly, and threw his empty cup into the bin. 'I suppose when I was a little child, before I could walk or speak or even think, then I was really free. But once I started my education, the bosses singled me out. Gradually, with privileges and promises, they bought me. And I never understood.

It was only when I realised how people who own things are free to break them and throw them away, that I knew that I had become an object, not a human being.'

'You're being far too hard on yourself.'

'No,' he groaned. 'It's impossible for me to be too hard on myself. Think of what I have done!'

'But you've undone it now! You've developed an antidote! You have every reason to be proud of yourself. Millions of men, and women, will thank you for the rest of their lives. And anyway, it wasn't your fault that Seminon got out into the world. If anyone's to blame, it was Mort. Poor Mort, even in the Land of the Free he was no more free, in the end, than you.'

'To be ruled by corrupt men is a terrible thing, no matter which country you live in. I have a dream, sometimes, that I would like to live on a little island somewhere, be self-suffic–'

'Stop!' Jill cried, in sudden pain. 'Sorry. It's just that Brad and I had the same dream. We used to talk about living on an island, and catching fish for dinner, getting away from the whole damn mess.'

'Would you like to live on a desert island?'

'Only if it had a decent Italian restaurant!' she joked, to lighten the atmosphere.

'What's wrong with good Russian cooking, may I ask?'

'Oh, are we both going to live on the *same* desert island?'

'Well, I'd need someone to laugh with. And so, I think, would you. Yes, actually, I think it would be a very good idea. Don't you?'

'Oh, yes!' she replied. She expected the usual devilish grin, but the green eyes were unexpectedly serious, almost sad. For all his talk of being prepared to stay and work for Ramirez, Jill realised, Boris was desperate to get away, to be free to live a normal, even ordinary, life. For all his light-heartedness and sophistication, underneath it all he was desperately lonely. She reached out to take him in her arms. She was vaguely aware that her T-shirt was damp with sweat and that she needed a shower. Oh, what the hell!, she thought; I'm past worrying about that now. His skin was warm, and damp from his vigorous exercise, and the warm, animal scent of him was almost unbearably exciting.

He pushed her away from him gently, and gazed into her eyes. 'You have an extraordinary effect on me, Jill Peters,' he said. 'It's not only that I want you, more than any other woman I have ever known, but you give me courage.'

'I believe in you,' she told him, and meant it.

'Thank you,' he answered, gazing into her eyes. 'There's only one answer, I've decided. I'm going to try out the reversal agent on myself.'

Jill broke away from him, horrified. 'But, Boris, what if it has even worse side-effects than Seminon? If it damaged you, I couldn't bear it!'

'But you could bear it if some poor unfortunate man from a slum in Medellin was damaged?'

'No, of course not! But –'

'Jill, Jill. You must let me do this. I have to.'

She nodded, suddenly calm. 'Of course. I was right about you, from the very beginning. I know that now.' He raised his eyebrows enquiringly, and she told him, 'When I first met you in London all those years ago, I thought then that there was something decent, something honest, about you. And whenever I heard anything bad about you – and I heard lots – I had difficulty believing it. I was right all along. You *are* an honourable man.'

'Thank you,' he said. 'But I think it's time I justified your faith in me. If it goes wrong, I have a lot to lose. But if it goes right, I have everything to win.'

'Yes, you have. We both do.'

• • •

Jill spent the rest of the afternoon keeping track of the first batches of the vaccine produced with the pure water, and didn't see Boris again until they joined the rest of the scientists for dinner. As he handed her a glass of wine, he whispered, 'I've done it.'

Although his words were deadly serious, Jill found herself beaming mischievously over the rim of the glass. 'The patch in place, is it?'

'Yes, you horrible sadistic woman,' he grinned back. 'And before you ask: no, it is not at all comfortable. You were quite right. I just hope I don't have to wear it for too long.'

Jill looked him straight in the eye, raised one eyebrow – men had always told her they found it sexy – and went on drinking her wine. She too hoped it wouldn't be long.

• • •

But the next two days seemed to go on for ever. By tacit consent, neither Jill nor Boris mentioned the patch, though Jill would keep an improbably straight face whenever she caught his eye. She filled the time running tests, and collating the results with the figures on her NIH disks. At the end of the second day, she sat back in her chair with a sigh of fatigue. Maureen Cheng looked up.

'You must be tired,' she observed. 'You've been at it solidly for ten hours.'

'I think I'm getting somewhere, at last. Come and look at this, and tell me what you think.'

Maureen sat down at the computer screen, and scrolled through the columns of data.

'You were really close, back in 97,' she said in amazement. 'Did you realise how close you were?'

'It was just a question of finding a way of getting the sperm coat antigen to stay bolted on to the tetanus toxoid. But at the time it seemed impossible.'

'Well,' Maureen tapped the screen, 'I have to say it looks good to me now.'

'Monkey time?'

'Monkey time,' Maureen confirmed.

• • •

'My dear Jill, you are a genius! A miracle worker!' Ramirez enthused. 'This calls for champagne!'

Oh, God, not again! Jill never imagined she would get sick of the very idea of vintage Dom Perignon, but she was coming perilously close to it. Certainly, she would never again be able to think of champagne without a shudder. But she made a huge effort, steeled herself to smile sweetly and falsely at Ramirez's overwhelming bonhomie and heavy gallantry, clinked glasses and drank.

'Now, how long will it be before we know for certain that the vaccine is effective?' For all Ramirez's friendly enthusiasm, the brown eyes held a calculating glint. Jill decided to err on the side of caution.

'I can't give you a definite answer, only an approximate one. Your monkeys have the same fertility cycle as human females, so it could be several weeks, or even months before you know anything absolutely for sure. We've divided the monkeys to be tested into two groups. One is a control group, and I would expect the usual level of fertility among them. If none of the vaccinated monkeys becomes pregnant, then you'll know the new stuff is effective.' Jill very carefully said 'you' rather than 'we' or 'I'; she had no intention of still being in Ramirez's underground lab three months from now! She decided to try pushing her luck slightly.

'Liborio, could I ask you a great favour? Do you realise I've been here for three weeks now, and I've lived underground all that time? It's been wonderful; I've had everything I could possibly want. But what I'd really like is to go out into the fresh air for a while. Could I do that, do you think?'

'I would like that too, if it's OK, Liborio,' Boris cut in quickly.

Ramirez almost smirked. 'Normally, as you know, it isn't permitted. But since this is a special occasion, I don't see why not,' he conceded magnanimously. 'There is a full moon tonight. Very romantic. But, I regret, no nightingales. Shall we say, after dinner, ten o'clock? I'll tell Arturo to take you up in the elevator. But you must be sure to be back by midnight, my children.'

• • •

The air was hot and damp, almost solid, but Jill breathed it in like someone who had been held underwater for as long as they could bear. 'Just *smell* it!' she told Boris. 'You can smell earth, trees, *life*!'

Boris sniffed sceptically. 'To me, there is something rotten and rancid in the atmosphere, a smell of death. Like this whole place.' He gestured at the tiny, low building that housed the elevator gear, almost hidden in the trees.

'But look at the moon! And the stars! The sky looks quite different in the southern hemisphere, doesn't it?'

'Ah, another quality I hadn't suspected! You have the ability to take pleasure in small things, no matter what the situation. How very English!'

'Are you getting at me, Volkov?' she joked.

'Of course not. I wish more people had it, that's all.'

They sat down on the ground and leaned against a tree.

'It's exactly three weeks since I arrived here,' Jill observed. 'I couldn't believe such a place existed. Did they bring you here by helicopter too?'

'How else?'

'Did you see the chopper being towed down a ramp to an underground hangar? I did. Somewhere over there, I think.'

'I've seen them being hidden away, often. Don't forget I've been here a long time.'

'Have you ever been down there?'

'Do you seriously imagine they'd allow –'

'Of course not. But it would be fascinating to see it, wouldn't it?'

'Well, you seem to have Ramirez eating out of your hand. Ask him.'

'Hmm. I might.'

They sat silent for a little while. The life of the rainforest pulsated all around them. The undercurrent of insect noise, moths and flying beetles filled the air, and far off they could hear grunts, snorts and screams as the creatures of the jungle mated, fought and preyed upon each other.

Jill suddenly jumped and screamed as a large flying insect blundered against her face and became entangled in her hair. She brushed frantically at it, trying to get rid of it. Boris calmly took the beetle out of her hair, and threw it up into the air. It buzzed away noisily.

'I'm sorry to be so silly. But I *hate* insects and bats, things like that.'

'That's OK.' Boris put his arm round her, and she snuggled up to him.

They sat there, companionably entwined, and watched the moon sailing above the clearing.

'Isn't it wonderful to be out here, away from those wretched cameras?' Jill sighed.

'Yes, I feel safer out here, where there is nothing more dangerous than a snake or a hungry jaguar, than down there with our host.'

'How far do you think we are from civilisation? I mean, a town, other people?'

'There are some Indians living near the river. But a town of any size – hundreds of miles, probably.'

'Babes in the Wood, aren't we?'

'What do you mean? I don't understand.'

'It's a traditional English nursery story, about children lost in a forest. Like us.'

'But we're not children.'

'No, we aren't.' Suddenly Jill couldn't bear it any longer. She turned in his arms and began to kiss him hungrily. He responded as if he had been waiting for her, and feelings and sensations dead for four years burst into life inside her like a flower. For the first time, she truly understood what it must be like to be a man who'd taken Seminon, and what it would be like when they took the antidote.

She broke away to catch her breath. 'Oh God,' she moaned. 'If that reversal agent doesn't work, I'm not going to be able to bear it.'

He said softly, 'I have reason to believe that it does.'

'Really?' She hardly dared believe it.

'Put it this way: I haven't felt like this for a very long time. What is it they say in America, your place or mine?'

Jill felt a rush of joy as she replied, 'Neither. Let's do it out here, under the moon!'

She reached for the buttons of his shirt, and flicked them open one after the other. For so long, she had fantasised about this man, about what it would be like to make love with him, knowing that it probably could never happen. And now, at last, everything she had dreamed of was, quite literally, within her grasp.

'Your turn,' he said, and lifted her T-shirt over her head. She crossed her arms as he lifted it over her head. As she did so Boris luxuriated in the sight of her firm, slender body arched backwards, her taut breasts, swollen from his caresses, just in front of his face.

As he admired her silky body, he drew her towards him, his hands firmly grasping her tight buttocks. Then he unzipped her jeans and eased them off. Jill rested his hands on her head and guided his face towards her trembling belly. Tantalisingly slowly, he ran his tongue around her navel and down towards her pubic mound. Her fragrance rose to meet him as he buried his face between her thighs. With care and skill he caressed her butt and hips with his hands and used his lips to trail kisses over her belly.

Jill now knelt in front of him. Pushing him back gently until he was lying on the ground, she lay on his warm, hard body, kissing his chest inch by inch. Boris moaned as the pleasure washed over him.

'I love you,' he whispered softly.

'I love you too,' she replied. 'These three weeks have been the best time of my life. I never thought I'd find love like this again.'

'Here,' he said, raising his butt so that she could remove his pants. Jill hurriedly undid the fastening and the zipper and pulled them off.

'Now these,' she said, tugging at his shorts.

Boris closed his eyes for a moment, enjoying sensations he hadn't felt for years. He'd almost forgotten how good his body felt in the hands of a woman. Jill trailed her hair over his belly and groin, nibbled and kissed his stirring organ.

Boris in turn caressed her passionately, his hands roaming over her curves, fingers seeking out her hidden wetness. She took him in her hand, removed the patch and continued gently caressing. Under her expert attention, he was soon ready for her. Slowly she knelt over him and leaned forward to kiss him deeply, their tongues engaged in a most intimate sword fight.

'Are you thinking what I'm thinking?' she whispered, hardly daring to mention it.

'I'm not thinking at all,' he replied. 'Just don't stop. Don't ever stop.' Jill leaned back to sit upright and gently lowered herself on to him. She shivered with delight as she took him into her.

Slowly, as if she had a precious piece of porcelain inside her, she moved on his huge trembling organ, contracting her inner muscles as she did so. She couldn't remember when she had last felt so good, her pelvis alive, her hips gyrating as if to devour him greedily into her soul. Moving rhythmically up and down now she gripped his penis, milking it with her aching pelvic muscles. Boris's hips started to rise and fall in tune with hers as his body strained to meet her.

Moving in perfect harmony, they approached mutual bliss.

'Aaargh,' he groaned, with a sound that originated in the depths of his belly as his pelvis jerked into action.

Jill let out an involuntary cry of delight as he thrust ever more deeply into her. 'God, that's beautiful –' she cried as they both came to a climax at the same time.

• • •

The moon had moved some way across the sky when Jill felt Boris stir in her arms.

'I should have asked you whether there was any possibility of you becoming pregnant,' he said, kissing her. 'But in all the excitement, I forgot.'

'I didn't,' she whispered. 'If I were pregnant with your child, I'd be very happy.'

'So would I. But my future is rather uncertain, you know.'

'Ssssh. Everything will work out just fine. You'll see.'

Boris looked at his watch. 'It's nearly twelve,' he said. 'Ramirez wasn't joking when he said he wanted us back inside by midnight. He meant it. And the security guards will be making their rounds soon. We'd better get dressed.'

A few minutes later they made their way back to the elevator block. Arturo took them down.

Ramirez was waiting for them, beaming ecstatically. To Jill's horror, he kissed them both with great enthusiasm. 'My dear friends,' he announced, 'you have made me very, very happy tonight. And, as I can see, you have made each other very happy too.'

He flung open the doors to the salon. Jill felt a tidal wave of embarrassment boil through her. There on the huge television screen, their love-making of only a few minutes before was being replayed before their very eyes, in glorious Technicolor and huge close-up! They'd been wrong about the damn security cameras! Even in the pale moonlight, the image-intensifier had picked up every single detail.

At the far end of the room, Jill heard the pop of a champagne cork. Oh shit! she thought. Ramirez, you *bastard*!

• • •

Later, by tacit consent, Jill and Boris spent the night alone in their own rooms. Ramirez's spying had unnerved Jill, and she was very angry. 'I'm sorry,' she said to Boris. 'But I'd rather be alone.'

'I feel rather the same way,' he agreed. 'Don't worry, there'll soon be a time when we can spend all our nights together.'

Lying awake in the small hours, Jill could just hear, through the thickness of rock on the far side of the wall, the thump and whirr of hydraulic machinery. The only thing she could think of that would cause it was the huge doors to the underground hangar where the helicopters were kept. She closed her eyes and tried to visualise the layout of Ramirez's underground empire and relate it to the little she knew of the world above. Maybe the hangar was really only a short distance away from where she lay. And, almost certainly, she reasoned, there was a way of getting into it without going up in the elevator under the watchful gaze of the taciturn Arturo. She would think about that in the morning.

• • •

'My dear Jill, surely you cannot mean to leave!' Ramirez protested. 'You have been here hardly any time at all!'

'Liborio, tomorrow I shall have been here for three weeks,' Jill reminded him gently. 'I'm due back at work this coming Monday. I can't do any more for you here, so I really shouldn't impose on your hospitality any longer.'

'But, Jill, Catalina and I would be so unhappy to see you go! And surely you can wait until the first control macaques conceive. I insist you stay. Boris, help me persuade our charming guest.'

'Of course I would like Jill here,' Boris said, with a palpable lack of enthusiasm.

Liborio Ramirez, you really are an evil sonofabitch! Jill fumed inwardly. But yet again, she forced herself to smile agreeably. 'Will you excuse me for now?' she asked. 'I would like to have an early night.'

'Of course,' Ramirez bowed graciously, and Jill made her escape. At the far end of the room, something in the smaller fish tank caught her eye. Outside, in the corridor, she slumped against the wall, feeling sick and faint.

'Jill, what is the matter?' Boris demanded.

'Didn't you see –?'

'What?'

'In the piranha tank –' she stammered.

'What, for God's sake?'

Jill gulped down a threatening wave of nausea. 'On the gravel at the bottom, a gold wedding ring. Quite a large one. It must be a man's.'

Boris grabbed her arm and marched her smartly along to her own room. He sat her down and fetched a glass of water. Then he turned the TV on loud, and came over and took her in his arms. It took Jill a moment or two to realise that this time he was doing so with no romantic intent.

'Be very careful what you say,' he whispered, so quietly she could scarcely hear him. 'This room is probably bugged, in addition to our friend there.' He glanced almost imperceptibly in the direction of the sinister-looking closed-circuit camera slung from the ceiling in the corner. Jill forced herself to relax in his embrace; since Ramirez's surveillance teams were fully aware of their interest in each other, this was the way they were expected to behave. And it meant they could whisper freely. 'You could be imagining something. Even if there were a ring in there, one of the people who clean the tanks might have dropped it.'

Jill shook her head. 'I don't think so. And neither do you. Listen, I think someone arrived here very late last night. I heard the hydraulic doors of the hangar slide open and shut again. But have you seen a single unfamiliar face here today?'

'No,' Boris admitted, stretching full length on the bed and pulling Jill alongside him. 'But that doesn't mean –'

'Well, I think it does! I think someone was brought here at about three o'clock this morning, and fed to those bloody piranhas! Boris, I've had enough of this place. I want to go home.'

'It might be wise to agree to stay until we can show that the new vaccine works. It would only be a few weeks.'

'What are you saying? Do you genuinely believe that if it does succeed – and we know your reversal agent works – Ramirez will just let us go, knowing what we know? Of course he won't!'

'You're right,' Boris said, his face drawn. 'As long as we were holding out promises to him, we were safe. But now we've delivered, we're expendable.'

'You could stay and synthesise designer drugs for him, if that's the way you want to live your life. I can't. It's not my field, and anyway I wouldn't want to. I'm no more use to him now. You're looking at a hundred and thirty pounds of piranha food here!'

'Ssssh,' he calmed her, hugging her tightly to him. 'The only thing that's going to get its teeth into you is me. If we can't leave here with Ramirez's blessing, we'll just have to leave without it.'

• • •

Later Jill's words echoed round his brain as Boris spent two hours lying on his bed, thinking, planning, exploring and rejecting possibilities of every kind. His KGB training was the sort that lasts for life, and he felt a pleasurable excitement at calling on skills long dormant and unused. Finally, his plan honed to his own satisfaction, he went to sleep.

• • •

'But Jill, when we get to Miami, I'll buy you all the clothes you want! If you leave your stuff in your room, it'll give us extra time. Maybe not much, but we'll need every second. Just remember to be up by five, OK?'

Jill nodded.

The day dragged interminably. Fortunately, the complex was so isolated that internal security was virtually nil. Apart from the ubiquitous surveillance cameras, it simply wasn't considered necessary. And, Jill realised, Ramirez wasn't reckoning on anybody stealing anything, because they were never going to leave alive. This meant she was able to make duplicate disks of the last three weeks' work without interruption.

Mindful of the all-seeing cameras, she carried out some legitimate tasks, all quite guiltless and above board, and every hour or two she ran off a duplicate disk and concealed it in the sleeve of her lab coat under cover of consulting a directory or pouring a cup of coffee. Shortly afterwards, she would go to her room, to visit the bathroom or to look for a Kleenex, and the disk would find its way into her underwear drawer, or her washbag. Every time she managed to hide one, her heart pounded so violently she felt quite ill. She must look so furtive and guilty, how on earth could Arturo's goons on surveillance duty not realise she was up to something clandestine?

At last all the disks were safely duplicated, and stashed away. As she showered and changed her clothes that evening, she contrived to put all of the disks in the pocket of her sweat pants. She couldn't bear to leave her ruby earrings behind, or her pretty tortoiseshell combs, so they went in as well. And she certainly wasn't going to leave Ramirez's fabulous emerald! She forced herself to act nonchalantly as she padded round the room naked, reckoning that if she gave Arturo's gorillas a real eyeful they wouldn't concern themselves too much with what she was actually doing. She emptied her purse out on the bed, as if to sort and tidy the contents. Her passport slid under the pillow, followed by her pocket-book, personal organiser and doorkeys. She made a great show of replacing her make-up bag, hairbrush, comb and mirror, of throwing away the used tissues and other mess, and slinging the strap of her purse over the back of a chair.

Finally, she dressed and went to join Boris and the other staff for the evening meal.

He winked at her imperceptibly as she came in, which meant he'd managed to complete his side of the preparations as well. As they had arranged, they steered the conversation round to sport.

Jill maintained that she had been on the university squash team – a total fabrication – while Boris declared that no American could possibly keep up with the fitness requirements of the Russian army. Inevitably, they ended up challenging each other to a game of squash, but far too early in the morning for anybody else to have the slightest interest in getting up to watch.

'Well, Dr Volkov, if I'm to thrash the living daylights out of you at dawn, I'd better get some sleep,' Jill said, on cue.

'You show him, Jill,' Shona MacIntyre growled good-naturedly. 'We'll hear all about it at breakfast. G'night.'

'I think I'd better do the same,' Boris laughed, getting to his feet.

'The honour of the male sex is at stake,' Raul Ibarruri said, lifting his glass. 'I drink to your success, Boris.'

'They're such a nice crowd,' Jill whispered as they made their way to their rooms. 'I feel awful about just leaving them here, knowing they'll never be free again.'

'Well, we can't take them with us,' Boris said shortly. 'We can try and do something for them once we're in Miami, that's all. Are you ready?'

'Yes. And you?'

Boris nodded. 'Sleep well. Until tomorrow.'

41.

Jill's alarm woke her a little before five. In the dark, before getting into bed, she had transferred her passport and other things into the pocket of her sweatshirt. All she had to do was wash and dress as though she were going to come back later for a proper shower after a game of squash. Carrying a towel to hide the suspiciously angular shape of the disks in her pocket, she walked briskly along the ever-lit corridor to the gym and the squash court beyond it, mentally measuring the distances between corners and memorising the number of stairs.

Boris was already at the court. 'Good morning!' he greeted her. Then, in a much lower voice, he added, 'I reckon we've got quarter of an hour, so let's make it look and sound good.'

Jill's nerves were strung so tight that she found herself playing rather well. Thinking of Ramirez, she slammed the ball viciously every time and Boris had to move really fast to hit it. 'Don't wear me out before we even start,' he muttered, as he knelt close to her to pick up the ball. 'We're both going to need every shred of energy.'

'Come on,' Jill shouted for the benefit of anybody who might be eavesdropping. 'Defend the honour of the Russian Army!' And she sent a stinging serve ricocheting off the wall. At that moment the squash court was plunged into darkness. Flinging their racquets down, Jill and Boris raced for the door. Pitch black greeted their eyes instead of the usual glare of fluorescent lighting, but they went pounding down the corridor, along another at a right angle, down the stairs – ten, twelve, fourteen, Jill counted mentally as she blindly took them two at a time – and along yet another passageway.

Within a couple of minutes they were crouched by a locked door marked PROHIBIDA LA ENTRADA. Boris switched on a tiny but powerful flashlight, shielding it with his hand.

'Just another couple of sec –'

There was a metallic click from the keypad beside the door, which echoed from hundreds of keypads throughout the complex. At that instant, the ever-present hum of the air-conditioning died, to be replaced by a terrifying silence.

Boris punched a single button on the keypad, and rammed the door open with his shoulder. He raced down a rock-lined tunnel, with Jill hot on his heels. The stud-rubber floor sloped slightly downwards and led to a metal walkway, with steps zig-zagging upwards and downwards. Boris flashed his torch briefly. The beam glinted off helicopter rotors twenty feet below them.

They clattered down the iron stairs, not caring how much noise they were making. The computer-generated failure of the lighting and the electronic locking system would have alerted everybody anyway. The largest of the four helicopters was stationed at the bottom of the ramp, already coupled to the lifting gear.

'Get in!' Boris panted. 'I'll have to find the manual override for the doors and the winch.'

Jill obeyed, and sat there gazing fixedly at the huge steel door that stood between them and freedom. They were insane to be doing this! For a split second, she saw again the gold wedding ring, glinting among the gravel of the piranha tank, and her heart pounded so violently she could scarcely breathe.

It seemed an eternity before the massive sheet of metal began to move upwards, and a strip of grey light appeared under the door. Slowly, *so* slowly, the door rose six inches, a foot, two feet, three –. The jungle was eerily silent, the metallic rumbling terrifyingly loud.

At last the door was completely raised, and the helicopter, towed on a steel hawser, rose inch by agonising inch out of the dark and into the colourless light of early dawn. Boris darted out and swiftly uncoupled the winch.

To Jill's horror, he disappeared back into the darkness. She heard a series of harsh blows echoing up from the hangar – what the *hell* was he up to?

Then he was there again, beside her in the cockpit, his face set and anxious. He hurriedly scanned the unfamiliar flight instruments, swearing in Russian under his breath, but in a few seconds the rotors were whirling.

There was a deafening racket behind them, as Arturo and his security guards crashed shouting down the stairs. Suddenly the helicopter lifted off and they lurched sideways, just skimming the tops of the trees at the edge of the clearing, and gaining height rapidly. Jill flinched as a bullet smacked against the Plexiglas bubble of the cockpit, leaving a crazed star-shaped scar just above her head.

She twisted in her seat to glance back at the almost-invisible maw of the helicopter hangar. 'How long before they come after us?' she demanded shakily.

'They won't,' Boris said drily. 'I found a monkey wrench and smashed the control panels of the other helicopters. Not elegant, I admit, but it worked. However quickly they repair them, they won't be able to take off in less than an hour. And by then –'

'Where will we be?'

'Right now,' Boris grunted, looking at the fuel indicator, 'I'm simply thankful that we have a full tank.'

'How much is that?'

'Enough. Well,' he said, relaxing visibly as they left the clearing far behind, 'this is the second time in my life I've escaped in a stolen helicopter in a hail of bullets.'

'Just don't ask me to do it again, *ever*! The 007 lifestyle doesn't suit me! I died a thousand times back there!'

'Nonsense!' Boris grinned. 'Do you know how long it all took, from the moment the electronics crashed, to take-off? A little over two minutes. My KGB instructor would have been proud of me.'

'Mira Harman once accused me of being attracted only to men who liked to live dangerously,' Jill muttered between gritted teeth.

'I'm sorry to hear that,' Boris answered. 'I can assure you, I no longer like to live dangerously at all. Those days are behind me. But I do like to live, and I intend to.'

Jill almost jumped out of her skin as a sudden, deafening burst of static flared from the radio, and resolved itself into curses and howls of rage.

'Ramirez,' Boris said grimly.

'Do you understand what he's saying?'

'I don't speak much Spanish, but I get the general idea. Keep quiet for a minute.' Boris scowled intently as he strove to make out what Ramirez was screaming at them.

'I think he's saying he'll blow up the whole facility and everybody in it. And their deaths will be our fault.'

'Oh, no! He wouldn't!'

'Wouldn't he?'

'Boris, we have to go back!'

'Are you crazy?' Boris's voice rose angrily above the static. 'Can you turn that off? He's gone anyway.'

Boris flipped the switch. 'There's no way we're going back.

'Boris, *please*! Think of them all – Shona, Raul, Maureen – and Catalina! They don't deserve to die!'

'And how are we going to save them if we do go back?' Boris snapped.

'I don't know. But we can't simply abandon them. Look, can't we just circle round once, just to see? We've got enough fuel, haven't we? Boris, I'll never forgive you –'

He darted a sideways glance at her. 'You mean it, don't you?'

By this time Jill was weeping with despair. 'Yes,' she gulped, sniffing inelegantly and wiping the tears off her face with the heel of her hand. 'I love you, but I do mean it.'

Without another word, Boris swung the helicopter round. Below them, the ridges along the Yari river were just starting to gleam green in the light of the rising sun, while the river itself was still in shadow. Boris set a course down the valley, and they flew in complete silence, the tension between them tangible, for several minutes.

'It's down there somewhere,' Boris said tersely.

Jill scanned the carpet of jungle to try and make out the tiny landing-area. 'No sign of an explosion, at least.'

'I'd say that was an empty threat. If you think about it, how could he risk having explosives permanently wired up to an installation that cost as much as that? Anything could go wrong. He was bluffing; I'd put money on it.' Boris took the helicopter in a wide arc up and away from the river. 'Now can we resume our journey?'

'I'm sorry,' Jill said, in control of herself once more. 'You were right. I should have realised he wouldn't really blow the place up. Let's get out of here.' Abruptly the helicopter swerved to the left and slid down a few hundred feet. 'What the – ?'

'Look down there. Do you see what I see?' Boris, his face set, flew at high speed back towards the Yari. The wake of a powerboat, heading fast downriver, appeared like a growing white slash on the sluggish green surface of the water. 'The bastard's saving his own skin!'

'Can we stop him?'

'We can have a damn good try. You belted in? Good.'

The helicopter plunged into shadow, and the river banks rose like green walls on either side, the whump-whump-whump of the rotors buffeting back like blows. Jill could feel every nerve and muscle in her body tense and rigid. The water seemed to be only inches below them, and they were going so fast that it looked solid; a little lower, and they could easily flip over and explode into a million fragments. Several hundred yards ahead of them, Ramirez's powerboat was shooting like an arrow along the broad expanse of the river. Boris zoomed in low to close the distance between them, and throttled back to keep pace with the boat as it skimmed the glassy surface.

'Let's hope we have more fuel than he does,' he muttered, buzzing the powerboat to un-nerve Ramirez.

'Won't he have a gun?' Jill whispered.

'I'm hoping not to give him time to use it. Hold on!' Boris deliberately waltzed the helicopter from side to side, directly above the boat. Ramirez started to jink and weave, the boat leaping out of the water and crashing back again, like a horse trying to throw its rider. Jill felt quite ill as the trees, the water, the sky, all reeled in a crazy dance. She'd never been a fan of roller-coasters and this was far worse than anything a theme park could offer.

Boris's face was set like granite as he called on every ounce of skill he had ever learned while, mere feet below them, Ramirez, his hair whipped back from his head by the speed, snarled ferociously, one hand on the wheel and the other fumbling in a compartment below the controls.

'No, you don't!' Boris muttered, and edged closer still, almost nudging at Ramirez with the right-hand skid to force the boat away from the broad centre of the river. 'Get over!' he growled. Ahead of them lay a broad bend as the river curved westwards, a bend Ramirez should have taken as widely as possible, given the speed he was going. But Boris was cramping him into the offside bank.

'Oh, my God!' Jill gasped, when she realised what Boris had seen, what he intended.

As they flew under the bluff on the inside of the bend, Boris jabbed the helicopter viciously at the powerboat, forcing it, and them, perilously close to the flashing cliffs of green to their right. Then, without warning, he rose high above the river, and Jill felt her insides lurch painfully. She realised she had been holding her breath for the last two minutes, and was starting to feel light-headed, as though everything was happening to someone else, or in a dream.

Way below them, Ramirez rounded the bluff. The current was narrow and fast-flowing at that point. He had now found the gun he'd been scrabbling for, and looked back to take a shot at the helicopter. His timing could hardly have been worse.

Beyond the bluff, a ridged bank of gravel and rock angled out into the river. Ramirez ploughed into it at full speed. With a ghastly balletic grace, the boat took off like a fighter plane, turning over and fragmenting in mid-flight to fling Ramirez out, before arrowing into the trees.

'Maybe the fuel tank will –' *Boom*! A billowing fireball rose above the jungle, and burned itself out in seconds leaving an oily plume of black smoke.

'He can't have survived that, surely?'

'Let's go and see.' Boris turned the helicopter in a tight circle above the gravel bank. Ramirez was thrashing feebly in the current, obviously stunned, and probably injured.

'Do we grab him? Leave him? What do we do?'

'Let's stay where we are for the time being,' Boris said drily, as the helicopter continued to circle. 'We may find the decision is made for us.'

Jill forced herself to breathe normally, and looked anxiously at Boris. His face was tight with strain, and furrowed with lines she had never seen before. Once more they spun in a narrow circle between the banks, watching the helpless figure drifting in the water.

Suddenly, Ramirez began to twitch, then to thrash desperately.

'I thought so. Piranhas. The river's full of them.'

• • •

'Feeling better?' Boris asked.

'A bit,' Jill said, sitting up and rubbing her eyes. After Boris had pulled the helicopter up out of the river valley and had set a northerly course, a stunning weariness had knocked Jill out for half an hour. She was thankful that it had; Ramirez's horrific death had now taken on the aspects of a nightmare – something that had happened in another time, another dimension. Now was now. 'Where the heck are we?'

'Half an hour north of where we were,' Boris grinned mischievously. 'We're OK for fuel; the reserve tank was full, thank God. We'll have enough to get us to civilisation.'

'There are so many things we haven't thought through,' Jill said. 'For instance, when we get back to the States with all the data, what do we do with it?'

'Well, for a start we could hold an auction among the multinationals and sell it to the highest bidder –'

'*Boris*!,' Jill almost shouted. 'If we did that, we'd be no better than Ramirez!'

'Do all American women interrupt like that?' Boris teased her.

'I'm *English*, you bastard!' she snapped back, grinning.

'Half an hour of freedom, and already my life's a misery! What I was going to say –'

'– when I so rudely interrupted you –'

'– was that we could then set up a trust-fund with the money to help people whose lives have been wrecked by Seminon.'

'And we could impose all sorts of conditions and restrictions on whoever buys it, to make sure they don't abuse it! Boris, forget being a Hero of the Soviet Union, you're going to be the hero of the United States!'

'I wouldn't be so sure. You'll be showered with Congressional Medals and Nobel Prizes; you're bringing home the information they want so badly. However, not only am I ex-KGB, but as far as your government is concerned the whole Seminon mess was also my fault, exclusively! I don't see them welcoming me with open arms!' Boris told her, his face grim.

'I do.'

'What do you mean?'

'In a safety-deposit box in my bank, I have something very damning on the FBI, to do with Mira Harman's death. I'd only have to *mention* this tape's existence, and I can pretty well guarantee the US government would fall over itself to give you whatever you want – citizenship, money, you name it.'

Boris gave an amazed shout of laughter. 'Jill Peters, you really are the most extraordinary woman! Pity you weren't born Russian. The KGB lost a really good operative in you!'

'The only thing is: won't you be bored? Living in a little house with a nice green lawn and a nice white picket fence, being Mr Suburban America, isn't going to suit you, is it?'

'Probably not,' Boris agreed. 'So, it looks as though we have only one choice.'

'What's that?'

'Using even just a tiny percentage of the money your data and mine will fetch, we could buy that desert island.'

'You *are* joking?'

'What do you mean, joking?'

'That money is going to be blood money! Don't you see – it'll be a sort of penance, paid by governments and multinationals as compensation for all the suffering there's been! There's no way I want to touch even a *cent* of it!'

'Actually, I agree with you completely,' Boris said seriously. 'But I have one immediate problem, which is that right now all I have in the world is the clothes I am wearing. Ramirez promised us all vast sums of money, and kept telling us how fat our bank accounts were growing. But, of course, we never needed money, so it was only ever an idea. Now I realise, without any doubt, that he never intended any of us to leave that place alive, so he would have had several years of our lives and our expertise for free!'

'I'd be happy for the DEA to napalm the place,' Jill said grimly, 'once we made sure Maureen, Raul, Shona and the others were OK.'

'I promise we'll do our best for them,' he said, reaching to take her hand. 'They won't be sent home scot-free, but at least we can testify in their defence.'

'You know who I worry about the most? Catalina.'

'Yes. I liked her. She deserved much, much better than Ramirez, for all his money.'

'Will she be lumped in with the others, do you think? Considered guilty, I mean?'

'I don't see that the DEA will be interested in her. If they arrest her, we'll do our damnedest for her. My guess is that the family network will close round her, protect their own.'

'I do hope so.' Suddenly, Jill sat bolt upright. 'Do you know what I've just realised? That sandbank back there in the river? It's been worrying me why it was there at all, above the bend like that. Do you remember Ramirez telling us how he dumped all the spoil from building his underground kingdom in to the river? Do you think that could have been it?'

'It seems likely. It has a certain symmetry to it, if so.'

Leaning happily against Boris's shoulder, Jill sighed, 'For the first time in years, everything's starting to look good.' Then she sat up again. 'Can you put this thing on automatic pilot for a while?'

'Certainly. But why?'

'Don't ask silly questions, Volkov – come here!'

• • •

After a few minutes, Boris drew back, and said, 'I'm sorry, but this is like cuddling a sackful of books! What have you got in your pockets?'

'I completely forgot!' Jill started systematically to empty the pockets of her sweatsuit. 'One box of floppy disks. One passport. One personal organiser. One pocket book. Doorkeys to Apartment H, 1209 Nebraska Avenue. Two tortoiseshell combs. Two ruby earrings. And – an emerald!'

Boris gave a great shout of laughter. 'I'm glad your scruples didn't extend to leaving *that* behind! You earned it, after all.'

'I wouldn't want to keep it, though. Boris, look at it! What do you see?'

'What do you mean? It's a very large, very vulgar, very valuable emerald!'

'Is that really all it is to you?'

He thought for a moment. Then he put his arms round her. 'No, of course not. It's much more than just an emerald. It's our passport out of suburban America. In fact, it's a desert island. *Our* desert island!'